Falconfar

falconfar

ED GREENWOOD

SOLARIS

First published 2010 by Solaris
an imprint of Rebellion Publishing Ltd,
Riverside House, Osney Mead,
Oxford, OX1 0ES, UK

www.solarisbooks.com

ISBN: 978 1 906735 61 6

10 9 8 7 6 5 4 3 2 1

A CIP catalogue record for this book is available from the
British Library.

Designed & typeset by Rebellion Publishing

Printed in the US

The Story Thus Far

ROD EVERLAR, A successful author of Cold War-era action thrillers and fantasy novels set in his imagined world of Falconfar, is astonished one night when Taeauna—one of a race of good winged warrior-women he created for his fantasy books—literally falls out of his dreams, onto his bed. Badly wounded and beset, she pleads with Rod to aid her and Falconfar.

Rod discovers the world he thought was created only in his imagination is all too real—and that its people believe he, Rod Everlar, is its Lord Archwizard or Dark Lord, the most powerful of the "Dooms," powerful wizards who can literally change Falconfar with their magic.

Plunged bewilderingly into a medieval fantasy world that's familiar but also dangerously different from his imaginings, Rod is swept into a civil war in the kingdom of Galath. One of the Dooms, the wizard Arlaghaun, is controlling the King of Galath, and seeking absolute tyranny over the Galathan nobles.

For years, the three other Dooms—the wizards Arlaghaun, Malraun, and Narmarkoun—have fought each other, in a struggle that none of them could win. Rod's arrival shatters the stalemate between them, just as Arlaghaun is on the verge of seizing control over Galath.

There are signs that a long-dead wizard of matchless might, Lorontar—the only Lord Archwizard of Falconfar before Rod—is stirring, somehow still alive (or undead), and seeking to control the living.

At the end of DARK LORD, the first novel of the Falconfar saga, Arlaghaun is slain in Ult Tower. The wizard Malraun appears, snatches Taeauna, and magically whisks her away as his captive, leaving Rod Everlar raging helplessly, desperate to rescue her but not knowing how.

As the second Falconfar book, ARCH WIZARD, begins, Rod tries to follow Taeauna, using magic he doesn't understand, but instead arrives in the distant vale of Ironthorn, where three self-styled Lords (Hammerhand, Lyrose, and Tesmer) are locked in a struggle against each other for rule of the valley—a long-term struggle that has just flared up again with the slaying of the Hammerhand and Lyrose heirs in a forest skirmish.

Taken to Lord Hammerhand, Rod asks for help in finding Taeauna and ends up taking part in an assault on the castle of the rival Lyrose family, where Lord Hammerhand insists Taeauna must be. Hammerhand secretly intends to use Rod's powers as Lord Archwizard to destroy or greatly weaken his hated foes the Lyroses, then have Rod killed, considering wizards far more dangerous than rival Ironthar.

During the assault, Rod and the band of Hammerhand knights are magically transported to distant Malragard, the tower of the Doom Malraun (ally of the Lyroses). Its defenses kill the knights, one after another, but Rod manages to stay alive, and eventually manages to sleep and dream, "Shaping" (altering the reality of) Falconfar. He dreams, among other things, of Malragard collapsing around him—and it does.

Before their deaths, Hammerhand's knights had drugged Rod Everlar to compel him to tell the truth, and questioned him about where he'd come from. The wizard Narmarkoun used magic to spy on this questioning from afar, and so learned about our Earth from it; enough to pique his interest. He sends a lorn and some Dark Helms to Earth, to mount an attack on Holdoncorp, the computer gaming company that owns the rights to the world of Falconfar. Like Rod Everlar, some of its programmers have the unwitting power to affect "reality" in Falconfar, as Shapers, and Narmarkoun is determined to gain control of all Falconfar by controlling—or killing—all of the Shapers who can influence it. Through the eyes of Rusty Carroll, security chief of Holdoncorp, we see Narmarkoun's forces attack the company's corporate headquarters and butcher their way through Holdoncorp staffers.

Meanwhile, two rough, veteran and aging scoundrels and adventurers, Garfist Gulkoun and his longtime partner Iskarra Taeravund, have blundered into the midst of Rod Everlar's adventures and become captives of the Aumrarr, who repeatedly whisk them away from trouble but keep them captive because they will soon become "useful" or "necessary." For just what, the Aumrarr decline to say. As FALCONFAR begins, these Aumrarr have been reduced to two, Dauntra and Juskra, and they have promised to fly Gar and Isk across most of the vast forest known as the Raurklar to the land of Galath, for their safety and to await their future moment of usefulness.

The wizard Malraun has also been busy, with a captive, mind-controlled Taeauna at his side. He has been aiding the Army of Liberation, mustered by the Stormar warlord Horgul (who has been acting under his influence), and with Horgul's death, leading the Army himself. The Army has conquered hold after hold, heading for Ironthorn.

Unbeknownst to Malraun, the infamous Lorontar, the long-dead Lord Archwizard of Falconfar, still exists in undeath, and has invaded (and is hiding in) Taeauna's mind. After the army conquers the hold of Darswords, distant meddling by the wizard Narmarkoun (who, though he doesn't know it, has himself fallen under Lorontar's mental influence) unintentionally breaks Malraun's control over Taeauna, allowing Lorontar to control her instead. Not realizing this, and awakened by the chaos in his own mind caused by the ruin of his distant tower of Malragard, an enraged Malraun magically transports himself to Malragard, to destroy the cause of that destruction: Rod Everlar.

Back in Ironthorn, its third ruling family, the Tesmers, have long been the agents of the wizard Narmarkoun (just as the Lyroses were backed by Malraun), though they fight among themselves almost as fiercely as they strike out against their rivals. We see two of the many Tesmer children, Belard and Talyss, a brother and sister who've long hated each other, enter into a secret alliance, steal wealth from their parents, and depart Ironthorn. Which is when their mother reveals to her husband that he's not their father; of all their children, these two were sired by the wizard Narmarkoun—and, it now seems, have inherited his magical skills.

As the wizard Malraun appears in Malragard, to destroy Rod Everlar, Lorontar uses his control over Narmarkoun to make that wizard whisk the surviving Dark Helms he sent to Earth to Malragard, and take himself there, too, to do battle with Malraun. Lorontar has already broken Narmarkoun's control over his "greatfangs," huge dragon-like flying monsters he has been breeding and training—and all six of them are now racing toward Malragard, to attack and destroy their master.

Finding himself beset on all sides, Malraun reaches back to the mind of his thrall, Taeauna, to whisk himself to her side, back to Darswords and away from peril—and Lorontar gloatingly reveals himself and strikes at Malraun with spells.

The wizard goes mad, hurling magical destruction right and left—including blasting the wizard Narmarkoun.

As ARCH WIZARD ends, Malraun's body, now controlled by Lorontar, stalks toward Rod Everlar. Lorontar declares he'll now take Rod's body from him, Rod feebly tries to flee—and from out of the sky, six huge greatfangs swoop down, jaws agape, seeking to devour the wizards they so fear and hate.

For what happens next, read on...

Chapter One

ROD EVERLAR STARED into wide-mawed death.

Down out of the skies it came, hurtling at him six-fold, darknesses so large that they almost blotted out the sky.

Six creatures out of nightmare. Out of *his* nightmares, literally. The dragon-like, long-tailed, scaly bat-winged monsters called greatfangs.

In the forefront were the two largest wyrms, leviathans both larger than the wizard's tower had been before its fall. Their gaping jaws were large enough to swallow not just Rod, but hundreds of knights standing with him—if he'd had such an army.

Instead, he was fleeing quite alone, plunging frantically down a stone stair he was sure one of the greatfangs would swallow, railings and steps and all, stumbling and falling as he fled blindly on and down, head turned back over his shoulder to watch those huge mouths coming for him.

Neck straining, Rod couldn't look away, couldn't stop watching doom rush down on him, fangs as tall as trees framing dark red maws, the glaring eyes above fixed hungrily, angrily on *him*...

He was going to die here, die horribly in those chewing jaws, moments from now. There was no escape. Already the gaping maw of the foremost greatfangs was framing the blindly lurching body of Malraun, staggering after Rod down the stair.

It had probably swallowed Taeauna already; he could see and hear no sign of her, though he was still shouting her name to the skies.

And if she was gone, what was the point of going on? Why not just lie down and let a hungry greatfangs take him?

Taeauna, emerald eyes flashing as she swung her sword in battle.

Cat-graceful, raven-black hair swirling about her shoulders as she ran.

Laughing at him around a doorway, mouth crooked impishly... or eyes large and dark with fear, captured in a moment when she feared for his fate.

Gods, what beauty! What fire. Trusting in him even when she was contemptuous of his ignorance, or despairing of his failings. Watching over him, defending him, a veteran warrior protecting a foolish younger brother.

The one who'd dragged him here, who'd plunged him into Falconfar and kept him alive. His guide, his bodyguard, his... everything.

"Everything," he sobbed aloud, as he lost his footing and slammed into another landing, bouncing his chin and one hand bruisingly off unyielding stone.

He scrambled to his feet and fled downwards, seeing not the stair but Taeauna again, eyes fixed on his imploringly as he'd seen her last, from afar, a captive.

So beautiful... and gone now, no doubt engulfed and tumbled into the scalding innards of a greatfangs, drowning in the roiling acids of its gullet, silent forever and... and lost.

He loved her, damn it.

And was lost without her.

No Taeauna...

It had all happened so *fast*.

Rod had awakened from a dream of Malragard collapsing into ruin around him to discover he'd been Shaping in his dreams, and the tower *was* falling.

Then Malraun had appeared, raging madly at the destruction of his tower, and lashed at Rod Everlar with spell-lightnings—then burst into lunatic laughter and turned the lightning bolts stabbing from his fingers to felling all the Dark Helms.

Rod had been rolling desperately away over cracked and heaved stone tiles, fleeing snarling lightnings, but he'd seen and heard Malraun well enough.

With a roar of triumph, Malraun summoned glowing wands and scepters out of the rubble to his waiting hands, spurning most of them to choose and use just two: two horn-headed scepters that forcibly summoned the wizard Narmarkoun from elsewhere—and then tore him apart in a whirling, tightening sphere of clawing magics.

A calmness had fallen on Malraun then, though his eyes were burned away by the fiery magics he'd hurled. He'd smiled sightlessly at Rod and revealed himself as the returned Lorontar, the Archwizard of Falconfar. Who'd hidden in the mind of Taeauna for a long time, and now conquered the body of Malraun, searing that wizard's mind into mad ruin in doing so.

Still smiling, Lorontar had announced his intention of entering and enslaving Rod's body, to gain both Rod's power to alter Falconfar and Rod's knowledge of Earth—and stormed into Rod Everlar's mind.

Only to be beset by Taeauna, rising in sudden mental assault to lash out at Lorontar's sentience from behind. Either she'd been here at Malragard, somehow, or she'd savaged the ancient wizard through their mind-link, from wherever else she was. Freeing Rod to flee, as the six greatfangs plummeted down out of the sky, jaws opening.

Yet the Archwizard had rallied, seeking again to wrest control of Rod's body from him, as Malraun's body staggered on and the greatfangs descended.

Was Taeauna dead?

Rod Everlar cursed bitterly, wanting to pray but not knowing how.

Was he dead already, and just didn't know it yet?

Or did he have a few moments left, before dark, scalding oblivion?

"So what's this inn ye're taking us to?" Garfist growled, clutching the heavy coffer of gems tightly to his massive belly. It hadn't been his for very long, and he couldn't shake the feeling that it was going to be snatched away from him, somehow. Soon.

"The Stag's Head," Juskra replied, a little grimly, from out of the wing-beaten night just above him.

She was one of the strongest Aumrarr, and a scarred veteran of many battles, but the stout and bear-thewed adventurer dangling from her carry-harness was heavy, and the coffer of Tesmer gems they'd stolen from Imtowers not so very long ago wasn't light either. "We'll not be getting anywhere near that far this night, mind. If the Falcon smiles on us, we *might* get as far as Telphangh before dawn catches us, and we have to set down."

"*Have* to set down? How dangerous *is* Sardray, these days?"

"Dangerous enough," Juskra told him tartly. "They've heard of bows and arrows in Sardray, you know."

"Fat man," Dauntra broke in sharply, from where she flew a little behind Juskra and off to one side, bearing the far lighter burden of Garfist's bony companion Iskarra, "let Jusk save her breath for flying. I'm struggling here, just carrying Isk, and you must be more than thrice her weight!"

"An' it's all muscle, too, look ye!" Garfist grunted triumphantly. "Yet I hear ye, an' I'll leave off talking to my steed, an' talk at *ye* for a bit. So, what's this Telphangh place, hey?"

"An Aumrarr ruin that other folk shun. That we told you would be our first stop on our way to Galath, remember? It's what's left of an old stone tower, perched on a crag in the heart of the wild Raurklor."

"An' why's it shunned?"

"It's shunned," Juskra put in coldly, "because it's haunted."

"*Haunted?*"

"Haunted," Dauntra agreed firmly.

"Aye, I heard well enough. I mean, by what?"

"Ghosts. And worse things."

Garfist frowned, and kicked at the air to twist himself around to face Dauntra—a habit that made Juskra's shoulders ache and her temper smolder. "There're worse things than ghosts?"

"Evidently," Dauntra told him sweetly.

"Wingbitch," Garfist growled, "don't *toy* with me. Ye seem to need us to do yer dirtydark deeds, often enough, an' for that ye need us whole and willing. An' we'll not be so if ye treat us like prisoners, or friends who just happen to be idiots to be chided, an' lied to, an' *not told things*."

"Gar," Isk said warningly.

"Nay, Snakehips, I'll not be shushed! Who's up here in the night air rushing past to hear us, after all?"

12

"The lorn who just rose up out of those branches, back yon, to follow us," Dauntra replied quietly.

IN THE SUDDEN silence that fell after the man in black armor vanished in mid-sneer, Rusty stared across the littered security room at Pete.

Pete Sollars stared back at him, lower lip quivering and eyes wide and staring with fear.

After a while, he whimpered.

Which left him a less than ideal candidate for answering any question the Head of Security of Holdoncorp Headquarters might put to him, but Rusty snapped it out anyway.

"Are—are they all gone, Pete?"

"Ooounnh?"

"The *monitors*, Pete," Rusty snapped, using the flashlight in his hand to point fiercely at the bank of security screens. "Are they all *gone?*"

Tears were still rolling down Peter's face, but the security observer shook himself, gabbled something apologetic, and scrambled back to his desk, not bothering to pick up his chair or use it. At least Rusty hadn't had to tell him who "they" were.

Only seconds ago, he and Peter had been facing the sixth Dark Helm, large and menacing in his black armor and full-face helm, sharp and glittering sword in hand, stalking forward to murder them both.

Only to vanish, instantly and silently, in the proverbial blink of an eye. Very much there one moment, and gone the next. Like a dream.

But this had certainly been no dream. Across the room, the severed ends of the power cable that the calmly murderous Dark Helm had sliced through were still swinging gently, back and forth, spitting sparks almost lazily out onto the floor.

Rusty stared at them, trying to remember where the nearest guns were, and how many locks he'd have to get through to get at them. Behind him, the huge metal fortress-door of Brain Central stood closed and gleaming. Silent and immobile, with who knew what sort of panic going on behind it.

Well, Hank knew, for one—and it was his problem now.

Faintly, far away, the wail of a siren arose, and the Head of Security found himself smiling humorlessly.

Or he could just wait for the police. It seemed Derek had taken Rusty Carroll seriously for once, after all.

Which just left him the colossal headache of dealing with all of the injuries and deaths, which—if the six Dark Helms and the... the *creature* that had flown in with them had been half as efficiently deadly as they'd seemed to be—could be many, plus all the inevitable lawyers, and shattered glass windows that until recently had been the outside walls of the company's corporate headquarters, and all of the electrical damage, too, and...

"No sign of them, Chief!" Pete said excitedly, whirling from the screens with fresh tears leaking from his eyes. "We're clear!"

And Rusty Carroll let out a deep breath he hadn't known he was holding until that moment, and smiled a smile so broad he thought his face might hurt.

The parade of colossal headaches ahead were nothing, nothing at all.

THE MAGIC SEIZED hold of him like a fist, bruisingly hard. He choked, trying to fight it, and—

Narmarkoun. The voice thundered in his head, coldly hostile and gloating. It was Malraun, and yet it was not only Malraun. It was older, deeper... colder.

The world whirled and flashed around him, and he found himself suddenly blinking in the changed light. He was in the open, under the sky, standing amid rubble on ruined stone tiles. It was somewhere he'd seen before, only never so smashed and ruined as this. Malragard?

Malragard, tower of his hated foe Malraun, and it had been Malraun who'd so tauntingly called him here.

Blinking as he called on all the magic he had left to him, gathering it for the coming fight, he stared all around.

Yes, it was Malragard, and here were his own Dark Helms, striding grimly through the tumbled stones with swords drawn, coming closer. Through billowing smoke they came—and greater darkness gathered overhead. His greatfangs were gliding through the sky, converging overhead... all six of them. But how—?

"Narmarkoun!" Malraun crooned. His voice came from behind Narmarkoun, not far off.

Even before he turned to face Malraun, fighting to stammer out a warding spell, Narmarkoun knew what he would see.

And what would happen to him.

Malraun was holding two horn-headed scepters, smiling faintly. The moment their eyes met, he unleashed those scepters.

And Narmarkoun screamed.

Could not help but scream as magic thrust into him, as sharp and as painful as any saw-bladed lorn sword. Then the claws of Malraun's cruel magic tore at his body, tugging it open, and he had no breath left to scream.

He was spun around, helpless, unable even to cry as the clawing magics tore at him and spiraled, whirling around him in a tightening sphere, drawing in close as they raked and tore.

His blood sprayed out of him in a mist, his legs wobbled and failed beneath him, a red fire of agony slashed across his world as one of his arms was torn away, and Narmarkoun sobbed as he fought to focus on one rune in his mind, the relic of a spell memorized long ago. His last hope, his only way out of this...

He was a helpless, bloody wreck already, armless, stumbling on shattered legs, whirled along by magics, reeling back... back...

He was vaguely aware of striking something hard, his shoulder and ribs giving way, collapsing into shards that stabbed through his smashed and broken body.

It was what was left of a wall, and the whirlwind of clawing magic moaned through it as if its cracked stones had been mere butter, or no more than smoke.

His body crushed, Narmarkoun writhed in agony, sobbing in the heart of a cloud of gore, clinging to one thing in his thoughts, a rune that blazed brightly...

By the time the whirling cloud of blood reached a second wall and collapsed into a wet smear of gore across it, the pitiful remnant of the wizard was no longer at the heart of it.

"As we planned, Bel?"

"As we planned. Galath, departing just as soon—and as quietly—as we can. I'd rather not have to fight my way out of the home I grew up in."

"Not even if it means killing as many of the family as we can?"

15

NARMARKOUN PLUNGED INTO the rune, *became* the rune, and the agony suddenly ebbed away. He was whirling again, even faster than Malraun's savaging magic had spun him, rushing along far from the riven tower of Malragard, racing home.

His own cold castle. Its familiar silent chill unfolded around him and enshrouded him as he sped on, an eerily whirling glow whose approach made his undead playpretties turn to stare expressionlessly. On, on down long passages and through high, balconied chambers seared out of the solid rock, past many rotting shoulders and silently gliding legs, toward just one of his beauties, who awaited him on her knees, as naked as all the others, her mouth open and eyes staring in astonishment.

The glow of the rune he clung to was answered by an identical glow issuing from her mouth, from the matching rune that his spell had long ago left in her head for just this need.

A glow his rune raced towards, Narmarkoun whimpering in anticipation of the agony that was to come.

Rune met rune, and what little was left of his playpretty's mind died as her world, and that of her master, burst into soundless mage-light.

She writhed, jerked and flailed on the stone floor in the heart of the flaring and fading light. The other playpretties stared as Narmarkoun shuddered in the grip of greater pain than even Malraun's spell-clawings had brought him, fighting to master his new body while still unable to control his own reeling mind...

After what felt like a very long time, Narmarkoun felt his agony ebb and the thrashings and spasms of his new body lessen. He slowly became aware that he was sobbing, a deep and ragged mewling that died away into a wordless whimpering.

Which was about the time he realized something else. A severed head had just struck the stones beside him, to bounce and then roll past. A headless but otherwise shapely body followed, toppling loose-limbed.

Narmarkoun blinked, his whimpering ending in astonishment. As a sword flashed past, not far from his nose, to slice deeply into the cold, bloodless body of another of his playpretties.

Narmarkoun blinked again, hardly daring to look up. He was fresh out of runes.

Chapter Two

ROD EVERLAR PELTED down seemingly endless stairs, step after racing step—how deep did Malragard *go*, anyway?—as he watched the open maw of the closest greatfangs looming behind him.

Half Falconfar, if they knew the Lord Archwizard was more than a mere fancy-tale, probably thought he could spin around, wave his hands, grandly declaim some thunderous words of magic, and in an instant blow the greatfangs—*all* of the greatfangs, all six of them—to a rain of blood and scales that would still be fading away as he dusted his hands together in satisfaction, turned away, and strolled down the last few steps.

Into what looked to be the cellars, or dungeons—*did* a Doom of Falconfar have dungeons, with prisoners or their forgotten skeletons dangling from walls in chains in every dark corner of them?—of Malraun's tower of Malragard.

Yet Shaping didn't work like that, and Rod was a Shaper, not a wizard at all. Still less a Lord Archwizard, able to lurk for centuries in the minds of others or in waiting magic swords or rings or crowns or suchlike baubles, just waiting for some unsuspecting person to happen along, pick the glittering lure up out of the dust—and get taken over by the ruthless Lorontar, on the spot.

Everyone seemed to think that he, Rod Everlar, was some sort of hero who would know exactly how to set Falconfar to rights and set about it, seeing into the minds of everyone, blasting the villains, lauding the gallant and aiding the oppressed. Hell, beyond the lorn and the Dark Helms and every wizard, he didn't even know who the villains *were*, though he was beginning to think every last knight and noble, except perhaps Velduke Deldragon and Baron Tindror in Galath, reveled in being as dastardly as they could be.

Taeauna had brought him here to be Falconfar's savior and hero. Rod knew she now knew better, yet liked him anyway. Even if her respect for him as the all-knowing Fixer of Wrongs was gone and she knew he was a bumbling idiot without her constant guidance, she knew he tried to be a good guy, and his blood was still useful for healing, too, and—

Oh, yes, that. He'd almost forgotten about that.

Falling bruisingly onto his left shoulder for about the fortieth time—it would have been his nose, if his head hadn't been turned around hard to look over his shoulder—Rod watched tumbling stones and heaving tiles and a darkness that might have been Malraun the Matchless vanish down that greatfangs' maw and wondered if drinking his own blood could heal him enough to bring him right back to life after he'd died.

Probably not, if he'd spilled it all.

NARMARKOUN STARED UP at sharp-bladed death.

The body that was now his was more shapely than most of his playpretties, and showed no signs of decay at all. His spell had long kept it supple and strong, not a decaying thing.

He could see in the eyes of the men confronting him over their drawn swords—a motley band of warriors, a score of them or more, all strangers to him—that the bared body he now inhabited was beautiful.

And that they were scared of him despite his whimpering on the floor before them, and his obvious lack of a blade. He—no, to their eyes, *she*; he must not forget that—was no grotesque horror to any gaze, yet her sleekness was the cold gray of undeath, of the sort they'd been seeing—and hewing apart in terror—since they'd arrived here.

Which had not been long ago, by the looks of them. He knew his holds held little in the way of warmth or food for the living, and this castle was no different from the rest. Nor treasure that could be easily found, for that matter. They'd come here seeking something they would not find.

Which made them doubly dangerous. He had no spells left at the moment with which to fight them, no things of magic near at hand that he could snatch up to blast them with, and no more runes to whisk him to the safety of another body elsewhere, if he was hewn down now.

In short, as the Falconaar saying went, if he walked not right carefully now, his striding would be straight to his final doom.

"Slay me not!" he pleaded, hearing the hoarse, long-unused voice grate out of his throat higher and lighter than his own speech. Their eyes bored into him, looking him up and down, seeing him as a woman one moment, and an undead *thing* the next... and then a woman again.

Well enough. He would *be* a woman, helpless and timid, and hope thereby to survive, to—

"Who are you?" one of the warriors demanded, waving the tip of his sword through the air right in front of the kneeling, trembling woman's throat.

"D-Daera, I am called," Narmarkoun replied, knowing it to be the truth. Even with the mind that had belonged to this body quite burned away and gone, the name clung to the skull. Even farmers' daughters knew their own names. "Daera. I am a slave to the wizard Narmarkoun, Doom of Falconfar. A pleasure-slave. This is his castle."

"So much we know," another warrior growled. "Where is he?"

"I know not," Narmarkoun replied, spreading her hands and inwardly marveling at how swiftly Daera's voice went from a dry croak to husky smoothness.

The men's eyes flickered at her lithe movements, and the cold, calmly calculating wizard within her took care to quell the little smile that this body now wanted to make. "I have not seen him in these halls for a long time," she added.

"Oh? How many days?" yet another man snapped suspiciously. They all seemed to want to wave their swords menacingly when they spoke.

Daera shrugged her helplessness, on her knees before them, her imploring eyes large and dark. "I know not. It is hard to tell the passage of days here, walled in by the rock. It *seems* a long time. Who..."

She hesitated, making her question, when it came, sound bewildered and fearful rather than any sort of challenge. "Who are you?"

"We're—" one warrior started, but fell silent when the man standing beside him waved him fiercely to silence.

"We are of Darswords," another man said, his voice very deep and grim. "We fled Horgul's army, and found this place."

"Sought shelter," the first warrior added tersely, and stabbed out with his arm and sword in an arc to wave at the stone ceiling overhead, indicating the entire castle. "Does the wizard spend much time here?"

"He always has," she almost whispered. "I—I can only think something's happened to him."

One or two of the warriors grinned at that. "Our hope, too," one of them muttered.

"Great lords," Daera asked, raising her hands very slowly to them in entreaty, and then crossing her wrists over each other to signify her submission and willingness to be bound, "will you spare me? Please?"

The reply she got was more murmurings than words, as the men of Darswords looked at her and at each other. Most sounded undecided, a few suspicious, and a few—just a few—pitying. Yet Narmarkoun was most used to dealing with his own spellbound slaves, not fearful warriors of a small upcountry hold. In recent years—decades—he'd had as little to do with the living as he could.

"You are..." It was the deep-voiced man again; the rest fell silent. "You are the wizard's creature. Dead by magic, yet kept walking and talking by magic. How do we know he cannot control you from afar, even hurl spells at us through you?"

Falcon *spit*. Narmarkoun fought to keep all hint of anger from his—her—face.

"I am *not* dead!" she made herself say fiercely, turning to look at him. "No! I live, I breathe—only the eldest of the slaves here are kept from crumbling to dust by the wizard's spells! Take me out of this place, and you'll see! Out under the sun, in the wind and the rain, I'll crumble not! I will laugh, and kiss you for your kindness, and *live!*"

There. As pretty a piece of acting as he'd ever seen any deceiving woman do, in all his years. That ought to do it.

"You avoid answering me," the deep-voiced man said grimly. "I asked this: how do we know your master cannot control you from afar, and cast spells at us through you? I ask it again, and await your answer."

Narmarkoun made Daera stare up at him open-mouthed, a weakling rather than a challenger.

"I am patient," the deep-voiced warrior added, after a moment, "but my sword is not."

Daera drew in a deep breath, and replied with a hint of fierce desperation, "You don't know, and can't know—because I can't be sure, and I have been in his thrall for years. Yet he has never done such to any of us. Cast magic through us, I mean. He controls us by his hands, or magic in his gaze, or lashes us with spells—magic he casts *at* us, not through us at another."

The deep-voiced warrior took a pace forward, the tip of his sword rising ready at her throat, and stared hard into her eyes, as if he could read truth there, or falsehoods.

Daera stared back at him, seemingly unafraid now, almost defiant.

After a long, silent moment he nodded and took his sword away. "You mean what you say," he granted, "yet you have more you want to say. Fear of us and our swords is holding your tongue. Say it, whatever it is, and I'll not strike you down. I would rather know what is in your mind than have you cowed but simmering. Speak, woman."

"I will," Daera told him grimly. "You asked me where my master Narmarkoun is. I know not, but will help you search this castle to find him. I do not think he is here, but I tell you this, men of Darswords: if you do find him, you should not be too swift to swing your swords at him. He is a wizard, and all wizards are dangerous, yes—but if you faced a dragon, and knew where there was a sword that could slay dragons, would you not go and fetch it? I know Narmarkoun fears another wizard, one called Lorontar."

"Lorontar," one warrior breathed. "The Lord Archwizard of Falconfar."

"Night-fright legend!" another man snapped.

"The Ghost Wizard," someone else said uneasily, and shook his head in a dismissive grin that did not hold much bright confidence. "Dead, yet working fell magics still."

"Dead but not dead," Daera told them, "as I am not dead. If you do find Narmarkoun, you should work with him, as allies, against Lorontar's far greater evil. If you cut down Narmarkoun, and then think yourself safe, you will have broken your Archwizard-slaying-sword, and will someday face the Archwizard empty-handed. Darswords will be no refuge, even if Horgul is gone and no armies ever march again. Not with Lorontar the only wizard left in the world."

"So it's time to ally with wizards?" the deep-voiced warrior asked, in slow and heavy disbelief.

Daera lifted her head to stare hard into his eyes, nod, and reply firmly, "It's time. For the good—nay, for the survival—of Falconfar."

"YOU HEARD WHAT happened to Jaklar?" Talyss purred smugly.

"Torn to death by wolves," her brother Belard replied, turning from an open leather shoulder-satchel on the table before him. "Led by Amteira Hammerhand, who could not stop calling on the Forestmother all the while, as they snarled and bit and savaged him to pieces. Ate him alive. A fitting end, I'd say—and I'd say something else, too: the goddess of the Raurklor has changed holy servants. In an impressively bloody fashion, I might add."

His sister nodded, leaning against the door frame of his bedchamber with languid grace. "You're fully informed, as usual. Ready to leave?"

Belard sighed. "Yes, but without the gems I was planning to take with us. It seems someone robbed our dear parents before I could."

Talyss nodded. "Aumrarr, according to one of the maids who got a glimpse of them leaving from the battlements. Though how they got past the warning spells, I know not."

Her brother shrugged. "And I care not. The gems are gone—and we'd best be, too, just as swiftly as we can hustle ourselves along. Nareyera isn't the only one looking for us."

"Kin?"

"Of course. Father was so aghast at what Mother told him last night that he couldn't keep his mouth shut."

"For a change," Talyss told the ceiling sardonically. They had both lost count of the number of times Lord Irrance Tesmer had let slip things he shouldn't have—within the family, to servants, and even to foes. "What choice blundering has he set crashing amongst us all *this* time?"

"The news, first admitted to him by our darling mother in bed last night, that two of their oh-so-close-and-fond Tesmer children weren't sired by father, but by the Master."

"And would the names of those two be Belard and Talyss, by any chance?" his sister asked quietly.

Belard lifted one eyebrow. "You knew."

"I suspected. The Master has always given us far more attention than the others, and it certainly wasn't because our magic is so enthrallingly superior. Maera is strong enough that we should all fear her, and even Nareyera—admit it, Bel—can hold her own against us."

"*I* fear Kalathgar," Belard replied quietly. "He just might be the only one of us who could outwit the Master."

Talyss nodded. "Let's hope we're halfway across fair Falconfar if he ever tries. Right now, let's be going." She drew a long, heavy leather carry sack into view from behind her long and shapely legs, swung it up onto her shoulder as she stepped past him, and adjusted its baldric across her chest.

Belard turned and reached out to smooth the leather strap where it slid between her breasts. His lingering fingers earned him a smile. "*Later*, brother mine."

"If there *is* a later for either of you," a voice said coldly from the doorway behind him.

Belard sighed, even as he stepped past Talyss—who was growing a sharp-eyed frown—and turned.

"Delmark, of course," he said wearily. "Who put you up to this, brother mine? Feldrar? Nareyera?"

"Nar— It matters not. What *matters* is that no sooner do we learn that the two of you are not true Tesmers at all, you both prepare to flee Ironthorn with as much Tesmer gold as you can carry. Making you not only traitors to your own kin—your half-kin—but thieving outsiders in our very midst."

Delmark's voice was harsh, his face was pale, his eyes glittered, and his sword was out and ready, sharp point leveled at Belard's chest.

Belard rolled his eyes. "Well, now, which is it, Del? Are we kin or not? Common thieves or traitors to the family? Can you spit out a coherent reason at all, or did Nareyera just tell you to rush up here and butcher us as fast as you could run?"

"She has nothing to do with this," Delmark said curtly. "*I* decide when I draw blade, and why. This is a matter of honor."

He took a careful half-step forward, flicking up the point of his steel in a clear signal that Belard should draw his own sword and defend himself.

"Oh? Whose honor? Mother's? Father's? Isn't it more than a few years too late to be fighting over that? And shouldn't you be seeking out a Doom of Falconfar to pick your quarrel with?"

"Clever words, Bel; always, clever words! Words that're no match for my blade," Delmark snapped. "Defend yourself, or I'll put this steel right through you!"

"You'd have been much wiser to just stride in here and *do* that, instead of all this snorting and blowing about honor and traitors," Belard replied, turning back to his open, half-filled satchel. "You bore me."

Delmark snarled, and shifted his feet to make ready to lunge. "Men of *honor* deal with each other face to face."

"*Precisely*," Talyss said cuttingly, from behind Belard. "But then, your strong sense of honor hasn't yet risen to the notice of any Tesmer *I* know. Nor is it particularly apparent now."

"You keep out of this," Delmark snapped in reply, not shifting his gaze for a moment from his gently smiling brother. "Slut."

Talyss lifted her left hand, fingers clawing the air in a brief, wriggling pattern—and the air in front of Delmark suddenly shimmered. Then it seemed to flow toward the floor like a silent waterfall.

Delmark gave his sister a look then, and it was a sneer. "You think I came unprepared? Or that you're the only Tesmer who knows a little magic? Narmarkoun taught the rest of us, too. Taught us more than enough to deal with—"

Belard whirled and flung the satchel into his brother's face.

Delmark staggered back, the weight of the sack bearing his blade sharply to the floor—and Belard sprang across the room like a striking snake, to slap at a small, oval picture on the wall. The picture rattled and with a loud *clack* the floor under Delmark's boots gave way. The stumbling Tesmer abruptly plunged knee-deep into the floor. Harsh, mechanical sounds promptly arose from beneath it.

Delmark jerked sideways, one leg almost severed by the blade that had snapped across the trap. The blade quivered as it bit deep into bone and sliced on, deep into his other leg.

He'd just started to scream when Belard's fist crashed into his face, snapping his head around like a doll. Delmark slumped into silence, his dropped sword clanging into the shallow trap, blood pooling beneath him.

Belard calmly plucked his satchel and two items that had fallen from it—a tankard and a ladle—out of the recess in the floor before they got drowned in gore, and turned to Talyss. "Shall we go?"

"Unless you'd care to fight a lot more of our kin all at once," she replied, strolling toward him. "He's wearing his locket, isn't he?"

Before she bent to pluck it from around the sagging Delmark's throat, Belard laid a hand on her arm. "Leave it. They can trace us through it, you know."

Talyss smiled. "I do know. In fact, I'm counting on it."

Belard looked at her, and slowly smiled.

She smiled back at him, beautiful mouth curling smugly, as she tugged viciously on the fine chain around Delmark's throat. It drew blood as it broke, leaving his head lolling loosely.

Belard and Talyss left together, not looking back.

Behind them, the unconscious Delmark jerked and then shuddered as the relentless blade sheared right through one leg, and bit more deeply into the other one.

Chapter Three

ROD WAS GASPING for breath now.

How many God-damned stairs did this wizard's tower *have?* Did this endless flight of steps go down clear through Falconfar, and out into some unknown lands on the far side of the planet?

Or was Falconfar a planet, a sphere in space, at all? He hadn't—

At that moment, with the image of the world as a great flat slab of earth and stone with mountains and trees on it—just on the top, or on both sides?—the great jaws behind him closed on a dark, half-seen form that must be Malraun.

Gore spurted in a wet spray—and the weight of Lorontar's relentless assault was abruptly gone from Rod's mind.

Blurting out a sob, he staggered, feeling suddenly as light as air. Free!

Happy, even, despite the imminent death sweeping down the stairs after him, crunching the dying wizard's body as it came. Lorontar's invasion of his thoughts had thrust darkness into them, bringing despair in its grim and heavy wake, and now it was—suddenly, so suddenly—gone.

The stair shook under him, and he fell again, tumbling down the hard stone steps in a whirlwind of bumps and bruises. When it ended, he shook his head dazedly, and looked back up behind him.

The greatfangs had bounded aloft again, beating its great sky-filling wings in mighty, ponderous, but steadily quickening sweeps, lifting it up and away. Rod watched something tumble from its working jaws, plummeting to bounce wetly to a stop on the steps just above him.

It was what was left of a man's right arm, bitten off below the shoulder, its fingers spread in a claw of pain. Malraun's arm, by the looks of it.

Rod stared at it numbly, then looked up again. Things had grown dim; the greatfangs was passing over him now, a scaled, leviathan tapering to a tail that could fell castle towers with a single lazy slap. It was chewing, with the same satisfied gusto that Rod had seen at Deldragon's feast table, as his knights worked away on favorite foods.

So Malraun was dead—chewed to pieces, and Lorontar with him. Which meant Taeauna must be dead and gone, too...

So who was making the faint echoes at the very back of his mind?

Someone shrieking, someone far away and swiftly getting farther, someone high-voiced and desperate...

"Taeauna?"

Rod could scarcely believe it, but the moment he gasped out her name, staring at the other five greatfangs sweeping menacingly out of the sky at him, he was certain.

It was Taeauna crying out to him. She was shouting his name.

"*Taeauna!*" he bellowed back, as loudly as he could, staggering and waving his arms for balance as he turned wildly in all directions, to stare into the distance in hopes of seeing her. "Taeauna? *Where are you?*"

The cries in his mind were getting fainter. She hadn't heard him, couldn't hear him, of course, was so far away now that—

"Taeauna!" he shouted, so hard and loud that his head rang and his voice cracked into a hoarse, wordless trailing-off. "I'm coming for you!"

As if the most useless Archwizard on two worlds could rescue anyone at all, with wizards and greatfangs everywhere, armies on the march, and—

The second greatfangs, almost as large as the first, was gliding down the stairs at him, its barbed chin brushing the edges of the stone steps, its maw open wide and looming darker and larger by the moment.

Rod Everlar sank into a crouch because he thought he'd fall over if he didn't, and watched it come for him.

Taeauna's voice was gone from his mind now, and—and if he didn't do something Archwizardly and heroic in his next few breaths, there wouldn't *be* a Rod Everlar to come for anyone.

And the Dooms, the ruthless sneering God-damned spellhurling Dooms, would win after all.

"THOSE LORN STILL back there?" Iskarra asked quietly.

"Yes," Dauntra sighed, "and we're very soon going to have to set you down so we can deal with them—or fall out of the sky, too weak to do anything but watch *you* try to deal with them."

"Hah!" Garfist Gulkoun barked gleefully, from where he hung beneath Juskra, a wingbeat or so ahead, "that's just what we'll do! Let me at them! My blade is sharp and my fists swift and hard, to be sure! Just *let* me get my—"

"Rump onto the forest floor, so you can stand up and swagger— and make of yourself a juicy, helpless target for lorn diving fast at you," Juskra interrupted him sharply. "They can *fly*, remember?"

"Aye, lass, aye. I'm not a *dullard*. How far's this Telphangh place, hey?"

"Never mind that," Isk told him sharply. "Is there a good spot near us, up ahead, where you can land?"

"Hope so," Dauntra replied grimly. "Jusk?"

"Not a good one," Juskra said slowly, "but I believe we're already past waiting for good ones. Shield your face and pull your arms and legs in, fat man."

"Are ye addressing *me*?" Garfist asked, in mock anger, even as he obeyed her.

"Nay, I was talking to the small *army* of fat men I seem to be lugging through the night," Juskra told him with a grim smile. "Hold tight!"

Before he could reply, they crashed through a tangle of branches. She winced—and then groaned aloud as Garfist got caught among them for long enough to yank her over on her side.

Growling, he let fly a lusty kick at an unseen bough, thrusting them free. Juskra wobbled like a drunkard through the sky, hissing curses, almost slamming into the next tree before she righted herself and drew in her wingtips in time to plunge between two thick stands of gallart-tops, and burst through the upper branches of a pine.

In grim silence, Dauntra followed her, keeping higher to spare herself and Iskarra the battering. Juskra was ducking and darting down a narrow, tree-choked cleft between two ridges, somewhere in the heart of the Raurklar, and a wet flatness that might be water—or just might be a bog—could be seen somewhere ahead.

"Here?" Gar growled at the battlescarred Aumrarr above him, waving a hand at it.

"*Don't* do that," she snapped back at him, as his gesture set them to rocking in the air and turned a smooth banking glide into frantic flapping. "No, *not* here. I've no wish to try to fight lorn up to my neck in sucking mud."

"So why not—"

"Garfist Gulkoun," Juskra growled fiercely, "shut your endless roar and *listen* to me. I'm about spent. That ring I gave you? Think of a sunrise, remember? Once it glows, it can strike someone—yes, it works on lorn—senseless at a touch. It won't glow again right away, though, and each time you use it in the same fray, it'll be a little slower to awaken than the last time. Oh, and one thing more: it seems to only work once on someone. So if you send a lorn to sleep, don't try using it on the same lorn a second time. And *don't* use it on me."

"Oh? Why? Ye'll get upset?"

Juskra rolled her eyes. She couldn't see Gar's grin, but she could hear it in his voice.

"Yes," she replied evenly. "I'll get upset—and we can't have that."

Despite herself, Juskra was grinning as she ducked around a huge old pine tree, misjudged the space beyond—and slammed hard into a gallart-top that had been tall and strong when Highcrag was built.

And was now old, hollow, dead, and the size of a small castle keep.

Juskra moaned in pain as she crashed through a dozen lichen-cloaked, long-dead branches and into the main trunk beyond, winding her and smashing something small in her left wing—and shattering the rotten trunk in an explosion of dead-dry wood.

Garfist's cursing, as he crashed along in her wake, ended in helpless coughing and choking as he breathed in a cloud of wood dust, and the air around them echoed with the dull snap of the trunk breaking right through and the rest of the tree starting to topple on them from above, breaking apart as it came.

Which was a good thing for the startled Dauntra and Iskarra, who flew right into it all with identical startled shrieks.

Already beyond the tree they'd destroyed, Juskra and Garfist were tumbling helplessly through a sharp tangle of other branches that broke loudly as they fell. Juskra was too breathless and pain-wracked to say anything, her wings snagging and tearing and snagging again, and Garfist was strangling as he fought to breathe.

The lorn diving after them would have smiled in triumph, if they could have. Not having mouths to smile with, they did it with their eyes.

As they swooped down, jostling each other in their haste to reach their quarry first, and personally do the killing.

It was no use. He *couldn't* Shape with greatfangs after greatfangs sweeping down on him, blotting out the sky, couldn't concentrate—

Shaking his head, anger rising, Rod Everlar threw himself sideways and up a few steps, rolling and curling up into the hard stone corner where a step met the side-wall.

The talon that had just stabbed out to slice him open from throat to crotch sliced the air above his shoulder and swept past, its owner hissing out its anger like a deafening, castle-sized kettle.

Rod cowered down, hugging the stone, and felt rather than saw the huge bulk pass over him, the tail of the irritated greatfangs lashing the steps above him, shattering them and showering him with rubble. He risked a glance up the stair—and saw the next two beasts swooping down the stairs at him.

They were much smaller than the first two—which meant that they were as long as a dozen horses, each, and their jaws would have to bite him in half to swallow him. Which they looked more than capable of doing.

The one that was in the lead was already angling over to one side as it flew, so it could come along the step he was cowering on rather than across it, and simply scoop him up with fang and talon.

Bite, bite, chew, chew, and that'd be it. No more Rod Everlar, no more Archwizard of Falconfar, no more... *anything*, for him.

Spitting out a curse, he sprang to his feet, whirled around, and started running down the endless steps again, barely aware that the fifth and smallest greatfangs was circling high in the sky above, and that the largest of them was disappearing into clouds in the distance. Presumably with Malraun and Taeauna in its belly. There was no sign of either of them, and her cries had been moving farther and farther from him so *fast*...

Below him, farther down the steps, the greatfangs that had missed eviscerating him let out a roar—and started lashing out with its tail and talons like a dog digging in sand, smashing what was left of the walls of Malragard right around it.

As if that had been a signal, the two smaller greatfangs swerved in opposite directions to wreak mayhem on the stones of Malragard, too, and the last, smallest greatfangs plunged down out of the sky to join them.

As Rod watched, mouth open in astonishment, the five greatfangs swarmed angrily over Malraun's tower, tearing open roofs, tumbling walls, and shredding the contents of the rooms with great raking sweeps of their talons.

Had Narmarkoun worked some sort of commandment into these monsters, to make them destroy the abode of his rival Doom? Or was he somehow sending them orders right now?

Whatever the reason, Rod doubted he'd be spared forever; if they got done reducing the tower to rubble while he was still standing here on this stair, they'd likely come for him again.

So where, with the roofs of Harlhoh yonder—a small village with plenty of folk cowering, pointing and running in it; fellow targets to lure greatfangs talons, all of them—and tilled fields stretching everywhere else to the dark and distant line of the surrounding Raurklor, could he go? Or hide?

Deep in the forest would be best, but there was no way he could outrun *five* of the beasts, across all that farmland.

The alternative was to find rubble, hunker down in it, and hope by the Falcon that he didn't end up crushed or buried alive, if the huge flying beasts kept at it after leveling the tower, reducing Malragard from rubble to gravel.

The largest of the remaining greatfangs whirled, in a sinuous twisting of its scaly bulk that Rod wouldn't have believed possible if he hadn't seen it, to hook its talons under the roof of the lower levels of the tower, and tug as it flew overhead.

Stone and slate shingles tried to bend, with an almost human shriek, and then shattered into scores of pieces and fell apart, creating a brief rain of tumbling shards and leaving the ponderous beast holding nothing at all.

Its latest attack had wrought something else. Well down the stair from Rod, below a landing now choked with tumbled ceiling-beams, a long sliver of ceiling had been torn away, so that someone running down the stair could leap sideways through the tapering gap, into the darkness below. Where there was a room, presumably—quite possibly a ready-made tomb, if the greatfangs' assault kept up—but better shelter than the open air he was standing up in now, alone and prominent on the stair, with two smaller greatfangs headed his way.

Rod dashed down the stairs, leaping heaps of rubble or skidding through them on his boot heels, like an out-of-control skier about to crash, where they formed drifts too large and deep to jump over or dodge. One of the greatfangs was definitely heading for him, veering from what it had been doing to open a fanged mouth that wasn't the huge cavern of its two bigger brethren, but still the size of a grand pair of double doors.

And definitely large enough to bite him in two in one swift lunge.

Rod had time enough to get a very good look at that mouth, and its fringe of sharp fangs—the largest were as long as his arms—before he had to duck and wriggle and bruisingly slam his way through a tangle of fallen beams. Whereupon, as he struggled free of them, gasping, the greatfangs looming up like a huge dark curtain overhead, the narrow gap was right in front of him.

He launched himself into it head-first, quickly raising his hands to shield his face and throat.

One wrist banged numbingly on the edge of the gap as he went through it, but he had time, in the long plunge that followed, to get both hands up.

He fell a long way in the darkness. His landing—

—Was a crash through an unseen awning or canopy, which held him for the merest of moments before tearing with an angry sound and choking and blinding him with swirling dust. Then he slammed into what felt like a mattress—cloth and straw and ropes that groaned and held for agonizing moments ere they snapped with strange singing sighs—and slammed with it into something beyond, something hard, flat and unyielding.

The floor, Rod concluded brilliantly, in the last moment before the worst of the choking took him, and he writhed and spasmed helplessly in the dust, lungs and throat afire and precious air nowhere to be found. He rolled desperately, blind and in agony and just wanting to get away from the dust.

Once, long ago, on a school trip, Rod had spent a few memorable minutes wallowing in a great box of foam mattress stuffing, giggling but helpless, and the dust roiling around him now felt about like that. He rolled and rolled, clawing at the floor to try to move faster, shuddering at the agony in his lungs, panting but unable to sob...

Until it all ended, and he could breathe.

And cough. And cough some more, curling up in a helpless ball to hack, and retch, and then spew his guts out.

Or so it felt, as he rolled weakly on into the darkness, just trying to get farther from the dust—and the faint light of the sky he could now see, through swimming eyes, somewhere above and behind him.

Timbers groaned, a little way off in one direction, rising to a shriek and breaking off into dull, floor-shaking crashes. The greatfangs demolition crew were still at work.

Another crash, this one closer. Tomb indeed, brought right down on his head, if he didn't move.

Still coughing, Rod forced his eyes open and tried to sit up. The crashing he was hearing was coming from right *there*—and there, in this now-dimly-seen room, was a place where the wall was bulging outward as he watched.

To break, jaggedly, showering the room with fieldstones, mortar dust, and splintered wood that a moment ago had been paneling; a tumbling cloud of wreckage that fell away from a row of dark, curving knives that Rod recognized all too well as greatfangs talons.

Talons now sweeping across the room at him, even as a scaly

and sinuous neck looped in the air above, to bring one cruel eye to peer in at him.

Sighing out a curse, Rod Everlar stared back at it and made a rude gesture before hurling himself into a frantic roll again.

He was heading for the unseen, unknown far end of the room— but he was really just striving to get *away*.

It was all happening so *fast*.

The talons swerved toward him, the body of the greatfangs blotted out all light, and Rod tried to console himself with the thought that the beast was flying overhead; it would be past and gone in another moment.

The trick would be living through that moment.

Chapter Four

I T WAS STILL raining broken branches, amid the gunshot cracks of dead limbs as they struck lower trees, when the lorn swooped in.

Straight through all the shards and showers of rotten wood and disintegrating bark, plunging toward where they'd last seen Dauntra—with Iskarra grimly clinging to the carry-harness beneath and behind her.

The Aumrarr and her cargo were now nowhere to be seen, though there was much thrashing in tangles of dead wood, below. The lorn found nothing but endless trees, and circled back to the chaos. Quieter, now, with only a few branches falling free from where they'd caught to descend amid smaller crashes. The dust of disintegrated wood hung in the air in a heavy cloud, drifting to the forest floor.

Where the two winged women must already be, barring some strange Aumrarr magic. Gliding cautiously lower, the lorn waved to each other to get right down under the wooded canopy so as to get a proper look.

There were well over a dozen of them, Garfist concluded sourly, peering up through the drifting dust. He stood above an untidy pile of dead branches, many of them still bearing leaves or needles, that he'd heaped over Juskra.

Who was now glaring up at him fiercely for doing so—and for planting one of his boots firmly on her chest, to keep her there—but seemed too dazed to even hiss a protest, much less struggle to her feet. Garfist had already plucked her sword out of its sheath and planted it point-first in the rotten trunk of a fallen tree right beside him, to have ready in case he needed a replacement for his own blade. Her wings—bruised and worse—were so tangled up in all the fallen tree-wreckage that she couldn't hope to get herself upright without help, even before he started tramping all over what was holding her down.

He gave the scarred Aumrarr a twisted grin—just as she went limp, and her eyes closed.

Garfist shrugged—and then stiffened, going into a crouch, as something moved behind the trunk of the huge tree behind Juskra. A living tree, as solid and unyielding as a castle wall—that she might have flown them both face-first into if her collision with the dead forest giant hadn't set her to tumbling instead.

Two faces slid into view, peering cautiously around opposite sides of the tree trunk. Fortunately, they were faces Garfist knew: Dauntra and Iskarra, both with worried frowns on their faces and drawn knives gleaming in their hands.

They pointed unnecessarily at the sky to warn him of the lorn; Garfist nodded and waved at them to get their backs against the tree and move around its trunk to stand on either side of him.

He was still waving one large and hairy hand when the first lorn bounded down out of the sky to land feet first in heaped dead branches with a loud snapping and crackling—and Garfist swung wildly at it with his sword, and slashed its throat out before it had time to catch its balance or do anything else. Lorn might have mouthless skull-faces, but they had throats that could be cut. In fact, aside from the skull-faces, the bat-wings, and the tails, they were built very like men.

And men, Garfist knew very well how to kill.

With brutal, growling efficiency he launched himself across the tangled deadwood, swinging his sword as he went, and succeeded in slicing open a slate-gray lorn forearm that had been hastily raised from the scabbard it had been tugging at, to shield its throat. Then a bough suddenly rolled over beneath his boot and Garfist crashed helplessly down against the lorn's shins.

The creature toppled helplessly forward onto him, leaving its throat an easy target for Dauntra, as she sprang forward with her dagger.

Behind her, Iskarra whirled in another crackling of dead branches, and swayed aside from the charge of a second lorn. Who suffered the same fate as Garfist, off-balance already from slashing at a woman who was much slimmer than it had thought, and who could twist and sway with uncanny balance. Iskarra sprang onto the lorn's back, stabbed down into its wing-muscles and jerked her dagger back out again, and prepared—as the lorn she'd just wounded bucked and wallowed under her, shouting in startled pain—to meet an onrushing third and fourth lorn.

One of whom promptly fell, only to roll back and well away from the fray before anyone could reach it with a knife, leaving her facing just one. It hesitated, slowing to draw a dagger to go with its sword, and crouched cautiously behind them both as it advanced.

This won Iskarra time enough to plunge her dagger hilt-deep into the lorn she was riding—and her second stab went into the back of its neck, causing it to spasm violently and slump into stillness.

By which time Dauntra was charging up and past her, amid snapping and thrashing branches, to slash aside the cautious lorn's sword with her own, driving it back.

A dozen more lorn had just landed, giving the withdrawing creature hisses of scorn, and shouldered forward in a group. These skull-faces, too, were trusting in swords and daggers rather than their own formidable talons, and they were eight strong now, with the lorn already on the tree-top both joining them.

Dauntra stood her ground alone, facing them with apparent unconcern. Iskarra shot a glance behind her—in time to see a similar group of lorn advancing in menacing unison on Garfist. He was murmuring curses under his breath in a non-stop flow; a sure sign he was beginning to feel afraid.

He retreated a step, and though mouthless skull-faces can't grin, something gleeful spread across the lorn faces facing him—and one lorn, a shade larger than the rest, strode forward out of the carefully advancing line to challenge Garfist with a flourish.

Garfist pictured the rising sun, struck his own "Have at ye!" pose, and when the expected lunge came, sidestepped with deceptive speed for his bulk, saw the glow of the ring on his finger, and launched himself into his own lunge, reaching—and slapping—the lorn's swordarm.

The ring flashed and went dark, the lorn collapsed in a limp heap, and Garfist announced loudly and in the most satisfied tone he could manage, "There! *That's* the one I'll eat first."

The lorn facing him shied back like so many frightened horses, jerking up their heads and shooting questioning glances at each other. Humans ate lorn?

"With *sauce*," Garfist added with relish, as if anticipating the most flavorful feast in all Falconfar, striking a nonchalant pose as he leant on his sword and drove it through the downed lorn's slate-gray neck, nigh-severing it.

Then something seemed to occur to him, belatedly and suddenly. "Ah, but I'm remiss in my manners!" he exclaimed aloud. "I have companions, and they'll be hungry too!"

Tugging forth his blade, Garfist swung it high with a flourish, flicking blood from its freshly drenched tip, and announced, "I'll need to slay *more* lorn, by the Falcon! And, look ye! By that very favor of the Hunting Soarer, here be some, right handy to my steel!"

He let out a roar of laughter and started wading forward through dead and fallen tree-boughs in a deafening cacophony of sharp cracks, whirling his blade around him as wildly as a Stormar tavern-dancer flourishing her discarded garments. Despite themselves, the lorn gave way, hissing in uncertainty and alarm—until one of them tossed his head, let out a growl that sounded astonishingly like Garfist's own growls, and charged to meet the burly onetime panderer.

Gar slipped, staggered, sagged under a thrusting lorn blade as if by accident—and surged up under the lorn's guard with a triumphant roar, to slide his sword across its throat with sudden vigor. Then he seized hold of the skull-like head as blood spurted all over him, and thrust it back until the neck snapped and the lorn hung lifeless and loose from his hand.

He let go, leaving the dead lorn to crash down in front of his boots, bounce, and roll to a stop, and announced briskly, "Well, that's a beginning, but there're more yet, by the Falcon, an'—"

With a chorus of shrill cries, the lorn facing Dauntra and Iskarra charged them, those facing Garfist took heart from that and plunged forward too—and Iskarra deftly caught hold of Garfist's elbow and tugged him aside, back against the wall-like trunk of the tree. For the briefest of moments, lorn charged headlong into lorn, slashing and stabbing. Collecting themselves, they turned, amid an ugly gurgling chorus, to face the Aumrarr and the two humans.

Dauntra gave them a sweet smile, slid the only ring she wore off her finger, kissed it, and murmured, "Death steel, before me and—away!"

The ring faded away in her fingertips, trailing into nothingness in a wisp of smoke.

As the lorn surged forward again, the air in front of her shimmered, became bright with whirling sword-blades arranged in a plane before her—and moved inexorably away from her breast, straight back through the lorn toward the trees beyond.

The lorn suddenly become staggering, disembodied legs and a bright, drifting mist of blood. The darkened but still whirling swords moaned on, across the empty air until they were shredding leaves and branches and another huge tree trunk.

With a deepening groan, the vast garandarwood gave way, vanishing in a swathe of destruction that filled the air with bark-shards and sawdust. Lorn legs toppled grotesquely—and a moment later, in a slow and ponderous lean, the trunk fell, too.

Straight at Garfist Gulkoun, who was busily dispatching the only lorn to avoid Dauntra's deadly magic, and only looked up when the tree's shadow fell on him.

"Gar!" Iskarra cried. "Get over here! *Now!*"

Beside her, Dauntra was clawing aside branches to try to uncover Juskra. The falling tree shouldn't strike anywhere near them, but if the projecting branches catch and the tree rolls—

With a deep and ground-shaking crash, the garandarwood struck the bed of fallen boughs and crushed them, bouncing only once amid a pinwheeling cloud of broken branches, ere it sank solidly down into the damp leaf-mold of the Raurklor. Echoes of its crashing fall came back to them from distant trees, and then near-silence fell, a sudden calm in which the moan of the conjured swords could be heard dying away as the magic of the ring exhausted itself. The swords claimed another sapling, but it caught in other trees in its fall, making almost no sound at all.

"Any more lorn?" Iskarra asked Garfist accusingly, as if their attackers had somehow been his fault.

Gar looked around, hefting his sword and trying to hear anything suspicious, then shrugged. "Sneaky silent ones, perhaps. No others."

"Keep watch," she commanded crisply, and turned back to helping Dauntra unearth the senseless Juskra. She'd been trodden on many times during the fray, under her blanket of fallen branches, but looked no worse for wear.

Once they had her clear of it all—her wings stretched a long way, and Dauntra insisted on lifting everything clear of them, not dragging her fellow Aumrarr out from under anything—Iskarra caught hold of Dauntra's wrist and stared hard at the long, shapely Aumrarr fingers.

"No," Dauntra told her in a dry voice. "Unlike what you'll hear in most fancy-tales, I'm not wearing any more magic rings. Not even invisible ones."

"You weren't wearing *that* one, earlier," Iskarra snapped. "I looked."

"No, I wasn't. That wasn't Aumrarr-work, mind. It's something House Lyrose left lying around carelessly unattended—but, I'll admit, fairly well hidden; 'tis just that nobles are so *predictable*, when they try to be clever—that I, ah, confiscated for the greater good."

"Ours, you mean," Iskarra said wryly.

"As it happens, yes," Dauntra agreed almost smugly.

"And have ye any more little magic tricks ye've, ah, *forgotten* to tell us about?" Garfist growled, from right behind her.

Not rising or turning her head to look at him, the most beautiful of the Aumrarr smiled sweetly. "No. From now on, fat roaring man, you're on your own."

TALONS SHRIEKED ACROSS flagstones not far behind him, then tore away the last of the ceiling as the greatfangs flew on. There was now enough light in the room that Rod could see two plain, dark, and narrow doors set into the stone wall. He scrambled to his feet and tore the left one open.

The door groaned open, its frame creaking, to reveal another dim, unfamiliar room beyond. Nothing alive looked to be moving or turning to look at Rod, and he could see more doors, so he plunged into the room and hastened across it.

Behind him, there were more—thankfully distant—rending sounds, followed by smaller crashes, and the unmistakable hollow noise of a wooden beam bouncing on stone. The greatfangs were still tearing Malragard apart, like beggars swarming over a food-basket.

Rod tore open another door, and then the one beside it, but both of the rooms revealed to him looked much the same. A few chairs and tables, otherwise empty, bare stone walls...

He chose the one that looked to have more doors in its walls and rushed on.

More talons burst through the ceiling by his head and sliced their swift way across the room, with a shriek like a table saw in pain, as Rod reached one of those doors at the far end of the room and tugged it open.

Or tried to. It was stuck, its frame sagging down onto it as the fitted blocks of stone above broke apart and shifted. He'd have had to be a greatfangs to be strong enough to shove it open more than the few inches he'd already managed.

Rod reeled away from the door—as slabs of stone crashed down here and there, freed from above by the busy greatfangs—and tried the next one.

It opened so easily that Rod's mighty tug almost spilled him helplessly across the room, under a quickening fall of stone that was shattering the flagstones and sending jagged shards tumbling through the air in all directions.

Rod winced, clinging to the door with frantic fingertips, then growled up at the groaning, bulging ceiling overhead, or rather at the greatfangs now beating its wings thunderously somewhere beyond it. "*Hell* of an inferior desecrator you are!"

As if it had heard him, the unseen greatfangs let out a deep, bubbling, angry sound between a roar and a snarl—and did something that caused a bouncing, ground-shaking roar, almost flung Rod off his feet, made the upper hinges of the door he was clutching part from the door frame with a splintering crash, and flooded the world around him with swirling, choking dust.

Despite himself, Rod exploded in helpless coughing, dimly aware in the midst of its wrackings that he'd found the floor in a hunched-over ball. He tried to be quiet about it, so as not to draw talons stabbing right down at where he was, and tried, too, to roll blindly forward through the door so those fearsome dark daggers would miss him, but—talons loomed suddenly out of the swirling haze, raking the air so closely that one caught the very edge of his boot and spun him around like a child's toy.

And into the room beyond, banging bruisingly off the door frame and into a room that seemed to be all cupboards and pillars and dangling, swaying ceiling-tiles.

Cupboards that leaned and toppled, crashing into pillars or other falling cupboards right above Rod, wedging themselves against each other to form ungainly, improvised roofs above him.

Still coughing helplessly, his eyes beginning to stream, Rod barely saw what was spilling out of one cupboard, to rain down on his face. He did notice—couldn't help but notice—that it included something that was glowing like a lamp, warm and yellow and flickering—in the brief and painful moments before something hard and heavy greeted his head with stunning force, banging his chin on the floor and leaving him seeing all sorts of things. Galloping horses, nude and shapely Aumrarr with two pairs of wings each, like dragonflies, who as he watched grew horrible skull-like lorn faces to grin at him... and wizards, Lorontar and Malraun and Arlaghaun alive again, all of their floating faces grinning sneeringly at him...

Then the ceiling fell, and all Falconfar went away in a hurry.

Chapter Five

"**Y**OU ARE KEEPING watch. *Remember?*" The look Dauntra gave Garfist was every bit as sharp as her words.

The burly onetime panderer threw up his hands in a mutinous shrug, but turned obediently on his heel to glare around into the darkness of the Raurklor.

"Not a tree has moved—and I can't see aught else *but* trees," he growled, a long breath or two later. "Strikes me I'm a better target, standing here gawking at nothing, than a watcher."

"I'll not dispute that," the beautiful Aumrarr replied in a bitingly dry voice. "Yet humor me a little longer. I need to finish with Jusk."

She and Iskarra were on their knees beside the unconscious Juskra, turning the battlescarred Aumrarr slowly and carefully so as to run their hands over her thoroughly, seeking wounds, the roughnesses that might be broken bones, any sticky wetness that might be seeping blood, and—

"How far are we from Galath?" Garfist demanded abruptly, peering off into the endless trees in the direction of that realm.

Dauntra shrugged. "A long way, yet. Its border mountains look nearer than in truth they are."

"And if she can't fly?" he asked, stabbing a finger down at Juskra's limp form.

Dauntra shrugged again. "Then we walk. I'll fly when it'll help us—to cross chasms, and the like—and we'll get to Galath. In time. Mayhap a long time, what with hunting for food and all, but we'll get you there; Aumrarr keep their promises."

45

"Aye," Garfist nodded—then swung to face her, leaned forward, and growled, "But tell me now... why did ye make this promise? I'm not so lovely as all that!"

"True," came her reply, more gentle than dry, "yet you—both of you—still have parts to play, in time soon to come."

"So ye say." Garfist was turning again, peering slowly and carefully in one direction and then another. "Yet how do Aumrarr *know* that? Do ye dream? Pray to some hidden god for guidance? Or is it just grand an' empty words about all folk having some part, great or small, in what befalls Falconfar?"

"Some Aumrarr see things. Most of us *feel* things, from time to time. We *know*, just as surely as Stormar sailors in port know when the tide will next turn. Now belt up, watchguard; sentinels who flap their jaws make too much noise to hear what they should be listening for, outside their camps."

"Huh," Garfist rumbled. "This forest never *stops* handing us suspicious noises." As if his words had been a cue, something hooted in the distance, there was a sudden and abruptly-ended shriek even farther off... and something started rustling in leaves and underbrush, very near where they were standing. Something that sounded small, but began to circle them.

Garfist cursed and hefted his sword, turning to face the unseen source of the sound as it moved. It proceeded in a series of short, scuttling runs, separated by pauses. Small, yet near. *Very* near.

He strained and strained to catch some glimpse of eyes staring back at him, or a flicker of movement, but he might as well have been staring into the innards of a sack, in utter darkness. Nothing. Nothing at all. Except other rustlings, a little farther away... but heading closer.

Seemingly unconcerned, Dauntra bent her head again to Juskra. After a moment, Isk stopped listening intently to the rustling as she watched Garfist, and did the same.

As suddenly as it had begun circling them, the rustling sounds turned away, heading off into the forest, growing fainter.

Then there came a very short, strangled *eep*, a furious thrashing of leaves and splintering twigs, and... nothing at all.

Garfist Gulkoun took two swift, darting steps toward the source of the brief sound, jaw thrust forward, sword held low behind him. Then he froze, listening hard and peering even harder.

The darkness did not surrender.

The silence held, though there came faint and distant stirrings from several other directions in the deep, endless forest.

"If I stare much longer, my glorking eyes'll start to bleed," Garfist muttered at last. "Enough of this. If something comes charging out of the night, I'll worry about it then. And feed it this—" He hefted his sword. "—or this!" He flung up the hand that bore the ring Juskra had given him.

Dauntra and Iskarra ignored him. Under their hands, Juskra was starting to stir, murmuring something faint and wordless.

Gar gave them all a glare, then growled at Dauntra, "Mind telling us now, before Ironhips wakes, just what ye intend to use us for?"

Dauntra didn't look up, and said nothing beyond sighing loudly.

"Revenge, is it? Revenge on someone formidable, that ye want old Gar to wade in an' get all bloody doing? And die, mayhap, whilst ye stay safely far away?"

Dauntra shook her head.

"Well? What, then?"

Dauntra kept her eyes on Juskra's face, cradling it in one hand and gently stroking it with the other, and said quietly, "The best revenge is one you simply wait for, and let your foes bring upon themselves. Manipulate them a little, perhaps, but otherwise do nothing but watch and wait—and get on with living your life. Letting them sway you not at all with whatever they did to you. *That's* the best revenge."

"Hunh," Garfist grunted. "I'm not as clever as you, lass. I'll settle for just sticking my knife into the ones I hate and twisting it, so they die in pain. That's more the sort of revenge I can really enjoy."

"I... feel the same," Juskra whispered, turning her face toward him. Her eyes were still shut, and she shuddered a little, under Dauntra's hands, then groaned aloud, arched her back, and beat her wings against the ground like a man beating his fist in frustration.

Then she went limp again, and opened her eyes. "Nothing too badly broken," she told her fellow Aumrarr, letting Dauntra gently boost her into a sitting position. Leaning back against Dauntra's knee, she gave Garfist a sour look. "I think."

"Tell truth," Dauntra replied quietly. "Your left wing..."

"*Yes*, my left wing," Juskra snarled. "Falcon *spit*, it hurts."

Garfist trudged over to her. "What about yer left wing?"

Juskra sighed, rolled her eyes, and turned to Iskarra. "Must I *really* lug yon tub of lard through the skies, all the way to the Stag's Head?" She gave Garfist a glower. "Trim little lass that I am."

His reply was a grinning snarl—that broke, by way of a cough, into a helpless chuckle.

After a moment, Dauntra giggled, and then all four of them were laughing.

Juskra sank back down onto the forest floor, closed her eyes, and announced, "So those of us with wings are utterly exhausted. And in my case, a little worse. Where are we?"

"Lost in the Raurklor," Iskarra said promptly. "Well east of Ironthorn but not yet in Galath. Which lies beyond the mountains yonder, that night now hides from us."

"Well, *that's* reassuring," Juskra replied. "Just where I'd thought we were. You took care of the lorn, I presume?"

"Of course," Gar told her proudly.

She slid open one scornful eye. "'Of course,' my left teat."

She'd meant her words to be crushing, but Gar gave her an eager smile, winked at her, and leaned forward, flexing his fingers.

"*Don't*," Dauntra told him warningly. "Even as she is now, I'd not bet on you, against her, in a fray."

"Huh. Even bareskinned wrestling?" Garfist asked hopefully, grinning into Juskra's flat stare.

"I have maimed several men," she announced flatly, apparently addressing the sword Garfist was now using like a walking-stick, "with my right knee."

"Oh, aye?" His reply was casual, unimpressed.

"My left knee," she added, "is even sharper."

"Ah, but do yer knees stretch wide apart, now?"

Juskra rolled her eyes again, then looked at Iskarra and asked sourly, "Am I going to have to strike him senseless just to get a little quiet, so we can all get to sleep?"

"No," Garfist's longtime companion replied sweetly. "Just order him to stand first watch, so his snores don't keep us all from slumber. He's all flirtatious roar, this one, and no true menace."

"Hoy!" the former panderer protested. "I'm—"

"About to belt up," Iskarra said sweetly. "*Now.*"

Garfist started to reply, then thought better of it and just nodded.

Somewhere close by in the darkness, something small started rustling again.

At least, Garfist hoped it was small. Not something large and sleek and dangerous, that padded so deftly it only sounded small.

He tensed, dropping into a crouch with his sword out in front of him, listening intently.

"Ahhh," Juskra said contentedly, stretching and then relaxing. "You'll take care of it, stout—very stout—man, whatever it is. Of course."

ROD EVERLAR CAME awake shaking. No, strike that; he was *being* shaken. Along with timbers and crumbled plaster—at least, it looked like plaster, though it had crumbled away into mostly dust, gray-white and chalky—and stones with mortar still clinging to them, and smaller splintered spars of wood, and... stuff.

All of this wrack was under him and around him and strewn over him, both shielding him and weighing him down, shifting and bouncing noisily as the floor beneath him trembled again.

Trembled and *heaved*, cracking and crumbling with a muffled groaning of timbers somewhere under it.

Ah, Rod thought, *that'd be the joists of the floor, or the beams of another ceiling below...*

Which reminded him; there'd been something glowing that had fallen on him, hadn't there? Something smallish and hard, spilling out of a cupboard with a lot of other stuff—bottles? Little boxes?—straight at his face...

He hadn't been off in Dreamland very long, Rod decided, as he struggled to prop himself up on one elbow, turning painfully amid all the chunks of stone and grit. At least there were no nails to stab him, in all of this; hereabouts, builders used wooden pegs of massive size. He tried to keep his head low, well aware from the rumblings and sharp splintering sounds that the greatfangs—two of them, at least—were still busily tearing apart the wizard's tower. Not all that far away from him.

Not that there was much left of Malragard just here, right above his head.

He'd have to be cautious, disarranging all this debris as little as possible. If a greatfangs spotted him, there was nothing left to stop its jaws reaching down out of the sky and ending his life in one swift, painful bite.

Rod shivered, hurriedly banishing an all-too-vivid image of that from his mind. Bumping his knee on something jagged and painful, he wobbled to his feet, almost falling, caught hold of a leaning beam just long enough to get his balance, then won free of the tangle of wreckage that had been hampering him.

Whereupon he promptly slipped, rushed ahead for a few helpless, staggering steps, and dropped to one knee—his other one, thank whatever gods or angels there might be—to regain his breath and calm, and have a good look around his new location.

There! That glow, yonder; it must be from whatever it was that had fallen on him, earlier. It *was* small, and metallic, but from what he could see of it, looked more like some sort of ornamental turned spindle of the sort that adorned cheap imported brass bedsteads, rather than a tool or a weapon.

And a glow almost *had* to mean magic.

Which would have been great, if he'd known the first damned thing about using any Falconaar magic. Oh, he'd dreamed and seen wizards point wands and suchlike, and unleash leaping lightnings and roaring flames and worse, but it seldom seemed to work when he, Lord Archwizard of Falconfar, tried it.

That meant it was only a matter of time before a greatfangs talon, or another wizard, or some six-year-old holding a sharp knife, killed him. Painfully.

A death that wouldn't please him at all, even if he had found that magnificent Falconfar, the land of his dreams, was real—all *too* real—and walked its ways. Nor would it help poor Taeauna any, and he'd promised her he'd rescue her. Before that, he'd promised her he'd deliver Falconfar from the Dooms, and their Dark Helms.

She knew better, now, what a powerless idiot he was, but he was tired of disappointing her, too.

So he was going to get up, fetch that glowing thing and anything else that looked useful—all the stuff that had fallen out of that cupboard looked to be there, strewn around amongst what was left of the cupboard and the wall it had been fastened to—and go play the storybook hero.

It was time, damn it. It was way *past* time.

His stomach rumbled suddenly, so loudly that he stiffened, afraid a greatfangs would come diving at him.

Thinking of 'time,' when was the last time he'd eaten?

It was past time for a lot of things. He rose cautiously and picked his way forward, keeping low. He probably wouldn't like a meal of raw, dripping greatfangs flesh any more than he'd like a greatfangs enjoying a meal of raw, dripping Rod Everlar.

He reached the glowing thing, bent down to take it—it did look like some sort of spindle, which probably meant it was either utterly useless or could destroy kingdoms if he waved it the wrong way—and then paused, fingers only inches from its gentle, steady glow.

What if Lorontar—if any wizard—could trace him in an instant, if he was carrying it?

Hell, what if all the *greatfangs* could trace him, sensing just where he was trying to hide?

"Hang it," he muttered. Reaching down, he took firm hold of the spindle-thing, and found it to be warm and somehow *alive*. Or containing slow pulses or waves of energy, or... something.

It flared into sudden brightness, and he hastily curled his body around it and wished fervently that it would go dark.

And it did.

"Son of a *bitch*," he hissed under his breath, and willed it to glow again.

Silently, obediently, it did, but he was already firmly ordering it to go dim again, in his mind.

It did that, too, instantly and silently, without the least fuss.

"Well, now," he whispered jubilantly, crouched in the wreckage. "I've got me a flashlight!"

Now why, with dragon-like beasts that could bite him in a half in an instant tearing apart his hiding-place around him, did that make him feel so suddenly, wildly happy?

"Huh," he told the solid, heavy spindle-thing in his hands, idly noticing that it didn't look like any metal he recognized, being somewhat like the old chrome trim on the first car he'd driven, gleaming something like silver... but silver that was the bronze color of vintage champagne. "Guess I am a Lord Archwizard after all. Or a mad idiot. All happy over a frikkin' flashlight."

He cast wary glances up and around, to see if any greatfangs were gliding nearer. He hadn't heard anything nearby, but...

No. No huge dark bulk with wings or jaws. Good. He reached for the nearest of the small, unrecognizable items the spindle had been lying among, wondering what it would turn out to be. A dishmop, perhaps?

"I HAVE NO particular liking for wizard's gates that whisk you far away at a single step to somewhere unknown, either," Talyss Tesmer snapped at her brother, "but the alternative is *walking* across the entire damned Raurklor. With all its bears, and snakes, and—and worse. Day after day, fighting our way through dagger-sharp thornbushes and under leaning trees that could fall on us and through swamps full of lurking things and dung-reeking mud. Don't be a fool, Belard!"

"Sister," came his cold reply, "I've spent more than enough years acquiring a hearty distaste for being called that. 'Fool' is a name I got tired of ten-and-six summers ago. Care to choose another word?"

"Stonehead?"

"That will serve, yes," Belard replied evenly—and grew a sudden grin. "So where's this gate, then?"

AROUND HIM, EVERYTHING shuddered again, and a wall crashed down in a thunderous roar of falling stone. At least one greatfangs was still tearing Malragard apart.

Hidden—he hoped—in the shadows of two fallen ceiling-beams under a tangle of split and splintered boards, Rod peered at the meager collection he'd retrieved. Most of the cupboard had been full of things that were now broken, and some of them didn't look as if they'd ever been interesting. Six objects, however—the spindle-flashlight one of them—he'd kept, and carried across the room to his newfound refuge to get a better look at.

There was a hexagonal mottled brown stone that filled his palm, worked to a glossy-smooth finish and graven with some complicated-looking runes or designs. It certainly *looked* magical, and it had been wrapped in what had once been an opulent-looking cloth, and stuffed into an ornately carved coffer that was now so many shards of polished purple-white bone.

And there was a—

Something that was half-roar and half thunderous gurgle of hunger rang out suddenly, from above and behind him.

Rod Everlar didn't wait for the world to turn darker as the great bulk of a surging greatfangs blotted out the sky again. Cradling his loot against his chest, he flung himself across the littered floor in a stumbling, slipping run, put his shoulder to a door he'd looked at on his way to the corner, and kept right on running.

Behind him, walls that no longer had a roof over them, and bared, sagging beams that had once been part of that roof, were driven aside in a loud, approaching thunder.

Crashing into half-seen furniture and hoping by all the fiends in Hell that Malraun hadn't left any traps waiting just ahead, the Lord Archwizard of Falconfar sprinted on into the unknown, fresh fear clutching coldly at his heart.

What would it feel like, to be bitten in half by teeth longer than you were?

Chapter Six

THE WINGLESS AUMRARR blinked at a bedchamber ceiling she'd seen before, wondering why it seemed to waver so much.

"Taeauna," she murmured, after a long and dazed time during which the ceiling ceased to cascade past her eyes. "I am Taeauna."

Her face was wet with tears. They dripped from her as she sat up, probing with her fingers at a stinging pain just above her chin. Her fingertips came away laced with blood; she'd bitten through her own lower lip.

Hunh. Small wonder, by the Falcon. The mind of Lorontar had been a dark and terrible thing, and it had been riding hers long enough to leave deep wounds. Even before she'd won herself deeper ones, lashing out at it.

She shuddered at the memory of that awful, awful...

Taeauna found herself up and staggering across the room, feeling ill and wanting just to get *away*.

She slammed into a wall and clung to it, tugging at it and then caressing it as if it had been the comforting chest of a lover, leaning her cheek against it and gasping out her pain and confusion and the urge to empty her guts...

This was the bedchamber where she'd lain with Malraun, in Darswords, yes. Malraun who was now... no more, his mind blown out like a candle, his body taken over by Lorontar.

Lorontar who was gone, too, but not dead. Somehow she knew that, just as she knew she was Taeauna. Oh, there were shadows in the corners of her mind that were still Lorontar—enough to tell her he yet lived, and enough not to let her forget the cold truth that he could reclaim her mind and body at will, that she was like a child with a knife to his darkly triumphant host of leering, battle-ready warriors—but for now, she was Taeauna.

Free of Malraun's thralldom forever. And for now, free of Lorontar's far deeper and mightier mind-slavery. For now.

Though she had never left the twisted, sweat-drenched tangle of the bed behind her, for a few fierce moments she had stood on the topmost floor of riven Malragard under the open sky, with greatfangs wheeling across it like gigantic bats above her, and Rod Everlar—kind, bumbling, *good-hearted* Rod Everlar, the only hope Falconfar still had, but little more skilled than a child, for all the fury of his resolve and the might of his Shaping, when he could manage to Shape—fleeing like a terrified rabbit from the lightning-hurling triumph of Malraun. She had seen Malraun seized, hollowed out and enslaved by Lorontar.

The *true* Lord Archwizard of Falconfar, a mage stronger than any she'd ever felt before, who lived beyond death in a horrible cold, malicious patience... who'd been awaiting Rod Everlar's coming, luring him with spell-spun dream visions.

And with her.

She, Taeauna, had brought Rod here to Falconfar, and Lorontar had made her do it. He'd been at work on her for season after season, twelve winters and more—probably her whole life—without her knowing it.

For all she knew, he'd been at work in the minds of all the Aumrarr, perhaps even seeing to who they bred with, to fashion them into his unwitting tools—ever better tools—to turn up Shapers as miners turn up gems amid rocks. To find Shapers, and bring them to him.

So Lorontar could use them to reshape Falconfar to what he wanted it to be, and in time to come leave undeath for full life again.

Taeauna blinked, turning away from the wall to find herself panting, knuckles at her mouth. Now how had she known *that*?

He hadn't managed it, though. Yet.

He was still stealing the bodies of others, burning out their minds and riding their bodies until death came for them or he tired of them. Or a better body came within reach.

What body was he in right now? Malraun's—or had something better happened along?

Taeauna stared down at the bed, forever empty of the cruel wizard who'd forced her upon it—then shook herself to put such thoughts behind her, and strode away.

Her armor was a tangle of straps and plates, in the corner where she'd so hastily torn it off under his mind-goading, to bare herself to him. She plucked up the shiny-worn, smooth, sweat-soaked leather jack she wore beneath its plates, and pulled it on.

The straps still needed mending, the buckle that rode on her left hip still bit into her. Familiar, reassuring; she reached for her crotch-cloth, with its long laces.

She had to get to Malragard. Malraun was gone—and that was *one* good thing for Falconfar, even if a worse wizard than he'd ever been was now striding the kingdoms in his body—but the man he'd been trying to slay, that any one of the six greatfangs might well have been about to devour, might yet live.

And that man, that bumbling Rod Everlar, was the last hope of Falconfar.

She believed that still, even if that belief had been something Lorontar had birthed in her, had nurtured into a fierce certainty over years of deft dream-weaving. Seeing Rod's face before her now, conjured up out of memory—mouth agape in astonishment, eyes full of that familiar, infuriating helplessness, as lost as a rabbit in her grasp—Taeauna found herself smiling.

Even when the armor-plate that always dug into her ribs did so again now, bringing the familiar raw pain as it sliced anew into the deep weal in her flank, she smiled.

She believed.

Oh, yes, she did. That helpless, bumbling idiot was the hope of Falconfar.

If she could keep him alive long enough to destroy Lorontar—for he was the only one who could, if anyone could—and become the Lord Archwizard in truth, that hope might just become something more.

Giving her—giving *all* Falconfar—a world free of wizards fell and mighty enough to be called Dooms, and all their hosts of lorn and Dark Helms and greatfangs. A place where veldukes like Darendarr Deldragon could rise to rule well, and the gruffly honest likes of Eldalar of Hollowtree and Tindror of Tarmoral could flourish in their smaller domains, and folk could enjoy seasons of peace and good harvests again.

"My thoughts," she told herself huskily, finding herself about to choke on fresh tears—she didn't have the Falcon-be-damned *time* for them, just now—"are like a bad ballad. A proper weepwailer."

She swung her heavy shoulder-plates over her head and into place, smacking herself across the face with at least two of their dangling buckles. As usual.

"Ow," she said. *True Aumrarr suffer in silence*, the saying went. A stupid saying, now that she thought about it. So was that more of Lorontar's meddling, or herself, freed of it?

She shrugged and set to work finding straps and buckles and mating them up properly. Being as there was no nimble-fingered maid or Stormar shieldguard to do that for her.

Malraun would probably have bedded them and then blasted them to ashes, if there had been.

Just as he would have served her, if she hadn't been useful as a lure for Rod Everlar, a handy lass in which to slake his lusts—and a thrall he could send into peril, or escape if need be into the mind of, just as Lorontar had done.

Now, *that* would have been utter doom, if Malraun and Lorontar had each found her mind a mite crowded with the other one there, and decided to fight it out inside her head.

She shuddered at a brief, vivid image of her head bursting on her shoulders like rotten fruit, drew on her gauntlets, shifted the hilts of her scabbarded blades and reached for her helm.

With all wizards out of her head for the moment—forever, if she could manage it, though that was more grim determination than anything she had any power to prevent—it was time to get back to work. She had to salvage all she could of Falconfar from *all* wizards. Which, right now, meant rescuing Rod Everlar.

She strode across the room, flung wide the door—and came to an abrupt halt. The room beyond was icily silent, and the men in it had swords drawn.

Two of them, whose tense shoulders were right in front of her, were the guards charged by Malraun to let no one approach the bedchamber. They were facing down five warriors; four expressionless bodyguards and their burly, glowering master—who was one of Malraun's army commanders. Korauth of Belamber, fearless but with a temper to match his flame-red hair, scowling brows and full beard. He was scowling right now, his helm in the crook of his arm just as Taeauna's was, and full, freshly-polished armor gleaming on him.

He hadn't been one of Taeauna's favorites when at his best, and he was far from at his best now.

"Wench!" he snapped, "where's your master?"

"Elsewhere," she flung back at him, and to the guards added a curt, "Stay your blades."

The doorguards obeyed her, but Korauth's bodyguards did not. She gave each of them a long, cold stare, but all that accomplished was to make them shift their swords from raised in general menace to pointing right at her.

"Disobedience," she observed softly, "tends to end in death."

"*Enough*, bed-lass; *you* don't command here!"

Taeauna turned her stare to Korauth. "As a matter of fact, Korauth, I do. You can dispute that with Malraun if you'd like to... but I'll wager much you won't like to." She raised an eyebrow in mocking query. "Well?"

"Well, there's no *time* for this foolishness!" Korauth started to pace, waving his helm for emphasis. It took him only one sighing whirl around back to face her to tell Taeauna that he was deeply worried beneath his bluster. "We have troubles!"

"Troubles, lord?" Taeauna lowered her voice and stepped closer, like a confidante rather than a challenger. This man was scared.

"Lorn have been seen lurking," he blurted. "Not once, but scores of times now. They're spying on us, following us—drawing back from battle when we try to cross swords with them. They all have swords, too!"

"And?" she asked gently, knowing there was more. Lorn in the Raurklor were a real danger, but hardly something new.

"Greatfangs have been seen in the sky! A line of them, low down yonder—" He waved an arm at the wall behind him. "Winging their way, straight across. *Six* of them."

He started pacing again. "More than that, small magics cast by Lord Malraun have been fading away; the glow-lamps, the horse-calmings. The men are unsettled."

He waved his other arm, and added heavily, "And none of us battle-lords know what to tell them."

Then, as she'd known he would, Korauth whirled around to face her and snarled, "*So*, woman: where by the flying Falcon *is* Malraun? Rutting takes not that long, he's never been seen to need much sleep, and we'd have felt it if he'd been spinning mighty spells in there—so what have you done with him?"

THE GLOW BOBBED with Rod as he ran, clutched against his chest with everything else. He should be using it like a flashlight, but that would draw the greatfangs right to him—

Behind him, the ceiling was torn away like a kid tearing aside cellophane to get at a toy underneath. No, not a toy. Chocolate. A big hunk of rich, succulent chocolate.

And he was that hotly-sought treat. Never mind the glow from the spindle, it was after him anyway!

Get lower down, deeper into Malragard, down into the lowest cellars where the ceilings would be layers of solid stone, not timber beams and cross-boards and—

Rod blundered into the edge of an unseen doorframe and through it, running on until the floor suddenly opened up under his boots and he fell—headlong down bruisingly-hard stone steps.

It was a long and steep flight of steps. He'd never been so happy to fall down stairs in his life, but the third bounce spilled some of his loot out of his grasp. Rod let it all go, making a grab only for the spindle-light, raking it in as he fetched up in a ball on a stone step with a chipped, saw-sharp edge.

"I'm a writer," he gasped into the darkness, feeling that edge biting into his shoulder, "not a fucking warrior—or cross-country runner, for that matter!"

Rod's breath ran out before he could vent any more, and he lay there panting for what seemed a long time—as more of the tower groaned and shrieked and was torn away, somewhere back above him—until he could find strength and air enough to roll over, banging his knees and elbows, and aim the spindle-light.

He willed it brighter, and it obligingly showed him that these stairs ran down not to a door, but into the open darkness of a lower level, with passages running off—cold, dank stone, all blocks of different sizes, fitted together, with old mold everywhere on them—in several directions.

Not deep enough. He needed solid stone around him to be safe from the talons behind him, though there was always the risk of being entombed by all their digging. Surely the greatfangs wouldn't keep after him forever, when there must be easier prey around? After all, *he* hadn't done them any harm; their rage *couldn't* be at Rod Everlar.

Oh, shit. Unless a wizard was guiding their thoughts. Using them, like trained dogs, to do his digging for him. No, worse than trained—mind-thralled, enslaved to be as controlled as the knives and forceps a surgeon held in his hands when cutting into a patient.

Urrgh. Enough of *that*.

Rod banished thoughts of spurting blood and steaming red innards and got himself down the rest of the steps just as fast as he could scoop up the things he'd dropped. One of them had broken in half, and he stopped long enough to peer hard at it in the light of the spindle, then shrug and toss its pieces away. It didn't look as if it had ever held magic, but if it had, all that power was fled now. It was just broken.

Someday, if he ever became Lord Archwizard in truth, he'd come back and find those two pieces and Shape them back together and *make* it something magic. Someday.

If ever.

Right now, he had four—no, five; one of them split into two about three strides along it—passages to choose from, and a greatfangs right at the head of the stair now, its long talons reaching *down*...

Rod chose the largest-looking passage and sprinted along it, arms wrapped more securely around his loot. What need would a powerful wizard have to hide the way to his lower cellars? Who would dare go snooping after his secrets, when an invisible, silently waiting spell could turn them into frogs if they reached the wrong place?

Wait. Turn *him* into frog, too?

"Shit," he gasped aloud, running hard. "Shit shit shit shit *shit*." Ah, we writers; *so* eloquent, aren't we?

He found himself grinning at that—a grin that widened as the passage came to an end in a stair leading down, a stair that for the first time had walls and—yes!—a ceiling of rough, chisel-scarred stone. Solid rock at last!

It could end up being his tomb, yes, but then so could any patch of grass or castle room in all Falconfar, with a greatfangs—or six—chasing him. And the one fate might lurk in the future, whereas the other awaited him right now.

The stairs started to curve, angling around to the right and becoming even steeper. Colder, too—and for the first time it occurred to Rod that the magic that gave the spindle its glow might have limits. He'd better know how to grope his way back to this stair in utter darkness, from wherever he ended up at the bottom of it.

Which was going to be someplace pretty darned *deep*, by the looks of things. A vast labyrinthine world in the darkness under the earth, like in so many fantasy novels he'd read; so many endless copies of Moria?

The stairs took a last abrupt hook to the right and ended, in another level of passages and doors that looked very like the one he'd just left.

It was cold here, and very quiet; the noises of Malragard being destroyed had faded away entirely, leaving him alone in stillness.

Where Rod stood, not fleeing anything for the first time in ages, realizing suddenly how tired he was.

Bone-effin'-weary. Oh, his thoughts were racing along (here I am, not knowing where I am or what to do next or what all this stuff is that I'm carrying—as usual); he felt no urge or need to yawn or anything like that. It was his arms and legs, bruised and numb from all the unaccustomed work he'd demanded of them, that were tired right out.

Not that anything like a soft bed looked likely, down here in all this stone. Still, perhaps behind one of these doors there'd be a heap of—of—turnips, or something, that he could just flop down on, making sure he propped the door open with a lot of them, and...

The nearest door was black, blackness that crumbled and flaked off at his touch. Iron, or something like it, painted black. Counterweighted, so loose in its stone frame that it couldn't possibly be rusted shut—or ever rust shut, for that matter—and adorned with the symbol of the Falcon in flight.

Which meant... what?

A temple? Something sacred? He had no idea.

Rod sighed, hoping he'd not be facing some fearsome monster in a moment, and tugged the door wide.

Silence. Dark, chill, still silence. A smallish stone room—no other doors—with irregular dark heaps all around its walls. Had he found his turnip-pile? He couldn't smell anything particularly bad, or for that matter anything at all...

He took a cautious step closer to the pile on his right, aiming the spindle-light as if it was some sort of weapon, to get a better look at it. Were those cobwebs, or—?

The pile moved, not just in front of his eyes but all around him. Rod backed away hastily, choking on sudden fright.

All around him things were erupting, shedding the enshrouding darkness. It was crumbling, falling away like loose black dirt—to reveal brown and yellow bones.

Bones now standing upright, moving in eerie silence. No, not standing, attached to each other but *floating*, dangling in the air like marionettes without strings. Hanging-on-nothing arrays of bones, with dark and eyeless skulls hovering in the air above all the rest.

Skeletons, dozens of human skeletons, all of them clutching rusted, jagged remnants of swords.

Swords they were pointing at him.

Chapter Seven

"**H**OW DO WE know you're telling us the truth?" Norgarl growled, waving his hairy hands. "How *can* we know, with the Lord Malraun nowhere to be found? Why, you could have murdered him and rolled his body under the bed, and we'd be none the wiser!"

"No, she couldn't," one of the brothers Esdagh said flatly. "I sent in some good men to look around. No bloodstains, no one hidden anywhere, alive or dead. No sign of the wizard, either, beyond what the two of them did to the bed—fair tore it apart, they did. And yes, we looked under it."

The other Esdagh—Mulzurr, the silent one—leered at Taeauna, but she ignored him, glaring coldly at Norgarl and Korauth. Hairy, unlovely, coarse old Norgarl had brought the largest band of warriors into Horgul's host, and everyone saw him as the senior commander in the army. Korauth, with his fiery temper and fearlessness, was the loudest of the army commanders, the most feared. The most likely to cause trouble.

The other battle-lords standing around the fire—Lanneth and Mulzurr Esdagh, ever-present axes at their belts; tall Tamgrym Buckhold, staring out at the world through his mass of scars, as terse as ever; and the old, hollow-eyed Stormar, Dzundivvur, who looked more like a worn-out merchant than a warrior—watched Taeauna to see what she'd do. What she said and did now would decide them, for her or bloodily against her. And with no wings, she couldn't just flap out of reach and avoid these butchers—

yet with all of them knowing she was an Aumrarr, she already had their mistrust. Men who live by the sword grew up hating and fearing the winged warrior-women who won battles serving themselves, disdaining kings and coin.

They were all suspicious of her, too, and no wonder. Malraun had been firm enough in his oft-repeated orders that after his army took Darswords, they'd be pressing on to Ironthorn. Right swiftly, too; just as soon as they'd rested, eaten, seized food and a little plunder, and done enough to their wounds to be trudging on again.

Not that they were quite ready yet. If they turned and started striding right now, charging on to Ironthorn, they'd be thrusting their noses into a *real* fight, quite possibly a battle or three more than they could win. Standing over this fire now, with Darswords just fallen and blood still wet on the ground, every last battle-lord felt he was too worn out to take Ironthorn, just yet.

Taeauna knew this, but also knew they'd be slow to admit it. Warriors of their ilk stood iron-strong, cursing all misfortunes by the Falcon, and never admitted mistakes or weaknesses—or much in the way of prudence, either.

If they did not, they were not battle-lords for long.

"My lords," she said crisply, keeping her voice as deep and hard as any of theirs, slowly and deliberately moving her stare from one face to the next as she spoke, "we all heard Lord Malraun's commands regarding Ironthorn. We all know his intentions. Yet I should not have to remind any of you that he *is* a wizard, one of the mightiest in all Falconfar, and that the affairs of wizards can change in an instant—and that wizards can travel across Falconfar in the instant after that. I say to you again that my lord has done just that, departing the room we shared by means of his magic, hieing himself to his tower of Malragard *and ordering me to lead this army to join him there.*"

She fell silent, waiting, to let them consider the wisdom of disobeying a man who could blast them to ashes in an instant, too—but the moment Norgarl's rising rumble told her he was gathering himself to speak, she added, "So let us ready ourselves for march, as speedily as we can, and take ourselves to Harlhoh, and Malragard. To do battle, if need be, when we arrive there.

These are Malraun's orders, and I will follow them. I should have thought there would be no question at all of you not doing the same. Certainly I would not want to stand in that man's boots, who dared to defy Malraun the Matchless, and then found himself facing Malraun to answer for it."

"We have only *your* word, wench, that he *gave* such orders!" Korauth burst out, leaning forward in the trembling eruption of his rage. "And I for one trust not an Aumrarr—"

Taeauna yawned, sighed, and let boredom slide clearly onto her face, shifting to settle herself into a comfortable pose for a long, patient listening. This raised a smirk from the brothers Esdagh and from Tamgrym, but brought Korauth around the fire in a lurching charge, roaring in fury as he flung out both hands to throttle her.

Tamgrym moved not a muscle, standing like a statue as Korauth tried to bull right through him, and their collision sent the burlier man reeling. He kicked his way through the fringe of the fire in a shower of snapping sparks, waving his arms wildly to keep from toppling into it—and avoiding the flood of hot broth that spewed out of the blackened cauldron as it lurched on its fire-frame—and so reached her off-balance and seething.

Taeauna ducked low, more to get beneath his belly and avoid his hands than to menace his cods, but Korauth flung down one arm to shield himself from any blow she might land. Which allowed her to twist as she kicked herself upright, pinning that arm against him with her hip, and punch him in the neck and throat with all the strength and weight she could manage.

Only the sidelong, upthrust angle of her strike kept Korauth's throat from being crushed. His bearded chin snapped up, head twisted around and roar becoming a shriek, and he took two awkward steps and flopped down on his face, bouncing limply, and lay very still.

No one went to check on him, though his bodyguards turned sharply from their cooking-fire, not far off, to stand uncertainly with hands on the hilts of their blades, and stare.

Taeauna ignored them. "My lords," she told the rest of the commanders flatly, "I have been given clear orders by my lord Malraun. I *will* follow them. I trust you'll do the same, because unlike Korauth, I deal in trust. Fighting alongside men who stand true makes me trust them."

She looked around at the battle-lords, one after another, keeping her eyes moving as she added, "If you decide to defy Malraun's orders—whether you seek to pass this off as spurning my lies about those very clear commands, or for your own reasons—you will disappoint me greatly, but I'll not seek to strike you down, or make war on you and the warriors you lead. Unless you offer violence to those of us still loyal to Lord Malraun, of course. Otherwise, to spare lives and preserve all I can of this army, I shall stay my hand. However, knowing Malraun as I do, more closely than all of you, for reasons you very well know—" She waved one hand across her chest, then down at her crotch. "—I do not think it likely that he will stay *his* hand, having learned of your treachery, when next he sees you. Govern yourselves accordingly."

She went to Korauth's sprawled form, faced them across it as she knelt to roll him over, and added, "I will be gathering all loyal to Lord Malraun to march out of Darswords just as fast as we can. Set the guards at the wells to taking turns drawing water to fill flasks and skins."

Norgarl frowned. "Many streams cross the trail to Harlhoh," he growled, fresh suspicion clear in his voice.

"The faster men march, the more they need to drink. I mean to be *hurrying* to Malragard," Taeauna told him.

Under her hand, Korauth stirred and groaned.

Norgarl bent closer. "Is he—?"

"Struck senseless, but coming out of it. Though I rather doubt he'll have more sense than he did before," she replied, stroking Korauth's cheek as if he was her son. "He might not have much of a voice for a time, either, but I suspect I'll not be the only one to welcome that."

Every one of the men around the fire chuckled.

WHEN MORNINGS WERE bright and rainless, it was the habit of Tethtyn Eldurant, youngest underscribe to Horgul's new Lord of Hawksyl, to invent an errand—or more often, trumpet a task deliberately left undone from the day before, to save on expensive candles—that would take him from the market hall to the records rooms up at the

Hawksylhar. Not to dawdle or hide from work, but just to walk in the sun and have a few moments to himself to think.

Thinking aloud, usually, murmuring some of the thoughts that rose unbidden in his mind and tumbled all over each other in their usual flood. Ideas—crazed notions, those who knew him called them—had come to him for as long as he could remember, and just as often had come tumbling out of his mouth.

Yet everything had changed when the Army of Liberation had come riding into Hawksyl, and not just the changes all knew about, the fires and death and local lords swept away. No, something had changed for Tethtyn, in an instant and forever, his body catching fire inside at the mere sight of a spell hurled by the wizard they called Malraun the Matchless.

Or perhaps more than mere sight. That crawling magic had sent men staggering all around him, and felled dead the warriors it had been aimed at farther off, but it had left young Tethtyn quivering. Staring in helpless longing at the distant dark-robed mage, Tethtyn had found his body shuddering from ears to fingertips with a power that thrilled him utterly, a tingling that would not fade, as the blood in his head pounded and warmed as if it was afire.

The sweating heat had gone as suddenly as it had come, but the tingling hadn't faded for days, until long after the army had marched on and Tethtyn's quill had been put to the service of Lord Bralgarth, the cold-eyed, limping warrior who'd been given the lordship of Hawksyl "until Horgul rode back in."

Bralgarth had needed a few folk able to read, write, and count to keep records for him, and by the time he'd finished executing those who tried to steal from the treasury and flee, and those who tried to poison him and all his warriors at table, there were only three Hawksarn left who had such skills—and stammeringly young, workshy Tethtyn was one of them.

Oh, folk didn't scorn or begrudge him serving Bralgarth—one did what one had to, to keep one's hide intact—but his new position left Tethtyn even more alone than before. Not many Hawksarn could freely enter the gates of the small but formidable Hawksylhar on its high ridge, and those within were usually grim warriors from the army, cooks and maids who did their work with fearful efficiency, keeping to themselves, and a succession of terrified local wenches whose doom it was to share Bralgarth's bed until he tired of them, and whose bruises showed every eye how ungentle he was.

The chief scribe was old Lythrus, who spent much of his days drunk and whose watery eyes were failing by the day, and the other underscribe was a bitter, ugly-as-a-jug woman with no head for tallies who wrote crudely. Which left Tethtyn doing most of the work, but doing it alone, sought out by his surly superiors only to demand the surrender of his work and give him more.

Which was a good thing, considering some of the things he was mumbling these days. That spell, and another minor magic he'd seen the Lord Malraun cast with casual ease, had set his dreams and waking visions alike down new trails.

He dreamed now of hurling such power, of working magics to awe warriors and topple castles alike—and every time Tethtyn thought of such things, the merest ghost of that tingling came back, an echo of power that made him feel warm again and sent his mind racing through strange skies in imaginary flight, swooping and darting along on surging powers that whirled up forces he could almost *feel*, hues he'd never seen before, that—

Lost in the thrill of remembrance, he trudged perhaps a dozen paces on up the steep lane before he realized that all around him in Hawksyl, folk were shouting or screaming.

What, by the Falcon—?

He turned, rather vaguely, to peer about for the cause of all the alarm. No fire, no half-hoped-for bright cloud of hurled magic and Malraun the Matchless standing fearlessly behind it, no charging army... Hawksarn seemed to pointing or looking up, into the sky...

So Tethtyn did, too—and felt his jaw drop open, just like the minstrels always said jaws did.

Huge and dark and bat-winged, looming up with frightening speed as it blotted out half the clouds, was a dragon.

Or no, no, it was... a greatfangs!

Falcon Above! If this was a greatfangs, how big would a dragon be? As large as the entire hargrauling *sky*?

It was diving down, headed more or less for him.

Great wings swept back, only the edges curling here and there as the gigantic, sky-filling beast tilted slightly to alter its course, then deftly rolled and tilted again, as gracefully as a hawk. Its talons were out, ready to grab...

It was swooping down to pounce on someone, to be sure.

Who? Tethtyn stared into its great eyes—gold, then blood-red, then he knew not what hue, as he met its cruel gaze and was lost.

Standing frozen and agape as the black, razor-sharp talons, every one of them longer than he stood tall, curled around him as deftly and gently as a nurse takes up a beloved baby—

And snatched him into the sky, a sudden roaring of wind in his ears, the stillness broken in a rushing that wrenched his breath away and bore him aloft again, the huge body above him surging as the great wings beat and then beat again, like a man at his oars, *pulling* through the sky, rising above the ridge crowned by the Hawksylhar, leaving the screaming behind.

Climbing into higher and colder sky, hastening on into the unknown so swiftly that the only part of Falconfar he'd ever known was already a dwindling spot amid the endlessly rolling green darkness of the Raurklor behind him. This impossibly huge beast, this monster as big as the Hawksylhar itself, was taking Tethtyn Eldurant—struggling to breathe, but bearing not even a scratch—away.

To whatever places lay beyond "away."

Or, no...

Dark fear boiled up in Tethtyn. Lacking air enough to scream, he started to tremble instead.

It wasn't taking him to fabulous new lands. Oh, no. Rather, it was heading straight to wherever greatfangs went to feed on scrawny young underscribes. Fast.

"STAY BACK!" ROD Everlar snapped, trying hard to sound fierce and commanding—and not shriekingly terrified.

Which he sure as damn-it *was*. He backed away half a step from the skeletons he was facing, before he remembered there were skeletons right behind him, too, and whirled hastily around.

Their brown, crumbling stumps of swords were almost in his face. The weapons were more rust than steel, now, yet looked plenty sharp enough to deal death. By sliding right into the bodies of lone idiots who came blundering into their crypt, for instance.

"Get away from me!" Rod commanded, hearing his voice rising in fear. "I am the Lord Archwizard of Falconfar, and I *command* you—"

Skeletons were evidently unimpressed by Lord Archwizards, or at least by quaking men claiming to be Lord Archwizards.

They were all shuffling toward him now, freeing themselves from the black cobwebs of what looked to have been their shrouds and converging on him in slow silence. They came floating unhurriedly ahead with a curious side-to-side gait, for all the world as if an unseen puppeteer was somewhere above them beyond the solid stone ceiling, making sure all of the bobbing, floating pieces of his marionettes kept together when they moved.

The spindle-light's beam did nothing to them at all, not even causing one of them to slow in caution when he shone it right at its gaping eyesockets, and willed it to get blinding-bright.

"I'll blast you down!" Rod threatened firmly, waving the spindle's light-beam around wildly, and at the same time trying to look at the four other things he'd scooped up without dropping and breaking any more of them in the process.

There was the hexagonal magic stone that he didn't know how to use, or even if it really had any magic at all; what looked like two finger-rings, or perhaps very short lengths of small plumbing pipe, both pierced and joined by a fine chain that ran through those piercings; and two cubes like very large dice, two inches across on a side, that had no markings or number-dots or anything on their sides, and seemed to be made of something hard that was glass-clear in streaks, and opaque blackish metal elsewhere. One of them was slightly larger than the other. No, no markings on either.

Now, just how or what any of these—

Coldness touched him, on his shoulders and hips and arms, and intense cold lanced through him in a gasping instant.

He was right out of time to try to play with his toys.

Chapter Eight

ROD GROANED, SHIVERING uncontrollably, doubled over and feeling helpless. He was so *cold*...

Wherever the skeleton's swords touched him, he felt as though he had just been plunged into icy water. It was a cold so harsh that it *burned*.

He stiffened, hissing in startled pain.

Steel had bitten into the strange sort-of-armor Rod was wearing—into a joint or gap in it, that is—and sliced into the worn leather padding next to his skin.

They were going to kill him, and there wasn't a damned thing he could do...

He could barely stand. He was shuddering uncontrollably from the utter biting cold, bent double and reeling blindly.

Rod blundered forward doggedly. He kept on clutching the maybe-magic gewgaws to himself, but lashed out wildly with the flashlight-spindle, seeking to smash some of those rusty blades away and maybe into ruin. They *looked* as if they should disintegrate into rusty flecks and dust.

They did, some of them, as he saw when he slipped and fell on his side. A moment later, a forest of converging swordpoints hung above his face, with more thrusting in to join them, the skeletal arms that wielded them seeming to *pass through* each other, strings of floating bones that could intersect without getting tangled or harmed—but two of the swords, less rusty than the rest, were being swung at him to cut.

The rest just poked at Rod, almost gently, as if trying to guide him, or warn him to stay down.

Skulls glaring eyelessly at him, a cold barrage of unblinking gazes he could *feel*...

Clenching his teeth to quell their chattering, Rod tried to get up again. They let him, but their swords gathered in a flicking, stabbing cloud at his arm. The arm holding the gewgaws.

Aha. There was something he had there that they didn't like, eh? Well, then...

He turned sharply away, as suddenly as he could—and gasped as the edge of a blade that was slicing along under what was covering his flank sank through it, just for a moment, and touched skin.

No, *cut* skin.

Rod shrieked.

If he'd thought he was feeling utter cold before, he now knew better. That sword hadn't gone into him—he might have a shallow cut a few inches long, at best—but the *pain!* Ohhh, the God-damned *pain!*

Blindly he staggered, vaguely aware that skeletons must be dancing aside to keep from collisions or impaling him on their swords... Slowly, as he shuddered against the chilling pain— Falcon, but this was a cold that didn't numb, it only bit deeper and deeper!—he became aware of something else, too: the two or three swords slicing at him were cutting away clothing, mainly what was covering his arms and the side of his chest and gut where he was holding those magical gewgaws—they *had* to be magical; this proved it, or why else would a bunch of skeletons want them so badly?—baring his upper torso strip by strip.

The other swords, the rusting stubs that just poked delicately at him, never boldly enough to pierce, were concentrating on the arm clutching the gewgaws—all but a few that were jabbing at his other hand, the one holding the spindle.

The cold brought Rod to his knees, sobbing for breath, and the volley of needle-like prickings became a hard, swift barrage. In the space it took him to pant out one ragged breath, Rod's arm was so chilled that he found himself grunting in despairing pain, his forehead pressed against the stone floor.

Quite suddenly, that arm gave way, the gewgaws bouncing and rolling—and the pokings ceased.

Only to resume all around his spindle-hand, jabbing and drawing back, darting in and jabbing again.

They wanted him stripped of the magic, all of it, but weren't killing him when they so easily could. His neck and throat, now his chest—they could have stabbed right through him, dozens of times, and hadn't.

Yet. Were they just waiting until all the magic was gone from him? Before they all stabbed into him, hilt-deep, and—

Rod shook his head, trying to wave away that grisly image, but it wouldn't go. He was writhing, dying slowly and horribly, impaled on dozens of swords with more sliding in to stab through his tongue and pin it to the back of his throat... then more sliding into his *eyes*...

He waved the spindle, one last feeble time, before the tip of a blade kissed his thumb so coldly that it spasmed—and his flashlight was gone, clanging off the stone floor with a bell-like ringing as it bounced, bounced again, then skirled to a clinking stop.

And the skeletons stopped.

Rod fell on his face on the cold, dank stone, groaning as the shivers claimed him, slamming through his body in waves that slowly faded away. He was lying alone in the cool silence, aware now of a gentle steady glow off to his right—the spindle, of course—and much fainter glows, that shifted silently and constantly, above him and all around him.

Coming from the skeletons?

He didn't want to look, didn't want to do anything except lie here and wince as the searing cold ebbed into a mere uncomfortable chill, taking stock of his hurts. His side throbbed faintly where it had been cut, and he was undoubtedly bleeding there. He felt tired, bone-tired, which was probably from all the shivering, not to mention the pricking swords...

He lay there until all the pain was gone, hearing nothing but silence, and feeling nothing but the faintest of cool breezes and the endless chill of the stone beneath him against his bare torso.

Then, gently and gingerly, a lone blade pricked his shoulder.

He lay still, though feigning death was probably futile when dealing with skeletons who could probably smell death—and life, too, for that matter.

The blade pricked him again, still tentatively.

He sighed, but didn't move.

Did they just want him to lift his face, so he'd see his doom—and then stab him, right up his nose and out through the back of his head?

The blade pricked him twice. Nudge, nudge.

Oh, all *right*, damn it. If he wasn't even going to be allowed to *die* in peace...

Rod rolled over, away from the blade, shoved against the floor cautiously, and sat up. Moving slowly, mindful of the forest of sharp sword tips he'd stared up into before.

Nothing touched him. He opened his eyes.

Skulls were still staring down. Not blinking, of course. Swords were still raised and ready—but when he looked up at the skeletons, they moved those blades in slow unison.

Pointing. The way out of the tomb.

As Rod stared at them, several of the blades turned back to point at him, jabbing toward his chest but not touching it, then swept back to point out the door again.

He was being commanded. Ordered out.

Well, they could slice him into little pieces—perhaps only a few at a time—if he defied them. So he might as well...

Rod found his feet, a little unsteadily, discovering he was still wearing his breeches and boots, but nothing more above his waist except a tattered scrap of leather trailing away from what was left of a leathern cuff and sleeve around his left forearm.

Well, now. If he wasn't so scrawny and stoop-shouldered, and didn't have the beginnings of a pot belly—or did he still have those beginnings, after all of the running and suchlike?—he might look a little like Doc Savage.

A little.

Blades waved, pointing again at the door, and there came the faintest of prickings—two or three of them—in his back.

"All right, all *right*," Rod growled. "Any chance of just talking to me? Anyone?"

There was, of course, no reply. But then, he hadn't really expected one.

He stepped out of the tomb, back into the passage, wondering if they were just going to let him go, once he was out of their resting-place.

He wondered, too, whether or not he dared whirl around and try to snatch up that flashlight-spindle. It was *dark* ahead of him.

Dark, but not pitch-dark. All around him, skeletons were glowing. A faint eerie blue, more like a series of half-seen, whisper-thin moving edges than steady lights.

Some of them moved ahead.

Surrounded by his cold and silent escorts, Rod Everlar started walking.

Well, at least he wasn't stumbling at random around the underground roots of Malragard.

He was being herded.

"No," DAUNTRA GASPED, her wings faltering again. "Too cold. I'm too stiff... must land, get a fire going... warm up."

Hanging in the harness beneath her, Iskarra tried not to sound too alarmed. "Glide lower, then, so we can see a good place to land," she snapped, voice quavering despite herself as Dauntra suddenly lurched sideways in the air.

They wobbled sickeningly for a moment before the Aumrarr caught herself, ducking her head and flapping grimly on.

"*Not* too cold," Juskra snarled from just behind them, spitting out words through teeth clenched in pain. Her left wing was something less than all right, and Garfist wasn't getting any lighter. At least the great lout had seen sense enough to stop kicking and waving his arms about, and contented himself with hanging in the straps like a lifeless lump, grumbling steadily. Thank the Falcon for small blessings.

"Not too cold," she said again. "Cramping! From not enough to drink... find us water!"

Dauntra nodded, but the nod turned into a shudder—and suddenly the Aumrarr and her burden were falling out of the sky, tumbling helplessly.

Juskra snarled a curse and bent herself into a steepening dive, sculling with her wings to make herself plummet faster. "Spread your arms!" she shrieked. "Spread your glorking *arms!*"

Iskarra was already spreadeagled in the air, but still tumbling. Dauntra seemed lost in spasms of pain.

Juskra screamed something else at them, but the words weren't half out of her mouth before the forest floor greeted the falling pair in a terrific crash of dead, snapping branches, bouncing arms and legs, and crackling, whirling leaves.

"Flaming feldrouking *dung!*" Juskra cursed. "Hold *on*, fat man!"

She and her complaining burden flashed over the tangle of dead trees that had greeted Dauntra and Iskarra, going too fast to land in it, and the wounded Aumrarr flung herself desperately over onto her side to avoid slamming face-first into a huge old gallart-top.

Through its side-branches she tore, Garfist kicking and cursing fervently in her wake, and found herself headed straight for another.

Juskra veered desperately, pulling her wings in tight, and slammed into two branches too stout to break. They sent her spinning, Garfist's snarled oaths rising into a fearful shout—and then, quite suddenly, they found themselves uprooting a sapling as they slid down its length to the ground.

Or rather, onto a little ridge of sharp rock that left them both groaning.

"Wingbitch," Garfist growled, inevitably finding his feet and his breath before the sobbing Juskra could, "did ye never learn any *gentler* sort of landing?"

"Fat man," she gasped back at him, still writhing on the rocks in pain, "go glork yourself." She spat out a sob that turned into a hiss, rocking back and forth in pain.

"Get up," he growled. "If ye can curse me that glibly, complete sentences an' all, ye're not sore hurt."

Juskra gave him a murderous glare. "No, but *you* soon will be!"

Leaving a chuckle behind, Garfist turned on his heel and lurched away, heading back to where light lancing through the trees marked the tangle of deadfalls Isk and Dauntra had crashed through.

He found them sitting together against the moss green trunk of a large and ancient gallart-top, clutching at themselves and wincing. Whipping branches had sliced more than a few cuts across their faces and ears, but they were as small as they were many.

"Anything badly broke?" Garfist greeted them cheerfully.

Two bent heads moved in rather weary unison to tell him "no."

"Need... to rest..." Dauntra gasped, not looking up.

"Aye," Garfist agreed sourly, feeling his own bruises and wincing—those rocks had been *sharp*, and trust Lady Icycurses Wingwench to find them, in all this muddy forest. "But why *here?*"

"Because it's near a spring," Juskra said sourly from behind him. When he turned, she tapped his shoulder and then pointed at a glimmer of water racing past nearby. "Water," she explained brightly, as if to an idiot child. "Water. That we can drink."

Then she turned to Iskarra, who was wobbling to her feet, wincing, and asked despairingly, "Doesn't he think of *anything* besides stealing, eating, and rutting?"

"No," Iskarra replied crisply. "In our modest little army, thinking's my job."

THESE WERE PASSAGES he'd never seen before.

They were halls he could barely see *now*, in the fitful glows of the skeletons bobbling along so silently beside him. Still deep enough to be carved out of bedrock, but rising. As he walked, ringed about by his eerie escort—his captors, Rod reminded himself—he was ascending. He must be moving up into the hollowed-out innards of the hill on the far side of Malragard.

Or rather, the hill beside and beyond the exposed roots of the place, now that the tower had been toppled and roofs torn off the wings and buttresses. He wondered if the greatfangs had gone, or were perched on broken walls and high places around the ruins, like so many buzzards in a dead tree.

Then he started to fervently hope the skeletons weren't marching him up to where he'd find out. Probably by promptly serving as a meal to the nearest greatfangs.

Or would they share him, all tugging and tearing at different limbs with their teeth? Pulling him apart, arms and legs and his *head...*

Rod shuddered, quelled a sudden urge to be sick, and told himself angrily to worry about whatever crises he was facing, not imagine new ones for himself. For one thing, this would be just the sort of time when his Shaping *would* work, for once—and he'd literally become the author of his own doom.

How large *were* these tunnels? It seemed to Rod that he'd been trudging for a long time, and it had certainly been long enough to have risen a level or two, and to get a little warmer, with the gentlest of breezes blowing in other scents than just mold and cold stone and damp dirt...

Cross-passages opened in the walls on either side of the hall the skeletons were moving along, and Rod could see that the hall opened out into an open space ahead. That was about all he could see, in the dim glows from the bobbing bones around him... and all of a sudden, he felt very weary.

Tired of it all. Tired of being always scared and lost and not knowing what he was doing. He'd been that way since being parted from Taeauna, and he was heartily sick of it. In all the stories—heck, in books he'd written—the hero moved steadily on toward completing the quest, saving the world, claiming the throne, winning the princess. Here, where fantasy was too damned real, they called him Lord Archwizard or Dark Lord and expected him to wave his hand and blast his foes to win all battles. And all he did was blunder along like some helpless child, too stupid to even know what the right thing was, let alone do it.

The floor under his feet rose more steeply, and the open space was just ahead, now. The dark mouths of side-passages grew more frequent, as if he was heading through a storage area.

Though it could just be a series of regular rooms separated by passages. It might be... well, *anything*.

Here he was, captured by a bunch of skeletons who couldn't even talk to him. They knew where they were going—they were certainly headed somewhere definite, and brooking no delays; when he'd tried to slow, feigning weakness, the swords jabbing him from behind had been neither gentle nor hesitant—but Rod didn't. As usual.

"Falcon take us all," he said wearily, more to hear his own voice than to make any of these silent skeletons answer him. "Off I'm being marched *again*. Now, where to, this time, and why?"

"To the place Malraun first bound us all," came a cold and sour voice from behind and to his right. "To unbind us, of course."

Rod whirled to face the speaker—and found himself staring at a floating head.

The head of a grim-looking, grizzled man whose rotting forehead bore a long white sword-scar, and whose neck had been crudely severed by axe-blows, ending in a ragged mess of flesh. A man who had died long ago, judging by the complete lack of blood and the shrunken, shriveled eyeballs.

It had drifted out of one of the side-passages and, as he stared at it, floated nearer to him.

"Well, man?" it asked irritably, sunken eyes flashing. "Have ye never seen a talking dead man before? Are ye *sure* ye're the Lord Archwizard?"

Chapter Nine

ANOTHER MAN OF Darswords stumbled, slammed into the passage wall with a curse, and came back to his feet a little unsteadily.

"Mind out!" the deep-voiced warrior said sharply, but before anyone could reply, the nearest man—the one who'd first menaced Daera with his sword, and was still doing so, trudging close behind her as she led the line of grim warriors deeper into the cold stone heart of the mountain—snapped, "Baerold, Laeveren's not clumsy. He's tired. We're *all* tired. Too weary to go on. If the wizard attacked us now, half of us'd be dead before we even knew what was happening. We *must* stop—and sleep."

There were emphatic nods of agreement, and some who nodded were yawning hugely as they did so. The deep-voiced warrior with the broad shoulders stared around at them all from under his bristling brows, then slowly nodded his head too.

"You're right, Roar. Back to that last cavern, then? Smooth stone there, underfoot." There were murmurs of agreement.

"Back," Taroarin agreed, his sword still close to Daera's neck. When he hefted it meaningfully at her and pointed back the way they'd come, she stood still for a moment, staring into his eyes, and breathed a kiss at him.

His habitual frown sharpened, but she kept her eyes on his as she turned, slowly, to obey him, following the shuffling warriors of Darswords back to the smooth-floored cavern.

Baerold was frowning at her, too. She met his narrowed eyes for the briefest of moments before bowing her head submissively, and was pleased to see some of that malice ebb before he turned away.

Only these two were wary of her; the rest kept stealing glances at her bared curves, when they looked her way at all.

She waited until he looked back a second time—a suspicious man indeed, our Baerold—saw nothing to alarm him, and returned his attention to trudging back to where he could rest.

Then Daera turned, nude and magnificent despite her graying skin, to whisper to Taroarin, "I know where rich treasures are hidden, man—but spells have been laid on me by the great wizard Narmarkoun. My tongue is bound, unless I speak to one who has mastered me. To him, and him alone, I am free to speak."

"One who has mastered you," Taroarin echoed, his whisper as ghostly quiet as hers, and gave her the merest crooked hint of a smile. Hint taken.

Men were already settling themselves as best they could on hard rock, with a chorus of sighs, muttered curses, and groans, by the time Taroarin led Daera to the back of the cavern, where it branched into three narrow fissures curving off into the darkness.

As Baerold watched wordlessly, he forced her to her knees on the sharp rocks there, took off his sword-belt, and used it to strap her arms together behind her back, winding it around and around them from elbows to wrists before buckling it tight. Then he did off his half-cloak, wound it around Daera's head, lowered her face-first onto the stones, and arranged stones on the trailing cloak-tails to pinion her head where she lay.

Two swift kicks spread her legs apart, and he growled, "Don't move. Or else." Half a dozen swipes of his boots raked loose stones away from all around her into a ring, so his captive lay on cleared stone but surrounded by a little wall of rock. Reclaiming his blade, Taroarin turned his back on her and returned to Baerold.

"I'll stand first watch," he said, but the deep-voiced man shook his head.

"Second," was his terse response. "I'm first. Wake Sargult to relieve you."

Taroarin shrugged, nodded, and sought the far side of the chamber, where he sat down and curled himself up against the wall.

He had barely begun to snore when Baerold went over to Daera, squatted down, and gave her trussed body a baleful glare.

"I want to trust you," he muttered quietly, "but I can't."

His hand closed over the solid, reassuring pommel of his dagger. "It'd be best if I just cut you apart right now. Though that just might mean severed arms and legs and a head all bouncing around, clawing at us and working mischief. We should burn you. Not that I've seen any wood since we got in here."

He drew his dagger, hefted it, and leaned closer.

"Well, dead woman? Wizard's monster? What if I started cutting you up right now?"

From inside the cloak enfolding her head came a soft snore.

THE LANDINGS WERE heavy but precise, the two weary Aumrarr thumping down on a high mountain ledge half a breath behind their harnessed burdens.

It was a big ledge, but not so large that four sprawled, tired folk—two with wings—didn't feel crowded.

"We're in Galath," Juskra announced faintly.

Garfist Gulkoun looked up at the peak behind them, then the other way, down over the lip of the ledge.

It was a sheer drop, a long way down to many jagged rocks heaped below. This had been the smallest of the marching mountains, but more than large enough to be deadly.

A cold breeze whistled past. He gazed out at the dark treetops ahead, and smaller rock ridges beyond that, then turned to stare at his steed.

"I fail to see your promised inn," he growled, as the wind rose. "Or for that matter, any safe way down from here." He reached for Juskra's throat.

Rather than pulling away or snatching out her sword, she leaned forward to let him take hold of her, sinking into his ungentle grip as if welcoming oblivion.

"Surrendering, Aumrarr?"

"Gar," she murmured, "I'm too tired to do anything else. We're worn out. Yes, even with all these shorter flights, and resting between. You're not getting any lighter."

The burly warrior growled at her, his hand tightening.

"Well?" she managed to gasp. "Are you?"

"Gar," Iskarra said sharply, "let go of her."

Garfist shook Juskra by the throat, then thrust her away with a snarl of disgust. "Ye'd get yer rest better in a good bed, in an inn."

The Aumrarr nodded. "We'll get to it soon enough," she mumbled. "A little patience, please."

Then, silently and suddenly and without any fuss, she leaned toward him—and went right on leaning until her face struck his chest and slid down it to an awkward stop nigh his lap.

She was out cold. Garfist gave her a little shake, but she didn't rouse, lying heavy on his thighs, one wing furled and the other open and trailing over the edge of the cliff.

Garfist looked helplessly over her at Iskarra. Her reply was a shrug, and a look as helpless as his own.

In unspoken unison they looked over at the other Aumrarr. Still tangled in the harness attached to Iskarra, Dauntra was fast asleep, draped limply against the rising face of the mountain.

"Is there anything we can hook any of this harness around, to keep from rolling off?" Gar growled.

Iskarra shook her head. The chill wind tugged at them.

They sat in motionless silence for a breath or two, as Garfist swallowed several curses, and then Iskarra made mimicry of laying her head on her hands in slumber, pointed at the mountain at their backs, and crawled over to it.

Garfist followed her, shifting himself awkwardly under Juskra's weight and dragging her with him. He shuffled along on his behind toward the rising rock at the back of the ledge; safer, perhaps, but by no means secure. Or warm.

"The quality of inns favored by the Aumrarr is slipping, to be sure," he grumbled to the wind, as he tried to settle himself into a slightly more comfortable position against sharp and unyielding stone, to seek a little sleep.

The wind rose into a little wail, just for a moment, as if in mocking reply.

IT HAD BEEN some time since Baerold had roused him, shaking Taroarin awake while growling his name in his ear.

The big man had lain down in Taroarin's spot against the side wall. He'd only sheathed his dagger reluctantly, and taken a long time to settle down to sleep, but he was snoring now, loud and long and regular.

Rubbing arms and legs that still ached from sleeping on hard stone, Taroarin picked his way carefully around the chamber in the dim, ever-present radiance—the wizard's magic, of course; had to be—peering at one sprawled man of Darswords, and then another. They were all asleep.

When he was quite sure of that, Taroarin drew in a deep breath, nodded as if to reassure himself he was going to do this and it would be all right, then went slowly and quietly to the back of the cavern and stepped carefully into the ring of cleared stone. After a last, wary look around, he knelt between Daera's spread legs, and tugged down his breeches.

She trembled when she felt his fingers at her nethers, but raised her behind up off the stone before his hand could. Taroarin brought his other hand around and closed it roughly about her throat to throttle any outcry—but she made no more sound than a muffled gasp as he forced his way roughly into her.

The cloak around her head hid her real responses. A flash of her eyes that would have made Taroarin stiffen in fear. A widening smile of soft triumph that would have had his sword out, trying to hack it off her face.

A smile that looked not at all like Daera's, but was all Narmarkoun's.

"Down swords," Taeauna said sharply. "Let them go."

Old Roreld nodded unhappily, and turned to wave at the bowmen hastily readying shafts—the brutal chopping signal that told them to leave off doing so.

As their bows were lowered, the last of Norgarl's men gave Roreld a few waves of their own—much ruder ones—and headed down the other trail, vanishing into the trees.

Taeauna watched them go, calm and silent, hand on the sword hilt riding her hip.

"Better they're gone, if they don't want to be with us," she added grimly. "Have Olondyn keep his best foresters back behind the rest of us, watching and listening to make sure none of the traitors skulk along behind us. We'll camp well off the trail, both sides; you know. See to it."

"Lady, I will," the bearded veteran rumbled, and tramped away.

Taeauna watched Roreld go, keeping a trace of a smile on her face, well aware that more than a few of her dwindling army would be sneaking looks at their commander, watching for fear, or anger... or tears.

"A pack of dogs waiting for any weakness to show, before they spring," she murmured almost soundlessly, making the sign of the Falcon calmly and slowly, so anyone watching would take her words for a prayer.

First it had been Korauth, of course, taking his men back the way they'd come, loudly and profanely.

Then Buckhold, slipping away as silently as he did everything else, taking rearguard as they marched on and falling behind slowly, until he and his warriors were just *not there* any longer, nor anywhere to be found.

The trail to Wytherwyrm, it seemed, was far less popular than the way to Ironthorn—and both roads paled before the allure of heading back home, through the long string of holds they'd already conquered and plundered.

"So many dripping pendants on a bloody necklace of war," she murmured, recalling a snatch of mournful song she'd heard an old Aumrarr sing at Highcrag, long ago.

Now she'd lost Norgarl, with all his warriors; more men than she now had left. The old boar himself was no loss, a beast of a man who thought that Aumrarr were far less than human and that women were good only for cooking, rutting, and tending wounded, but his men obeyed him as if he was the Falcon himself, and...

She shook her head impatiently, turned, and started walking back to the front of her host, strung out along the winding, shady way to Wytherwyrm. Dwelling on might-have-beens was a luxury no prudent Falconaar could stoop to, in this time of Dooms unleashed and Highcrag made an open grave and war in the Raurklor... and likely in Galath again, too, before the snows flew, if she knew anything about the ambitious ardukes and barons of that land.

So, would it be the brothers Esdagh next, or Dzundivvur the coin-counter, cutting his losses?

She grimaced sourly, then twisted her lips into a smile as she passed Lanneth Esdagh. She gave him a nod and said lightly, "You're rearguard now, Lan. Norgarl's not the man he used to be, it seems."

She walked on without waiting for his reply, keeping her shoulders square and her gait jaunty, trading jests with the veteran swordsmen and giving winks and smiles to the younger ones.

She did not hurry. It wasn't *that* far to Wytherwyrm, and even Lanneth Esdagh would have a hard time managing to steal away a host of warriors when she was actually striding alongside them.

Though she had no doubt he'd find a way.

TAROARIN ARCHED BACK from the cold beauty he was clutching to his loins, threw back his head—and made no shout at all.

For the space of a long breath he reeled, on his knees and trembling, mouth wide open for a scream that never came.

Then he blinked, closed his mouth again, and bent down over the woman he was clutching, letting go of her hips and putting his hands to the floor.

Where he hesitated, trembled again, and slowly bore her back down to the cold stone under his weight. When the trembling died away, he drew back from Daera in utter silence.

With gentle fingers he arranged her just as she had been lying before, and with the same deft stealth buckled up his breeches and rose swiftly away from her.

He was back at the front of the cavern, with most of the sleeping men of Darswords between him and their undead captive, when Baerold suddenly sat up and looked around, awake and suspicious, delivered out of the terrifying depths of a dream of a grinning Narmarkoun taking the shape of a dark serpent, and slithering among the sleepers to bite them all.

Chilled and unsettled, the burly man was, truth be told, a little surprised to see Taroarin standing watch nowhere near the dead-she, blade in hand and with his back to his companions. The way he'd been eyeing this Daera...

Too beautiful to be trusted. Dead but walking, a creature held up by the wizard's hand, just as a minstrel at a feast thrusts a little carved head of a king or a dragon or a dull-witted knight onto his fingers to make folk laugh. Why, the mage could be watching us right now, out of her eyes...

Baerold peered about, but the undead woman lay sprawled and motionless in her ring of rocks, head still shrouded in that cloak, arms still bound. He saw no black serpents, either, nor any sign of death among the men of Darswords.

He glared around the chamber for a long time, but nothing moved except young Taroarin, peering along the passage in one direction and then another.

With a sigh, Baerold laid himself down again and sought slumber.

Falcon take all wizards, and their marching armies and mad schemes, too.

"LADY TAEAUNA!"

Between gasps for breath, Zorzaerel's voice was sharp with alarm. "Lord Dzundivvur demands word with you! He and all his men press forward into us—and behind him, on the trail, the men of Esdagh are hastening back the way we've come!"

Taeauna nodded, giving the youngest and boldest of her warcaptains—still panting from his haste to reach her, and looking as if he'd seen the death of the Falcon itself—a smile she hoped looked calm enough to be reassuring.

"Well, now," she said lightly, "the Esdaghs managed to make a deal with the old Stormar coin-grasper. I'm astonished they could afford it."

"*We* can't afford it," he growled, surprising her.

She clapped him on the shoulder, laughed merrily, and wondered what she'd tell him next. Or the men beyond him—Malraun's men, faithful blades all—who to a man were staring at her, deepening worry etching their faces.

They were waiting for her to give them hope.

TAROARIN SMILED—OR rather, Narmarkoun made the lips he now controlled smile, taking some time over it to make sure the result looked like Taroarin of Darswords smiling.

The man's ruined will was struggling feebly in the depths of the mind Narmarkoun had just seized, but it was a futile fight, a battle already lost. Lost forever; there was not enough left of Taroarin to ever regain control. When Narmarkoun departed this strong young shell, there would be no more than a staggering, drooling husk left behind.

This close to her, he could still control Daera's body, too.

For that matter, with a stride or two he could conquer every one of the sleeping men of Darswords, right now. Not that he particularly wanted the mind-deadening weight of riding so many mounts at once. He already had more agile and able slaves, and each and every one of them was more pleasant to the eye than these hairy louts.

Who still lived because they would soon have their uses.

Doomed men, every last one of them, though they knew it not. Taroarin's smile turned wry. Aren't we all?

Choices. Most of us don't even get to choose the manner of our dooms.

Chapter Ten

THREE OLD MEN with swords and a boy with a rough-hewn spear stood in a tense line across the trail, barring the way. The sunlight of Wytherwyrm was at their backs, and the steadily marching army before them, bearing down on them without hesitation. Their faces were gray with fear.

Olondyn put a shaft to his bow with a sneer on his face, but held his fire, and looked to Taeauna.

She gave him a tight smile and lifted her hand, staying him for now, then turned to give proud Askurr a nod.

The tall warcaptain unfurled Malraun's blood-red banner and held it high. At the sight of it the four defenders of Wytherwyrm sighed as one and stood aside, lowering their weapons and waving Taeauna's army into their hold.

Taeauna looked for changes since the last time she'd been in Wytherwyrm—flying, then—and saw none.

It still wasn't much of a hold. Little more than a muddy clearing where two streams met at a pond, with a smithy and a ramshackle inn and a dozen-some log huts hard by. But then, this wasn't much of an army anymore, either.

After the Esdaghs were well and truly gone, she and Dzundivvur had talked out their short, weary parley. The old, hollow-eyed Stormar had told Taeauna bluntly that he didn't mind fighting under a wizard, but there was no way by all the feathers of the glorking Falcon he was going to try to fight *against* a wizard, with no more aid than "an Aumrarr who's lost her wings and brave blades who have no more magic than I do."

Taeauna knew very well that amid all his crisscrossing baldrics, pouches and targes, the Stormar merchant was wearing enough enchanted things—old and mean as they might look—to defeat three or four hedge-wizards, given a little luck. Not to mention several score weary bowmen and swordswingers, with ease and magic to spare. Wherefore she very politely told him she understood, stood aside, and let him—and his motley, hardbitten band of hireswords with him—depart unhindered.

Leaving her with what was left of Horgul's seekers of liberty, and Malraun's own warriors. Fewer than a hundred men, all told; Wytherwyrm's ale-casks ought to be sufficient.

That wry thought took Taeauna into Wytherwyrm, to stand watching as Roreld waved his arms in commands that sent warriors hastening everywhere in search of foes hiding in the trees, the cabins, and the inn, with pairs or threes of Olondyn's bowmen right behind them, arrows ready.

She didn't expect them to find anything, and by the casual stances of the warcaptains standing around her watching the scouring of Wytherwyrm, they didn't either.

When she turned toward the inn, however, they did not walk with her—or get out of her way. Taeauna found herself in the center of a grim, silent ring.

So she lifted her eyebrows at them in silent question.

"Lady," Askurr said almost gently, furling Malraun's banner, "we must talk."

"Say on," she replied calmly, keeping her eyes on him rather than looking around at the faces now intent on hers. Olondyn, Zorzaerel... Roreld had joined them, too. All of the warcaptains, and the eldest and most trusted of Malraun's guardsmen, too.

Askurr hesitated, then blurted out, "We want some answers, all of us. What with all who've left, we... Well, tell us plain: what's become of Malraun?"

She waited, calmly. There would be more. There was.

"Why're you leading us to Malragard, and not on to Ironthorn? And, and—forgive me, Lady—why should we obey you? You say you follow the Master's orders, but we all heard him say it was to be Ironthorn after Darswords; those are his orders we *know*."

Taeauna nodded. "Well enough. Fair questions, all." She tossed her head, looked around at them, and raised her voice a trifle.

"Let me say first that I have been, ah, *closer* to Malraun than the rest of you... yes? In a manner I trust you'd prefer not to outdo me in."

Her dry declaration brought murmurs from them, but not—quite—any grins. They were troubled, all right.

"So I know Malraun's mind well. We've talked a lot together, and we speak frankly to each other. *Not* as fearful underling to feared master. Though I know very well what a Doom of Falconfar can do to a foe. Or someone who is disloyal."

She paused to look around her, trying to meet gazes, to show them she was calm, not angry. And certainly not afraid of them.

"I know his will and his intended road ahead better than any of you. And I remain loyal to him, and so am trying to follow his orders and desires. I heard him speak of taking Ironthorn next, too. However, that was before... Lorontar."

A murmur of soft curses and despairing remarks arose, and she waited for it to die down before continuing.

"I know the first Lord Archwizard of Falconfar lived—and died—a long, long time ago. Yet all my life I have heard the same rumors you have: that he survives, somehow, and will rise again when the time is right."

She stared slowly around the ring of men, letting them see the truth in her eyes.

At least, she hoped they'd see it as truth. They gazed back at her in silent dismay, every one of them.

"Know that he *has* risen," she went on, "and has struck at Malragard, seeking to seize the Master's magic. Lord Malraun used his magic to hurl himself from Darswords to his tower, to stop Lorontar the Terrible before the risen Lord Archwizard became too powerful for all Falconfar to defeat, standing together."

"And?" Olondyn barked.

"And my head took fire with that battle," she told them all grimly. "Malragard did not fare well, I believe. The *third* Doom of Falconfar—Narmarkoun—saw the battle as a chance to seize power from the both. I know not if my Malraun survives, or Narmarkoun... but I fear greatly that Lorontar, somehow, still exists."

"And you've... you've been walking down the trail with us this day with *all this* in your head, telling us not a *word* of it?" Askurr's voice rose as high as a terrified young girl's. "Marching us into a battle of *Dooms?*"

Taeauna shrugged. "*We* are Falconfar's last hope. We and a man who was captive there, and may yet survive, too. Rod Everlar, the Dark Lord."

"So," Roreld rumbled slowly, "if we can rescue him, you mean..."

She nodded, wordlessly, and waited.

The storm was not long in coming. One moment they were all staring at her in silence, aghast, and the next they were bellowing and wagging their fingers in her face and waving their arms around. Rages born of terror, a roaring of frightened men.

She stood like a rock, silent and patient, and let the tumult break over her. When they all ran out of curses to shout, it was Olondyn who spat at her, "And *you* were marching us right into this, scheming wingbitch!"

Taeauna nodded. "I was."

"Rushing us to our slaughter!"

She shrugged and faced him squarely. "Perhaps. I know that we have a chance to destroy Lorontar, however slim. I know that if we slink away, scattering to our lairs and strongholds across Falconfar, that chance is lost—and that he'll come for us, one by one, and we'll be too few and too weak to cling to our lives. One by one he'll have us, like a night-cat pouncing on rats. Would you not want the chance to save your life, and all Falconfar? Rather than hurling it away, to live the rest of your life in fear, awaiting the doom you know will come?"

"I *know* nothing of the sort," Olondyn snapped. "A doom *you* proclaim, that I foresee not at all. Any wizard will need bodyguards, warriors to fight for him; why should he not choose Olondyn of the Bow?"

Taeauna shook her head. "You do not know Lorontar. *I* know him all too well. Dark Helms and lorn are his preferred troops—and hedge-wizards whose minds he burns out, so he can ride behind their eyes. Put all thought of paid service out of your head, Olondyn. Anyone who may have thought Lord Malraun cruel and imperious, consider this: what manner do you think a wizard will have when dealing with the world, when he *prefers* to be served by the dead?"

"Words," Zorzaerel growled. "All we have of this is your words, Lady. This Lorontar could be a kindly old sit-by-the-fire, for all we know."

"And if he is, and everything I say is a lie," Taeauna replied gently, "how much better a place will be Ironthorn, where three rival lordlings make war on each other every day, and have tested and ready armies, alert for any foe—when we are so few, now?"

"You," Askurr told her bluntly, "are crazed. I'll not listen to a word more from you—and I'll *not* follow you to certain doom."

There was a general rumble of agreement, and men started to move. "Bah," one warrior growled. "Give me swords any day, not spells I can do nothing to stop."

Taeauna stood still, turning only her head as she watched for a sword or two lashing out at her in anger.

None came. They drew back from her, not turning their backs until they were well away, then started tramping off in all directions, seeking their men.

"Hear me, all who are loyal to Falconfar," Taeauna called after them, keeping her voice flat and firm. "Rally to me, and walk with me to Malragard. Your swords can carve out our last chance."

None of the warcaptains even looked back. Except, after a few reluctant strides, old Roreld, who stopped and shook his head slowly at her.

Malraun's own men, the bodyguards who'd served him the longest—Eskeln, Gorongor, Tarlund, and Glorn—alone came to Taeauna, to stand with her, guarding her back and flanks. All of them stared at Roreld, who stared back and shook his head again.

"This... this is madness," he muttered. "Ironthorn's our death, I know, but a wizard's tower, now..." He shook his head again. "We could end up as Dark Helms, doomed to fight on after we die, until our very joints fall apart."

"Or we could save Falconfar, every lass and hearth of it we hold dear," Taeauna replied softly. "Instead of turning our backs and leaving that fray to others and dooming us all."

"So you say," Roreld said, sounding helpless. "It sounds so... unlikely." He waved empty hands, as if beckoning the Falcon to show him some sign. "Fighting wizards and dead things is not how I want to die."

Taeauna snorted. "We're warriors, Roreld. We could all be dead tomorrow. So don't wait for the morrow. Be magnificent *today*."

Roreld gave her a crooked smile. "You sound like a merchant trying to sell me something. For too high a price, and a thing I don't want, besides." He shook his head again—but turned and trudged toward her.

"I'm in," he said simply.

They embraced, chest to chest and thumping backs as warriors do, and in the heart of it he muttered, "Don't make me regret this. Tay, *please* don't make me regret this."

"I'll try not to. By the Falcon we all hold dear, I'll try," she murmured back, as they broke apart.

Taeauna looked around the ring of men. It was smaller now. Much smaller. Ten men, in fact, including Roreld's five. Veterans all, but still... ten men.

Ten men, against the greatest archwizard Falconfar had ever known.

She shrugged. Fewer graves to dig.

"If there's enough left of any of us to need burying," she murmured under her breath.

Gorongor, who had the keenest hearing, turned his head sharply. "Sorry, lady? What was that?"

"I said," Taeauna told him with a smile, "that I'm for yonder inn, for meat and drink before we start hurrying."

They nodded in agreement, and started across the clearing, ignoring the warriors everywhere who avoided their eyes, men hastening this way and that, making ready to start back to their own holds.

Horgul's army hadn't lasted long, after all.

So much for Liberation.

Taeauna smiled thinly. There'd be no liberation until all the Dooms were dead and gone, and Falconfar had no Lord Archwizard.

None but Rod Everlar.

"LORD ARCHWIZARD? I—I—some call me that," Rod stammered. "Who're *you*?"

Sunken, shriveled eyeballs glimmered angrily back at him. "I'm a *real* wizard, 'Lord Archwizard.' The mage who built—and dug—this place, spell by spell. Back when the world was young and men kept their word—and all that sort of bog-twaddle. In the days when the Falcon flew our skies and was seen by all."

"The Falcon is real?"

"Of *course* it's real. Who d'ye think hears our curses, and heaps misfortunes on our heads for uttering them?"

"Lorontar," Rod said wryly. "Except when he's busy. Then Malraun and the other Dooms fill in."

The head dropped open its jaw—green-white flesh quivering—and made a hearty rattling sound that could only have been meant to be a laugh. It drifted closer to Rod.

"I *like* ye, man. Ye can't be a wizard. Ye lack the imperious rudeness, the spurning of humor. Yet... yet ye wakened all the Sleepers, just by blundering into their midst, and only one who can wield the most powerful magics can do that."

"The Sleepers?" Rod looked at the bobbing skeletons, who had now paused to stand in a ring around him, every skull turned toward him, the rusty remnants of their blades held so as to point to the ceiling. "These?"

The floating head sighed loudly. "Ye *are* an idiot, aren't ye?"

Rod managed a thin smile. "Guilty as charged."

"'Charged'?" The head backed away, eyes flaring up in rage or alarm. Then it seemed to relax, slumping down in midair. "Oh. Ye really *don't* know the first thing about magic, do ye?"

"No," Rod admitted quietly. "No, I don't."

DLARMARR WAS FAR from the largest and wealthiest port on the Hywond Shore, but it was one of the best.

In the oh-so-worldly opinion of Morl Ulaskro, tomekeeper of Lord Luthlarl's private library. Not that Morl had ever been farther from Dlarmarr than the village he'd been born in—Esker's Well, just the other side of Mralkwood Hill

Yet Morl was the tomekeeper, and so had read more about the Stormar ports than almost anyone he could think of, even if he'd never been to any of them but Dlarmarr. From the lord's highest tower, he could see Hywond itself, as a distant smudge down the coast, and what he *thought* was Telchassur beyond that, but at night the twinklings of their lights, the ship-fires lit atop their harbor-towers, were clear enough.

Hywond had the best shipyards and the largest fishing fleet on all the Shore, and Telchassur was supposed to be old and even wealthier, but neither of them had anything to touch Lord Luthtarl's library. Hy-folk used books as ledgers, writing coin-counts of the moment over the fading words others had written long ago, and Telchassur was a city where tales were told in tapestries and paintings and sculpture, or sung in long, eerie chants, not set down in books.

So Morl was quite content to stay snug in Dlarmarr—not even ducking out of the familiar warm dust and quiet of the library except when he was sent—and read, dreaming of places he would never see. From here, he could look out over the world—if only the world limned so colorfully on the fading maps that covered the top of the Shrouded Table—and know all. It was as good as commanding all.

Not that Morl had the slightest desire to become lord of anywhere, or was in any danger of becoming so. He *did* want to become locklar of the library, some day, when blind-and-deaf old Urvraunt was carried off by the Falcon. Urvraunt had never been a pleasant man, and as his senses failed and he increasingly needed Morl not just to scramble up ladders and fetch hard-to-reach tomes, but to find the right title among the rows even at chest level, hard by the reading table, his irritability was becoming a constant, snarling thing. Besides, he was beginning to smell—and not just of strong everember wine.

There was something else Morl would gain by Urvraunt's death, someday. The library keys, of course, but more importantly just one of them: the long black key that gave admittance to the Black Chamber. Where the books of magic—the books that *lived*, some of them, moving around by night, and reportedly even draining those who stole in to peer at them in the hours of darkness to withered old age—were kept.

Just once, when the locklar had been interrupted by a message from Lord Luthtarl, Morl had seen a lone book of magic lying open, and it had been an ordinary-looking, slender tome Urvraunt had sneered at as "poor and paltry enough." Yet the black and red, angular runes that made so many folk ill just by glancing at them had *flowed* under Morl's gaze and thrilled him, kindling something in his mind. Trying to read them—he took in no more than a line ere Urvraunt had come snarling back into the room— had thrown up vivid, half-glimpsed visions that had kept Morl awake and quivering all that night, and left him aching for more.

He was one of those who could read magic, could *wield* magic— and by the Falcon, one way or another, he would taste that flowing fire again before he died, and cast spells, and sweep past cowering folk in dark and splendid robes, and be a wizard.

Wizards could change the world.

Chapter Eleven

"**M**ASTER ULASKRO," THE locklar greeted him with heavy sarcasm, "it seems the gulls have been relieving themselves all down the windows again. The windows outside *my* office. Do you therefore go out upon the balcony—*now*—and speedily perform such scrubbings as are necessary to let the sun shine once more unimpeded across my desk."

Morl knew better than to reply with anything except a bowed head and the words, "Of *course*, Locklar Urvraunt!"

He put all the toadyingly submissive eagerness into them he could, because he knew such a manner pleased rather than irritated the old man—and life ran more smoothly for them both when Locklar Urvraunt was pleased.

Brushes, bucket, and soap flakes were old, familiar friends, and so was the roof-cistern tap. Urvraunt seemed to find a lot of things around the library for his tomekeeper to scrub. In fact, it seemed as if Morl did a lot more maids' work than keeping of tomes.

Not that Morl particularly minded. It set him to seeing new things, getting some fresh air, and making little trips down to shops in Dlarmarr he'd never have seen otherwise. Which brought to mind a certain bakehearth on the steepest part of Orshandul Street, and fishcakes that melted in the mouth with a sauce that... that...

"Tomekeeper Ulaskro," Urvraunt snapped, "you're *drooling*. Stop standing there dreaming of feasts, boy, and get out there and *clean my windows!*"

Hastily Morl nodded and obeyed. Oh, so they were "my" windows now, were they? And all these years, he and everyone else in Dlarmarr had been so stone-cold sure that they were Lord

Luthtarl's windows. Stiffnecked old toad. Urvraunt, that is, not kindly old Luthtarl. Of course, Luthtarl had been something less than "kindly" down the years, in dealings with pirates—personally gutting them before all his court—and visiting merchants who dared to feud in the streets of Dlarmarr through the daggers of their underlings, and even the haughty lords of Hywond, too—

Morl noticed the sun had suddenly gone out.

Now, storms were wont to strike Dlarmarr suddenly, but there was always a great roaring and moaning of winds, first, and the air turning either sultry-hot or icy, and—

He turned from washing the windows and gaped in utter disbelief.

The largest monster he'd ever seen—a dragon or a greatfangs or something else that had scales and huge raking talons and bat-wings broader than an entire wing of the lord's castle—was looming up over him, blotting out the sky.

Its wings were spread wide, slowing it, but it wasn't a heart-beat away from slamming into the balcony, and the library beyond the balcony.

Which meant that Lord Luthtarl was going to need a new library—and a new tomekeeper, too.

Morl tried to scream, but all that came out was a sob. There was a young man struggling feebly in one of the monster's massive, cruel claws—and the other claw was reaching out for him.

With all his might, Morl swung his bucket of soapy water at the creature's talons. The brush he'd dropped into it bounced off one tree-trunk-sized talon and fell away.

And then he was snatched into the air, a fire in his ribs and all the breath slammed out of him.

Stone shrieked below him as the gigantic creature raked at it, thrusting itself aloft, and Morl saw the balcony and some of the wall above it breaking away and falling, tumbling down into the courtyard he could no longer see. There were great bright gouges in the weathered castle stone.

This thing can shear through stone with its talons.

Someone was shouting and pointing, from a tower nearby. "Greatfangs! Falcon deliver us! A greatfangs! It's snatched someone!

A greatfangs. Winging its way strongly out over the Sea of Storms, now, rising higher, its tail lashing the air behind it.

Still fighting to try to breathe, Morl turned his head enough to see the man gripped in the monster's other claw. Their eyes met.

No comfort there, only despair.

They were both doomed.

THE FLOATING HEAD acquired a peculiar expression—a mixture of dismay, a little disgust, a hint of incredulity, and a certain grudging respect—as it regarded Rod Everlar. "So ye admit it. Ye don't know the first thing about magic at all."

"No," Rod admitted, wondering if he'd just made the worst mistake of his life. "I just write about it. Making things up as I go along."

"*Falcon*. Well, at least ye know how to speak plain truth. That's more than most every wizard I've ever known could bring himself to do."

Rod shrugged, smiled, and spread his hands. "I've not met all that many wizards, but I wouldn't—*couldn't*—trust any I did meet."

"Oh? And just who have ye met?"

Rod drew in a deep breath. "Well, all the Dooms: Arlaghaun, Malraun, and Narmarkoun. And Lorontar, too. Oh, and there was a wizard in Wrathgard, and another—one of Arlaghaun's apprentices, I think—who conjured a gate in the cellars of Bowrock, and—"

"Enough. Well, now ye've met another. I am Rambaerakh, Slayer of Dragons."

Rambaerakh fell silent, beaming. Rod, feeling awkward, blurted, "Oh."

"Well, I see ye really did speak truth. Ye *do* know nothing about magic at all."

Rod managed a lopsided smile. "I was supposed to be impressed, learning who you are, I take it?"

"If by 'impressed' ye mean 'awed,' yes, ye were. I built this tower around and above us, and for many seasons ruled a kingdom from it. Rauryk, 'twas called. The Realm of Tall Trees."

"The Raurklor?"

"The Raurklor. Alone I slew a score of dragons—one at a time, of course, save for that night above Har Rock when two wyrms took wing against me. *I created the first Dark Helms.* Not that sneering pretender Lorontar, who killed wizards he got drunk and took their magic for his own, one after another, until the rest of us noticed—and then killed enough wizards more that we finally saw fit to seek him out. *I ruled here,* until I got just careless enough to make one mistake too many—guarding too much against Lorontar and mages he had his hands up the backsides of, and not against others. Which was when Malraun wrested my Dark Helms from me, hurled them against me until I was forced out of this tower, and there in the fields beset me with spells until dragons found me and took their revenge on me for their slain kin. Leaving me like this."

"Torn apart?"

"Torn, eaten, burned, and clawed. These aren't sword-scars below my chin."

"How... how did you survive at all?"

"Magic. *Real* magic, man, spells piled deep and true. I laid more on myself than on my Helms... and look at them."

Rod frowned, glanced around in vain, then stared at the bobbing, silent skeletons. "These? These are—were—your Dark Helms?"

"Are again, though there's not enough left of them to be my Helms any more. No, their time is done, and mine too."

"Meaning?"

"Meaning we need ye, Lord Less Than Archwizard."

"To—?"

"Work a little magic for us."

"But..."

"Oh, I'll guide ye, man. Ye don't have to know what ye're doing; if *that* was a requirement, there's few enough Falconaar who'd ever do anything."

"So what is this 'little magic'?"

"Unbind us."

At Rod's puzzled look the severed head smiled sourly and said, "Malraun the Matchless bound us here, to keep us from marauding through his tower whenever his back was turned, or out across Falconfar. He's dead now—must be, for my Helms

106

to be walking and me to be free to depart my tomb and trade words with thee—but the same spells that keep the very stones of Malragard in place, that he added atop my wards and bindings, also tether us here."

The head drifted a little closer. "So, Rod Everlar, I charge thee to come with us now and do what is needful to unbind us."

"I—"

"We'll not slay thee. Lord Archwizard of Falconfar, if ye care for Falconfar at all, *unbind us.*"

The shrunken eyes were ablaze, glaring at Rod now from close beyond his own nose. "Unbind us."

Rod swallowed, trying not to look horrified. The promise not to kill him could be so many empty words; this was, after all—or had been—a wizard. Lying is what wizards *do.*

And try as he might, Rod could not banish from his mind scenes of bobbing bones swinging swords to hack down ardukes and fleeing farmwives alike, bloodily hewing frightened guards apart and—and Taeauna, alone and beset and going down in a welter of spraying blood and screams of agony...

As he heard their mocking thanks for being so duped, as they cut off his hands and feet to let him bleed to death, and surged forth from wherever he was lying, helpless and doomed. With no one at all left to stop them as they went marauding across all of Falconfar...

TETHTYN HAD LONG ago exhausted the contents of his stomach; there was nothing left in him to spew into the whistling wind. He was cold, shivering, miserable, and barely awake, sinking into dozes time and again and starting awake, usually when an especially chilly gust of wind or a wet cloud engulfed him, or the talons around him tightened.

He didn't want to think about how his life was going to end, when the greatfangs decided to land and needed the claw that was wrapped so thoroughly around him.

Right now, he didn't want to think about *anything.*

Tethtyn was vaguely aware that the great dragon-like beast above him had flown far and fast, east and south to the coast and one of the smaller ports there—where it had stooped to snatch someone else, in its other foreclaw—then swung briefly out over the open sea before it soared back up into the rolling, wooded uplands behind the Stormar shores. He didn't doubt it could easily have flown higher, and crossed over the towering mountain range that girded southern Galath, but it had turned east again, into lands he barely knew.

Not that he'd ever been anywhere near here, of course; he "knew" these parts from maps. The greatfangs was flying lower now, its wingbeats slower—but they seemed more unhurried than tired. Not that he was much of an expert when it came to greatfangs.

Through the gap between two of the talons encircling him, Tethtyn glanced over at his fellow captive, hanging as motionless and huddled as he was in the monster's tight grip. He couldn't tell if the man—it looked like a man, no older than him, thin where he was big-bellied—was looking back, or even if he was awake.

Nothing much to hold his interest there. He looked ahead again; the greatfangs was certainly flying purposefully, heading for some definite destination, and had gone still lower.

They flashed over a landmark he knew, from the maps: the twin lakes of Sarth and Redgelar, glimmering side by side like the print left in mud by a large cloven hoof. Which meant that the rising ridge beyond—under him now—was the Darserpent, and that hold ahead was Marclaw.

They passed over the green and rolling Marclaw low enough for Tethtyn to clearly see folk gaping up at the greatfangs, and turning to flee.

And left it behind, stump-fenced farms giving way to tall, trail-laced forest again, the greatfangs flying even lower now, treetops rushing up to meet it. It must be about to land.

Which meant Tethtyn's life was going to end here, in... in... he struggled to recall the map in his head, suddenly furious that he couldn't name the place where he was going to die.

Kathgallart! Aye, that was it. Kathgallart. The place where they bred the horses.

The best horses, the ones lords and knights and the wealthiest merchants paid so much for. It must be a wealthy place, and a big one, too; farms as far as the eye—

The wind rose to a thunderous roar as the wings above him curved and beat against it, the greatfangs shuddering in the air as it slowed with breath-taking speed. They were below the treetops, men were shouting and running, and a paddock full of horses—densely packed, and snorting in alarm as they struggled to turn and run—were dead ahead.

The greatfangs came right down onto them, rearing up at the last as horses surged and screamed under it, its captives held high and clear in its foreclaws as it slammed down, bounced amid a horrible thudding and crunching of crushed, shattered horses, and slammed down again through a solid-looking fence that vanished like smoke under its bulk. Then it *twisted*, back-and-forthing itself in the air with awesome strength, dragging one straining wingtip along the ground as it turned—and whipped its tail around in a great slash that hurled broken men high into the air, reduced a front porch to kindling, and brought it facing back the way it had come, where its long neck could lunge to greet the screaming, terrified horses with ready jaws.

Horses bucked and shrieked and fled in all directions, and the greatfangs bit at them and flung out its wings to spill them over on their backs and snapped around to bite at them again. Not to eat, but to take off both forelegs or a head, or tear open a horse's side, to bring it down, helpless, into the churned-up dust.

In the heart of all this blood and pounding hooves, Tethtyn Eldurant found himself set down on the ground almost delicately, the claw opening to leave him behind and then thrusting forward to drive those long dark talons right through three bucking, plunging horses.

The greatfangs turned, shifting sideways with astonishing speed, and before Tethtyn could do much more than shake his dazed head and raise himself on trembling arms to try to crawl, the other claw was upon him, opening to sweep him with breath-dashing force against the other captive—and its talons had closed around them, in an all-too-familiar prison.

"M-Morl," the young face now pressed close against his left hip gulped, after a moment. "And you are—?"

The fight to just breathe was too much of a struggle for Tethtyn to manage either the astonishment he felt or the sudden wild urge to laugh that followed. It took him a while before he could speak at all, and gasp out, "Tethtyn. Tethtyn Eldurant, of Hawksyl."

By then, the greatfangs had bitten down on the three impaled horses, and with blood still spurting amid many horrible crunching sounds, was busily thrusting those dripping but now unencumbered talons into the front of a barn, and tearing through it, shredding wood as if it had been old and brittle parchment. Men fled shrieking in fear as the wall they'd been hiding behind vanished in front of them, or fell in bloody silence, sliced in half by the swift talons. Massive posts and pillars groaned and parted, spilling the roof of the barn forward in an ungainly slide to the earth. The greatfangs had already turned—past another barn, the keep, and what looked like a wagon-shed—to a porched house.

It seemed to know where men were hiding, and tore apart their hiding-places, its eyes flashing in glee. Again men sprinted away in wild terror, and again the talons lashed out to slice and smash them down, leaving them feebly writhing in spreading pools of gore, or sprawled in unmoving silence.

The greatfangs never paused. It turned back to the second barn and tore it open, too, spilling more men and horses in all directions. This time it rose, talons tightening around Morl and Tethtyn, to lunge forward over the sagging ruins of the barn so its long neck could reach the farthest, fastest escaping prey. To let no one and nothing escape. Even a yapping barn dog was silenced.

Without pause the greatfangs turned to Kathgallart Keep, a modest stone tower rising four levels above the ground. Square and unadorned it rose, thick walls pierced by narrow slit windows, the one sign of life a lone, cowering guard crouching behind the merlons of its battlements as if they could somehow hide him.

The greatfangs bit him first.

Then it turned its head away, arms and legs tumbling from its jaws, and drove its scaled shoulder against the stone. Which shivered with dull booming sounds.

Folk promptly fled from the keep gates and a back door that led into a walled garden, but the greatfangs was large enough to curl right around the keep and deal with those running through the garden with its jaws, even as its wings and scaled bulk crushed and corralled those issuing from the front. Then it rolled against the keep again, crushing those it had trapped before the gates— and this time, the tower shuddered visibly.

Again it struck... and with a slow rumbling noise the keep swayed, groaned, and gave way, toppling away from the rolling greatfangs in a slow and terrible fall.

The echoes of the crash rang back from nearby hills, and then, amid the rising dust, a silence fell.

A silence broken shortly by agonized screaming.

Chapter Twelve

SOME OF THEM roused at a touch, and others had to be shaken roughly, but every last one of the twenty-two warriors from Darswords came awake cold, stiff, tired, and in a foul temper. There was much groaning and grunting and muttering of curses: on soldier grumbled, "So it's daybreak now? Just how can you tell?"

There was no food, and nothing to make a fire with—and the only consolation, if it was one, was that their trussed captive seemed to have moved not a muscle. Men gathered to admire her bared behind until Baerold almost regretfully rumbled, "Stop staring and rouse her. Laeveren, you do it. We must be getting on, to find treasure or to get ourselves back out of here. *I'm* thirsty and hungry, if none of you are, and it's only going to get worse."

There were grudging mutters of agreement, and the men of Darswords started to move. At Baerold's direction, Laeveren took the silently obedient captive to the front of the line, and set Taroarin with Albrun and Tresker to guard the rear.

"Swords out, keep alert, and keep *quiet*," he barked at them. "If we're all a-chatter, all the time, we warn anyone ahead of our coming, and we can't hear them getting ready to kill us."

"Baerold, 'tis a good thing you're always right," a sour-faced Darsworder spoke up. "Or I'd be getting to hate you about now."

"Aye, it is a good thing," Baerold replied with a glare. "Or you'd have been dead long ago, Norgan. Long before you could even begin to get around to the luxury of hating me."

Norgan started to say something, but Taroarin spoke up from the back. "By the Falcon, let us *not* fall to arguing with each other now! Start walking. Laeveren, were I you, I'd do off that useless bow-baldric—seeing as you forgot your bow—and put it around the captive's neck like a leash, so she can't lead us into some trap or other and dart off. Then prod her with your sword and get her to lead us to some cavern or other that has treasure—and once we're all rich, she can right swiftly guide us out of this curséd place!"

A chorus of agreement arose, drowning out anything Baerold or Norgan might have said, and trailed off into murmurs of wonderment as Daera turned back toward them, went to her knees before Laeveren, and put back her head to offer her throat to him.

"Gods, I'd not mind having *that* waiting for me when I got in from the fields!" a farmer said feelingly, not far from Taroarin.

"She's *dead*, Gorult," another man reminded him.

"Oh? Doesn't smell," the farmer grunted back, as they watched Laeveren rather awkwardly tighten his baldric around the nude woman's throat. "*Falcon*, Merek, look at her!"

"I am," Merek muttered. "Oh, I am."

Then they were on the move, trudging warily through the caves once more, leather creaking and swords out.

Behind Gorult, Taroarin stiffened. "What was *that?*" he hissed to Albrun and Tresker, who frowned.

"I heard nothing," old and thin-lipped Tresker replied, as they all turned, blades rising in their hands.

They could see nothing behind them, nothing but the motionless stones. Taroarin silently waved the other two back the way they'd come, and followed behind them, glancing back at the rest of the Darsworders.

Gorult and Merek had just shrugged and turned away from him, and everyone else was heading the other way, on down the passage following the leashed Daera.

Taroarin smiled a tight smile and slowed his advance, falling behind Albrun and Tresker as they peered into darkness behind the band.

He knew they'd soon stop and look back at him, but he only needed a moment to tuck his sword hilt under his arm, turn away from them, make two swift gestures as he turned, and whisper a few words.

Whereupon, ahead of the main group, a bright and fell blue radiance suddenly surrounded Daera. Men shouted in alarm as the magic blossomed—a fire that burned not, but seared their vision—and flashed through the air, expanding to cover them and race on before they could react.

"You *bitch!*" Baerold bellowed, across the cavern. "What have you blundered into? Laever—"

The terrified Laeveren wasn't listening. Even as he hauled on his baldric hard enough to break Daera's neck and snatch her off her feet, bright blue fire flared around them all.

Fire bright enough that the cavern all around the Darsworders was gone, everything was gone but blue star-shot fire, fire that—

—Faded as swiftly as it had come, leaving all the men of Darswords blinking at—at—

Sky overhead, and unfamiliar surroundings, the roofless ruins and tumbled rubble of a stronghold. Greatfangs were wheeling overhead and, espying the dumbfounded men, turning almost lazily to swoop down...

Norgan screamed, and suddenly everyone was screaming and trying to run, sliding and falling in all the scattered stones and corpses—the bodies of monsters, raked and bitten open and lying in sticky, fly-swarming lakes of blood.

The frantically running Darsworders saw a sprawling web of dead, splayed tentacles, a curled-up, frozen chaos of spider legs as large as a wagon, and great wolf-like heads on long necks, whose severed tongues trailed into the dust and rubble underfoot.

They did not have time to see more as they panted past, scattering in all directions, heading for—for—

The sun vanished, blotted out by the descending greatfangs, the first two hulks each as long as the main street of Darswords...

Men howled and wet themselves and ran blindly in terror.

All except three men. Laeveren was weeping openly in terror and trying to hide under the body of Daera, that he'd draped across himself. Baerold was crouched flint-eyed against a corner where two walls met, sword in hand as he peered this way and that, seeking somewhere to run to and hide in.

And Taroarin, wearing a smile that did not belong to him, was striding to where two dented, riven grand entry doors sagged open and plucking a misshapen staff from the great black hinges of one door.

A staff that seemed much lighter than it could possibly be, as he hefted it in his hands and its dark twisted metal lit up with small lights of various hues, from end to end. Lights that winked like watchful eyes, or stared steadily and balefully out at the world as Taroarin let fall his sword at his feet, raised the staff over his head in both hands, and said something harsh and unintelligible to his fellow Darsworders.

Flames sprang into life at both ends of the staff, snarling up into angry spheres.

Taroarin pointed down the roofless hall at Laeveren, and murmured something. A moment later, the limp, lolling body of Daera rose into the air and hung out of Laeveren's reach, shapely and gray and lifeless.

Taroarin said something else—and the snarling fires at the ends of his staff flared and burst through the air like bolts of fire-red lightning, faster than the descents of the greatfangs, scorching lines in the air behind them as they flashed across the ruin to smite Laeveren and Baerold.

Both men vanished in pillars of flame, giving one brief shriek before they collapsed and went out, spilling ash to the littered flagstones. No bones were left to tumble with them.

Men who'd run out of places to run stared at the twin pyres in horror, and then slowly, reluctantly, turned to behold their source... and found themselves gaping at Taroarin.

Who beamed at them as the five greatfangs landed with stone-shaking force all around the great roofless hall—beyond its walls, but with force enough to cause one shattered wall to slump forward, dashing a Darsworder to the flagstones, broken and dying even before the tumbling blocks buried him—to pen it in with their great scaled bodies and spread bat-wings, living walls that towered above the broken stone ones, making the hall as secure as a tyrant's prison.

A tyrant like the man standing at the head of the ruined hall, wielding the staff. Not that the men of Darswords yet realized who he was. They were still mindless with fear, and peering up and all around at the looming greatfangs, living mountains whose jaws bristled with fangs each longer than a blacksmith stood tall.

One by one the men who'd dared to go wizard-hunting looked down from their captors and stared, however reluctantly, at the one Darsworder who now stood apart.

Taroarin the cooper.

He held the staff over his head with fresh fires blazing at both its ends, smiled at them from under it, and told them all politely, "Welcome to the great entry hall of Malragard—or what's left of it. The wizard Malraun is fallen, and so are these his creatures, this carrion at your feet. The greatfangs all around you, however, are mine."

A silence fell.

"Tar—Taroarin?" Tresker stammered, daring to break it.

By way of reply, the smiling cooper murmured something under his breath, then lowered his staff into his arms and embraced it like a lover.

It flared with a rose-red glow that raced down his arms and throughout his body. The watching Darsworders saw him close his eyes, gasp, shudder, and throw back his head.

Then the glow was gone, leaving in its wake a body that was taller, more slender, blue-skinned, and bald.

A sharp-eyed man who didn't look like Taroarin at all. Many of the lights winking on the staff in his hands had dimmed, and some of them now went out.

"Men of Darswords," he announced, "I am Narmarkoun. Doom of Falconfar, and the wizard you were so bold as to visit. Behold, you have found me."

He waved one long-fingered blue hand almost lazily, and Daera came walking through the rubble to join him, striding demurely as if she was whole, and her head didn't hang loosely from her neck.

When she reached him, Narmarkoun's hand briefly glowed rose-red, the staff in his other hand winking with the same radiance, and he touched her neck.

As the Darsworders watched, trembling and silent, Daera's lolling head slowly righted itself to stand on her shoulders again.

She stepped into the crook of his arm, Laeveren's baldric still trailing from her neck, and he rested his hand on her hip.

Staff in one hand and gray-skinned woman in the other, Narmarkoun looked around one Darsworder face after another, a grim smile steady on his face.

After he'd stared into all of their eyes, he said calmly, "I require your loyalty, here and now—or your death. And it will be a slow passing, as you lie here for days in helpless torment, every bone in your bodies smashed, the flies and rats and hungry dogs of Harlhoh dining on you at will, while my magic keeps you from sleeping or falling senseless. Which shall it be? Will you kneel to your new lord? Or be struck down where you stand?"

Tresker wavered, then sank heavily to his knees. "Tar—Narmarkoun, I will serve you. *Lord* Narmarkoun, I am your man."

A great sigh arose from the other Darsworders.

One by one, trembling in terror in the shade of the greatfangs looming over them, the men of Darswords went to their knees to submit themselves to him.

One by one, staring into their eyes, the wizard Narmarkoun surged into their minds, long enough to *make* them his.

When he was done, Narmarkoun turned, leveled the staff at a point where the flagstones met the base of the nearest wall—and blasted it.

The greatfangs perched there rose smoothly into the air, but the other flying wyrms sat like statues, watching as the smoke cleared, the rubble clattered to a halt... and a new hole was revealed.

"Forward, men of Darswords," Narmarkoun ordered pleasantly, gesturing at the opening with the staff. A few more of its lights had gone out. "Or rather, loyal warriors of Narmarkoun. You sought a wizard's treasures, and that's just what you'll find. For me. So on, and down—and mind the heat of the stones. If my suspicions are right, Malraun's caches of magic will be at least a level deeper than this."

He waved the staff again, watched the reluctant men shuffle forward, and started to hum a happy tune.

No MEN OR maids screamed in Kathgallart any more. The last cries of dying agony had ended, the greatfangs padding ponderously around a few ramshackle cottages to silence them in a brutal flurry of smashes.

Now the gigantic wyrm lay sprawled at its ease in a field, atop the splintered remnants of the paddock fences, and leisurely swooping its free foreclaw or its long neck into various stalls, to bite and drag forth and chew.

Now it was horses and mules and oxen that were screaming, shrieking as they died, while those not yet dead snorted and kicked at their stalls and stamped their hooves, frightened by the reek of fresh blood and the cries of their kin.

Still clamped bruisingly together in the grip of the greatfangs' talons, Tethtyn and Morl shuddered at the grisly noises and the smells of fear and blood. They could not help but think they would be next, the moment the last horse had vanished down that huge maw.

And why them? Well, why did anything happen in Falconfar? Fell magic or blind stupid savagery, a wild beast snatching an opportunity to fill its belly.

"Why—" Morl got as far as whimpering, once, before Tethtyn hissed at him and moved his knee urgently. Not that he could harm Morl much, pinioned as he was, or silence him, but Morl understood, and said no more.

More biting and chewing, the flailing hoof of a dying horse flashing past their eyes... then real silence.

The greatfangs rolled over, and suddenly their ears were battered by a force that also made the talons around them tremble, and the very earth thrum.

So a greatfangs can belch. Loud and hard enough to nigh-deafen men.

The greatfangs rolled again, the talons around the two young men loosening. It was... *yes*, by the Falcon, it was curling itself up in the ruined paddock like a cat before a warm hearth.

Bloated after its huge feast, no doubt. The talons suddenly fell open, spilling Tethtyn and Morl out into the light and air, on blood-drenched grass under a sky of tattered high clouds and merry sunlight. Rolling hard to get well away from the great claw, they saw the head above them yawn drowsily, great fangs flashing... and then sink down, ignoring them both utterly as they stared at it.

The greatfangs rested its barbed chin on the talons of its other claw, eyelids drooping. The eyes widened again, once—Morl and Tethtyn hardly daring to breathe—and then closed.

They half-opened a long moment later, showing only a crescent edge to silent Kathgallart, then shut again.

It was several long, shallow breaths later when Morl and Tethtyn dared to look at each other.

Whereupon they promptly discovered—possibly at about the same time as the neighboring holds of Marclaw and Indrulspire—that a sleeping greatfangs snores.

The snores echoed from distant mountains. Tethryn Eldurant and Morl Ulaskro stared at each other in the heart of the deafening roar, open-mouthed... and then found themselves giggling, shaking helplessly in high-rising mirth that no one could have heard three paces away amid the all-pervading thunder of the greatfangs.

They were still giggling when something rose up within them and took hold of them, right behind their eyes.

Something that had claws keener and stronger than the black talons of the greatfangs. Something that they somehow knew had come out of hiding in the mind of the greatfangs to drive into both of theirs.

Something that now had hold of them in a grip they could never hope to escape. Lorontar.

Lord Archwizard of Falconfar, age-old and gloatingly patient, a mind mightier than mountains, easily strong enough to dwell in both of theirs at once and hold them in helpless thrall.

A dark sentience that had plunged into the mind of Malraun the Matchless himself, burned it to quivering ruin, then leaped from the doomed wizard to the greatfangs that swept him up in its jaws, and took *it* over.

Just as it was now residing in the minds of Tethtyn Eldurant and Morl Ulaskro, whom it had selected—had been watching for years—because they had the raw, untempered talent to become great wizards.

Fitting vessels for the greatest wizard in the world. Soon to be the greatest wizard in at least *two* worlds.

It had boiled forth from the greatfangs now because the great wyrm was a beast of hungers and rages and urges, who felt more than it could think.

Wherefore it had served its purpose, and must now die.

Morl and Tethtyn obeyed with alacrity, because they could do no less. Inside their heads, Lorontar guided them both.

To select suitably sharp fallen fence-rails, large enough for their purpose but not so large that they could not control them. To aid each other in moving these rails to just the right places in the blood-soaked paddock, heft them in unison—and rush forward to pierce both eyes of the sleeping greatfangs at once. Then to keep running hard, driving the sharpened wood deeper through all the gouting wet gore, deep into the wyrm's brain.

They were hurled high and hard in the creature's wild, convulsive thrashings, its squalling attempts to scream, wild talons slashing air and turf and a nearby tree in futile, blind frenzy.

As Tethtyn and Morl landed wetly on heaped human corpses, slid and rolled to their own separate stops, then found themselves dragged to their feet in unison by the relentless claws in their heads to watch the last feeble thrashings of the wyrm they'd slain.

Then, heedless of the blood all over them, the death underfoot, and the swarming flies, they limped into what was left of Kathgallart's buildings to take cheese and cooked stew, sausages and hardbreads, tearing gowns off sprawled and gnawed goodwives to bundle the food into, so they could set forth without delay.

It was a long way to Indrulspire, through the deep woods.

Not that Tethtyn and Morl would have the chance to rest, or any desire to, until they reached what they were now seeking.

They could both see it clearly in their minds, around Lorontar's sinister smile, though neither had ever been anywhere near Indrulspire in their lives.

It lay at the near edge of that hold, overgrown and forgotten in the trees: a certain old and moss-covered tomb... and in its dark depths, a lone casket that held not bones but books of magic.

Tomes that had lain hidden for centuries, their stamped and graven metal pages glowing faintly as they waited for wizards to come.

Chapter Thirteen

RAMBAERAKH, SLAYER OF Dragons, regarded Rod balefully, shriveled eyeballs ablaze.

"Well, man? Ye hesitate! Why?"

Rod felt the gentle touches of swords—or the rusting, broken remnants of them—on his shoulders, chest, and back. He did not have to look—hell, did not *want* to look—to know that grinning skulls would be floating above both his shoulders, facing him with unwinking stares. And that the velvet-soft, yet chill feelings now at the back of his neck—momentary touches, no more—were skeletal fingertips that would move snake-swift to strangle him, if he gave the wrong reply.

Yet he wasn't a good liar. Never had been. The truth was all that came readily to his lips, and...

"*Tell me*, Rod Everlar!"

Die for truth, not for a lie.

Rod swallowed, ducked his head a little, and blurted, "I—I fear unbinding you will mean you'll slay me, as swift as it can be done, then go hunting all living things across Falconfar, killing everyone and everything. And I—"

He let out a deep, unhappy sigh, then drew himself up and added firmly, "I can't allow that."

"So *ho!* Decided 'tis time to play Lord Archwizard again, have ye? Well, now, I can tell ye plain and straight that we intend to kill no one, that we'll not do either of the things ye fear—but ye seek proof, don't ye? Trust no floating severed heads this month, aye?"

"A-aye," Rod agreed hesitantly, managing the trembling beginnings of a smile.

"So name thy proof! What will it take to convince ye?"

"I don't *know*." In exasperation, Rod waved his arms and started to pace, ignoring sudden warning taps from many sword points. The skeletons moved with him, smoothly and precisely. So did the scarred, rotting head.

"I believe you're who you say you are," Rod told it, "and that these are indeed your Dark Helms, or the forerunners of Dark Helms, rather... and I certainly believe you urgently want me to work some sort of magic that you for some reason can't, but... but I don't even know how it is that you know my *name*, and I'm heartily tired of being lorded over by wizard after wizard since I got here! Why, I..."

"Aye?"

"Nothing. There's nothing you can swear by that I can trust in. Nothing."

"Oh? Not even Taeauna, whom ye seek so desperately? In the name of the wingless Aumrarr ye cherish, and by the Falcon itself, I promise ye—"

"*How do you know about Taeauna?* Are you reading my mind?"

"Of *course*, Shaper. How else would I know ye're called Rod Everlar? 'Tis not a name I'm likely to hear, bound down here in the coils of Malraun's spells, now, is it?"

Rod shook his head. "Then you should see why I can't trust *anything* you say! You can just read whatever it is I want to hear from my mind and say it to me! Yet now that I know that, I can't—"

"Hold a bit, man, hold a bit! A little calm, a little less shouting and waving the hands about! Some of the dead down here are still asleep, ye know! This reading of minds can work both ways, mind, if I draw aside my mindcloak."

"Mindcloak?"

"Letting ye read my sincerity, even as I read thy memories and the fiercest of thy passing thoughts."

Rod hesitated, trying to stare into those sunken, angry eyes.

"Afraid of stepping into the mind of another wizard? Well, ye should be, of course. I'd hesitate, too, if the last cesspool I'd been wading in was the mind of Malraun the Matchless. And if I didn't want oblivion so sorely."

"That's what this is all about? Suicide? You want to be unbound so you can die?"

"Aye, though I know not this word 'suicide.' I can see in thy mind that it carries fear, that death is bound up in it, and that 'tis a crime—and that ye worry about doing crimes. So what, exactly, is suicide?"

"Taking your own life. It's *wrong*."

"Well, so 'tis, unless ye spend thy life to save others, or slay great evil, or do much good. Otherwise, thy death is a waste, and the Falcon is displeased. So, know ye, man, that neither Rambaerakh nor his loyal warriors—" The floating head revolved slowly, its moving gaze seeming to make the bobbing skeletons glow wherever it was looking, then regarded Rod once more. "—hold with suicide."

"But—"

"Pah! This oblivion we seek is *not* suicide! Our lives were torn from us years upon years ago! We have been dead and beyond dead for more seasons than ye can count! Rail at us not of crimes and guilt and morals! Man, we *ache* to be alive again, but cannot, so ache all the more to seeing and talking with and being near those who are! *Ye* cause us pain right now, by being here and being alive!"

Rod tried to step back, but the points of swords gathered behind him in an unyielding wall.

"I—" He swallowed. "I'm sorry."

The grizzled, much-scarred head bobbed rapidly up and down, as if in exasperation.

"Man, man, be not *sorry!* 'Tis the dead who have time and cause to be sorry! Just waste not the life ye have!"

Rod stared into those sunken, burning eyes. "Show me your mind," he said quietly.

The wizard's floating head rose and drifted nearer, closer than it had ever been before, until it was hovering right in front of Rod, their noses almost touching. Not that Rambaerakh had all that much of a nose left.

"See, man. *See...*"

Rod quelled a sudden urge to giggle. That hollow voice had uttered the exact words used by a femme fatale to entice her lover into her arms, in an old and very bad movie he'd seen once on late-night television—and in the same low-pitched, earnest manner.

Then he seemed to *slide* forward and down, down through those burning eyes and into cavernous darkness beyond, all thoughts of giggling gone in his wake...

He was in a place of labyrinthine, crazily-tilting passages, all dark blue and purple against black, with tattered drifting shadows everywhere and thick pillars too smooth to be stone.

So this was what a dead wizard's mind looked like.

One who wasn't afire with the need to destroy you...

Rod was gliding along, slowly and uncertainly, seeing nothing but passages and pillars, and hearing nothing at all. If there was proof here he was supposed to see, there was no sign of it at all, not even—

The wall beside him seemed to ripple and billow like a black curtain. Sudden dread rose in him, as he pictured an unseen horror straining at the barrier, ready to lunge out at him...

The curtain faded away, leaving a slender man in black, ankle-length robes facing him. A man whose head was severed from his shoulders, and floated above them. It was a head Rod recognized, of course.

"Rambaerakh, Slayer of Dragons," he greeted it calmly, and the floating head bobbed in a polite nod.

"At your service," it replied, "Behold what you came to see."

The darkness fell away, and Rod now seemed to be standing on nothing at all, with bright shards looming above and beneath him, each showing a different scene, like so many windows into films that were all playing at once. It resembled what he'd imagined a satellite television control room must be like, all—

His gaze was caught and held by the image of a breathtakingly beautiful woman, welling up on his right, from below. He felt a surge of affection for her, then all the love in the world; he was fighting to stare at every last inch of her looming face through a sudden waterfall of tears as that love turned to despairing grief. Then her face was gone, melting into a yawning skull surrounded by her flowing hair, with a spade tossing loose dark soil onto it...

and as it all fell away behind him, another face was looming, a man with an infectious, lopsided smile, and Rod found himself grinning, too, in friendship this time, just in time for that smile to become a scream, and flames to roar through the head and leave it a blackened skull, collapsing into bone shards and revealing another woman, younger and even more beautiful than the first, beyond. Love danced within him again, leaping to the fore once more and leaving him sobbing...

On his knees on cold stone, within a ring of lowered, rusted blades, with a severed head hovering above him.

"Ye're out again, Everlar," it told him, almost kindly. "Did ye see enough?"

Rod managed to nod, through his tears. He felt so desolate, so...

"I've lost many," Rambaerakh murmured. "Too many to go on. So have we all, my Helms and I. We're too *tired* to go marauding across the Raurklor, let alone Falconfar. Unbind us, and let us rest at last."

"Oblivion?" Rod asked dully. "Just... nothing?"

"Not quite," the wizard's head replied, smiling a crooked smile. "Thy releasing of us will accomplish one thing. One last revenge. Spending our passing doing something, after all."

"Revenge on whom?"

"On Lorontar. Who intends to school younglings in wizardry, and return here riding their bodies to hold the great magics he knows are hidden here. Magics we can rob him of, and give the foundation of all his gloating plans a good shake—perhaps, just perhaps, one that will shatter them and bring them tumbling down."

Rambaerakh sank a little lower, until he was nose to nose with Rod again. "Well, man? Will ye?"

Rod Everlar set his jaw, wiped tears away with an impatient swipe of the back of his hand, and said grimly, "I'll do it."

"FAUGH! DID YE *have* to set us down in the shit-heap?"

Garfist staggered as he spat those words, holding his nose. Then he slipped in something slippery, windmilled his arms desperately for balance—and dropped into a low, braced stance to keep from falling over in the waiting muck.

"No," Juskra replied sweetly. "We thought you'd prefer not to take a sword through that ample belly of yours right away, wielded by some Galathan who happens—like nigh *all* Galathans—to be suspicious of anyone who consorts with wingbitches. But we can certainly snatch you up, flap over yonder, and dump you right on the threshold of the Stag's Head, if you prefer. Losing most of that belly *would* improve your looks—and balance, too, by the looks of things."

Garfist responded with a loud, coarse description of Juskra's character and anatomy. Some of his phrases made both Dauntra and Iskarra wince, but Juskra merely smiled broadly, sketched an elaborate, exaggerated bow, and waved him in the direction of the inn.

The Aumrarr and their passengers had landed amid much broken old furniture and rotting remnants of carts and casks. This refuse was almost hidden in the tall grass, clinging vines, and various wild and thorny bushes that bordered the deeper forest around the reeking midden behind the inn.

From where they stood, they could peer around the shoulder of the dung-heap that so offended Garfist, to see the sagging, ramshackle chaos of the Stag's Head's back kitchen.

Almost disappearing in overgrowth of its own, it was a crudely-built, low wooden wing that seemed to have been assembled by drunken carpenters in fits and starts over the decades, always disagreeing in style and direction of expansion or repair with what had been done earlier. The result had many corners and mismatched joinings, at least one set of steps up to nowhere at all, and several warped and buckled doors, some obviously so unusable that old tables had been piled against them to rot or boards had been nailed across them. However, the back kitchen thankfully boasted no windows.

Which meant the four travelers had hopefully thus far passed unnoticed, both upon their arrival and during the pleasantries exchanged since.

Garfist finished stripping off the leather straps of his carry-sling, flung them in Juskra's general direction without looking back, and started picking his way carefully around the edges of the muck, snapping off branches and trampling down vines with a series of

deafening crashes that left Iskarra and the two Aumrarr—who
hastily folded their wings and crouched down—wincing.

"Garfist Gulkoun," Dauntra said quietly but firmly, after him.
The fat man paused for a moment in his noisy lurchings and
stumblings, but did not turn.

"Garfist," the Aumrarr repeated, no more loudly.

This time he swung around, a furious expression on his face.

"You should know what's afoot in Galath, just now," Dauntra
offered, her voice quieter than ever. He leaned back to hear her—
and almost slipped into the muck doing so.

Spitting curses and waving his arms for balance, Garfist started
stumping back toward them, circling through the grass and thorns
to keep out of the muck.

Iskarra and the Aumrarr waited nervously for someone in the
inn to hear the din and peer out a window, whereupon they could
hardly miss the lurching, tramping warrior.

No one did, and Garfist fetched up against a nearby sapling—
which sagged visibly under his weight—to glower at Dauntra and
snarl, "*What?*"

"You and your lady should be aware of some things," Juskra
said crisply, and waved at her fellow Aumrarr. "So listen to her."

Garfist nodded curtly, and glared at Dauntra.

The Aumrarr smiled and murmured, "Right now, Galath is just
one or two killings away from erupting into civil war. Bands of
knights are riding across the realm, bloodying their blades in each
other in the name of this challenger for the throne or that one.
Every man is suspicious of every other—and strangers, it should
come as no surprise, are mistrusted more than most."

She leaned forward and held up a quelling hand as Garfist drew
himself up to speak. "So hear me, Gar and Isk. We are Aumrarr,
and Aumrarr try to be fair, and more than fair, with the few we
consider friends. We will remain near for the rest of this day, and
until the sun rises highest on the morrow. Should you need to
be plucked away from the inn in a hurry, call on us. Shout these
words: 'Old king or no king!' Twice at least, and as loud and slow
as you can. We shall hear... and we shall come."

"The day will be dark and strange," Garfist replied sourly,
"when I'll either need or want rescue from wingbitches—though

I'll grant that if Aumrarr are to come flying to my aid, I'd welcome yer faces more than others I know not. A little, at least."

"*Gar*," Isk said sternly, "be civil. More than that, be *grateful*, glork you! 'Old king or no king!' Yes? Well, *I* can remember that—and so can you, Old Ox. Or else."

Garfist grunted by way of reply, faced the inn, and started crushing undergrowth again.

Iskarra sighed, and turned from him to the two Aumrarr. "Ladies Dauntra and Juskra, have our thanks. Mine and, yes, his, too, if he did but know the most basic of graces, so as to tender it!"

Juskra's grin was wry. "*You* are most welcome. As for him... well, we'll accommodate him. For your sake."

Iskarra smiled crookedly, nodded, rose, and darted after Garfist, who was already well on his way past the midden, heading for the front of the inn.

The two Aumrarr watched them go. When they'd turned the corner onto the muddy King's Road, Dauntra and Juskra sighed in unison, exchanged looks, shook their heads—and sprang back into the sky, beating their wings furiously.

Their flight was a short one, almost straight up, to a broad bough overhead.

It belonged to the tallest tree around, a towering saberwood that overlooked the patched and uneven roof of the Stag's Head. If all went well, they'd perch on it until full night fell—when it would be safe, if they were careful and watched where the moonlight fell, to relocate to the roof of the inn.

Three vaugren were already roosting on the bough. They flapped up in clumsy, noisy alarm when Juskra loomed right up into their very beaks, reaching out with both hands for the largest of the trio.

That vaugril shrieked out his surprise and fright as he fell off the bough, squawking loudly and long. The other two vaugren joined in as they fluttered away.

Settling herself on the bough, Juskra glared at them, then put her hands on her hips and spat out a long, low, rolling *caaaaww*.

That brought immediate, startled silence—and the vaugren fled faster, flying frantically.

Juskra gave Dauntra a satisfied smirk. "Mating-call gets them, every time."

Joining her on the bough, Dauntra folded her wings behind herself, plucked out a flat, slender flask from somewhere under her belt, and offered it to her sister Aumrarr. "And if one of these vaugren ever tries to take you up on it?" she asked teasingly. "What then?"

Juskra shrugged. "They'll get a surprise. Save for the smell, it might be an interesting experience. Those hooked beaks have to be good for *something*."

Dauntra rolled her eyes. "Yon fat man has gone inside the inn, Jusk. You *don't* have to try to outdo him, just now."

"Oh? And just when am I going to get a chance to practice outdoing him, if not now?"

Chapter Fourteen

To Rod's surprise, the large chamber the skeletons had been marching him toward wasn't their destination.

Beyond it were more tunnels, a maze this time rather than any sort of ordered layout. The air here was moving, and although quiet and dark, these passages had a lived-in air, where the earlier passages had felt like silent storage for the dead and the forgotten.

As far as Rod could tell, they must be just under the surface; any rooms above these must be the roofless chambers the greatfangs had just ruined.

Quite suddenly, Rod found himself facing an ordinary-looking door, with a honor guard of two rows of skeletons on either side of him, flanking it and all staring silently his way. Rambaerakh was floating beside his shoulder.

"Open it," the wizard said calmly. "What's beyond is quite safe—so long as ye touch nothing."

The door had a simple metal latch no sturdier than what you might find on a suburban garden gate back home—an old one from the fifties or sixties, when no one had heard of motion-activated lights or perimeter alarms, and gates were more adornment than barrier.

Rod wasn't expecting what he saw when the door swung open, away from him, into the space beyond.

It was a small, low-ceilinged room, with no other doors or windows, and everything was of stone: the walls were lined with massive stone shelves, and they were the only furniture. It was lit by an eerie, multi-hued glow, pulsing gently in places. The air itself crackled with unseen, restless energy, as if scores of unseen presences were waiting breathlessly for something momentous to happen.

That hair-raising—literally; Rod lifted one hand into the room, and watched the hairs all over it quietly stand out from his skin—energy suffused the room, but the glow was coming from the objects lying on the stone shelves.

Things of magic. Wands, and staves, and metal one-piece war-helms with upthrust horns sweeping up and out from their foreheads. As well as a lot of, well, *stuff* Rod had no names for, and couldn't even begin to know how to describe. So he settled for the blindly safe village-idiot comment. "Magic."

The floating head nodded, by way of reply.

"Malraun's?" Rod felt emboldened to ask, taking one step forward into the room, and stopping to look up for any yawning trap, and listen for clicks or grinding sounds—or worse. Nothing. Just the straining, unseen, *crawling* energy all around. "Was this his private treasure-store?"

"One of them. Almost all of my craftings lie here—which is why the unbinding must be here. Let me warn ye again, Rod Everlar: to touch the wrong thing here is to die. Touching *any* enchanted item will send warnings ye will not want heeded and answered."

"But if Malraun's dead..."

"Lord Archwizard, I hardly think any man can be called a wizard who does not prepare some web of spells or bound guardian beast or spell-thralled apprentice to act for him after he is dead. I say again: touch nothing."

Rod nodded, taking another cautious step forward. He cast a swift look back to make sure nothing was hiding behind the door. "The staves and wands and such I know. I wrote a lot about them—and those gauntlets, too. I know what a helm looks like, but what do these do, exactly? Why these brow-horns, if that's the right term? And what are *these* things? The spheres with the hand-holds?"

Rambaerakh drifted smoothly across the room to hover above one of the largest, most polished helms, and turned to face Rod. "This is a sarn-helm, and so are all the rest. Any man or maid can use one. It is worn, and the mind of the wearer urges forth beams of harmful magic from the brow-spur. This one bestows fire."

The floating head moved along above the shelf until it hung over an orb of gleaming, polished stone.

The orb was brownish granite or some such speckled rock, as shiny as a brand-new curling stone. It rested on a flattened base—and between there and the curve of the sphere it was pierced right through with a smooth, sculpted grip. Obviously it was carried around by the handle, and whatever magic it exuded or fired or gave off came from the rounded part of the...?

"Lurstars," Rambaerakh said helpfully. "They're called lurstars. One holds them up as if the rounded top was a posey of flowers, murmurs the right word, and they give forth their magic. They can all glow, as brightly or dimly as the holder wills, but they have only one real power per lurstar. Usually it's warmth, to save on firewood all winter, but sometimes it's cooling, if instead ye need to keep meat from spoiling. Fewer still hurl deadlier effects; battle magic. Rarely—very rarely, and I see not the one I had, here—they can heal."

Holdoncorp, Rod thought. Lurstars were new to him, so they almost had to be—

"So now that ye know what a lurstar is," the floating head added, "thy curiosity is satisfied, and ye can *leave them be*. Like all the rest of the magic here. Just leave them alone. Don't touch them. Or else."

Rod nodded. In truth, he was more than tired of magic, and would just as soon never see a wizard—or a wizard's staff—again in his life.

"So just what do I do, in this ritual of unbinding?"

"The Helms will line up, and come to ye one after another. Touch the skull and say aloud: *Thaeth arcrommador ezreeneth*. It is important that ye think of leaping flame, or bright sunlight, while doing so. Then stand back and wait for that Helm to be done. Ye'll see what I mean. When ye are ready for the next one, beckon him forward. I'll be last of all."

"That's *it*?"

"Aye, Lord Archwizard, that's it," Rambaerakh said wryly. "Not everyone can do this, but *ye* can."

"But I—"

"Don't know magic, aye. Rod Everlar, cozen me not. Have our minds not just met? Think ye I saw nothing of thine? Ye can."

"But—"

"Ye seem overly fond of that word. The Helms are waiting." So they were; as Rod had been staring rather helplessly at the hovering head, the skeletons had silently formed a line, around and around the room. They were waiting, bobbing slightly.

Rod swallowed. "And so it begins," he murmured. "Death." He lifted his hand to beckon the first skeleton. "The doom of kings."

The hovering Rambaerakh darted forward. "What's that?"

"The doom that comes even for kings," Rod explained gently. "Stealing in like a hooded lady in the night, or falling suddenly, like lightning from a clear sky. Death. At least, that's how I described it in a poem I wrote once." He shook his head. "It wasn't a very good poem."

"I'm not so sure of that, man. Those words, at least, strike me as apt indeed. Remember, now: 'Thaeth arcrommador ezreeneth.' That's right."

Rod swallowed again, stretched out his hand to touch the cool, smooth skull—there was an unpleasant thrill, as if the Helm was alive with low-voltage electricity—and said the words, remembering only at the last instant to think of roaring flame.

And the skeleton fell away from him with a sigh, plummeting to the floor as if it weighed a ton but disintegrating into dust as it reached those flagstones, in a spreading cloud that claimed not just the skull but every last bobbing bone in its frame. Unseen amid the rising dust—it was like so much rolling, billowing gray smoke—the skeleton's sword clanged, clattered noisily as it bounced... and then shattered with a discordant shriek of metal.

Not that Rod heard it. He was too busy staggering backward, momentarily blinded by memories rushing through his head—memories that weren't his. A great cavalcade of bared and gasping women, bloody swords swung at shouting foes, dying men falling away with screams or groans, glittering cold coins, great meals by firelight, and—

He fetched up against something that jabbed against the small of his back and held.

"Stand!" Rambaerakh snapped, from right behind him. "Stay where ye are! Another step back and ye'll be lying atop a dozen lurstars and I don't know how many wands!"

Reeling, Rod nodded hastily, went down into a crouch, and waited for the worst rush of the flooding memories to subside. Faces, all those faces—furious, anguished, bawling, leering... All the triumphs and worst moments and emotional times in a long, long life. It was *exhausting*.

"How many Helms are there, again?"

"Just one at a time," the wizard told him curtly. "If ye start counting, ye'll never get anywhere near done. Beckon the next one."

"No, I—can't! I—"

"*Beckon the next one!*"

Trying not to show his disgust and weariness, Rod took two steps forward, straightened up, and solemnly beckoned the next Helm forward. Bobbing in that eerie, comical manner, silent and grinning eternally, it came, casting its sword aside with a skirling clatter.

Rod reached out for it, staring into the empty eyesockets as if he could meet the eyes that weren't there.

And trying, by the Lone and Flying Falcon, to smile.

"Must catch my breath!" Roreld panted, reeling to a halt beside Taeauna and clapping a heavy hand to her shoulder to steady himself. "Not young enough for this... anymore!"

"Aye," usually silent Tarlund agreed. "Walking I can do, all day and all night, but this trotting like horses—are we in *that* much haste?"

Taeauna gave him a grim look. "We should have been there half the day ago."

Eskeln left off his own panting long enough to grin. "Well, now we know why grand Olondyn of the Bow said ye nay. I can't see him running anywhere—not if the Falcon itself was swooping down for him! 'Tis *hard* to sneer at the world with idle disdain while ye're sprinting along gasping!"

"Come," Taeauna told them all, with a toss of her head. "Onward! Start out at a walk; we're near enough now..."

"Malragard's just over this ridge," Gorongor called, from ahead. "Or what's left of it is."

They all scrambled to join him. Among them, Taeauna was quick to hiss, "Keep *low*. I don't want us flashing steel as we gawk along the ridge-top!"

They went face-down to the ground amid tangled bushes, to peer over the crest of the ridge at the next hill over—the one that had a riven, roofless stronghold atop it, whose tower had toppled.

"Look!" Glorn snapped, throwing out an arm that still bore stained bandages from the taking of Darswords. "Look there!"

On that far hill, approaching ruined Malragard ahead of them, was a band of armed men in motley array. In strength, about twice their own. Counting them was hard, because some of them were already half-hidden amid the outermost walls and rubble of Malraun's tower.

"Thieves," Gorongor growled, darkly.

"Mage-slayers," Eskeln suggested.

"Men we must stop," Roreld summarized.

Even as Tarlund was asking, "Say—that one, there! Isn't that Tresker, of Darswords?" Taeauna was heaving herself upright.

Turning to face them, she announced crisply, "Too late to keep hidden! We must get down there, ready to fight, just as fast as our legs can take us!"

Beside her, struggling to his feet, Glorn groaned.

There were some chuckles. Everyone was already on the move, over the ridge and loping down its other slope.

THIS WAS A nightmare. A nightmare that went on and on, and that he couldn't wake from or change in the slightest. He was trapped, his head a great cage that everyone else was stuffing their lives into... until he gagged. Retching helplessly as the surging, overwhelming flood went on.

Rod didn't have time to enjoy the good memories or savor anything—heck, he didn't have time to *understand* what he was seeing, as the torrent of lives went on and on.

The floating head of Rambaerakh was holding him up now, butting against his back and shoulders, thrusting him upright as he sagged and shivered, babbling encouragement and threats and anything else it took to keep him reaching out with trembling hands for the next bobbing skull.

Frightened faces, shrieking as they died; castles burning, flames flaring hungrily; bared flesh by candlelight... the flood of memories raged on, crashing through him no matter how much he whimpered or fought to scream them begone—all that seemed to come out of his trembling mouth was sobs and a soft, wordless keening—as the bobbing bones fell into dust and the swords rang and crashed on the stones at his feet.

There were only a few skeletons left now, or so it seemed, the line a mere shadow of what it had been. Rod could barely tell—no matter how much he shook his head, it was getting harder and harder to banish the memories jostling behind his eyes. He tried to peer past them, tried to—to... *what* was he trying to do, again?

"Bear up, Everlar," the floating head said into his ear. "Almost done. Ye're feeling maze-minded, but it won't last. Minds bury and forget, so they can go on. *Ye* will go on."

"Really?" Rod mumbled, reaching forth with a wavering hand for the next skeleton—and wincing, despite himself, as it advanced. "*Wonderful.*"

"Sarcasm ill becomes ye," Rambaerakh told him tartly.

"Oh? Going barking insane won't suit me too well, either." Rod started to say more, but it trailed away in less than a breath into helpless babbling, all control over his tongue lost under the vivid onslaught of *another* set of memories, another parade of loving faces and dying ones, mourning and lust and surging hatred, grand and sordid moments, triumphs and disasters...

This Helm had killed his own dog in a drunken rage, and regretted it for the rest of his life. Now Rod was going to regret it too. He found himself plunged into the man's, raw-edged tide of sorrow, and swept away from the twinkling lights of all he knew and loved—that is, all that this Helm had known and loved, in life—into a deepening night and a rising gale. The seas rose and his gorge with them, and Rod vomited and wallowed and reeled helplessly in the false remembrance of a storm twenty summers past, and an early blizzard that had come in its wake...

Another skeleton was approaching, bobbing almost jauntily to loom out of the swirling snows...

"I did *not* dream all of *this* up," Rod told himself grimly. "I only wanted to tell stories that would keep pages turning and readers smiling."

Obligingly, the skeleton grinned into his face, a rictus of yellowing teeth it always presented to the world... until this instant, as it sighed away into trailing dust before Rod's eyes, leaving the Lord Archwizard blinking at nothing but the dark room—and seeing a fresh tide of memories not his own.

When it was done, he was crying again, the streaming tears blinding him as he stared and peered, hand held out... but there was no skeleton to touch.

Nothing but the severed head of the wizard Rambaerakh, floating slowly around to face him.

"Death," it whispered. "Death at last."

"GREATFANGS!" GLORN SHOUTED hoarsely, dropping from a run to a face-down skid in the grass.

"*Dungfire!*" Esklen cursed, seeing five of the huge beasts descending from the sky to the distant ruin they were sprinting toward. "Down! Down, or we're dead men!"

"Taeauna," Roreld growled, from where he was sliding to a halt hard by her heels, "what *now?* Surely we should turn back—"

"Go, then," was her cold reply. "*I'm* going on. They're only overgrown lizards with wings—just as we Aumrarr are only women with wings... as I've heard a man of my company tell all warriors who'll listen, more than once."

Roreld groaned. "I might have known..."

"That I was listening? Yes, you should have. Let us crawl, men, until yonder wyrms fly off again. They will—you'll see!"

"I don't doubt it," Gorongor growled, from nearby. "But who'll they be carrying in their claws when they do, hey?"

"*You* listen to too many minstrels' tales," Taeauna told him severely. "Drink less, sleep earlier. Maybe even alone, from time to time."

He gave her a mournful look. "And what price my life then, hey?"

RAMBAERAKH'S ROTTING, SCAR-CROSSED face was wearing the same grim expression as always, the shrunken and shriveled eyeballs aglow with terrible life.

"My turn at last, Everlar," the severed head told him quietly, eyes flashing eagerly. "I wanted to stay long enough to see all the Dooms—and Lorontar, too—go down, to outlast them all. Now, though, for the first time in too many seasons to remember, I just want it all to end. Have all I know, wizard with no magic. Have it all—and rescue Falconfar for me. *Rescue Falconfar for us all.*"

And with that fierce whisper still ringing around the room, it sprang forward, right at Rod's face.

He shouted, or thought he did, as he felt the wizard's skull shatter against his nose and forehead. Then a deluge of memories choked him in a flood of dancing white fire, that roiled and echoed thunderously inside him, sending him staggering and flailing about blindly...

The severed head had disintegrated like all the Helms, and Rod heard himself calling Rambaerakh's name again and again.

There was no reply. Not that it mattered... not that anything in the dim room around him mattered, anymore.

In Rod's head, *real* terror and wonder were unfolding, as he saw what Rambaerakh had seen and learned what Rambaerakh had learned—sometimes triumphantly, sometimes disastrously—about wielding magic. Across seventy summers he was watching spells go wrong or sizzle forth, their magic maiming or transforming Rambaerakh's foes and rivals. He *was* Rambaerakh, and he could—

No. He was Rod Everlar.

Now he knew a lot about magic, but there was a vast difference between knowing and doing. Unless, of course, he could Shape what Rambaerakh had once cast...

Rod barely felt the crash as he slammed into one of the shelves, already off-balance and falling. It caught him under the ribs, then under his armpit... he scraped his nose on the shelf-edge as he went down, still wandering in surges of recalled magic, of memories not his own...

Rod must have hit the floor, but didn't feel it at all. He dimly heard a loud metallic clanging that must have been one of those horned helms striking the floor nearby... and beheld, with calm disinterest, one of the lurstars tumbling in velvety silence toward the stone floor.

The stone struck, and shattered.

The white fire behind his eyes was joined by a flare of crimson flames in front of him—and in the leaping teeth of that sudden blinding roar all Falconfar went away.

Chapter Fifteen

THERE WAS A sudden, soundless thrill in the air, a prickling of hairs on arms and necks. Before the men of Darswords could do more than stiffen warily and peer about for some mighty magic awakening, all that was left of Malragard rocked beneath their boots.

The greatfangs shrieked and hurled themselves untidily into the air in a flapping frenzy of haste, screaming in shuddering convulsions of agony that almost tumbled them from the sky.

Narmarkoun spared their squalling, dwindling forms not even a glance. His head had snapped around to peer in another direction, and down. The men around him could see that he was staring at the flagstones underfoot as if he could see right through them—and was frowning and looking delighted at the same time.

There was a chance Malraun had survived, or had been able to hurl himself into the body of someone else, who had just worked a spell in the cellars of Malragard. There was a better chance that Malraun had taken apprentices, or captured and held mages, unbeknownst to his rival Dooms, and they had just unleashed magic... or that captives or looters incapable of wielding magic at all had blundered into a magical trap, or triggered some guardian spell or other.

He'd been expecting this. *Someone* was bound to start trying to hurl Malraun's magic before Narmarkoun could secure this ruin for himself. It could be a formidable foe, or an utter fool stumbling into a trap or ambush Malraun had prepared—or anything in between.

Which was why these twenty-one men of Darswords around him were going to be so useful. It might cost a few lives to find and deal with the cause of the magic. By the Falcon, it might cost a few lives just to get down through riven Malragard to get anywhere *near* the cause of this magic.

"Come," he ordered curtly, pointing with the staff at where a ruined wall turned a corner, away from them all. "That way. You—Merek—to the fore, and lead us all. You'll find a stair on the other side of yon wall, not far."

Slowly, staring at him doubtfully, the men of Darswords moved toward the wall.

Narmarkoun smilingly sloped his staff down and made it spew forth fire, erupting from the flagstones just behind the boots of the slowest Darsworder. The man staggered forward with a startled shout, echoed by the next slowest man a moment later, as another flagstone erupted in shards and flame.

"*Move*," the wizard ordered all the warriors, as they stared at him. "Haste is required."

And he gave them a pleasant smile.

"We wouldn't want to miss any treasure now, would we? Or tarry so much that something unfortunate befalls us? Hmm?"

"No one lurking about?" Zorzaerel growled, looking not at his master-of-scouts, but almost longingly down at the racing creek.

The veteran scout, his face sour, shook his head in silent reply. Zorzaerel grunted pleased acknowledgement, nodded dismissal to the scout—who returned across the water to fill his own belt-flasks—and sat down heavily on the bank of the stream.

By the time Askurr arrived beside him, he was already dipping his helm into the flow.

Askurr drank thankfully. Even in the Raurklor shade, trudging along a trail in full armor is wearying work.

"So, now," he said with a gasp, once he'd slaked himself, water streaming from his stubbled chin, "whither next? Horgul's dream died with him, and I've no stomach for hacking my way clear through the heart of Tauren without Malraun standing at my side to blast down every self-proclaimed duke who has the hairies to stand up to us!"

"Well, now, there," Zorzaerel rumbled, raising a finger to wag it. "I've been thinking..."

Askurr waited.

"Aye?" was all he said by way of prompting, when it became clear Zorzaerel really was waiting for leave to say more.

"I've no stomach for being led to my slaughter by Malraun's bed-lass, no matter how fair on the eyes she may be," the youngest of the warcaptains growled, "but if I'm free to skulk and watch and hide—if there're to be wizards hurling lightnings and the Falcon alone knows what else at other wizards, hiding is what we'll be doing most of, hey?—I'm thinking there just may be some spoils, after 'tis all done, worth having."

"Aye," the master-of-scouts put in sourly, chewing on a water-reed. "All of *us*, turned to pop-belch frogs. Spoils indeed. We'll go good in the stewpots of whichever's wizard's left."

Zorzaerel shook his head. "No, *not* blundering out into the heart of their quarrel, yelling and waving our swords, ripe to be turned into anything. Keeping quiet and hidden, rather, to see what happens. We *must* see what happens!"

"Oh?" Olondyn asked incredulously, reaching his own helm down into the creek. "*Must?* Life gone too quiet for you, Zorz?"

The youngest warcaptain lifted his head to glower, and waved one finger at the archer. "If Malraun had caged monsters and someone's going to let them out to prowl and breed and eventually show up hungry at *my* back door, I want to know about it!"

"You're sure we can't learn all that from a good safe distance away?" someone else asked. "Right here, for instance?"

"No," Olondyn snapped, not bothering to look up. "We must see what happens at Malraun's tower for ourselves. Would *you* trust someone else to tell you, true and full? Wizards have more ways than we can count to fool our minds, or take beast-shape, or show us something that's not there. I'm with Zorz; I want to be there, and *know*."

"Know that trees and castle stones and little pieces of wizards are raining down on our heads?" Sortrel of Taneth snorted. "What's to know? You been hit so often above yer ears that you can't feel it now?"

"You're thinking the wizards'll blast each other to blood-spew, and fuddle-headed Tay and her warriors," Askurr said slowly, "leave just one of them still standing for us to take down."

"Aye," Zorzaerel growled, "and we *will* take him down, whoever it be. No more wizards!"

"Aye to *that*," Sortrel echoed.

"No more wizards!" Askurr agreed loudly.

"See for ourselves," someone else muttered.

"Treasure!" someone else barked, as if in reply.

"No more wizards," Olondyn and Bracebold of Telchassur thundered.

"Aye!" Zorzaerel shouted, standing up and waving his helm excitedly, slopping water all over Askurr. "Whichever mage prevails there, we slay or hunt down. Let's be rid of them all!"

"Now *that*," the master-of-scouts snapped, "I'll drink to. Pity this is but spring water!"

Suddenly everyone was up and moving; hoisting packs, settling helms back into place, and stowing bulging water flasks.

"We're not turning back to Wytherwyrm, are we?" Olondyn demanded disgustedly, looking hard at Askurr in the heart of all this tumult.

"No, no—we go on. We'll take the Downwagon Trail at Wolfskull Ford, and get to Harlhoh right on Taeauna the Wingbitch's shapely heels!"

Olondyn nodded, waved an arm to his archers, and tramped across the stream.

Ahead of him, Bracebold and his men had already set forth. If they wanted to be make Stag Hill before nightfall, and camp somewhere that wasn't deep in the misty bogs of the wolf-haunted heart of the Raurklor, there was ground to cover. Many strides of it.

THE TOMES HAD been right where their minds had told them to look, the tomb unguarded and overgrown in the deep forest. Seizing what they suddenly hungered for had been swift and easy, no more than a few moments tugging a heavy, grating stone lid aside.

Now, panting hard over metal pages that glowed and tingled under their eager hands, Morl and Tethtyn were back in the trees, much farther out from Indrulspire than the tomb was, sitting on adjacent stumps at one end of a woodcutters' clearing that didn't look to have seen an axe swung all this season. They were a good long ramble along a narrow log-drag trail distant from Indrulspire, which might be a good thing; they had no idea how much noise and disturbance their magics might cause.

Lorontar was there, at the back of their minds. They could both feel him, and dimly sense each other's thoughts, too, through a link that could only be him... but the Lord Archwizard, though awake and watchful, was lurking beneath and behind their thoughts, not riding their minds like the conqueror he'd been back in Kathgallart. For now at least, they were themselves.

Tethtyn supposed they had to be, to truly *learn* the magic, rather than merely casting it as obedient thralls. He looked up at Morl, and read the same mounting excitement in the Dlarmarran tomekeeper's face as he could feel tingling inside himself, rising insistently, almost chokingly.

"Translocate," he blurted, an instant before Morl could. They were seeking the same magic, Lorontar was making them want it...

Morl's face lit up. "Translocation!" he hissed, stabbing a finger down on the glowing blue metal pages in front of him.

Tethtyn sprang up, turning in the air to face the right way and not miss an instant, as he crouched to look over Morl's shoulder. They peered together at the dark, wandering script; characters that had been stamped—punched, with anvil, hammer, and dies— deep into the glowing, enchanted sheets of metal. The spell was surprisingly simple, just two words to be spoken aloud as the mind pictured two things: the intended destination and a whirling of forces—thus—and brought them together, *thus*.

Blinking and sweating, his magical tome almost falling from his suddenly numb fingers, Tethtyn abruptly found himself on the other side of the clearing, right beside the untidy pile of brush he'd been staring at as Lorontar made him visualize those whirling forces.

Morl was gaping at him in astonishment—and then was gone, leaving only an empty stump.

An instant later, he was swearing in delighted incredulity right at Tethtyn's elbow. "This is—this is—"

"Yes," Tethtyn agreed enthusiastically, the words almost bubbling out of him with glee. "It is!"

The book quivering in Morl's trembling hands spent two pages exhaustively describing precisely how the forces were supposed to "look" in their minds, and Lorontar was now doggedly marching them through that text, guiding their thoughts from delighted astonishment to ordered thinking, and to visualizing, step by step, moving from an indistinct remembrance of whirling forces to a clear mental image of the whorl of forces he'd put into their thoughts moments ago.

When those whirling energies were vivid and clear in every detail, the lurking Lord Archwizard firmly put images into their minds of where they'd come from: the trodden twigs and dirt right in front of the two stumps.

Abruptly, that's where they were again. Right back across the clearing, without taking a single step.

Translocated, teleported... just like that. They were wizards, or magelings, or whatever one called novices who had already worked magics some hedge-wizards never mastered in long lives full of trying.

"High... thundering... Falcon," Tethtyn swore aloud, slowly and wonderingly. Could it be this easy?

Well, they had Lorontar guiding them, to be sure, making them masters of magic swiftly and surely... Lorontar, who must be preparing them for...

There was a sudden pounding fury behind Tethtyn's eyes, a rising flame and pain that shattered all thought in a flare of unfolding agony and left him staggering, dimly aware of Morl staring at him in concern, and of something else rising out of the pain, something bright and soothing and wonderful, something better than translocation, something he *had* to have...

He could see it looming, see it but not yet know it for what it was... an idea, a power magic could give him, something a spell could do...

"Bloodsteel," he whispered, as it unfolded in his mind at last. "Armor against any blade..."

Morl was grinning at him, eyes alight, seeing the same thing Tethtyn was seeing.

Swords slashing through their innards, slicing deep into their bellies in ways that should have slain them both, killing wounds that should be making Morl and Tethtyn shriek in utter agony as steel sliced through their guts, spilling everything out into a steaming mess around their legs as they began the descent into oblivion.

Swords that were instead bringing no pain at all, and no spurting blood, but only a thrilling sort of chill... and blue glowing smoke in their wakes rather than gore, the blades slicing through them and on, leaving no trace behind.

They were both unwounded, the swords of their unseen foes cutting right through their midriffs but doing them no harm save sliced clothing. Steel could not shed their blood or cut their innards, so they could stride through any number of blades unscathed, as if those swords and thrusting spears weren't there at all.

"Falcon *above!*" Tethtyn swore delightedly, as he and Morl grinned at each other in disbelief—and then with one accord peered down at their spellbooks and started turning pages, peering hard and knowing that they'd recognize the bloodsteel spell when their eyes met with it.

It was in Tethtyn's book this time, and Morl leaned on his shoulder as they both murmured the words and lifted their hands to trace in the air with their fingers, leaving two identical glowing blue symbols floating in the air for a long breath before fading away.

It was Tethtyn who got out the little quill-trimming knife from his belt, and Morl who extended his hand. The steel plunged in with such ease that it was hilt-deep against Morl's palm before he could even gasp.

And shiver with the cold as Tethtyn apprehensively snatched the knife back out, and they both bent close to stare at the blue smoke curling up from the glowing, swiftly closing wound.

"Son of a Stormar!" Morl hissed delightedly. "This is... too splendid for words! What will we cast next?"

"Handfire," Tethtyn said firmly, without thinking. The word had just thrust itself into his mind and come out of his mouth, like that.

He smiled wryly. Lorontar, of course.

Morl wasn't asking what "handfire" was. They were both picturing it at the same time: cold flame that burned nothing, but provided light around the caster's hand, some of which could be left behind on anything non-living that was touched—a table, the pull-ring of a door—or hurled through the air, as one throws a fruit, until it struck something it would stick to, or stopping to hover when the caster speaks its word of mastery.

They shared a grin, and started flipping pages again. And there it was, this time in both books, the very same spell. A radiance, nothing more, never strong enough to blind but quite bright enough to read by, or sew or do exacting work with quill or lockpick or—

Morl's hand flared into silent flames, rising soundlessly to nowhere.

Tethtyn smiled, nodded, held up his own hand, and filled it with the handfire from his own spellbook—a steady glow that had no heart nor flame-like raging. They brought them side by side to compare, thrilling at the thought that they could—could—

"Falcon *shit! Get them!*"

The roar was as loud as it was sudden, a hoarse voice exploding in fury. Tethtyn and Morl barely had time to look up before a wave of strong-smelling attackers was upon them.

They saw swords, and hard-faced men wearing helms and well-worn leather armor, with hairy hands and pounding boots.

Blades plunged into them, leaking cold and blue smoke, then were pulled out to stab and thrust and stab again, the men wielding them snarling in rage and fear.

"Wizards! Falcon-damned *wizards* skulking to bring doom to the Spire! *Die*, you lorn-spawned vaugren-rutters!"

Swords met in them with wild clangs, thrust through them wildly and repeatedly enough to stir a breeze, as all-too-solid fists gathered two lots of clothing chokingly under their wearers' chins, and ungentle hands snatched away glowing metal books.

A sword slashed at one tome—and its wielder shrieked out his life and toppled slowly, lightning crawling along his limbs, the unblemished book falling from blackened and smoking fingers.

There were fresh shouts of fear, and swords came ripping up and out through the faces of Morl and Tethtyn, up through their bodies from beneath, to leave them blinking and gasping from the surging, thrilling chill, blue smoke billowing from their mouths.

Then came the fists, swinging hard.

These *did* hurt, the world rocking and darkening, Morl spitting out blood and teeth as Tethtyn tried to watch him through welling tears, head ringing, fists looming again...

A will that was hard, clear, and swift was suddenly *there* in Tethtyn's mind. He saw Morl's eyes go dark and glint like drawn steel in the same moment, and knew Lorontar had arisen in the tomekeeper, too.

Then they were both spitting out words they had never heard before, and flinging up their hands to claw the air with spread fingers—and the men with the swords and fists were bursting apart, heads exploding off shoulders in dark red, wet clouds, hands bursting off wrists in spurts of blood that left grotesquely twitching, staggering bodies behind.

They were saying more words, harsh declamations that carried Lorontar's dark smile... and more men died.

Then it was all over, as swiftly as it had begun, and Tethtyn was standing with the fingers of his left hand knuckle-deep in the streaming eyesockets of a whimpering, dying man, searing ruthlessly into the fading welter of terror that had been the forester's mind, seeking... seeking...

They were the Guard of Indrulspire, such as it was, one of two patrols who walked the forest verges of the Spire seeking wolves and thieves and unwanted travelers, men of the Spire who'd fought in wars before and wanted nothing at all to do with wizards or lorn or knights and their war-making lords, and... and...

It all went dark, and Tethtyn found himself staring at Morl, feeling empty and sick, Lorontar sinking back down into his mind satisfied. They had slain all of the Guard, whom no one would come looking for all the rest of the day, if not longer, and the bloodsteel was still cloaking them until moonrise.

Morl was snarling something, his eyes dancing flames, and suddenly the sprawled bodies erupted in hungry flames of yellow and green that raged in brief silence until there were no minds left for another wizard to read anything from...

With mounting disgust, Tethtyn watched Lorontar's firm control recede from Morl, leaving the tomekeeper as weak and empty as he felt.

They stared at each other then, across all the smoking, shattered bodies, dismay on their faces... and hunger, too.

They saw that hunger in each other's eyes. Then, with one accord, they were both retching. Bent over, before they could stagger one step more, almost knocking their heads together as they convulsed and groaned, spewing everything in their stomachs all over the corpses.

Chapter Sixteen

S THE ROLLING echoes of the great crash faded, the dark-cloaked noble storming toward its source—and towards the men who'd come running to the accident and now stood before him, aghast and shaking—came to a stop and glowered at them, hand clenched white on the ornate hilt of his sword.

"If Galathgard isn't finished—or at least the great rooms and guesting-chambers, and the stables—by Falconfall, when the King rides in yon front gate to hold his first Great Court, heads will roll," Klarl Annusk Dunshar said icily. "By *my* hand, not his. And using the bluntest of my old blades, so I have to *saw*, Falard. Or that one of the necks won't be yours, unless you have a *very* good excuse to proffer. And Falcon damn me if I can think of one, just now."

Shaking his head, Dunshar stepped around the stone block that had crashed to the floor of the throne hall, sparing not a glance for the tangle of hoist-ropes bound it—or the fresh blood running out from under it, along a web of fresh cracks in the flagstones.

An unfortunate prentice-mason had just made the last discovery of his life, regarding the difficulty of catching a stone block the size of a horse in one's bare hands.

The senior hoist-jack, Falard, stood trembling with fear beside the block, staring down at it—if the truth be known, seeing not the spreading blood, but the broken flagstones beneath them, and wondering where in the ruined east wing he could best glean replacement flagstones, when the klarl's back was turned.

Without looking back, Dunshar stalked off to the robing room he was using as an office, cursing all stupid prentices and hoist-jacks as he went.

He needed a drink, and he needed it now—and hargraul it if the Falcon-be-damned *nightwine* wasn't running low, too! All the way from Yandaltur that had come, and there'd not be any more to be had for coin nor firstborn *this* season, in all the Stormar ports, or any other market he could think of.

Lost in a momentary idle fancy of executing some of the klarls and marquels he particularly hated and raiding their cellars for the nightwine that might well lie therein, Dunshar never noticed the two smiling strangers watching him.

Belard Tesmer looked at his sister with a question in his eyes, and she nodded her answer.

Yes, this one would do.

Klarls weren't the lowest of the Galathan nobility, but the rank was base enough that ambitious men chafed under it. Being as House Tesmer had heard of his doings in distant Ironthorn, there probably wasn't a noble alive in Galath who didn't know Annusk Dunshar was an ambitious man.

Ambitions that had in the past made him loyal to King Devaer, and to the wizard Arlaghaun behind Devaer. Which meant Dunshar could also be made their puppet, if he saw a way higher under their banner.

"He disgusts me," Talyss purred. "Arrogant, unpleasant, full of empty and unearned pride, expendable, predictable... in short, he's an untidy bundle of all the qualities that make Galathan nobles hated far and wide."

Her brother nodded. He, too, had heard all about Annusk Dunshar. The klarl was a cruel, aggressive, unlovely man, unable to resist bullying his lessers and finding fault with his betters. He was widely disliked, even among fellow nobles.

A drink or two still bought an outlander in a Galathan tavern the gleeful retelling of how the burly klarl had won himself the ridged sword-scar across his high, bare forehead. Arduke Halath Lionhelm had given him that, in the battles among Galathan nobles below the walls of besieged Bowrock, after word had spread of the death of King Devaer Rothryn—and Lionhelm had only been prevented from beheading the blubbering klarl on the spot by the need to slay Dunshar's mountainous pair of bodyguards; Dunshar had fled headlong as he did so, and so managed to salvage his life.

Below the scar, Dunshar sported bushy eyebrows, side-whiskers, and a jutting jaw that Belard Tesmer would heartily enjoy slicing right off the man's face, when the time came. "So, d'you think you can seduce him without spewing in his face?"

"Brother," Talyss murmured, "I can do *anything*, if I must." She winked. "If I've judged him rightly, he'll be slaking his thirst right now. Let us go and learn with what. Remember, I'm nobility from our distant, downtrodden Raurklor hold, and you're my servant. Let's not give old Bulljaws any impediments on his path to enjoying my fair form."

Belard rolled his eyes. "And if he fancies men?"

"Then I'll make him stand taller in the eyes of his fellow nobles—as I let him enjoy my servant. He'll be my lapthing, or yours, soon enough, once the braethear starts its work."

She pushed off from the wall and strode through the arch, every inch the imperious noble, and had already slapped a hurrying mason out of her way before Belard could catch up with her, keeping carefully head down and a pace behind.

Catching the eye of the guard who advanced on them then, hand on sword hilt, Belard shook his head warningly, keeping his face stern. The guard froze, nodding uncertainly.

Belard nodded in reply, as if he was the man's commander, and turned to follow Talyss to Klarl Dunshar's office. He restrained himself from rolling his eyes once his back was to the guard.

Although it looked as though he would be doing that a lot in the days ahead.

"I DON'T MUCH like the look of this," Roreld muttered, as Taeauna waved everyone down into the grass, to regain their breaths and ready their swords.

They had sprinted across the open land, down from the ridge and then up the broad, exposed slope to the riven wall of Malragard, as if the Falcon itself had been chasing them. Roreld had caught sight of fearful faces peering at them from windows in Harlhoh, but seen no reaction at all from Malraun's shattered tower.

Aside from five greatfangs suddenly bursting up out of the ruins in terror, of course.

That had sent them plowing their faces into the dirt right swiftly, and left them hugging the grass in cods-wetting fear for a good long time, though the wyrms had taken themselves off with no sign of returning, and they'd never seen a hint of what might have set them to flight. Perhaps they'd escaped some spell-cage.

"Old one," Eskeln panted from beside Roreld, "ye never much like the look of *anything*. Now, this before us is an infamous wizard's tower that's been torn apart—in spell-battle, I doubt not—with greatfangs roosting in it until *something* scares them away, and twice our count of warriors from Darswords blundering about inside it, to say nothing of whatever twisted, crawling things Malraun may secretly have magicked into life down the years, so, aye, I'll grant ye it bids fair to be perilous. Yet the Lady Taeauna—"

"—Would appreciate it greatly, Eskeln, if you'd *belt up*, right now," Taeauna hissed at him. "Just this once. We can't count on the Darsworders being deaf, you know."

She glanced around at them all, huddled in the grass around her. "It seems we can now stride right in, through any number of gaps in the walls, and we know that the Darsworders, at least, are in there ahead of us. So, any suggestions on where we could best enter, and head for?"

They stared back at her thoughtfully; old Roreld, who knew even less about Malragard than she did, and the nine from Malraun's bodyguard. Eskeln stirred, but it was Gorongor who spoke first. "Yonder, as far as we can get. The kitchens, the pantries—as far from the entrance hall and all the traps as we can get."

Tarlund and Glorn both shook their heads vigorously.

"No, no," Glorn hissed, "that's foolishness! Go in by the garden door, and straight across, to where the Master liked to work on his enchantments! If any magic still protects the place at all, that's where it'll be, or was when whatever did this struck or—"

"Which means that's *just* where we *don't* want to be," Roreld growled. "Give me beasts I can put a blade through any day, not crawling spells I can only gawp at—before I start screaming. Why, I—"

Taeauna rolled her eyes, stood up, hefted her sword in her hand, and snapped, "Come!"

Then she turned, without a backward glance, and strode through a gap where a stretch of wall had fallen, into the nearest smoldering chamber of Malragard.

"A JACK OF ale, o'course," Garfist growled, digging in his pouch for coin. "Something dark and rich, from a keg that doesn't kill dogs that drink from it."

The tavernmaster gave him a dark look. "You're not in Tauren now, trader. Nor the Stormar ports, neither." A battered, patched wooden tankard thumped down beside Garfist's row of coins, a thin thread of foam spilling down its side, and the man selected one coin with a finger and drew it across the smooth-worn bar. "We brew *good* ale in Galath."

"Oh?" someone called, from the far end of the dark, low-beamed room. "Where'd *this* come from, then?"

The tavernmaster turned with a good-natured snarl, forgetting Garfist, who swept up his coins and took his tankard to a back table where Iskarra was waiting.

She thrust a finger into it, lapped at her nail like a kitten, then nodded—whereupon Garfist drained it with a satisfied sigh, turned, and belched his way back to the bar in search of more.

"*Food*," she reminded his back firmly, knowing he wasn't listening. Well, at least the ale was good—and free of any of the poisons she knew the taste of, too.

Gar was turning back to her with his second tankard when a nasal voice said sharply out of the cluster of tables in the center of the room, "I *know* that man. Garfist! Garfist Gulkoun!"

Garfist shot a look toward the voice, and it promptly added, "So it *is* you! Gulkoun, you owe me a new ship—and a new wife, too, damn you!"

In the wake of those words a stool came hurtling across the room, which Garfist batted aside with a scornful sweep of his arm. Iskarra snatched up the crumb-strewn platter the last diner had left on their table, and flung it hard and fast to catch the dagger thrown in the stool's wake—and sent it singing and clanging across the bar. The tavernmaster ducked, roaring out an oath, and the feasting room of the Stag's Head was suddenly full of men jumping to their feet, shouting, toppling stools, and throwing dishes and cutlery.

"Outside!" the tavernmaster roared, over the tumult. "*Outside!*"

Swords were hissing out of scabbards now, and knives were being snatched from belts. Iskarra caught up the candle-lamp from the table in front of her and plucked a tiny cloth bag from a clip at her throat.

There was a scream, a crash as someone was shoved aside and lost his footing amid the tables, and five traders were plunging across the room, swords out, heading for Garfist.

Gar took a swig from his tankard and watched them come.

"Three seasons I searched the Stormar ports for you—*three seasons!*—you morlraw's backside!" the foremost man snarled, his nasal voice rising higher with rage at each word. "And all the while you were *here*, hiding like some scuttling *rat!* Getting fatter and richer on what you stole from me, rutting with my woman like—like—"

"Like someone she *wanted* to have her legs around?" Garfist rumbled, reaching for his sword with one hand and bringing the tankard around with the other, shattering the drinking-jack across the nose of the glaring tavernmaster, who'd been stalking up on him from behind. The man fell like a sack of stones.

"Instead of someone who beat her and took her by force and hauled her hair out by the roots, night after night?" the burly former panderer added. "*Now* I know ye, Markel. Murderer of rival merchants and anyone else who got between ye and the nearest heap of coins—including at least one Stormar heir I know about. Come to Galath where they don't know that about ye yet? Or are the Stormar lords coming for ye with their swords out, hey?"

"They'll come too late to save *your* lying hide, that's for sure!" Markel spat. "Take him!"

The bodyguards at his shoulders charged forward, swords slashing the air to drive Garfist back, and then dropping into vicious lunges. The second pair of bodyguards swung wide to try and flank him. A table of armsmen in matching livery hastily drew their feet in out of the way, and leaned back in their seats to watch the fun, casting glances at their knightly master at the next table for direction. The knight himself was smiling thinly and leaning his chin on his hand, for a better view.

The bodyguards closed in on the fat outlander.

Garfist dropped back, closed his hands around the edge of a table, and hauled on it, hard. It came around in a great arc and crashed through two swordarms, sending the bodyguards sprawling and their blades clanging to the floor behind the bar.

He charged forward in its wake, took one man by the throat and broke his neck, kicking the other viciously in the face to keep him on the floor.

As he turned to deal with a third bodyguard, Markel came at him with a shriek, sword and dagger out and high—and vanished in a gout of flame as Iskarra's bag, trailing flame, struck the point of his dagger and burst, igniting with a roar.

A moment later, Isk thrust a needle-thin blade under the edge of the last bodyguard's codpiece. The man shrieked and crashed to the floor, clutching himself.

Garfist knocked aside the cornered bodyguard's sword, and slammed a fist into the man's throat.

He turned away without pause, knowing he'd slain his man.

"Isk, Isk," he said then, watching the blackened Markel collapse to the food-littered floor and writhe in strangling agony, "ye didn't have to do that! I'd have had him down in a trice, look ye, an'—"

The bodyguard Garfist had knocked to the floor tried again to rise to his feet. This time the burly man put real weight behind his kick, ruining the man's face and snapping his neck around at a crazy angle. The warrior sagged back in silence, mouth gaping, his one visible eye staring fixedly at the ceiling-beams overhead.

"Right," Garfist said in satisfaction. "That's *that* done and gone. Now, is there any chance of a hungry traveler getting some *food* on his table, before the night's out?"

He turned back to the bar. "Ho! Anyone?"

Iskarra's warning scream came a moment too late, and he was sent reeling by a stool hurled into the side of his head.

Fetching up against the bar, Gar grunted, shook his head, grimaced, and turned to face the direction whence the stool had come.

A dozen or more Galathans stood facing him balefully. Stools and tables had been flung aside, and some of them had knives in their hands.

"That man was hiring here, spending a lot of coin," one of them said, pointing down at the smoldering, gasping Markel. "Now you've snatched all that away."

Slowly and menacingly he caught up another stool, hefted it, and threw it at Garfist, who sidestepped and ducked, to let it tumble past him and crash into the tables beyond.

"*And* the good roast gelgreth I paid for is all over the floor," snarled the knight, as Iskarra darted around behind the bar, "and you've put Mrelbrand down and it's not looking like I'll be getting another meal out of his kitchens... so I think I'll just cut me one out of your *hide!*"

Another stool came hurtling. Garfist batted it aside, snatched up a stool of his own from nearby, and hurled it back at the armsman who'd thrown it, felling him. Both tables of armsmen came to their feet with a roar.

The Galathans already on their feet shouted in anger, and as the armsmen joined them, closed slowly in on him.

The lone man they were facing neither paled nor flinched. Rather than backing away, he strode almost insolently to meet them.

"So it's a fight ye're after, is it?" Garfist Gulkoun asked them, smiling like a wolf. "Good. *Now* we shall begin."

Chapter Seventeen

MORL AND TETHTYN blinked at each other. There were unfamiliar gardens all around them. Tranquil, beautiful gardens, quite deserted of people, with moss-girt stone statues of stern knights and gowned maidens standing on plinths dotted among the lush flower-beds. The towering walls and ornate oval windows of a grand mansion loomed over the lush little lawn where they stood.

No one shouted an alarm, and no war horns blew. Aside from the gentle buzz of a glimmerwings darting unconcernedly past, silence reigned.

They relaxed slightly.

This translocation was getting easier every time.

A confidence was rising within them, a certain cold, efficient ruthlessness that carried them on from small victory to small victory, the magic was starting to feel *right*; something that served them rather than something they were in the coils of.

Tethtyn knew the confidence must really be coming from Lorontar, guiding his thralls, yet even knowing that, it felt *good*. He felt more powerful, more sure of himself, than ever before. And, yes, the magic was working. Obeying his castings, as if he really was an accomplished wizard, and winning battles.

Already he and Morl—who wore the same slightly amazed, disbelieving look that he did—were using mightier spells than any hedge-wizard he'd ever heard of, and most every other mage he knew about except the Dooms.

They were two inexperienced bumblers, for all that—but when they found themselves in real trouble, *he* rose up inside them, forcing them to do what was needful to win the battle, crush the foe or get away unscathed.

Lorontar had done that more than a dozen times, now, as Morl and Tethtyn moved around Galath and the Stormar coast at his bidding, seizing books of magic and enchanted things from tombs and hidden rooms, blasting all who sought to prevent them. They were sickened by what they did less and less often. Now all the violent deaths made them wince or frown, not empty their stomachs.

It was a matter of calm, capable performance, as they did what their minds—that is, what Lorontar lurking in the depths of their minds—commanded them to do.

But we're good little puppets, Tethtyn thought to himself, turning to peer up at the ornately carved stone walls soaring above the gardens. There were no sentinels atop them that he could see... and still no shouts of alarm, nor challenges.

Something was making him look to one end of the garden, where the trees reached out to meet the end of the mansion. He knew better than to ignore these urges by now, and Morl was already heading in that direction; Tethtyn hastened after him.

The gentle music of running water cascading over metal chimes could be heard as they drew near, and irregularly shaped flagstones began to appear, set deep into the sward in a wandering path that curved around two smoothly pruned darsart trees to end at a modest stone archway in the shade of a spreading althantar, and an open door into a stone pavilion.

Tethtyn followed Morl silently through the arch, and beheld a stone casket styled to resemble a castle. It lay, high and dominant, down the center of the pavilion, and was already stained by rain. Massive stone pillars rose from the cobbled floor to the low roof, and the garden could be seen between them. The pavilion abutted the wall of the mansion, pierced here by no windows, but by a grand stone door.

There were no signs of anyone about as they stopped side by side to gaze upon the casket, which bore the inscription: "Haerelle Bloodhunt, Velduchess of Galath/Sleeping the long sleep cloaked in much love."

Morl and Tethtyn looked at each other, shrugged, and worked a spell they had used often this morning and the evening before. They heard the faint singing of its rising power, saw wisps of shimmering silver briefly blossom in the air and fade as the magic stole forth... and watched the gigantic stone lid grate off the casket, away from them.

The turreted slab hovered in the air just beyond the stone box as the mansion door burst open, and five guards burst out, shouting and grabbing at their swords. There were others—maidservants—behind them, and an old man in a splendid dark doublet and breeches, who lurched forward leaning on a gilded cane, his face black with anger.

"*Stop them! Cut them down!*" the old man roared, his tiny beard wagging on the point of his chin—and the guards surged forward.

Morl and Tethtyn, moved by the same cruel will and smiling the same ghost of a smile, thrust the lid forward like a battering ram, smashing into the chests of the guards and bearing them back against the mansion wall with bone-shattering force.

Maids skrieked and fled in all directions, the aging velduke ducked to avoid the lid and fell heavily, cane cartwheeling in his wake, and the guards screamed in agony—some spewing out thick blood as their ribs splintered. Then the lid fell, released by Lorontar's mages.

Fresh, shrill cries rent the air as the guards' knees were smashed and feet crushed.

"What a *din!*" Morl spat, wincing. "Enough of this!"

Tethtyn nodded, watching the same brief golden flicker in his fellow mage's eyes that was hazing his own vision. Lorontar was again handing them both the same spell, unfolding it in their minds for the first time and draining the power of the spells he'd readied in their minds to do so.

"Motherless, misbegotten despoilers!" Velduke Aumun Bloodhunt snarled, struggling to crawl toward them and drawing an ornate belt-knife as he did so. "Thieves, desecrators! *Wizards!*"

Morl and Tethtyn gave the enraged old velduke the same mocking smile, murmured the same incantation, curled their hands into the same spider-claws... and sighed as the guards, maids, and the struggling, hissing Bloodhunt all took on dark, flickering purple glows, shuddered uncontrollably in the tightening grip of the magic—and shrank away into black, crawling spiders the size of large mens' fists.

Most of the spiders scuttled right at Morl and Tethtyn, only to encounter something that drove them back, legs curling in pain, and sent them limping and lurching unevenly away, fleeing lopsidedly as if prodded or chased by something unseen.

"By the Falcon," Morl muttered, smiling a crooked smile. "It's getting so that one can't even plunder a velduke's dead wife's tomb undisturbed!"

"Indeed," Tethtyn agreed, wincing as brief regret flared in him—and was promptly washed away in a dark, eager flood of hunger. Magic! They were going to get their hands on more spells!

Powerful magic, too. The Lady Haerelle Bloodhunt had been a clever woman, not only younger and stronger than her husband, but quite wise and controlled enough to keep her mastery of magic secret from the velduke, all of his guards, and his servants. A pity winter-fever had taken her well before a boulder had crushed his leg at the siege of Bowrock. Even before Arlaghaun had noticed her accomplishments and come calling, as it happened.

So it had fallen to an ancient and doddering local hedge-wizard—gone to greet the Falcon himself, since—to discover her arts as he laid the usual spells on the dead velduchess that would keep her from rising as a walking skeleton or baleful ghost. Her magic was of sufficient power to frighten the hedge-wizard out of all desire to claim any of her tomes or scrolls for himself, and cause him to bind and conceal the magic beneath her, cloaked in the illusion of solid stone to make it seem part of the casket that held her.

It was the illusion that drew Lorontar. He could sense it half a realm away, and knew by the feel of it that it cloaked strong magic.

Consequently his two new hopes were standing before an open casket now, watching the terrified scuttlings of the spiders, and learning all about the hedge-wizard and his illusion as they thrust their hands into it, shattering it, rolling the mouldering, withering cage of bones that had been Velduchess Haerelle Bloodhunt aside to get at what lay beneath her.

More shouts came from within the mansion, and the pounding of boots. Morl and Tethtyn calmly thrust the corpse this way and that, making very sure they'd found all the magic, then nodded at each other and cast their translocations.

"Sleeping the long sleep, cloaked in much love," Tethtyn murmured sardonically, as the casket, pavilion, and all started to fade.

The guards and servants charging out of the mansion had just enough time to stare at the opened tomb, and at the two smiling strangers beyond it, then down at the spiders scuttling furiously everywhere, and start to scream.

Before Morl and Tethtyn were gone.

KLARL ANNUSK DUNSHAR thrust his favorite flask of nightwine hastily back down behind the heaped plans and papers on the far side of his desk, choked down a fiery mouthful, and gaped up at the unexpected visitor smiling down at him with one long-fingered hand on her shapely hip. Somehow he managed an attempt at a pleasant greeting.

"Who by the randy, hargrauling Falcon are *you?*"

The woman now bending lithely forward to smile at him—and afford him a generous view down the front of her soft leather bodice—purred, "I am the Lady Talyss Tesmer, of Ironthorn. And I like what I see. Tell me, lord—for you can be nothing less; no man so splendid could be—just what, by the randy, hargrauling Falcon, is *your* name?"

Annusk Dunshar gaped at her, sharp-pointed side-whiskers bobbing, jaw working as he struggled for the right words... or *any* words.

She licked her lips, gazing at him in open desire, and the klarl caught sight of the man standing behind her, also clad in tight, well-worn leathers and sporting a sword and daggers, and stiffened, grabbing for the hilt of his blade.

Slender fingers forestalled him.

"Gently, my lord, *gently,*" the woman murmured in soothing reproof, almost in his lap now. "No danger awaits you here. He who stands behind me is my sworn and loyal man, not some murderous thrust-knife or other."

That man promptly nodded, though Dunshar saw that the man's gaze kept carefully steady, looking past him at something on the far wall of his office.

"I—" Dunshar flushed, wallowing in confusion.

Stuttering for a moment, he lowered his head like a bull, put all thinking behind him, and snapped, "I am a klarl of Galath, Lady Talyss. Annusk Dunshar is my name, and I rule over the rebuilding of Galathgard, here around you, and this great castle once it stands proud once more, until the day the King rides in to once more sit the Throne of Galath. Which makes me the seneschal of this most royal of castles, wherefore I ask again: who are you? Am I to understand you rule this Ironthorn? Or is there a Lord Tesmer?"

"There is, but he lies near death, too old and feeble to rule beyond the door of his own bedchamber—if that. You've not even *heard* of Ironthorn?"

Dunshar waved a hasty hand. "No, no, 'tis west of Galath, somewhere beyond Tauren, is it not?"

"It is, and I have come *all that way* to see you," she breathed, lifting a knee onto the edge of his chair and thrusting herself forward until her breasts grazed his chest...

Dunshar shook himself, like a dog awakening, and managed to ask thickly, "Why?"

"Because I seek a *real* man, a man of power and refinement, a great man in the greatest realm Falconfar has ever known, not one of the slackjawed, stoneheaded hay-farmers of Ironthorn. A man such as *you.*"

Dunshar blinked. "But—but, lady, this is ridic—harrumph, highly un—ah, incred—uh, irregul—"

"Unusual, I quite grant," the Lady Tesmer murmured, her lips almost brushing his, her breath a warm zephyr carrying a hint of cinammon. "And I am sure that our rough, backcountry Ironthar ways seem clumsy to you, perhaps even striking you as akin to the blandishments of lowly coin-kiss lasses—not that you will have experienced any such personally, my lord klarl, *of course*, but men who rule hear much, and know much, and anticipate even more."

"Uh, indeed they do," Dunshar said brightly, daring to adopt something that just might be interpreted as a tease. He went so far as to wink.

A moment later, the lips so close to his were locked upon his mouth, and an eager, ardent tongue was thrusting in his mouth, leaving him—

Choking and sputtering, clawing at the air for aid that did not come and dignity that was quite lost.

Fingers that thrilled with their gentle touch were tracing his neck and up behind his ear, and toying with the curled hairs of his chest.

"Lord Dunshar, would you prefer that I beg you? For I will, and gladly; it has been long indeed since I have known the touch of a man, and—"

By some miracle or other, probably involving the Falcon, Annusk Dunshar heaved himself up out of his chair somehow, spilling the woman—gods, she was taller than he was, though now she was down on her knees gazing up at him with glazed eyes and parted lips—off of him. He reeled to his feet, clutching at his sword for fear the woman's unmoving manservant would suddenly lunge forward to thrust steel right through him.

"No, this *can't* be happening!" he snarled. "This is some sort of trick! Women just *don't*—"

He stared down. She was kissing his dusty boots, grinding herself along the stone floor like a serpent as she licked at them. "Ah, but *I* do," she murmured. "Yet I am well aware that men—great men, noble lords—have their dignity and their own entanglements. And are guided by manners prevailing here in Galath that I am woefully uninformed about."

Staring up at him with great dark eyes, she deliberately bent her head again and planted a wet, ardent kiss on the now-gleaming toe of his right boot. "I have, I fear, offended. Lord Dunshar, please believe me when I say it is not my intent to discomfit you—only to have you if you'll have me."

"I... I am flattered, lady," the klarl said stiffly, uncomfortably aware that anyone could walk by the open door of the office and peer in—to say nothing of the fact that nothing at all would stop anyone from overhearing all of this.

"Please, arise." He extended his hand. "I would like to meet with you elsewhere, after my work here is done for the day, when we can speak more freely. In the meantime, let me say that although your, ah,... *warmth*... has more than astonished me, it is not unwelcome, and I am not displeased. May I, ah, offer you some nightwine?"

Lady Tesmer's eyes flashed delight. "I'd be delighted!"

Dunshar retrieved his flask, started to hold it out, then hesitated, looking helplessly around his cluttered office for a goblet he hadn't spit into or used as a censer.

The Lady Tesmer came to his rescue. "Ah! No fears, my lord klarl! My man carries two slake-horns for the trail, if you mind not small quaffs!" She turned to her impassive manservant, and almost immediately whirled back, proffering two tiny cones cut from the tips of beast-horns.

Dunshar admired them with a smile. Better and better; they were small enough that he'd not diminish his precious nightwine nearly as much as he'd feared he might.

He poured with delicate skill, and not the slightest hesitation.

He'd never drunk nightwine while staring into the eyes of a woman who was staring back at him in obvious longing—by the Falcon, he'd never had so beautiful a woman staring at him with longing *at all*. Somehow the wine tasted brighter, more sparkling, and more warming than ever before. More *golden...*

"Wonderful," he breathed as they stood facing each other, lips almost touching.

"The nightwine is, too," she murmured back, eyes devouring his.

Klarl Annusk Dunshar smiled at her jest, finding himself amused, proud, and aroused all at the same time—and somehow warm and comforted and *safe*, too...

He was vaguely aware of being in his chair again, his face nestled against those warm, soft breasts, and the shapely mouth not far above them murmuring, "The braethear has full hold of him."

However, he was far beyond wondering what "braethear" might be, or why the manservant muttered back, "Good. Now, as long as none of our bolder kin come trailing along after that locket..."

"If they do, the trap is more than ready," the Lady Tesmer replied smugly. "Now help me with Lord Dunshar, here. *Such* a man of Galath."

Her laughter then was like the merry, mocking tinkling of many bells, at once high and carefree, and at the same time so deafening that Annusk Dunshar slid down and away from it into deepening shadows, wondering why every last man in Galathgard didn't come running to see what was making all the noise, and then turn to take those wonderful breasts for themselves...

Chapter Eighteen

H E WAS...

He was here. Wherever "here" was.

Chin-down on cold stone, surrounded by fresh wreckage, the air full of heavy, clinging dust.

Weird glows flickered and pulsed, here and there through the cloak of dust, silent and tireless radiances that weren't flames... and so, must be magic.

Magic. That was it!

Rod Everlar nodded feebly, the floor beneath him cold, and hard.

An enchanted thing—a lurstar, he remembered—had fallen to the floor of this room and exploded, right in front of him. He'd been... the memories of the wizard Rambaerakh had been flooding through him—

Memories not his own flared in his mind again; a bearded man shouting, clawing at the air in frantic patterns that trailed fiery lines—but too late, as the man choked and spasmed and went purple and fell away behind his floating tangle of fire...

A castle of dark stone looming tall and dark on a mountaintop, green fires bursting forth from the windows, hurling folk within to their deaths, then raging higher until the walls cracked and split and the fortress started to fall...

A woman with love in her eyes, and grief, rushing toward him in a darkened chamber, pleading...

Rod shook his head violently, slapped himself, and gasped in relief. He'd managed to thrust aside the dead wizard's memories somehow, and was himself again, lying in this shattered chamber in the cellars of Malragard.

"Light," he mumbled. "Must have light. Can't... see."

As if that had been a command, magical lights silently flared all around him.

Rod glared at them and raised himself onto his elbows. He couldn't quite believe that he'd been so close to a blast that scoured the walls bare and cracked the ceiling, and been untouched.

Or *was* he? He couldn't feel his legs or his left arm, although he heaved himself up off the stone readily enough.

He sat up, and put a tentative hand up to his face.

There was his cheek, and his nose... Everything felt very much as it always had. He was alone—he *felt* alone, though the memories of too many dead men to count were all in his head, just waiting for a chance to get out—and he felt whole, too. Unhurt.

He stood up, a little unsteadily, and peered through the drifting dust.

Most of the stone shelves were gone, blasted away in great jagged shards where enchanted things had exploded; it looked like a greatfangs had somehow managed to get just its head into the room, and bite the edges of the shelves. The glows were coming from shattered things of magic, or were playing back and forth between wands or lurstars that had fallen close to each other.

Rod shook his head. How *had* he survived? It just wasn't—no, he *couldn't* believe it. His face had been somewhere about *there*, and the lurstar just over *there*...

He shook his head in disbelief. Now, if the thing had just shattered like glass, maybe, but when it had obviously exploded with sufficient fury to vaporize itself and crater the stone floor beneath, and magic items all over the room had blown apart, too, turning Malraun's arsenal into all these shards and twisted chaos and dying magic and perhaps, just *perhaps* one or two things he might be able to salvage...

Well, perhaps there was something to this Lord Archwizard business, after all...

Salvage, that had been a good idea. Not that he knew the slightest thing about magic, or even how to turn on some of these items, but he could always trade—

Rod stopped then, and blinked. New memories were crowding into his mind as he stared along the benches, and he realized that he *did* know something about magic, after all.

Still not spells. Very probably, if he tried to cast one—even if he somehow found a profusely illustrated *Simple Spells For Kids* book, or some such, and everything else he needed for a spell, too—stone-cold nothing would happen.

He wasn't eager to try, either. Instead of "nothing," he might very well manage *something*. Like blowing off his own hand, or a bystander's head, or the towers off the nearest castle.

Yet as he looked at what was left of Malraun's things of magic, strewn along the benches—most of them blackened, twisted, shattered, or even melted and run down off the fragmented stone bench in long, tarry streams that had hardened again, like cooling plastic—he could now put names to things. As in: *that* hadn't just been some sort of magical staff, it was what was left of a Falconstrike.

And that wand, before its dangerous end had turned into a line of charcoal, had been a Taether's Talons, a weapon that conjured up raking claws out of thin air to rend one's foes.

These things, too, that looked like long spindles, with a handgrip centred between *two* tapering ends rather than just one like a wand; these had been mysteries to him before, but he knew what they were now. Very likely because Rambaerakh had known. They were called *undluths*, and they spewed magic from both points, in long, flowing lines that trailed behind a moving undluth-wielder, and could be used to lash foes or counter their spells, hurled between the wielder and a foe like a dancing, undulating barrier. Undluth-strands could parry enemy magic where nothing else could, luring and clutching at it where a sword or net or shield would be utterly useless against it.

Which meant he could now at least name what was about to kill him. Well, that was progress of a sort...

Rod drew in a deep breath, reached out his hand, and firmly took hold of the nearest intact undluth.

Nothing happened. It proved to be solid, cold, and smooth; touching it caused nothing to blow up, no sparks to spit anywhere, and nothing to boil up in his mind. It was like holding a splendidly carved stick.

Until a little window seemed to sigh open in his mind, showing him lines of bronze-hued flame spurting smoothly from the points of the undluth, and a word slowly appeared around the window: *nressae*.

Well, now...

Rod shrugged, held the undluth up and carefully out to one side, tilted it so neither of the points were aimed at him, and announced to the room calmly and clearly, "Nressae."

Bronze fire leaked silently out of the tips of the undluth with no fuss at all, as readily and simply as if he'd turned on a tap.

"Nressae," he said again—and the fire stopped, the fiery lines hanging down in midair slowly fading back up toward the points of the undluth.

No, no, they were *burning* their way back to the points where they'd come from, consuming themselves like a long fuse running to sticks of dynamite in an old movie. As Rod watched, they reached the points and winked out.

He blinked. A good thing, that; it hadn't crossed his mind until just now that the undluth could have exploded when they reached it, coming from either side, and met.

No, impossible, his mind told him rather scornfully—Rambaerakh, for all the tea in China—yet someone inside his head, some memory that hadn't belonged to the wizard, had fully expected that result. Probably due to seeing it happen once.

His mind hurled a severed hand at him, cartwheeling out of the darkness and past his nose fast enough to leave him blinking, trailed by a raw, throat-stripping scream of agony.

Then it was gone, and he was staring at the silent, reassuringly solid undluth in his hand again.

Rod shrugged. "Nressae."

Bronzen fire awakened once more. He watched it blaze for a moment, then drew his hand carefully up and to the right, with the exaggerated sweeping grace of a ballerina, so as to swing those lines of fire up onto the bench *around* a trio of pulsing, backlashing wands to where a row of burnt staves and scepter-like things lay.

So *ho*, he could do this! As deftly as a dancer, that had been...

The charred things sprang into the air, spitting sparks, at the first touch of undluth-fire. Rod flinched.

In prompt response, the lines of bronzen flame undulated like a snake, traveling along the battered bench like someone sending waves along a skipping rope. Enchanted items bounded up, spat spectacular showers of sparks, and flew apart—sending thrilling discharges of magic back down along the fires and up his arm.

Rod was trembling in an instant, caught in the thrumming heart of more magic than he'd ever felt before, power that lifted him right off the floor to hover a few inches above it.

"Wow!" he gasped aloud, then saw the lines of fire still snaking along the bench, toward a tangle of staves that still looked intact—

"*Nressae!*" Rod shouted desperately, hauling back on the undluth, hard.

Bronze fire danced above the bench, recoiling and lashing, reaching out writhing tendrils toward a staff that almost seemed to stir and then *bend* to greet them, as if yielding to the pull of a gigantic magnet in a Saturday morning cartoon—and faded back toward Rod, without reaching any of the staves.

Thank the Falcon.

Well, he'd certainly be keeping this. It was about time he had something in his hand to deal with evil wizards or veteran warriors— what had one of his history teachers called them, so long ago? Oh, yes, "well-practiced murderers with swords"—and he liked the *feel* of this. Or rather, he liked the way it made him feel.

Powerful, dangerous, and capable. For the first time in years.

Not that he particularly wanted to be dangerous to anyone. He just wanted respect. To be treated like someone it would be dangerous to casually mistreat, thrust aside with scorn, or use as a pawn.

Yes. Rod hefted the undluth. He'd certainly be taking this with him.

Which meant he dared not carry any other undluths away from here, or he'd be the one in danger. Undluths did bad things with other undluths carried by the same person.

Now, how had he known that?

From one of the memories that had flooded into him, yes, but whose? Who had those bobbing skeletons *been?*

Rod frowned, shrugged, and turned to peer at the tangle of staves. He already knew they didn't all look alike, but hadn't yet applied himself to finding out what they *did* look like.

Hmm. Not that just looking was going to give him much of a clue as to what each one did. They lacked handy labels, and though they had decorations of a sort, mostly carved collars bordering the smooth handgrip, the style of those borders told him nothing about the intended purpose or powers of the staff. One or two of the borders looked a little like Celtic knotwork, yet formed parallel ridges of different heights, like the flaring decorative bands on Staunton chess pieces.

So Rod shrugged, took hold of a staff that looked to be about the right height to serve as a walking-stick and that wasn't too badly tangled up with other staves, and pulled it free.

No revelations rushing into his mind, no stirrings of power in his mind. It was a stick. Smooth, heavy and reassuring in his hand, but still just a stick. Until, he supposed, he said or did the right thing.

Which he would never ever happen to blindly, mistakenly do. Probably.

Rod shrugged, lifted the staff and turned it to make sure there were no little inscriptions hidden anywhere on it.

No. Nothing. There was no way the repeating curves of this border could be letters, or hide words—or even a rune, unless the whole danged thing, all around the curve of the staff, was a symbol. He recalled being taught about an ancient wartime code that used a strip of paper wound around a staff, but there was nothing on this staff that would help tell him if a code like that would work with this staff, and no little cracks in it where pieces of paper—or anything else—might be hidden.

His father's perennial gruff Christmas morning question: "What? No instructions?" rose into Rod's mind, and he smiled wryly. Shrugging, he turned to look for a rod, or a lurstar, or a wand, to take along, too.

One of each, no more, one part of his mind was warning him.

Yet an instant later, someone else's memories showed him men trudging along with bundles of wands bound at their belts, and six or seven staves lashed together and slung across their backs in baldric-carriers.

Rod shook his head, grinned, and decided to look thoroughly all over the room, pick up everything that he really liked the look of, make sure nothing so much as brushed against anything else, rig up some practical way of carrying everything, and take it all. After all, he doubted he'd be coming back.

174

In fact, a restless part of him wanted him to get going, to get out of this scorched and battered room without delay. There wasn't really much left of Malraun's arsenal of magic, all crowded and gleaming and neatly arranged along the shelves as he'd first seen it. He was looking at an aftermath, and what little wreckage had survived.

Some of it for not much longer, by the looks of the awakened wands whose pulsing, arcing magics were still wrestling weirdly with each other and getting feebler. Most looked like they'd just go dark, fading away into spitting and then silent exhaustion, but a few looked angrier; more dangerous, as if they'd explode rather than fading. Perhaps that was behind his growing restlessness.

"Begone," he murmured, selecting a wand he liked the look of. "Begone."

He thrust it through his belt, judging the slightly bulbous ends—both of them flared the same way, both of them carved with squiggly grooves that might mean something significant, or might be mere decoration—would keep the thing from falling to the ground unnoticed, as he walked. Then he saw a lurstar, uncracked among a group of broken ones, and took it, too, thrusting it through his belt nigh his other hip. Which left him with no hands free, if he was going to carry the staff and the undluth and let none of them touch each other.

Right. Magic he hadn't time to master—even if he could. Time to go.

As if that decision had been some sort of silent signal, staves and wands and lurstars awakened, all over the room, kindling into insistent, pulsing glows—and Rod's head was flooded with memories not his own. Striding out of this very chamber and along the passage ahead—not rubble-strewn and collapsed, but lit by a neat row of flickering torches. Meeting with powerful robed men. Wizards. Regal and feared—and rightly so.

One turning to face him, in a high-collared robe of maroon, hair and beard flecked with white, with great dark eyes... Lorontar.

He shivered, although it was only a memory, and was almost wildly glad when the figure was gone and others stood in its place; younger, darker men robed in green and sky-blue and brown. Lorontar's foes, these, though they were all dangerous in their own ways, too, wizards with no one to govern them and little to recommend them save that they had banded together to stand against Lorontar.

Dead now, most of them, and the rest gone into hiding. A secret society of sorts, hiding all over Falconfar and in places beyond, behind dozens of hidden gates. The Moon Masked, they were called, for their ability to cloak their faces with pearly radiance like moonlight.

They survived still, whoever had provided this memory was sure. Yet he—not Rambaerakh, so it must have been one of the skeletons—also knew they had not been seen or heard from in the lifetime of any living Falconaar he knew of, and that many— priests and sages and Aumrarr—believed the Moon Masked gone forever, done with Falconfar and with their struggle against Lorontar.

Rod shook his head to put such distracting thoughts aside—not *now*, this room was about to blow apart, or something or someone was headed here to investigate the first blast—and headed out of the room, along the passage.

Not that he knew his way around Malragard all that well. He had a vague idea that he had to turn around, and ascend a floor, to get to ground level and to the parts of the tower he knew.

Which were chock-full of Malraun's nasty little traps.

Right. Burn that bridge when we get to it. Right now, *hurry.* So turn left here, and—

Rod came to an abrupt halt, hefting the undluth in his hand— and was very glad he was holding it.

Something *had* been coming to investigate the magical explosion. But this...

Only a fantasy game designer could come up with *this.*

It was too damned ridiculous.

Rod was staring at two tawny, muscular legs that ended not in the paws that should have been there, but sticky, splayed feet like a gecko's.

The beast moved carefully, planting each foot securely before unpeeling the other behind it from the stones, then repeating the process... for all the world as if the sticky toes anchored it to the ground. Maybe they did; its bulbous, tapering body was made of swirling smoke that trailed behind it as it moved.

At the front end were great fanged jaws and an arc of four eyes that seemed to float in the air above them.

A maercrawn!

A which? Several memories had rushed up into Rod's mind to hand him that name, and were now crowding and overlapping confusingly. *Deadly, for all its ridiculous looks,* another added helpfully.

The maercrawn took two more slow, silent steps toward Rod, who found himself thinking that the beast's legs looked as strong and sleek as a lion's—and opened its jaws impossibly wide.

Rod stared at them.

It was as if a construction site backhoe had opened its scoop-bucket, and was trundling towards him. Except that it was ringed by very long, sharp teeth, and was coming straight for him.

Chapter Nineteen

"Careful," Taeauna murmured, her voice so low and soft that the men with her had to stop to hear her.

Which was exactly what she wanted them to do. Rushing around Malragard—this floor of it, at least—was apt to be fatal. For those who wanted to live, caution and stealth were imperative. The traps were many, and Taeauna didn't know precisely where and what all of them were, or how they worked. She suspected Malraun's longtime bodyguards knew even less than she did, once they stepped past their simple, memorized warnings like "don't step here unless you want to die." She'd overheard Eskeln muttering that to himself, once, as they clambered over the rubble of a fallen ceiling, toward a gaping doorway beyond.

They were not alone in the ruins; they had all heard enough to tell that, even if they'd not seen Narmarkoun and his Darsworders plunge through the riven walls ahead of them.

As Taeauna had kept her ten warriors advancing slowly and carefully through roofless, rubble-strewn rooms, Malragard had been noisy around them. They'd heard screams and clattering noises, and once, the ringing din of falling roof-timbers.

The fallen stone underfoot was endless, and slipping through it a slow, noisy, and chancy process. However, they were now coming at last to passages and chambers that had retained their ceilings—and could hear scuttling sounds, ahead in the dimness.

"I—I like not the look of this," Roreld growled, voicing what it was clear they all felt.

Taeauna nodded, keeping her voice soft enough that they all had to lean toward her to hear. "This floor of Malragard is *thick* with traps meant to kill intruders. What little is left of the floors above holds scant interest for us; Malraun was well aware that thieves tend to believe the lord of any tower will keep his precious things up high, where he rests his head of nights, so he kept his treasures hidden low, instead. Wherefore we should seek a stair down; if they're not now blocked, two such are near. We want the closest one, ahead over *that* way, because getting to it is far safer than seeking the other."

Old Roreld rolled his eyes. "Saf-*er*," he emphasised.

Taeauna shrugged. "What better than that do any of us have? Were you a weaver who never left the back room of some Stormar shop except to trudge up to the loft above of nights, to snore, rather than out wandering wild Falconfar earning your coins and bread with your blade, you'd not be 'safe.' 'Safer' is all any of us can hope for."

"A cheery thought, to be sure," he growled, but gave her a grin. "All right, Lady Bright-Tongue, lead us on to glory. *Safer* glory."

"L-LORD NARMARKOUN," MEREK said uncertainly, halting in a doorway. "I mislike the look of this room, ahead. 'Tis... not safe."

"I tremble," the wizard announced calmly, giving them a smile of merry menace. "I quaver. Proceed, bold Merek. Tarrying now is even less safe. For you."

The men of Darswords stiffened silently. Narmarkoun shared his smile with all of them who dared look at him, and added, "Believe me."

One long-fingered blue hand strayed to his belt, and started to stroke the dagger sheathed there—the knife that had been Taroarin's—almost lovingly.

Merek stared at the smiling wizard for a moment, then bowed his head, hefted the sword in his hand, and without a word started trudging forward through the rubble. Tresker nodded as if agreeing with something that had just been said, and followed, right behind him.

Narmarkoun's smile widened.

THE MAERCRAWN PADDED closer.

Rod fell back, hefting the undluth. All he could think of was another vivid memory, welling up unbidden in his mind wreathed in excitement: a severed but not dripping dragon's head, floating in the air across a valley. The head turned slightly as it drifted along, peering at things as if very much alive.

Among other things, it was watching armored men fleeing it, clanking toward horses they would never reach—as the head opened jaws that gaped just like the maw of the maercrawn, and gave them fire.

The fire roared as it consumed, drowning out screams and all as armor smoked and blackened, and men within it ran in frenzy... and died.

A spell cast by Lorontar had conjured up the great draconic head from a tiny fragment of bone from the skull of a dragon. A spell Rambaerakh had always coveted...

Rod shook his head, trying to push the memory away.

Yes, yes, yes, but how was this going to help him *now?* He was going to be *eaten*, damn it!

"Nressae," he snarled, sudden fury rising to join his fear.

He drew back his hand and dashed it forward again, lashing the creature's gaping jaws with bronzen fire.

The maercrawn sprang into the air, hissing, but Rod was already scrambling in the wake of his strike, fearing the thing would rush and bite at him—and it did, snapping savagely at where he'd been standing.

It came so close that he could feel the air stirring along the side of its jaw, and smell a faint lemongrass scent that must be the beast's natural reek. But Rod wasn't stopping to sniff and marvel.

He kept running along the beast's body, keeping low, waving the undluth back and forth so fire raced along the quivering, floating length of the impossible thing.

In his other hand he waved the staff, finding a use for it: keeping his balance during all of this capering, as he cooked the maercrawn's body.

And it *was* cooking, as surely as if he was grilling it out on his back deck.

Like a maggot he'd once seen in science class, it started to writhe and twist, bending and spasming. He lashed it again with fire, and again, stumbling in loose stone rubble but keeping his feet somehow and not slowing down. He *had* to keep ahead of its turn, *had* to keep moving, or he was dead.

"So this is what warriors do, and this fire-spewer is my sword," he hissed aloud, feeling angry and scared and excited all at once. "*Hah!*"

Rod liked the sound of that defiant yell, so he did it again, seeing the monster shudder now. Where he'd slashed it earlier, lines of tiny flame licked and flickered.

Belatedly he wondered if he should have kept quiet, if there were worse beasts wandering Malragard right now that would hear him and come looking for food.

Then the maercrawn turned toward him, jaws low and closed and shaking in pain and in anger, like a bull lowering its head to charge, and Rod forgot all about whatever noise he might be making, turned, and dashed up and over a heap of rubble, yelling in fear. He ducked into a doorway, turned hard right and spun around to bring the undluth up without even looking at where he'd blundered into and what else might be waiting there for him.

And the maercrawn charged after him, up and over the rubble and plunged through the door to wheel and face him as he slashed it wildly with fire, again and again, just trying to stay alive. He had to last long enough to have a chance to turn and run again, before the massive jaws could close on him.

They clashed together very close to him, and Rod scrambled frantically on, slashing the air with the undluth in a frenzy, trying to slice the maercrawn right apart with the magical fires but knowing somehow that they did little harm to its jaws, and that he had to try to reach its floating body to really hurt it.

Then the stone floor suddenly gave way under him, and he was falling, plunging into darkness with a startled yell—with those backhoe-sized jaws open wide, and plummeting right after him.

TETHTYN FOUND HIMSELF standing on a hard, smooth stone floor, in a fortress chamber with only half a roof. The rest of what should have kept out the sun and rain and stars lay strewn in a great drift of stone that began not a handwidth from his left boot. As he peered at the mound of stone and across it, looking for doors but seeing only half-buried remains of crushed, once grand furniture, Morl suddenly appeared atop the heap.

Blinking, his fellow apprentice wavered, almost fell, waved his hands wildly for balance, slid down the stones a little way, and recovered himself. Tethtyn waved to him and turned to look in the other direction, where three gaping doorways awaited.

Malragard, this was, all around them. Or at least it was supposed to be, and the translocations hadn't taken them astray yet. So this ruin was the tower of the wizard Malraun, Doom of Falconfar for long seasons but now dead. Amid the rubble and the crumbling walls lay hidden much powerful magic, Lorontar was coldly sure in the darkest corners of their minds—if only Morl and Tethtyn had arrived in time.

So here they were, in haste and with their heads ringing with a dark warning to expect lesser wizards, warriors, and the Falcon alone knew who and what else hastening in to slay them and snatch up any magic that might be lying around.

"Seen any magic yet?" Morl asked quietly, wading down through shifting stone to join him—and looking back at it, hard. Nothing stirred under it, or erupted to tower over them in menace, as Tethtyn shook his head.

"No," he murmured, keeping his voice barely above a whisper, and turning to point sharply at two of the doorways.

Morl tilted his head to listen, then nodded, hearing it too.

From just the other side of the wall, beside the right-hand doorway, came the faintest of sounds: a slight shifting of stone on stone, as if something had crouched down on another heap of fallen stone, tensing to spring.

Both novice wizards kept their eyes on the doorway as they stepped apart from each other, shaking their sleeves back and flexing their fingers, readying themselves to hurl some of the spells from Indrulspire. The battle spells, rams of force and invisible blades and jets of scorching flame.

"Come," Morl muttered under his breath. "'Tis the *waiting* I hate. Come at us..."

At that moment a huge, scrambling, catlike beast, bristling with writhing tentacles that ended in jaws, bounded through the doorway and loped toward them, its claws shrieking on the stones.

"Falcon *spit*," Tethtyn gasped, as he spread his hands in a flourish and wreathed it in fire.

They were fast, but almost not fast enough. Lorontar was rising inside both of them as a ball of flame exploded around the loping tentacled thing, and it squalled and started to thrash and roll in helpless agony. The two novice wizards sprang away from it, tracing frantic symbols in the air.

Morl was a shade faster than Tethtyn, which proved valuable when the keening monster came lolloping off the heap of stones and right at him, still burning and mad with pain.

Morl's hasty spell hauled hundreds of stones out from under its racing paws to rise up like a curling wall in front of it, curling over its head and collapsing onto it like a breaking wave, burying it in stones with a thunderous, room-shaking crash.

"Over *there!*" someone shouted, from far off across the ruins, as flames leaped and danced under the stones, and the buried bulk surged, convulsed, and went still.

Move, came the cold command in both their minds, and Morl and Tethtyn obeyed. *Find magic. Avoid battle.*

With one accord, the two wizards rushed to the doorway farthest from where that shout had come from, burst through it, and sprinted across the room beyond. No rubble, no monsters, and an intact roof. Deserted and dimmer than the chamber they'd just come from, with closed, featureless doors in two other walls. Morl and Tethtyn exchanged glances and shrugs, then went to the door straight ahead.

"Up," Tethtyn panted, as they flung it wide and stared into another deserted room—this one dominated a by a grand feasting table with highbacked chairs drawn up along either side of it, and a matching credenza flanking it on its far side. There were closed doors in all three of the room's other walls. "We should look for a stair up. Wizards build towers to get up high, so they can feel safe, and work their magic in those high rooms."

"No dispute," Morl replied breathlessly, "but where *is* such a stair? I saw nothing but sky back there, where the ceiling was gone—no higher floors or side-towers. Do we try to scale a wall, somewhere, to look around?"

"And show ourselves to whoever shouted, back there? What if they have bows?"

"Dung of the Falcon," Morl snapped. "Did you *have* to say that?"

Magic. Seek magic. Go deeper. Little is left of higher.

The voice in their minds was cold and implacable.

"Deeper," they murmured in unison, hurrying again, down the length of the room to the door at the far end. Somewhere behind them, several rooms back, they heard the crash and rattle of the heap of loose stones being disturbed as several creatures charged through it.

Go deeper.

"Yes," Tethtyn replied, as his hand fell on the pull-ring of the door. He wrenched it open, heedless of who or what might be waiting beyond, and found himself staring at a flight of worn stone steps—leading down into darkness.

He plunged down them without hesitation, following them as they curved slightly to the left, with Morl right behind him.

"Where do you think," the tomekeeper from Dlarmarr gasped, as the light failed completely and they had to slow to avoid stumbling and falling into the unknown, "these stairs lead?"

"Down," Tethtyn replied, with sudden glee at his own wit. He laughed aloud—and then stumbled and fell as the steps suddenly ended and his feet found a flat stone floor he wasn't ready for. He crashed onto his face with Morl on top of him, and hastily conjured handfire, scrambling free and rolling over to see—Morl, chuckling wryly at him in the pale light of his own kindling light.

"Well, *that* was certainly graceful," the tomekeeper said. "We did close the door up there, didn't we?"

"No," Tethtyn replied. "Not unless you closed it."

Morl swore softly, then brightened. "There was that spell..."

"*No*," Tethtyn said firmly. "Casting's as tiring as digging; no wonder wizards are all so bad-tempered. Let's save all the energy we have left for battle-spells. We're going to need them."

Morl swore again, and added, "We are. *Look*."

His arm was pointing into the darkness. Tethtyn looked along it, saw the glint of large yellow eyes glaring back at them, and threw his handfire.

Its light exploded in front of a great leonine face, which narrowed its eyes in hatred—and exploded into a great bound forward.

Two frightened wizards hastily stammered out the same word—and two invisible blades plunged through the great cat's half-seen breast while it was still in the air, jaws opening, paws extended.

Instead of landing in a charge that would turn into a bloody rush, the beast shuddered in midair and landed belly-down on the unyielding stone with a great crash, already dying.

Morl and Tethtyn circled around it, running hard into the darkness whence it had come, lit by Morl's handfire as Tethtyn conjured a new flame as fast as he could.

Ahead of them, a musky, heavy beast-smell was growing stronger, and they slowed, still unable to see much of anything. The reek was everywhere, and they were heading right into it.

Something skittered underfoot, and they both froze, aiming their handfire and peering hard.

There was a bone, large and long and well-gnawed, still rocking gently on the stones where Morl had unintentionally kicked it. It looked very like one of the long bones of a man's leg.

They stepped forward even more cautiously, and soon saw other, smaller bones: ribs.

"A lair? Of the thing we killed?" Morl muttered, coming to a stop again.

"Or a whole den full of them, with the rest still waiting for us, somewhere up ahead?" Tethtyn murmured back.

He held up his handfire to see farther—and it seemed to catch fire on the passage wall beside him, tracing a straight vertical line.

Hastily he moved his hand away. The line winked out.

He looked at Morl. Who stared back at him, then shrugged and reached out with his own handfire.

The line reappeared, and Morl extended it by moving his hand along the wall. Tethtyn peered at the route the line was taking along the otherwise smooth stone, then moved his own handfire, and made another line spring into being.

They were tracing the outlines of a door.

Tethtyn looked at Morl again, remembering the last spell they'd looked at together.

"Do it," Morl whispered, and Tethtyn laid his glowing hand flat against the cool stone, and murmured the word he remembered reading. The wall melted away under his palm.

The space beyond the now-empty doorway was dimly lit from above. Flat stone floor, a large, silent room with many open doorways. The mages cast wary looks back up their dark passage of bones, then leaned into the new room to peer around.

As they did so, a man fell down into it from above, and a weird-looking monster—all jaws and smoke—plunged after him.

Their landing shook the room.

Tethtyn's fingers glowed blue, and answering glows flared up from where the man had fallen.

"Magic!" the two wizards shouted, as one—and flung up their hands to hurl the mightiest battle-spells they'd learned.

Chapter Twenty

ROD LANDED HARD, feeling a sharp pain below his left knee and high in his right shoulder and knocking all the air out of his lungs. His abandoned staff clattered loudly on the stone floor nearby, bouncing to a stop.

Not that he had any time to care.

Fire from his undluth seared Rod's leg for a moment, and then he was rolling desperately away across the floor, he knew not where, the rod held out away from the rest of him. He had to get clear—

Of the great stone-rattling *crash* as the maercrawn slammed into the floor just behind him, jaws first.

Its fangs and one jawbone shattered deafeningly, shards cartwheeling through the air, and the beast gave a gurgling, piercing shriek. Then the thrashing, roiling smoke of its body vanished in a roaring burst of purple flames.

The flames spat and spread in a crawling filigree to the corners of the room. By their actinic purple light, Rod saw two young, intent men in a doorway, now rushing forward into the room.

Apprentices of Malraun, or the first wizards to come plundering his tower; they had to be.

And his doom, right here and now, if he didn't get out of here *damned* fast.

He bent his head again and kept rolling, keeping low and trying to ignore his body's protests. There were open doorways everywhere, and right now he just wanted the nearest one on the far side of the room from these new arrivals, one that led not into a dead-end room but out to a passage that could take him—

The door he was heading for was suddenly full of grim-looking men with swords and knives in their hands, wearing motley armor or dirty clothes. Men streaming out into the room, seeing him but paying him no attention as they stared at the wizards—and then charged at them.

Near the rear of this flood of newcomers strode a man—bald, blue of skin, and cold-eyed—who cast a keen glance at Rod Everlar before glaring across the room to spit an incantation at the two mages.

Narmarkoun!

Shit! If it wasn't one Doom of fucking Falconfar, it was another!

Rod desperately slashed at the wizard with his undluth, knowing how feeble its fires must be against a Doom—but grimly aware that he had to do *something*.

Bronze fires lashed cold blue skin, and Narmarkoun stiffened, but didn't even spare Rod and his undluth a glance, keeping all his attention on the two mages across the room. Whatever magic Narmarkoun had cast was already bursting into being around them, with force enough to rock the room. Rod tried not to think of his own pains as he scrambled to his feet—*Christ*, that hurt!—and charged at the blue-skinned man, raking the air with his undluth.

Fire swirled and slashed at Narmarkoun, scorching his head. The blue wizard shook himself, and ducked as if to shield himself from rain, but was still facing the two mages across the room as he muttered another vicious spell, gesturing furiously.

The room rocked again, exploding into bright amber light amid ragged cries, as torn and blackened bodies came tumbling back through the air at Narmarkoun, hurled by the spell.

Most of them, Rod suspected as he kept pounding across the floor in his desperate charge, were Narmarkoun's own men. A human head with no body attached to it plunged past his nose, and a moment later he slipped in gore and found himself looking back across the room, into dying amber flames.

Outlined against them stood the scorched and blackened bones of the maercrawn, reduced to a skeleton but not yet fallen, still moving feebly toward Rod in its dying charge.

In the air above and behind it, Rod's lost staff was spinning wildly, pulling in the flames of Narmarkoun's spell and absorbing them. Beyond it, the two young men were still on their feet and casting spells, their hands shaping the air desperately in front of their pale, frightened faces.

Some of the warriors were still standing. Running, actually, charging at the young wizards in slow motion. Caught in the grip of a magic Rod had never seen, they hung in the air in mid-run, limbs moving inch by treacle inch as everything else roiled and flashed around them.

"Falcon *shit*," Rod murmured in amazement, dragging his gaze from them almost reluctantly to turn back to Narmarkoun. He was doomed, of course, but he might as well be looking at the man killing him, in the instant before they slammed into each other.

He was in time to see a tendril of bright magic form around his wrist, with Narmarkoun's cold blue smile behind it. A tendril that was tightening to crush Rod's wrist and force him let to go of the undluth.

Rod's hand spasmed and opened, but even as the undluth tumbled from his fingers, tongues of flame fading, he knew Narmarkoun's magic would go on tightening until it wrenched his hand off.

With his other hand Rod tugged the lurstar out of his belt, and swept it up to slash through the tendril.

He saw Narmarkoun's sneer falter at the sight of it—and then Rod drove into him, dropping his shoulder like a football player to take the necromancer low in the chest and try to knock him off his feet.

A fresh spell broke over them both, as cold as a torrent of ice water and so bright white it blinded them both for a moment—a moment in which Rod felt the wizard under him slam into the floor, and then his own body sink hard into Narmarkoun with satisfyingly solid force. Then the tendril was gone from his wrist, the lurstar torn from his hand, and the Doom under him was crying out in pain as rings and fine chain bracelets and more tore bloodily free from his blue-skinned body and flew away across the room.

Rod shook his head, fighting to see, and got a distorted, blurry glimpse of the undluth, lurstar, and a score or so of smaller things—rings and the like, some of them trailing thick blue blood—sailing across the room in a cloud that was converging on one of the two young wizards.

The other mage was staring triumphantly at Narmarkoun as he shouted another incantation—and the Doom sobbed and cursed in pain.

Of course, Rod's knees, elbows, and fists might have had something to do with that.

In one of his Cold War thrillers, Rod had written a scene where the hero stopped a guard from shouting a warning by punching him in the throat. Gritting his teeth, he punched Narmarkoun's throat as hard as he could.

It didn't seem to plunge the wizard into agony, or stop his increasingly frenetic struggles under Rod, so Rod did it again. Then he remembered something he'd written in his first Falconfar book: the difficulty wizards would have castings spells correctly once someone had broken all their fingers. And thumbs.

He bent one of the Doom's fingers over backwards against the floor and flung the whole weight of his body atop the man's hand—and felt the snap. Narmarkoun grunted under him, then kicked and wriggled, spilling Rod across the floor.

The Doom whirled to his feet, tall and slender and terrible, and Rod flung himself desperately back at the man's boots, to try to trip Narmarkoun or claw his way up the wizard or—or—

A new spell washed over the scene, a piercing emerald in hue, a rich green that filled the air across the chamber and turned it into an undersea grotto from a children's book, some sun-dappled never-never reef where pirate skeletons danced like seaweed among open chests of gold, and—

Rod's fancy vanished in a teeth-rattling impact with the stone ceiling that would have split his skull open if he hadn't started from flat on his belly on the floor, twisting while being hurled at the ceiling to strike it boots-first, with numbing force.

Elsewhere in the room, others weren't so lucky. Warriors slammed into the ceiling hard enough to break bones loudly.

The spell ended, the emerald cast winked out with dizzying speed and all those who'd struck the ceiling plunged back hard to the floor.

The two young wizards on the far side of the room were grinning openly as they hefted Rod's staff, and undluth, and lurstar.

In the wake of his landing, Narmarkoun writhed and shuddered on the floor right in front of Rod, in obvious agony. Somehow he'd managed to draw his dagger, but all he was using it for at this instant was to repeatedly pound the floor with its pommel in his pain.

"A good time to vanish," Rod whispered, wincing and shuddering. Breathless and fighting the pain, he spun around on his side on the cold stone and crawled as swiftly as he could out the nearest doorway.

As *more* warriors came charging in through that doorway, swords drawn and fear warring with anger in their eyes.

"Taeauna!" Rod gasped, seeing who led them. He stretched out his hand to her—and saw a gleaming blade swinging down at him.

TALYSS TESMER RECLINED at ease on the polished leather of the huge new lounge. Grand and magnificent, the lounge had been meant for the ease of the King of Galath alone.

"So tell me, Annusk," she murmured idly, sipping from the great goblet of nightwine that her watchful manservant kept refilling. "How soon, exactly, is King Brorsavar expected here at Galathgard?"

Lost in the warm caresses of the braethear coiling within him as he knelt at her feet, Klarl Annusk Dunshar left off tenderly licking sweat and journey-dust from between her bare toes with reluctance, to murmur dreamily, "I know not, Lady, for his arrival will be delayed by the visits to loyal nobles he makes along the road, as he journeys from his home castle to here. How long he tarries with each in feast and parley, and what time it takes them to muster their knights and ride on with him, you see. I have sent knights of my own house to many keeps, with orders to depart them and bring word to me of the unfolding royal approach. Yet I very much fear we'll not have time enough to remake this ruin into the grand seat it once was, and will be again."

"How soon?" Talyss asked again, gently.

"More than a dozen days, certainly. Less than two dozen."

She nodded, then pointed wordlessly at the cod-lacings of her breeches—but before the klarl could do more than lift his face hopefully, Belard stepped forward behind him and drove a boot so hard up between Dunshar's legs that the Galathan's body was lifted right off its knees.

The klarl crashed back down onto the floor, quite senseless, and slid on his face down one of Talyss's legs, his limp tongue leaving a damp trail.

She sighed. "Brother, another part of me *does* need licking."

Belard turned back from making sure the door was securely barred, and gave her a nod.

"My job," he said curtly, thrusting the unconscious Galathan aside to take his place on the floor, and apply his teeth to the lacings.

Talyss smiled fondly down at him.

"Bite me once or twice," she murmured. "I've been bad."

"This," Belard growled into her crotch affectionately, "I *had* noticed."

TAEAUNA THREW HERSELF desperately against the old, dark-bearded man running beside her, shoving his sword aside a scant inch or two before it struck Rod's hand.

"*Not* this one!" she commanded sharply. "Leave him be!"

The rest of the warriors with her swept past into the room, and noisily crossed swords with Narmarkoun's surviving warriors, who were hastening to form a ring around their master. The wizard rolled over and croaked out a spell, gesturing one-handed.

In the stamping, hacking heart of the fray, one of Taeauna's warriors plucked up a fallen sword and hurled it across the room—and the young mages ducked away, cursing and abandoning the spells they'd been weaving.

The blade clanged out the door behind them, and one of the wizards darted after it.

"Glorn! '*Ware!*" a warrior shouted, and the bodyguard grunted his thanks as he parried a Darsworder's blade and sent its wielder staggering back with a vicious slash.

A moment later, another Darsworder stiffened and gasped, eyes staring in horror and sword falling forgotten from fingertips. A bone white tendril of mist was rising behind him, probing into the cracks and openings in his worn and ill-fitting armor, as men on both sides of the fight shrank back from him muttering in fear.

Before their eyes, the man shrank and paled and shriveled, his eyes staring hollow cheeks stretched over his skull, mouth locked in a rictus of pain.

He collapsed, and Narmarkoun stood up behind him wearing a cold smile, tall and whole once more, the eerie mist writhing and curling restlessly around his ankles.

The mist spread and reared behind Narmarkoun's men, eager to drain another life—and gloatingly forbidding any thought of retreat.

The Darsworders groaned in despair.

The warriors arrayed against them pressed them with renewed fury. Those who'd fought together in Malraun's bodyguard worked together, Gorongor and Tarlund moving almost as one, Eskeln and Glorn calling warnings and intentions to each other through the flashing steel.

The healed Narmarkoun scowled, spread his hands, and hurled death at them, a storm of phantom swords that felled four men before they could scream.

The two young mages dispelled it, shattering the blades to nothingness, battering Narmarkoun and sending his warriors reeling.

In the aftermath of the dying spells a shimmering door opened in the air in front of the two young mages, revealing an alien sky, gray rainclouds retreating behind skyscrapers.

Narmarkoun's warriors charged at the mages and the door.

Right in front of their blades, the two young men plunged through the magical door and were gone. Their conjured gate winked out with them, and a warrior running towards it slammed into the wall and turned back, shivering in relief.

"Tay!" Rod cried, far across the room, oblivious to everything but his guide and guardian.

She reached down for him, smiling, and Roreld lowered his blade with a nod of understanding.

Then another spell broke over them all, driving the bearded Roreld clear out the doorway and dashing one of Taeauna's other warriors against the walls above it, leaving him limp and broken.

The spell hadn't even been meant for them; it was a thing of unseen hooks flung at Rod Everlar, to snare him and bring him to its caster.

The surviving Doom of Falconfar smiled at Rod in easy menace as the magic swept him helplessly up into the wizard's embrace— and then went right on smiling *inside his mind*, as Narmarkoun bored into his thoughts, recoiling only briefly at all the others' memories he found.

The dark and tattered remnant of Rambaerakh rose inside Rod to resist the Doom's mind—and the man who'd once thought he created Falconfar found himself back on the cold stone floor, sticky blood spreading under his left knee, blinking in bewilderment as Narmarkoun viewed and discarded memories, seeking skyscrapers against gray skies, and where—in Rod's world, the Doom already knew, but precisely *where*—the young mages had fled to.

Rod was helpless, his body moving at Narmarkoun's bidding. Enthralled—*enslaved*—he watched mutely as the Doom plowed deeper, finding what he wanted.

Holding Rod firmly mind to mind, Narmarkoun conjured up a gate of his own, using what Rod remembered of the office towers he could see in the distance from his back deck.

A cool breeze was blowing from behind them, whisking the storm clouds away, and the trodden grass was wet. The lawn smelled of mud and rotting leaves and... they were through, stepping out of Falconfar and into Rod Everlar's backyard, the tall blue wizard glaring around imperiously and Rod following him helplessly.

The writer stumbled abruptly forward, toppling the startled wizard face-first into an old gift from the neighbor's dog, a slobbering Great Dane named Sadly, who got free and roamed from time to time.

Someone had fierce hold of Rod's legs from behind, just below his knee. Someone who was hissing fiercely, in a voice Rod knew well, "Not *this* time, wizard! This man is *mine!*"

Chapter Twenty-One

"**H**o, dogs! Can ye *dance?*"

The fat man bounding from the top of one stout table to the next, swinging his sword lustily at every face that came within reach, roared the challenge across the pillared feasting room of the Stag's Head like a battle cry.

There weren't all that many diners left to hear it. Bodies littered the floor, blood ran wet everywhere, and Garfist Gulkoun seemed to know within the width of his thick left thumbnail just how far the battered sword in his hand could reach, and had laid open more than a few unwary faces; a dozen men had fled staggering or reeling into the night, trailing blood and cursing.

Wherefore the Stag's Head was no longer the usual crowded, happy place of brisk chatter and feasting this night, but had become a battlefield. Cooks cowered in their kitchens or slunk out of side-doors before any swords were pointed their way, the tavernmaster was in no state to cry them nay nor send for what passed for the law in Galath—and the most brutal of the local lawmen, a cold-eyed knight and his score of armsmen, were already on the scene.

Their swords drawn and their tempers dark from having the prospect of their usual hot dumplings, overdone roast boar with hot horseradish, and tankards of ale snatched away from them, the knight and his men had thrice made a move for the kitchens. Thrice they'd lost an armsman at the merest scratch from the bodkin the bony outland woman had plucked from her boot.

"Poison," they'd muttered, and thrown stools, benches, and daggers her way—only to have them all miss their mark, and be calmly collected, the knives laid in a row along the far end of the bar ready for throwing, and the furniture tossed into a growing heap in the kitchen doorway.

Three had gone for her together, expecting her to scream and run when faced by their largest and best armored warriors, but she'd calmly snatched up and thrown her salvaged daggers coolly and accurately, felling one armsman with a dagger hilt-deep in his eye, and another with a knife sunk so surely in his throat that its pommel held up his chin as he choked his life away.

They now left the slimbones alone, and drew together to hack at the fat man atop the tables—who seemed not at all fearful of their numbers, but merely amused.

"I said take him," Sir Raenor ordered curtly. Reluctantly his armsmen shouldered forward again, swords and daggers held high, acutely feeling their lack of decent shields, and made to clamber up onto tables.

It was expected that the fat man would come racing along the tabletops to stab any man trying to join him atop them, and the armsmen on the floor drew together around every fellow making the ascent, blades ready to protect them—but Garfist Gulkoun had tired of doing the expected years ago. He was down off the tables at the far end to pluck up stools and benches, and hurl them merrily over the tables at the men.

They had been thrown his way earlier, and he was careful to use furniture that was cracked and splintered—and so disintegrated as it struck the armsmen. They reeled under this assault, then roared and rushed the tables, vaulting or overturning them as they came.

The chaos that ensued was no surprise to anyone—nor was Garfist's capering back and forth along the line of his foes, his sword flicking out to open throats or slash faces as he hastened.

"Always be merry," he sang, "never be glum! Her lips like a cherry, as red as her—"

An armsman sprang down on him from behind with a roar, arms spread to capture and pinion Garfist's sword and dagger, but even as his landing ended the fat man's song in a grunt, it became apparent that the outlander had seen the peril, and at the last instant neatly tucked his sword under his arm to jut up behind him—and gut his attacker.

The armsman fell away, blood spilling out of him. Garfist kicked his way clear without looking back, staggered along the line of tables once more, and with a slash of his sword swept both ankles out from under another armsman who was just gaining a tabletop with a roar of triumph.

The man crashed to the floor, screaming and clutching at his half-severed foot. Garfist trod on his face hard, in a bound that took him back atop the tables, knocked aside another sword, and sprang down into the open space in the midst of his milling foe.

Therein he landed—and not by chance—right in front of Sir Raenor, who shouted a challenge, waving his jeweled blade with a flourish.

The toe of Garfist's boot caught him not in the knight's ornate armored codpiece but *just* behind it, driving up and in with force enough to launch his foe forward in a wild lunge that allowed Garfist to draw his dagger across the knightly throat with calm precision.

Sir Raenor slumped to the floor and into obscurity, and the surviving armsmen all shouted in alarm—however hated their employer had been, the custom established under King Devaer was clear: when knights or nobles were slain by anyone except a wizard or another noble, their bodyguards or armsmen were held personally accountable for the death—and someone's wild sword-swing sent a flaming lantern off its hook and spinning through the air to crash at the foot of the common room's one drapery, an old, much-patched, and rotten window-cloth that burst into flame.

Garfist and Iskarra had both seen blazes like it often enough to know what fate awaited the Stag's Head. They started sprinting for the front doors, Gar waving his sword wildly to clear himself some running room, and Isk sweeping up her salvaged knives in a bundle, heedless of their edges, so as to have something to hurl at her assailants as she fled.

Halfway to his goal, with armsmen converging on him from all sides, Garfist abruptly stopped, spun around and gutted the nearest man, let the next two run past him in their haste, and slashed open a fourth man's forehead, blinding him with blood streaming into his eyes.

"Isk?" he roared. "Get out!"

"*Brilliant* idea!" his partner called back, as she raced down the room. "So favored by the Falcon am I, to have a man handy to command me into doing what I would *never* have thought of, if I'd been all alone!"

The front wall of the room, near the drapery struck by the lantern, was now aflame, and the armsmen entangled in the wreckage by the kitchen were starting to cough and curse.

Iskarra reached Garfist's side, stabbing her way through the knot of men surrounding him, and warned, "Lots of witnesses, Old Ox!"

"Aye, but I'm not leaving men to burn to death," he growled back. "Horrible way to greet the Falcon."

His partner ducked under a thrust and hamstrung the man swinging it in one smooth movement that then brought her bobbing to her feet behind Garfist. She turned her back on him to deal with an armsman trying to run him through from behind, and asked, "So?"

"So we'll have to slit every throat and spit every paunch offered to us," he replied merrily, watching yet another armsman back away and try to flee—only to encounter his own fellows and get cut down.

"You *know* there're too many to butcher them all," Isk pointed out, as they sidestepped in unison, trying to move closer to the front doors. "Just *look*—"

The tip of an armsman's sword caught her side and spun her against him, bleeding and gasping—and Garfist decided he didn't have time for his foes, any more. He snatched Isk up like a doll and swung her high around his head, her boots crashing into half a dozen faces, then ran right over the armsman in front of him, trampling him to the ground, and charged for the entrance.

The fat man had to tuck his partner under his arm as he reached those double doors, and twist around to smash the doors open with his shoulder.

He staggered two steps out into the road and dropped her, backing away from the men who'd followed him and swinging wildly at them.

Isk bounced in the dirt with a shriek, scrambled up and cried, "Old king or no king!"

Garfist bellowed the words a breath later, as strong and slender arms were already reaching down to pluck them aloft—leaving the dozen men of Galath who were bursting out of the inn staring up into the sky in dumbfounded fury.

As flames started to crackle angrily out of the inn behind them, and winged women bore their quarry into the sky, the Galathans found themselves standing in the road with no tankards, no feast, and no one to fight.

One of them spat into the road-dust and snarled, "Pah. Another good evening ruined."

"HAH!" GORONGOR CRIED triumphantly, striking aside a parry and slicing hard into his foe's neck. "That's *you* done, and down!"

The Darsworder he'd been fighting staggered away and fell, sword clanging to the floor as he tried to stem the fountaining blood. Gorongor turned away.

"That's the last of them," Tarlund grunted, at his elbow. "Except for the wizard himself, of course."

"Huh," Eskeln puffed, clutching at his arm where blood was seeping from between his fingers. "It's *always* 'except for the wizard, of course.'"

"The blueskin? Where's he gotten to?" Glorn asked them, gasping as he pushed out from under the bodies of two men he'd slain, and trying to wipe their blood out of his eyes.

Tarlund pointed, and they all turned and looked down the room.

The mage was striding away from them, stepping through a conjured door in midair that glowed with the gray light of a stormy day on the far side.

"Oh, Falcon *shit*," Gorongor whispered wearily, lowering his sword.

Through the magical opening, the warriors could see a lot of cloudy sky, and rising against it several strange, smooth rectangular towers, dark and slender and gleaming. It was an otherwhere none of them knew, or could even guess at from bards' tales.

Another man, the stranger who'd been with the maercrawn, was lurching along right behind the blue-skinned wizard—and as they watched, Taeauna, hissing fiercely, sprang forward to tackle the stranger around the legs, her abandoned sword clattering on the floor in her wake. Her dive took her through the glowing opening.

Which promptly winked out, snatching all three of them away from the watching warriors.

Leaving them in the trap-filled depths of ruined Malragard, staring at empty air where the gray-sky glow had been, and then at each other across the burned bones of the maercrawn and the sprawled bodies of their dead comrades and the warriors of Darsword.

Five men exchanged slow, grim glances. Of the ten who'd come here with Taeauna, they were all that was left.

Old Roreld, and four who'd been part of Malraun's bodyguard. Eskeln, Gorongor, Tarlund, and Glorn.

They stared at each other until Roreld broke the silence.

"Well," he growled, looking at the others sourly, "*now* what?"

THE BREEZE DIED a little, but the cold remained, and the grass around them was still drenched.

Not that any of it mattered much, with Narmarkoun rolling frantically out from under Rod and hissing out an evil-sounding spell through the old, graying dung decorating his blue nose and cheeks.

He slapped Taeauna across the face as she let go of Rod to grab frantically for the dagger at her belt—and just like that, strain though she might, she couldn't move.

By the Falcon, she could barely *breathe*. The pain was intense—it felt as if every muscle in her body was going into spasm, each one locking up after the next, relaxing just a trifle, then clenching again.

Taeauna gasped, or tried to, fighting to draw breath, helplessly frozen with her head up to stare now at nothing but a backyard, as Narmarkoun touched Rod and froze him, too.

The wizard rolled them both over with the murmured words, "Can't have you two dying on me for lack of air. Yet." Then he calmly wiped his face clean on the grass, sat up, looked at the house behind them, apparently saw nothing of immediate interest there, and turned to peer around the yard.

Watching and listening for anyone who might have seen us, Taeauna thought, her eyes fixed on the side of Narmarkoun's intent face.

Breathing was easier—a little—without the weight of her own body pressing down on her lungs, but it was taking all her strength to do it. She wouldn't be doing anything else while this magic lasted.

There was a weight on her right leg, just above the ankle. It must be Rod Everlar's foot, lying across hers. It was as heavy and unmoving as a rock. The only things that were moving, that Taeauna could see, were the racing gray clouds overhead, and the wizard's head, turning this way and that like a hawk's.

Narmarkoun seemed to satisfy himself that no watchers were nearby, and no alarm was about to be raised. He turned, thrust two of his fingers into the nostrils of the helpless Lord Archwizard of Falconfar, and lifted Rod's head to face his. The Doom's face went curiously blank.

He's plundering Rod Everlar's mind, Taeauna told herself. She dimly felt his thoughts being thrust aside as a ruthless will shoved and probed, ever deeper. She was sensing Rod's mind with her own somehow; something about this spell must be...

The feeling abruptly ended and the wizard let go of Rod, letting him fall back onto the grass. Then Narmarkoun straightened and strode purposefully down the yard.

He soon returned, triumphantly holding up a slim, dark little metal box between his thumb and forefinger and smiling down at Rod. Taeauna could read two of the words on it: "Soothing Lozenges."

What were Soothing Lozenges?

"Just where you remembered," Narmarkoun murmured, "safe in the crack in the back corner fencepost. Which is almost falling down now, it's so rotten. *Anyone* could have found this. Idiot." He turned the box so it was level, thumbed its sliding lid half-off, drew out a key, and gave it a cold smile.

Then he looked at Taeauna, and his smile sharpened. "Struggle not, Aumrarr. I have plans for you both."

Rod made a thick, incoherent sound, as if he was trying to speak.

The wizard looked back at him, shook his head dismissively, and murmured, "Not so mighty a Lord Archwizard after all. Certainly not much of a keep, this."

Another sound came from Rod, but it made no more sense than the first one.

The wizard smiled down at him almost indulgently.

"Don't run off now," he added mockingly, and strolled out of Taeauna's sight, heading for the house.

She lay on her back staring at the stormy sky, unable to even curse.

Chapter Twenty-Two

I T WAS AN old house, and had real shutters. Someone had drawn and fastened them across the windows, probably to discourage break-ins.

Narmarkoun learned that much from Rod Everlar's mind before he reached the steps up to the back deck. "Steps" was a rather grand term, he thought, for two railless planks leading up onto a platform, all made of mossy, green-tinged wood. On the deck was a round metal table, painted white with streaks of brown rust where the paint was peeling off it, a large pot that looked as if a plant had died in it some time ago, and a rusting black metal bulk on legs that Everlar thought of as "my old grill; long past time to replace it, but I like it, damn it."

The last Doom of Falconfar warily passed the old grill—it looked like something you'd animate into a clumsy but fearsome guardian—and strode straight across the deck to the back door.

Rod's spare house key stuck on the first try, but Narmarkoun knew enough about locks in Falconfar not to force it and break the key off in the lock. He jiggled it instead, and tried again.

Still stuck. He withdrew the key, warmed it in his mouth, then spat on it and tried it again.

This time it worked—whereupon it was the *door's* turn to stick. Narmarkoun sighed, worked the lock once or twice while thrusting at the door with his knee, then made sure he'd left it unlocked, took the key out, and put his shoulder to the door. Solidly.

He was here to find one thing, before all else: whatever magic this fool Rod Everlar had used—*must* have used—to make his Shaping reach from world to world. Whether the dolt had known he was using magic or not, he must have been. No one as weak-willed and as utterly *ignorant* as this Rod Everlar could send Shapings across a good-sized lake, let alone to an otherwhere. A gate *must* have been involved.

And he wanted it. More than that, he wanted to make sure neither Everlar nor any other bumbling idiot of this Earth happened across it, and did something that might threaten the imminent triumphant rule of the last surviving Doom of Falconfar, over all the Falcon Kingdoms and every desolate part of the wilderlands beyond. Every last dragon-haunted peak and frozen waste of it.

For he was Narmarkoun, the *real* Lord Archwizard of Falconfar.

Soon that would be truth, not merely a boastful title. Soon he would rule every last lord and lady of Falconfar, not just the Tesmers of Ironthorn.

If, of course, he fared well, in the days ahead. Which meant avoiding mistakes, and doing things right.

He shrugged, unsheathed Taroarin's dagger, and cast a spell he'd not used for years, that would send it floating ahead of him, to strike at any threat. Almost certainly unnecessary, but caution was best. A small mistake avoided, a small thing done right.

Under the goad of his thought, the dagger floated into the gloom ahead, point first, and he strode after it.

He moved cautiously, but expected to meet no one. The air was stale, hanging heavy and silent, the house dark and dusty. It felt empty, long deserted.

Books, books everywhere... There were bookshelves in every room, and books stacked atop them, and in untidy piles in front of them, and on chairs beside them, littering the place as if it was the home of an old, befuddled wizard.

No one would have so many books but a mage, or someone hoping to find magic hidden in books. Perhaps Everlar had succeeded, and what he sought was in one of these small, dim, cluttered rooms, hiding in the semblance of a book. Everlar's mind had told him there was nothing to be found, that there *was* no magic—or hadn't been, until a wounded Aumrarr had fallen onto his bed, with Dark Helms right behind her—but that meant nothing.

Less than nothing. This Rod Everlar was simply too stupid to recognize magic for what it was. *Something* must be augmenting his feeble Shapings, to make them reach to other worlds...

He just had to find it.

"DUNSHAR, A FEW of us are displeased by what we've been hearing of your progress here in Galathgard," the burly man in the shining armor and magnificent scarlet cloak growled, as he shouldered his way past the stammering klarl. "King Brorsavar is going to be here *much* sooner than you think, and right on his heels will come all the rest of us; there's not a knight in Galath that wants to miss old Bror's first royal court. Yet I hear you've not even yet rebuilt the kitchen chimneys, nor readied so much as a single bedchamber, and frankly, some of us are beginning to think you're just not the man for the—"

He blinked. "And just who by the Falcon are *you?*"

Velduke Mespur Hallowhond had rather been looking forward to humbling Klarl Annusk Dunshar, whom he'd never liked much. He had not expected to stride into an inner chamber and find a waist-down-naked—though undeniably beautiful, fair of face and, er, limbs—lass, reclining at ease on a lounge that by its size and magnificence could only have been meant for the royal backside. A doxy, moreover, who now had the effrontery to incline her head to him in regal greeting—for all the world as if she thought herself his equal! As she regarded him, her slight smile held not the slightest trace of fear at all.

"This is the Lady Talyss Tesmer, of Ironthorn," Klarl Dunshar said stiffly, hurrying around Hallowhond to interpose himself between the glowering velduke and the serenely smiling woman on the lounge. "Who has come here to—"

"To be your bedpretty, by the looks of things," the velduke grunted. "I know, *I* know, the pressures of such hectic work, all the demands on you and the hardships of luring good masons out here into this monster-haunted wilderlands with too little coins to entice them. Good thing you managed to find coins enough to pay *her*, now, isn't—"

Dunshar's dagger-thrust was low, brutal, and swift. He tugged his blade viciously upwards, right in under Hallowhond's ribs, ere he pulled it out and stepped back to let the noble crash to the floor.

The klarl paled, mouth falling open as he stared down at the fallen velduke, aghast. "What have I *done?*"

"I'm wondering the very same thing," Mespur Hallowhond snapped, scrambling up and drawing his sword. "Very stupid of you, Dunshar. *Fatally* stupid, in fact. But then, if you'd had any brains, you'd have expected any velduke riding across Galath right now, what with all the troubles, to be magically protected against swords and daggers."

Sword raised, Hallowhond advanced menacingly on the stumbling klarl. He set himself to lunge, but abruptly reeled and toppled, crashing onto his face, sword clattering from his hand.

There wasn't much left of the back of the velduke's head.

Belard Tesmer looked at the blood-drenched stone block in his hands, sighed, then let it fall almost regretfully onto the bloody mess it had caused. "Shoddy mason-work. The curse of every hasty rebuilding job. *Such* an unfortunate accident."

He bent down, his dagger hissing out, and cut off one of Hallowhond's fingers, sporting a ring that had begun glowing.

"So much for magical protection," he murmured. "If we must speak of fatally stupid behavior, my lord velduke, ignoring a mere servant standing behind you as you draw your sword and start to threaten folk with it is a striking example."

He calmly tossed away the bloody finger, then held up the dripping ring. "Useful little trinket. Talyss?"

"You wear it, brother," she replied with a sweet smile. "If you continue this career of going around killing Galathan nobles in front of witnesses..."

She lifted a languid hand to indicate the white, shaking Dunshar. "You're going to be needing it more than me."

ROD LAY VERY still, trying to think of the storm blowing away and how strange it felt to so suddenly be back here, in his own backyard, instead of wandering through ruined Malragard back in Falconfar...

He knew the mind-link was still firm and strong; he could feel Narmarkoun's mind at work as the wizard prowled the dusty, deserted house, peering alertly at everything. Thank the Falcon, Narmarkoun's attention was entirely on his exploration right now, but...

Rod was discovering just how hard it was to *not* think of something.

Something exciting, that he could feel happening to him, slowly and tinglingly. Something that so far was obviously, as writers say, "unbeknownst to" Narmarkoun.

Something he could tell, from the faint wet whisperings of the grass beside him, where Taeauna lay, was affecting her too.

Evidently some sorts of magic faded very quickly on Earth, magic that a wizard of Falconfar trusted in, because on Falconfar it lasted much longer. The muscle-lock was failing already, lessening its grip as the wizard moved from the nearer rooms at the back of the house to front rooms farther away.

Rod fought to turn his head and look at Taeauna—and managed to shift the section of sky he was staring at, moving his nose a few inches. It felt like shoving against a concrete wall, and seemed to take a straining eternity—enlivened, in the back of his mind, by Narmarkoun's observations, where the wizard had just about finished his first foray around the ground floor, and was debating climbing those open stairs to the few rooms above, or descending into the basement ("the cellars" to Narmarkoun, of course) first. Opening and examining all these books would come later, after more immediate concerns—such as anyone who might be hiding in the house—were dealt with. The mind-link let him see nothing of the wizard's thoughts beyond the most lasting and general images, though that might change if Narmarkoun turned his attention back to Rod, which was very much *not* wanted, and—

Something loomed up against the gray sky, very close by, and looked down at him. Taeauna!

"Tay!" he tried to cry, but managed only a wordless mumble. His jaws felt stuck together, as rigid as stone.

"Hush," she whispered soothingly, leaning close to his ear. "We're together again at last, yes. Lord Rod, I have missed you just as much as you have missed me."

Sounds like dialogue from a bad romance novel. Unthinkingly he tried to say that thought out loud, but his mouth was still frozen.

"Yes, the wizard's magic is fading," Taeauna murmured, as cool and crisp as any police officer Rod had ever heard, "but it may rise again when he comes back closer to us. If this gives us any chance for freedom at all, that chance is *now*. Come."

A stiff and fumbling hand took hold of Rod's shoulder and hauled on it, hard, rolling him over onto his side in the wet grass. Taeauna gave him the briefest of smiles and kept on tugging at him, rolling Rod right over onto his face—his nose meeting the wet lawn—and then, faster now, up to face the sky again.

Over, and again. Over and again; she was doing it! Dragging him away down the yard...

Rod grinned, thinking he was seeing more of his yard, close up, than he had in months. *Years.*

It was frighteningly slow, and Taeauna was gasping and panting as if hurling all her strength into back-breaking labor—but then, she was, wasn't she?—but they were moving.

Rod found he could now move his fingers, though he still couldn't feel them, and turn his head, too. Most heroic.

Well, he'd always known he was no hero, just a man who wrote about heroes. Yet thanks to Taeauna's dogged pulling, all of his movements were coming a little faster now... and he was losing the helpless feeling at last.

"Guide me, Lord Rod," she gasped suddenly. "Down to the end of your yard we must go, yes, but whither then?"

Rod tried to answer, but all that came out was a frustrating sequence of grunts.

Taeauna rolled her eyes, set her jaw, and grimly but briskly rolled him over twice or thrice more. "Guide me."

"Roll me," Rod croaked back, finally able to move his jaws and tongue properly; or almost properly.

"Lord Rod," she said almost sternly, obeying him twice more, "we don't have much time."

"For me to play the idiot, you mean?" Rod managed a smile. "Right down at the back, right-hand side, there's a gate. It opens right onto a little trail behind all the houses, where all the neighbors walked their dogs. The other side of that, forest, for quite a ways, down to the creek."

"Thick forest? Then we head down. Unless your neighbors—"

"No help there. Nice enough, but none of them own guns, and not one is likely to be much use against an angry wizard. They won't even believe he can use magic on them—until he does, and it's too darned late."

He could crawl on his own, now, and Taeauna dragged him to his feet and into a sort of stumbling run, that took him maybe eight strides at her shoulder before he fell onto his hands and knees. Yet those eight strides had covered a lot of ground.

"Again," he gasped, and without a word she hauled him up, into another shambling, off-balance run. This one took them clear down to the end of the yard.

It was a big backyard, overgrown by Rod's feeble attempts at a wildflower garden on one side and a vegetable garden on the other, both long untended. The back gate was just as he remembered it. Aluminum frame with bars and chain-link fencing stretched across them, held closed—no lock—by a bendable metal latch set into an old and rotten wooden post.

Rod glanced over at the corner post, where Narmarkoun had found his spare door key. It was just as ruinous as the wizard had said. One of the young wild trees growing on the outside of his fence had been blown over and fallen on the fence, bending it down, pulling the old thing right apart...

"Lord Rod," Taeauna said urgently, in his ear, "I know this place is dear to you, but our lives are dearer to us both, surely? May I suggest—"

Rod turned, gave her a grin, and tried to kiss the end of her nose. It might have worked better if she hadn't been pulling back and away from him, and hadn't looked so irritated. "Suggest," he told her. "In fact, command. It works better when you just tell me what to do."

Taeauna contrived to somehow look amused and irritated at the same time.

"Lord Archwizard Rod," she said, almost severely—and then stopped, with her mouth open.

For one horrible moment Rod thought Narmarkoun had just cast a spell on her, or Lorontar had arisen from somewhere in the depths of her mind to take her over, but then she pursed her lips, shook her head, and began again.

"Rodrel," she said, "I know not what to do. We cannot run and hide from a wizard who is linked to your mind; he will always know where you are and what you are doing—and see and hear everything you do if he wants to, even use you against me.

Close-standing trees that he knows not well can keep him from translocating at will to us, and hamper him in blasting us with battle-spells, but I *cannot* lead you through heavy forest if you are bound and gagged and blindfolded!" She spread her hands in exasperation.

Rod tried to check on Narmarkoun without thinking about him, but found it nigh impossible, so he snatched his mind away again. Whatever the wizard was doing, he was paying no attention to his helpless captives. Yet.

He nodded to Taeauna. "To say nothing of the fact that you don't have anything to tie or gag or blindfold me with," he agreed.

She gave him a disgusted look, and tugged at what she was wearing, miming that it could easily come off to be used as bindings on him.

"Geez, Rod, I had no idea you were into that sort of stuff," a hesitant but all too familiar voice said, from behind the dark, thick cedar that grew just outside the gate.

Up until that moment, Rod Everlar had thought only people in books jumped straight up into the air when they were really startled.

But for a beginner, he managed it very well.

Chapter Twenty-Three

WHEN HE CAME down again, Rod was facing the right way to stare.

He knew the owner of that voice, who thankfully was alone, and just as Rod remembered him: short, balding, with an untidy goatee, blue-stubble cheeks, thick black spectacles, and one of those bad suits he always wore, summer or winter, rain or shine. He was also wearing brown, buckled rubber boots, and carrying a crumpled, empty plastic bag.

It was Max, all right. He stood blinking through those thick, smudged glasses not at Rod, but at Taeauna.

"And who's this *lovely* lady? Ma'am, I'm Max—ah, Maxwell Sutherland. Ah, I'm in real estate. And I'm Rod's next-door neighbor."

Max turned his head back to Rod. "Speaking of which: Rod, where've you *been?* The cops and everyone were looking for you, and—"

"Mister Sutherland," Taeauna said crisply, opening the gate and advancing on Rod's neighbor, "do you have a dog? A large dog?"

Max looked a little alarmed. He stepped back a pace.

"You, ah, you *like* dogs?" he asked, a certain apprehension rising in his eyes.

"Not in conjunction with gags or blindfolds or play involving such things, if that's what you mean," Taeauna replied, as crisply as any severe schoolteacher. Then she repeated patiently, "Do you have a dog?"

"Well, yes, but it's not an outside dog. That is, it's really Muriel's—that's my wife—and it's a Chihuahua. Honeybell, we

213

call it, and it—er, she, but she's fixed, you know?—very much feels the cold, so she wears these little pink sweaters that Muriel knits her, but she *never* goes outside, and—"

"*Fascinating*," Taeauna said, witheringly. "*Thank* you, Mister Sutherland."

It was a clear dismissal, but Max merely blinked at her for a moment and then swiveled his head back to look at Rod.

"So, uh, Rod, where've you been?"

"Away," Rod replied brightly, and managed a wide smile. He really didn't know what to say. Everyone on the street thought Max was more than a little crazy, but the man was a blabbermouth, and if the police had been—

"The cops searched your house," Max told him excitedly, almost as if he could read Rod's mind, "and it's all locked up—I guess you found that out, huh?—because the lawyers for your creditors and relatives are all fighting about it. They said you couldn't be declared dead yet. And they were right, because here you are— and aren't! Dead, I mean, that is!"

"And here I aren't," Rod agreed. "So far, at least."

Taeauna reached back through the open gate, took firm hold of Rod's arm, and started towing him through it.

"I—uh—I hope you don't mind," Max said hastily, holding up the empty plastic bag. "I've—uh—I've been coming over and, uh, harvesting your vegetables sometimes. I mean, it seemed a shame to let them go to waste, and—"

"Max," Rod told him, "that's great. I'm *glad* you did that. I've been very busy, very far away, and it's good to hear that they ended up on your plate. You just go right on doing that, because I may not be back again for a while, maybe a long while, and—"

"Oh," Max said, and looked back at Taeauna. "'Cause of her, huh?"

"Well, yes and no," Rod replied, as the Aumrarr drew him to her side and started across the path, into the trees. "We've still got a lot to do together, you see, and—and—"

The jet of flame that roared down the garden then crisped two trees and a bush, set the old, wet posts and scaling-paint boards of the back fence aflame, and missed Rod himself only because the fire had also flared up in his mind—driving him to fall to his knees, to clutch at his head.

Narmarkoun was standing on the back deck, tall and terrible, his eyes blazing with anger. Letting fall an unfolded, yellowing piece of paper that looked like one of Rod's phone bills, and thrusting his dagger back into his belt-sheath, he raised his hands into the air, and started to spit out a long and ugly sounding incantation.

During which Taeauna plucked Rod bodily to his feet and raced into the trees with him, holding him up by main strength.

Max Sutherland stared not at her or his departing neighbor, but at the blue wizard. He listened to the incantation for just long enough to let his mouth drop open and his eyes follow the path of the now-vanished flame—a line of blackened tree trunks topped with ash, where all their upper branches were now simply *gone*—right down the garden, and started to shake.

A moment later, he wet himself, started gobbling like a turkey, turned, and fled wildly.

Right into a tree, slamming into it face first, hard.

He ended up on the ground, nose streaming blood, but picked himself up with remarkable speed, managed to catch—out of sheer habit, without really looking—both halves of his broken glasses as they fell from his nose, and ran blindly on, pounding past his own backyard and the Jenkins' and the Smiths' and the old Miller place that no one lived in now, dwindling into the distance.

GARFIST SHIFTED HIS behind to get clear of a particularly uncomfortable knob of rough wood—and almost lost his grip on the tree for the third time.

"Sit still, and you won't be in quite so much danger of falling," Juskra's voice came down to him, from the branch above. It did not sound all that sympathetic. "Tell me, when you were so enthusiastically killing patrons back in yon tavern, Gulkoun, did you happen to notice any badges or blazons, or hear any names? Sir this or Lord that?"

"Why?" the fat man growled, trying to find a more comfortable stretch of bough to sit on. "Are ye keeping score in some game of count-the-surviving nobles?"

"Yes, as it happens," she replied crisply. "And before you ask why, know this: it's just one more of those crazy, mysterious things Aumrarr do. That'd be those same Aumrarr who flew you to safety."

"Call *this* safety?" Garfist asked gloomily, looking down. It looked to be a long, long way to the ground.

"And the same Aumrarr you'll need to depart your current perch—er, *refuge*—safely," she added.

Garfist peered up at her. "No," he said sharply. "No, I did not. My killing enthusiasm must have gotten the better of me. Being a mere flawed human, an' all that. Does it matter?"

"Eventually. If they all go on behaving like arrogant idiots, Galath will run out of knights and nobles some day."

"Ye think so? Myself, I'm not thinking any realm'll ever run out of such pests unless they're all rounded up and put to the sword at once, every last one of them. They *breed*, y'see. All of them, hey? D'ye by chance wager on this, ye wingbitches?"

Dauntra laughed merrily, from the lower branch she was sharing with Iskarra. "Don't tempt us, Gar. Don't tempt us."

"Well, 'twouldn't be fair," Garfist growled. "Ye Aumrarr kill folk and suchlike, too. Ye can make a wager and then go out an' bring something about that ye've just bet on happening. *That's* hardly fair."

Juskra snorted. "You're how old, fat man? And you think life is fair? Well, you *are* an idiot."

STRIDING DOWN THE garden, Narmarkoun ignored the fleeing human utterly. What cared he for any hue and cry raised in this otherwhere?

His attention was bent, with the piercing stare of the hunting eagle, on a storm of hissing murmurs and crashing noises in the trees. They were thicker than he'd thought, almost a swamp thicket of bushes and dead saplings, and his storm of force-arrows might well do little harm to anyone who got down low, quickly enough.

The spell was fierce but brief, and he stood at the very edge of the trees and listened hard, hearing its brief echoes die away but trying to hear something else. Everlar's mind was still alive, but the fool was holding his hands over his eyes, or the Aumrarr was holding *her* hands over them, so he could learn nothing beyond the mere survival of the so-called Lord Archwizard.

Then he heard what he'd been expecting: faint but repeated crackling sounds as two bodies rose cautiously and started moving through dead leaves and fallen branches. Moving away from him, of course.

He took a step back, not even bothering to curse, and with unhurried care cast another, longer spell.

This time, the faint forest sounds coming back to him included a chorus of ringing clangs. Narmarkoun smiled faintly, picturing what he got to see moments later, albeit blurred and confusedly, through borrowed eyes: his magic was working, snatching at every last piece of metal they wore or carried, pulling it irresistibly back toward him. Small or loose metal things—daggers riding in unstrapped sheaths, keys and coins in unfastened pouches— would be torn away and whirled off into the forest, flying or bouncing or rolling toward him. To stop right about *there*, where the reach of the magic ended. If either of them wore armor under their clothing, or didn't get rid of all their daggers in time, they'd be hauled back to him as surely as fish caught in a net.

Probably about as naked, too; this magic often ripped buckles and pins right out of the target's clothes.

He retreated a few steps, to give himself time to cast whatever spell might be best, and waited, smiling coldly. Did these idiots know *nothing* about magic? Did they honestly believe they could hide from a wizard—much less a Doom of Falconfar—who was linked to the mind of one of them? They'd have done better to have split up, to have the Aumrarr lurk and slink and try to slay him with a lucky dagger-thrust, while Rod the Shaper played unwitting lure.

Not a challenging role, after all.

Everlar, so far as he could tell, hadn't moved since throwing himself to the ground when the spell erupted. The Shaper was still cowering back there in the trees, wondering how to hold his pants up now that his belt was gone. He was whimpering in fear, a singing dread that left him trembling.

Narmarkoun's lip curled. Lord Archwizard of Falconfar, indeed. A child could be more capable. Shriek and quake in terror, little mindless thing, as Narmarkoun comes for you...

A branch danced, right in front of his nose, and the Aumrarr burst out from behind it, leaping right at him. She was half-naked, and was whirling the torn remnants of her jerkin with both hands like a cloak as she screamed, "Rod! *Now!*"

In the wake of that shriek, she fell on Narmarkoun like a whirlwind, clawing and kicking and—and *biting*, damn her!

Narmarkoun tried to snap out a spell that would hurl her away, but her flailing jerkin caught him in the teeth. He couldn't see, couldn't hear, everything was a confused roaring. Punches rained bruisingly on him, and he was choking, his mouth full of wadded cloth and what felt like her fingers thrusting more in deeper.

He bit down hard, snarling in satisfaction—only to choke in sudden agony as she slammed the edge of her hand down on his throat. He tried to scream, then tried to sob, but couldn't find breath for either...

"B-b-but the Lady Talyss—"

Klarl Annusk Dunshar's protest was as frantic as it was feeble.

Belard gave him a tight, steely smile and murmured into Dunshar's sweating, quivering face, "—has *changed her mind*. Is there something wrong with your hearing, Dunshar? Must I find a slightly less deaf noble of the realm to take over rebuilding fair Galathgard? For if I must, that would seem to make you... expendable."

"Nononono! Wah-huh-who would—would—"

"Lick her toes clean? I'm sure a kingdom this large must hold *someone* else with a tongue, and knees to crawl on, hmm?"

He tightened his grip on the lace that covered Dunshar's gorget, gave the dolt a good shake—and then let go disgustedly, allowing the klarl's limp body to crash heavily to the floor. The fair flower of House Dunshar was out cold, and had wet himself, to boot.

"This is all becoming steadily more tiresome," a familiar voice murmured, from behind him.

"Sister, this was your plan, remember?" he replied, turning with a smile. "Blame none of its more tiresome moments on me."

In a snarling, seething frenzy Narmarkoun kicked out and rolled over, getting momentarily free of the Aumrarr. Clawing his way to his feet, he sprinted blindly away, treading on the cloth hampering him with his first stride, wrenching his head around over his shoulder, eyes watering too hard to see much more than a blur.

The closest shape was the Aumrarr, he knew, and she was *right* behind him. Narmarkoun kept right on running, glancing bruisingly off a fencepost and thankfully on through the open gate, back toward the house.

The house! In there, she could only come at him through the doorway, where he could turn and hurl quick spells through, to thrust her back. It would be his fortress while he prepared the right magics to deal with her permanently. Then it would become his shelter and Everlar's prison, while he leisurely searched it for its hidden magics and decided how best to leash this otherwhere and make it do his bidding, as he set about conquering Falconfar at last.

Lorontar was the only impediment left to overcome, the only—

Something fell hard on his legs, toppling him helplessly into a face-first skid in wet grass.

Falcon *take* this Aumrarr! She'd done it again! Even as Narmarkoun fought to get onto his knees so he could be back up and running, she was clawing and clutching at him like a hawk, fresh pain flooding him at her every blow.

"Taeauna!" Everlar was shouting, from not far behind. "Taeauna! I'm here! I'm—*urkkh!*"

Narmarkoun kicked out behind him viciously, struck something solid and heard the Aumrarr groan—and was free.

And up, sprinting toward the deck and the open back door. The idiot Shaper had obviously fallen on his face in his own garden, the Aumrarr was down and couldn't catch him now, and—

Something fast and heavy struck him between the shoulder blades as he rushed through the door, smashing him to the floor.

The Aumrarr, of course.

Enough! She was going to die, and she was going to die *now!* Not slowly and painfully, not pleading for her life or for a merciful death. No, she was just going to—

The spell that roared out of him was a simple thing from his youth, the only thing he remembered just now that was fast enough and free of any need for gestures or focal items. Feeble, but it did what he needed it to do. The Aumrarr's head and shoulders bounced off the wall with ugly sounding thuds, she gasped, and Narmarkoun was *free!*

He pushed her off, scrambled around the corner into a room that was crowded with discarded old furniture, stacked boxes of things, and of course books, and turned to *rend* her with a good sword-storm spell, like—

The kick swept Narmarkoun's feet out from under him and toppled him helplessly into one of the stacks of boxes. One by one, hard and heavy, they came down on him.

He couldn't even draw breath under all the bruising blows to curse. He fought to turn himself over and drag himself out from under them—as they started to spill all their contents all over him in a noisy flood of things that clanged or thumped or shattered like glass.

He managed it somehow, though, snarling out his rage and rising up to—

Be struck in the face by with a chair, breaking his jaw, sending teeth flying and slamming him back into *another* stack of boxes.

This one didn't collapse, but Narmarkoun couldn't even find his balance, let alone avoid the next swing, which hit him across his nose and forehead hard enough to make everything go momentarily dark.

He felt himself falling.

Then he felt nothing much at all.

Chapter Twenty-four

HE WAS TOO slow, as usual, too far back. He wasn't going to get there in time.

"I'm not a hero, damn it," he gasped aloud, smashing his way through tangled dead branches and caroming painfully off tree trunks that were little larger than his arms, but much, much harder. Then, very suddenly, he was out of the trees and pounding across the dog-walking trail and into his yard through the open gate.

"Taeauna!" he shouted, seeing the wizard almost at the deck and Tay sprinting like the wind to catch up with him. Maybe Narmarkoun would be distracted by his yell, or look back to see him and stumble. Maybe. "Taeauna! I'm here! I'm—*urkkh!*"

Yep, hero to the last. He never even saw what he tripped over— just uneven ground, perhaps, unseen amid the clumps and trodden twists of wet grass—but he went down, painfully, full length onto his arms and belly.

Goodbye, wind.

He bounced his chin solidly a time or two against the ground coming to a painful stop, in trying to keep his eyes on Taeauna and the Doom. Neither of them faltered or slipped or looked back, of course, and he watched them both fall through the back doorway, into his house.

Up, idiot Lord Archwizard. Up.

Rod was up again and running hard, the open back door looming up in front of him with surprising speed.

For once, an open door didn't slam in his face. He burst through the doorway in time to see Narmarkoun get free of where he and

221

Tay were struggling together on the floor, and hurry through the first doorway on the left; Rod's storage room.

Taeauna turned on the floor and launched herself after the wizard, without taking the time to scramble up. Leaving the hallway free for Rod to come running right in after them.

We have to hit him before he can get a spell out, or we're both dead. Right here and right now.

Boxes toppled, the mage going down underneath them, and Rod skidded to a stop to avoid trampling Taeauna, who was taking box after box in the face as they hit Narmarkoun and rolled or bounced right at her.

I'm responsible for this—for this wizard being here, on Earth. And if he gets me, he'll make Tay his slave forever! My fault—mine! Must do something, or we're dead. Must do something!

Rod stared wildly around the room, then snatched the nearest chair off a stack of chairs. They were old, heavy wooden chairs that scratched the floor if someone dragged them, and—

Old, heavy, and solid. As the blue-skinned wizard struggled to his feet, Rod set his teeth and swung the chair, a big roundhouse sweep with all his strength behind it. *Don't hit the ball, son*, his father's voice came back to him, from years and years ago. *Hit THROUGH the ball.*

So he did that, putting his shoulders into it, turning his whole body, and doing his level best to destroy Narmarkoun's face.

Wham.

A moment later, he was staggering sideways, dazed.

He'd forgotten about the mind-link.

It felt like a truck had just hit him—or no, no, like a God-damned *mountain* had smacked Rod right in the face.

Through swimming eyes, he saw the wizard staggering back against boxes, reeling but not falling.

Gritting his teeth, knowing how much it was going to hurt, Rod swung the chair again at the blue face, just as hard as he could.

Arrrgh!

No wonder Narmarkoun had been staggering!

Rod found himself staring blearily at the floor through a flood of tears as he staggered helplessly forward, not knowing where he was heading and utterly unable to stop.

Except perhaps by falling on his face.

Jesus, the floor was hard. It had rushed up to meet him so suddenly that he was on it, tasting the dust, before he could even blink.

So he blinked now, several times. It seemed to be one of the few things left that he still knew how to do. Lying still with the side of his face on the somehow comforting flatness was another.

Rod didn't *think* his nose was broken, but he wasn't so sure about his cheek. His head was on fire, and—

He screamed as his eyes seemed to burst, first one and then the other, driving needles of pure pain straight into his head behind them, leaving him blind as blazing agony spread—and then he was choking and gurgling, swallowing his scream in sudden fresh helplessness, as yet more pain seared his throat.

He was dying.

This was what it felt like.

Oh, God, no wonder people screamed so much...

MORL ULASKRO POUTED when he was concentrating. When he was frowning hard because he was thinking harder, he started to look just a little like a frog. Or, no... like a toad—yes!—an old and irritated toad.

On the other hand, despite the kindling danger they presented to each other, the fact that there were two of them, meaning Lorontar could discard either the former tomekeeper of Dlarmarr or the former underscribe of Hawksyl whenever the necessity arose, Tethtyn *liked* Morl. He wouldn't dream of pointing out to Morl what he looked like, at moments such as these.

Besides, he had no idea how ridiculous he himself looked, when it was his turn to cast the spell they were taking turns using. The spell that was guiding them closer and closer to—

Morl shivered, opened his eyes to stare at Tethtyn, smiled, and pointed past his left shoulder. "*This* way—and not far off, either!"

Tethtyn grinned, waved at his friend to lead on, and they plunged together through crowded saplings, down into the wooded valley they'd been skulking beside.

They hurried, excitement rising—yet feeling somehow safer in among these trees than out in all the blaring and rumbling noises and the glass-walled keeps and lights of this strange world where people seemed in so much of a hurry, and the armored boxes swifter than horses that seemed to be *everywhere*.

Tethtyn took a stinging branch across the face in the wake of his friend's noisy progress, thrust it aside, and grinned wryly. There was nothing like the frightening strangeness of another world to make one long for Falconfar, even with all its cruel rulers, fell mages, and murderous thieves and slavers. To say nothing of lorn and dragons and other horrid beasts.

Another branch. This one he broke off, and flung aside.

To think that wizards—the greatest and most powerful mages, that is, the thankfully few, like the Dooms and the fabled spellhurlers of old—walked these otherwheres all the time.

No wonder they went mad.

THE SECOND HARD swing of Rod's chair smashed Narmarkoun's head sharply to one side and left him shuddering—and then sliding limply to the floor in front of her.

Taeauna winced, remembering hits she'd taken that had been as hard as that.

In the other direction, Rod was reeling away too, obviously just as dazed, lost in the same pain that he'd just dealt Narmarkoun.

Both men were momentarily, but utterly, helpless.

Which meant her best chance to fell the last of the three Dooms of Falconfar, and save both their lives for a little while at least, was right glorking *now*.

It was the work of but a moment to pluck out the wizard's own belt-knife, and the next to plunge it into Narmarkoun's left eye.

Then out, even before he had time to more than start to sob in the breath he'd need to scream, to stab him brutally in his *other* eye.

Driving the dagger hilt-deep against his face just like the first thrust, so that it would pierce deeply into the brain. Rod would be in agony, but that couldn't be helped, and at least this was an agony that would end, and the wizard with it, not the first of the countless agonies Narmarkoun would have leisurely visited on them both with his spells, until he grew tired of it.

She snatched the knife back out again, trailing blood, as the wizard gurgled and started to sag.

Taeauna brought the knife down and under and across, cutting Narmarkoun's throat deeply, to prevent any last gasped words that might doom them all.

There would be magics tied to his death, of course, but Taeauna just couldn't count on managing to drag the dying man outside in time. In fact, she'd do better to fling down Narmarkoun's knife, turn and grab hold of the reeling Rod Everlar and get *him* outside—and then return to finish the killing.

So she did that, gasping in her frantic haste, running Rod halfway down his backyard before she let the wet grass claim him.

He sprawled on his face like a dead man the moment she let go of him, but she had no time to spare just now for gentling him.

The closed door that led down into the basement. The switch that her hand thankfully found before she had to slow on the precipitous, sagging old steps to search for it.

Duck low when springing, to avoid braining herself on the low ceiling beams. This was a "washing machine," and that was a "bicycle," leaning against another sagging heap of damp old boxes full of junk...

And there, beyond it all, was the workbench!

Hopefully, waiting on it would be what she'd so briefly seen in Rod Everlar's memories, what seemed now a very long time ago. Recollections she hoped weren't too old to still hold true.

Falcon be with me, they weren't! The hatchet was still there amid all the tools and old tool catalogues and lightbulbs and other clutter.

She snatched it up, whirled, and flung herself at the stairs.

'Twas time—if there *was* still time—to behead a wizard.

She rushed back up the stairs. Mages who retained their heads, Dooms in particular, were all too apt to rise and walk again, dead but not quite dead, and—

There was a tingling in the air, a weirdness wondrous strange that grew stronger and heavier as she ran, and Taeauna winced and clenched her teeth and ran on, knowing she might well be running right into the heart of a magical explosion that would dash her to bloody spatters on the disintegrating roof of this house, mere moments away—

Narmarkoun was just as she'd left him, lying face down in the long smear of his own blood, head at an odd angle thanks to his opened throat, his blood a spreading pool around it.

Falcon, be with me now. Swing just as if she was hewing wood in a hurry.

With all the strength in her arms, she brought the hatchet down.

STRIDING ALONG A passage in Bowrock, thoughts bent on the coming Great Court in Galathgard—or more precisely, on which of his fellow nobles would stand in support of the crowned head of Galath and who would attend, cloaked in false smiles of loyalty, with an eye to murdering King Brorsavar before he could tighten his rule over the realm—Velduke Darendarr Deldragon stiffened suddenly, blurted out a wordless snarl of pain, and almost fell.

"Lord?" an anxious knight called from behind him. "Lord Velduke, what's wrong?"

Fetching up against a cold, hard stone passage wall with a gasp, Deldragon managed to croak, "N-nothing, I believe. A sign from the Falcon, a little overwhelming in its suddenness, but no more than a sign of what I must do—or a warning, perhaps."

"A warning of what, lord?" the knight murmured warily.

His eyes still seeing, through a flood of pain, a blue mouth contorted in a silent scream, beneath eyes that were ruined wounds weeping blood, Deldragon shook his head.

Wincing at the head-pounding result, he replied grimly, "Trouble to come. In Galathgard, of course, and after. Perhaps even on our way there. I'll want every man full-armored, and as vigilant as if we were riding to war."

"Of course," the knight agreed. "After all, we will be."

Deldragon nodded, trying not to shiver. He felt suddenly *empty*, weak and weary and... and... as sad as if he'd lost someone near and dear.

Someone with blue skin.

Someone who—it seemed—had been camped in his head for a good long time, a watchful, weighty presence lurking unnoticed in the darkness at the back of his mind.

Someone he knew, but did not know. Hmmm.

The only blue-skinned man he knew of was the wizard Narmarkoun, third and least of the Dooms of Falconfar. Had—Falcon forfend—had a wizard been his master, without him even knowing it?

If so, what had Narmarkoun the undead-tamer ridden him into doing? Deeds he obviously recalled nothing about, at all. How did Galath see the Lord of Bowrock, these days?

On his journey to the Great Court, should he bring along every last armsman, knight, and hedge-wizard he could muster?

Were there enough of them in all Galath to keep him safe against his fellow nobles and the commoners of the realm?

And if what he'd just felt was Narmarkoun dying, who had handed the powerful mage his death?

Was it someone all Galath should fear, sparing not another thought for the fate of Deldragon or Narmarkoun?

Darendarr Deldragon sighed, smiled briefly, then squared his shoulders, reassumed his customary stern expression, and strode on, the knight a careful pace behind his left shoulder.

Before he'd walked very far, a rueful smile crept back onto his face. He was beginning to understand why his father and mother, for many a year before they'd found their graves, had so often been stern or confidently smiling in public, and behind closed doors had so often sighed and demanded of the empty air, "Why me?"

Not that he ever recalled the Falcon swooping down to favor either of them with an answer.

It had taken four brisk blows, but the eyeless blue head was now rolling away across the floor. Above it, the air itself was beginning to emit odd sounds—strange jangling, singing chimes.

Taking no time to curse, Taeauna hurled herself up off the headless body, flung down the hatchet, and launched herself at the door.

She rebounded off the wall outside the room and sprang headlong out the back door as the discordant singing noises rose into screams and the air thickened and swirled, becoming as dense as treacle above the deck as she crashed down on it and rolled frantically onward, then as light and clear as a desert breeze as her flight took her over the lip of the deck, onto the grass.

She was two running strides beyond the end of that roll when what she'd been expecting happened.

Behind her, much of the house blew up.

Pieces of wood and brickwork were flung high into the air as the blast slammed into Taeauna's back and flung her down the yard.

She had beheaded a mage of power, and magics tied to his death—spells he'd cast down the years, but left hanging until this most dire of fates should befall him—were finally taking effect.

She slammed into the ground hard, right beside the moaning, writhing Rod Everlar, but was hurled on, rolling and bouncing and rolling again, driving all the wind out of her, and finally came to a bruised, flailing stop.

She fought hard to resist just sinking into welcoming oblivion, and instead struggled up to one elbow and turned to see what was left of Rod's house.

The room where she'd slain the wizard was shattered, open to the sky and the passing breezes, the roof blown off and the back wall reduced to flaming shards and splinters all over the deck and the lawn.

There were no blue hands or fingers or anything gory among them, though; the wizard's dying magics would have seen to that.

Flames were quickening around the gaping wound in the house, but she spared them not a glance.

Rod Everlar was blinking blearily in her direction and murmuring, "Taeauna? Tay? Taeauna, are you there?"

"I am, Rodrel," she reassured him, crawling back to him and rolling him over to see how whole he still was.

Flight of the Falcon, could it be?

He seemed untouched, completely unharmed by the blast and all it had hurled.

His mind, though—enthralled by a wizard who'd died while linked to it—might well be another matter.

Narmarkoun might even be lurking behind those streaming eyes and murmuring voice right now, seething in hiding and awaiting his best chance to lash out at her.

"Glorking *wizards*," she hissed to herself, before she asked him whereabouts he hurt.

His reply was a weak smile, and the words, "All over."

Behind them both, flames started to rise and roar. The scorched interior walls of Rod's house—and all those books and papers, the work and play of his lifetime—had started to burn.

Chapter Twenty-Five

"**R**OD! LORD ROD!" Taeauna's voice beside his ear was insistent, her hands gently but firmly shaking him. She was trying to rouse him.

Rod stared dully up at her, still riding a long downhill slide of agony that was plunging into numbness... was this a dream? She *seemed* real enough—and agitated, too, her eyes sword-sharp as they peered into his.

"I need you," she said fiercely into his face, still shaking him. "We must leave this place, and return to Falconfar. Open another dream-gate, as you once did here for me, when we were beset by Dark Helms. Open a gate, Lord Archwizard."

"Unhhh?" he managed, intelligently. It would be so *easy* to slide down and away, leaving all of this behind...

"Rod, *open a gate*. Please. Now."

Through his daze, Rod heard another sound, distant but unmistakable. Sirens.

He could smell smoke, roiling up around them and streaming past. Smoke, coming from...

"My house is on fire, isn't it?" he asked faintly.

"It is." Taeauna's face, just above him, was grim. "There's nothing left for you here. Except a dungeon cell, when your— police?—get here. I need you to craft a gate, to take us back to Falconfar. Just as you did before, when first we met."

Rod stared at her. "Yes," he mumbled, "but help me. I'm... I'm drifting..."

Taeauna leaned close, as if to kiss him—and Rod felt a sudden, sharp pain in his ear.

"Owwwrah!" he blurted. "You *bit* me!"

"Yes," she said into his throbbing ear, her arms going around him to hold him tight. "Lord Rod, remember Falconfar. Hollowtree, and the map on the table there. All my dead sisters at Highcrag. The haystack, and Lord Tindror and that bedchamber of his high up in Wrathgard. Deldragon and his great keep of Bowrock—and the gate that apprentice of his conjured up in its cellars. Just such a gate as I need you to open for us both, now. Remember, Lord Rod Everlar? Remember? *Remember!*"

"Yes," Rod murmured, into a tangle of her hair. "Yes..."

He was seeing again the bright blue edge of the upright oval of magic in the dark cellars of Bowrock, its brightening glow...

"*Yes,*" Taeauna hissed, wrapping herself tightly around him. "Yes, Lord; it's opening! You've done it! Take us home! *Take us home!*"

"Where?" Rod asked, feeling blue mists swirling into his head from he knew not where, but seeing just one place through them: ruined Malragard, the very place they'd left not long ago.

Taeauna did not reply—for they were already bumping down, hip to hip, onto hard, sharp stone rubble scattered on a stone floor.

They were back in the riven chambers of Malragard, with blood and burned bones and sprawled corpses all around them.

The Aumrarr sprang up and hauled Rod to his feet, all in one smooth movement.

He blinked at her mutely, a little dazed and a little lost in the sudden deliverance from the pain in his head. It was gone as if cut off by a knife, vanished as if it had never been.

"Is—is—Narmarkoun's dead for good, isn't he?" he asked hopefully. "Are all the Dooms gone from Falconfar, then?"

Peering all around like a hawk expecting trouble and hoping to spy it before it pounced, the Aumrarr snatched up a sword from the floor and handed it to him.

"Lord Rod," she said reprovingly, "there's a very old saying you really should remember: the Falcon flies, day and night, and the world beneath its wings is seldom simple or easy."

Despite her grim tone and grimmer meaning, Rod found himself fighting down a sudden chuckle. Of *course* he should remember that ancient saying.

After all, he'd made it up, when writing his very first Falconfar novel. Or... had he?

KLAXONS BLATTED AND sirens whooped, rotating lights flashing great bars of ruby-red light across the two still faces time and again.

The two men neither moved nor flinched, not even when people burst into the nearby backyard and started running toward them.

It was almost immediately obvious they'd not been seen; the many men soon milling about the yard were paying attention only to the burning house. Those in the bulky flame suits and helmets were busy dragging and aiming hoses, and the ones in the dark uniforms who'd poured out of all the identical cars topped with lights were just circling around peering about them—though one did look hard at the gently swinging gate, for a moment or two.

Morl Ulaskro, lately tomekeeper of Lord Luthlarl's private library in Dlarmarr, and Tethtyn Eldurant, until recently the youngest underscribe to Lord Bralgarth, the recently installed Lord of Hawksyl, stood in the trees like patient statues, watching the house burn.

They made not a sound, and moved only their eyes. They were still several mind-prying spells away from knowing the large, loud red horseless wagons with the red flashing lights were fire trucks, and the men in the dark uniforms who rode the smaller, shriller wagons were police, but Morl and Tethtyn already knew what the wands called "guns" in this world were, and what they could do—and there were a lot of them at the belts of all those excited uniformed men.

So they stayed very still and just enjoyed the show, wearing identical mirthless smiles.

This new world was both strange and wondrous. Conquering it would almost certainly be a lot of fun.

THE LANDING WAS hard but not bad, a solid, jarring blow that snatched away breath, but left them unhurt.

Garfist trudged a few steps and then stopped and looked about in the moonlight. Just the four of them were on this bare hilltop, with dark stands of trees curving around on his left and behind him, and long, narrow farm fields running away in all other directions, to where the crests of various hills hid—except for the treetops—the rest of unfolding Galath from him.

Almost certainly including the barns and steadings of the farms these fields belonged to. Yet from here, the four of them stood alone in a deserted land, beholding no signs of settlement but the cleared fields.

No lights twinkled, and no men nor beasts moved, as far as he could see. All was serene and tranquil.

"Huh," he grunted, as the moonlight grew stronger around them. "So just where by the flying Falcon are we?"

Juskra gave him a smile. "Here," she said sweetly.

He favored her with a disgusted look. "Clever, clever Aumrarr! So where, exactly, is this 'here' we're standing in?"

"A part of Galath that isn't an inn full of angry drunkards trying to kill you," Juskra replied meaningfully, lying down in a stretch of the long grass after examining it carefully.

"Your point," Iskarra put in, sitting down beside her, "is taken. Isn't it, Gar?"

"Aye," the burly man growled reluctantly, lowering himself to the ground with a wheeze and a grunt. He peered over his shoulder to make sure of Dauntra's whereabouts, and found the beautiful Aumrarr in mid-yawn as she lowered herself onto her side in the grass.

"Tell us," she told him sleepily, "who you killed, and why, and who's likely to be looking for you henceforth."

"Why?"

"We're curious, prying wingbitches, that's why," Juskra drawled. "Who just might not decide to tell you just where in Galath we've dumped you—*and* might decide never to pluck you out of trouble ever again—if you're too thick-necked and generally unpleasant to answer a few of our questions right now."

Garfist sighed. "Right. I hear ye. My thanks for saving our behinds. Again."

"Accepted. So tell."

Gar looked over at Isk. "Where to begin?"

"The Aumrarr answer to that," Juskra said quietly, "is always the same."

"The beginning," Iskarra said flatly.

Both of the winged women nodded, smiled, and waved at her to start.

Looking from one of them to the other, Garfist noticed they'd both turned to face outwards, so they could see anyone or anything approaching from the trees.

Moonlight bathed the forest, as Isk said, "Men drinking too much. Curses, menacing glares, a few fists; the usual. Then the trouble started for us, when an old... friend... recognized Gar, a man named Markel."

Both Aumrarr nodded, startling Iskarra into blurting, "You *know* him?"

Juskra smiled wryly. "Isn't it 'knew' him, now?"

Garfist gave her another dark look. "Ye saw it all, didn't ye?"

"We saw none of it," Dauntra told him, "but we know *you*. Please, tell us all. Every name you overheard, every face you remember, who's dead, who might be... all of it."

"Why? Are ye trying to keep count of every glorking knight in all Galath?"

"Yes," Dauntra told him simply. "Haven't you been listening? We *are* Aumrarr, remember?"

Then she waited, giving him time for his jaw to drop, and thereafter for Gar to master his astonishment and then his mouth, and close it again.

Interestingly, it didn't take quite as long as she'd thought it would.

"*THAT'S* MALRAGARD?" SORTREL of Taneth sounded less than impressed. "It doesn't look like much."

"I daresay it struck the eye as a lot more impressive," Bracebold growled, "before some wizard dashed it to the ground with spells. 'Twas a *tower*, remember; see you any 'tower' now? Yon's a ruin, the tumbled bones of the place, not the brooding keep I've been told about."

"It was a tower, aye," Askurr said shortly. "I've stood right here, more than once, looking across at it. Rose like a beast's fang, right about... *there*. I've a mind to camp right here, going no closer, until morning. The moonlight's bright enough, but we can't trust it. Look at all those clouds."

"They're galloping across the stars in a fair hurry, aye," Zorzaerel agreed. "What about Harlhoh, yonder? Is there an inn?"

"No," Olondyn the archer said flatly. "As I discovered to my cost, once; had to spend an uncomfortable night shivering out in the woods somewhere yonder. It *had* an inn, once, aye, but Malraun wanted guests in his hold, right under his hand—or far away. So the inn burnt down, mysteriously. Thrice."

"And stopped burning down when they stopped rebuilding it, hey?" chuckled Bracebold of Telchassur.

Olondyn nodded. "Indeed. I stand with Askurr; right here is as close to Malragard as I care to get, in the dark. Let's camp—in a ring we can defend, from right under our boots here to yon dead tree, and stand strong watches, the night through. We can cross the valley on the morrow."

"When there'll be light enough to see what's killing us," Askurr agreed dryly.

There were nods and murmurs of assent. "A fair plan," Bracebold told them all. "A fair plan."

At that moment, a swarm of shadows with silent wings and gleaming swords came swooping out of the night. Two warriors fell dying, nearly beheaded, before Askurr roared, "*Lorn!* We're under attack! Lorn! Throw down your torches, out in a ring around us—there and there, like so! *Hurry!*"

Two lorn tried to silence him, diving in from opposite directions and slashing at his head, but the old warcaptain was faster than he looked. His worn and half-laced armor let him roll smoothly and swiftly away, taking care to be seen to stagger helplessly until the lorn had committed themselves to the kill.

They slammed helplessly into each other in mid-air, already hacking with their blades. Their dying screams rent the night in unison.

Olondyn smiled mirthlessly as he strung his bow. His men hadn't waited for his orders; shafts were singing through the night already. Good lads.

It had been a while since he'd heard a lorn scream, but it was a sound he never tired of hearing.

GARFIST RAN OUT of things to say, and looked to Iskarra.

She shrugged. "You left nothing much out, Old Ox." She turned to look at the two Aumrarr. "That's more or less how it befell."

The winged women regarded each other grimly.

"Raenor," Juskra said to Dauntra. "Hereabouts, already."

Her fellow Aumrarr nodded, her face somber, then looked at Iskarra and said almost gently, "Matters in Galath are worse than I'd—"

"We'd," Juskra interrupted.

"—thought, and our plans must now change."

"Is this a 'we four' our, or 'ye two wingbitches' our?" Garfist rumbled warily. "An' what's so dark and dire about this Raenor? He seemed as big a glork-nose as most Galathan knights, all 'obey me or die, scrapings-of-my-boots,' but if that's cause for gloom an' plan-changing, ye must spend every day weeping an' tearing up plans, over an' over again! They're *all* like that!"

"Raenor," Juskra said sharply, "dwells about as far away from here as one can get and still be in Galath, yet your telling suggests he and his armsmen have been hereabouts long enough to become known and settled at the Stag's Head—and to feel as if he can swagger it under its roof without answering to the knights hereabout. So someone brought him here who either gives orders to local lords, or *is* a local lord. *Someone* is preparing for trouble."

"A throne war," Iskarra said flatly. "Galath torn apart over who rules it."

Both Aumrarr nodded. "Indeed. Which means, Gar, you'll get butchered in short order if you wander about Galath right now trying your swindles and tongue-wagging. So plans have changed for us all."

"Suppose, before ye assume that much," Garfist growled, "ye tell us just what these new plans are. Leaving out no trifling detail— such as, for instance, occasions upon which we'll be fighting pitched battles against mounted armies, or besieging keeps. That sort of thing."

The ghost of a smile crossed Juskra's face, just for a moment, before she sat up, flexed her fingers, and announced, "We'll be staying together, we four. Flying as before, by night. So we have the day ahead of us to rest and eat and make ready—in a manner that *doesn't* draw Raenor or his like into hunting us—and we fly on after the next sunset."

"Fly where?"

"Galathgard. The famous ruined royal castle of the realm, aye. We must get there as swiftly as we can, to see how things stand with its rebuilding, and where we can best hide. In plain sight in its kitchens, if need be—which should please you, Gar. We must be there when the Great Court convenes, and I've a feeling it will be easier to get there now than it will be to try to fight our way across the realm when all the rival nobles and their armies are converging at its gates—with none of them wanting witnesses to what befalls."

"An' why care we for the first conclave of the new king of Galath?" Garfist sounded more wary than truculent. "Is he likely to ennoble Garfist Gulkoun? Or grant us immunity to his laws?"

"Hardly," Dauntra told the moon. "If he listens to even a few of the many, many tales about the scoundrel Gulkoun, a swift death for such a miscreant may seem the very height of benevolent mercy. And kings known to have been gentle as nobles often find it prudent, at the outset of their reign, to reveal how strong and ruthless they can be if the need should arise. Just to, ah, educate their nobility."

Gar waved a dismissive hand. "I'm familiar with both the tactics an' the necessity. 'Change or die' is hardly a new notion, hey?"

"Iskarra and Garfist, hear me," Juskra said then, gravely. "We may well need you—humans without wings and the unfortunate reputation that goes with them—to aid us or speak for us, if the need arises in Galathgard. As to why we need to be there, let me put it plainly."

"At *last*," Garfist grunted, as Iskarra said politely, "Please do."

Juskra nodded. "We need to see not only how strong Brorsavar's rule looks to be, and who seems to be favored and powerful in 'the new Galath,' and who's out of favor—but we also need to be there if blades are drawn and trouble erupts. Whether such open strife breaks out or not, we also need to see who's missing from the gathering—and perhaps already dead—and what mischief befalls after the Court ends and the nobles all head for home... or elsewhere."

Garfist started to grin. "Ye make it sound interesting. Like just the sort of time an' place me an' Serpenthips here should be loitering near, to seize spoils and opportunities."

The scarred Aumrarr gave him a crooked smile. "Well put. If things grow too... perilous, we can vanish in a trice, too. In one of the cellars of Galathgard there's an ancient spell-gate linking it to Ironthorn; we can be back there in a single stride."

Garfist blinked, drew in a deep breath, and then made it loudly and colorfully clear that he never in his life, *whatever* befell, wanted to see Ironthorn again. His bellows echoed back to them all from the dark forest as he wound down, lowered his voice again, and descended to a surly snarl.

"Nor," he said, after much other ranting, "am I all that Falconglorking eager to taste the delights of hiding like a rat in the walls of Galathgard, dodging haunts an' lorn an' ancient death-traps if we keep to the ruined wings—an' running the constant risk of discovery by all the arriving nobles an' their knights an' armsmen an' doxies, too, if we venture anywhere they've put a roof on—*ye* know, the places where the king an' the nobles we want to listen in on will be. Not to mention that hiding in ruins we'll find a distinct lack of easily procured food—or any strong drink at all. Why, I've a mind to—"

"Obey these good lady Aumrarr," Iskarra snapped at him suddenly, rising and glaring up at him. "And agree with their highly sensible schemes, and follow their very reasonable orders like a wise man. *For once.*"

Garfist Gulkoun blinked at his furious partner—by the Falcon, her eyes blazed like fires, they did!—and managed to say, "Uh. Um. Ah. Aye... aye, I will."

Iskarra pointed at the two Aumrarr, and Garfist obediently turned his head and repeated his promise to them.

The moonlight was full on their faces, so he saw their utter astonishment very clearly.

Chapter Twenty-Six

ASKURR DISPATCHED A lorn viciously, trampling and stabbing it until it spasmed and slumped limp and helpless, to bleed out its life. Then he sawed off its talons, on general principles. If you gave these glorkers half a chance to gut you, they'd...

Slashing the air around him as he rose, out of habit, Askurr heard the squalling of wounded lorn on all sides—and the heavy thumps and crashes of their landings. Good, good...

He looked around. *Four* lorn were converging on one of Olondyn's archers, over on his left, and another pair—no, three—of the beasts were already clawing and slashing at another one, yonder.

"*Guard the bowmen!*" he roared. "They're going for Olondyn's archers!"

"Hear you!" Zorzaerel cried in reply, from somewhere under a shrieking knot of lorn straight ahead of Askurr, perhaps a dozen strides distant.

A moment later, two of the bat-winged beasts fell away from the struggling mass, fronts laid open and spewing gore—and the young warcaptain surged up into view, throttling a third lorn as he slashed at a fourth and fifth wildly and tirelessly with his sword.

The two lorn reeled back, giving Zorzaerel room to spin and gut another charging at him from behind, swinging the helpless lorn he had by the throat around as a shield to be impaled by his new attacker.

Zorzaerel let go of the dying lorn, its writhing body carrying the blade thrust through it to the ground, and stepped over it to drive his own sword deep into the lorn crouched behind it, still struggling to free its blade. The creature stiffened, gargling wetly on its own blood, then slumped down atop its fellow that it had killed.

Thus freed of foes for a moment, but drenched in lorn blood, the young warcaptain hastened through the fray to Askurr. "Which archer?" he called as he came. "Which one d'you want me to guard?"

"That one," Askurr yelled, pointing with his sword. Then he spun on one foot, bringing his sword around in a great whistling slash to catch a diving lorn in the side of the head and send it sprawling, mewling in pain. The blasted beast had been swooping in to take him from behind.

Again he pounced, stabbing ruthlessly. A wounded lorn was a lorn who'd attack you from behind, given any chance at all.

He'd not gotten this old by giving lorn any chances.

"Wings of the Falcon!" someone cursed, in the fray nearby. Bracebold of Telchassur gave a great bellow from off to his left. Askurr spun to face him, and saw several lorn tumbling through the air, fleeing wildly amid a great flapping of wings.

Behind them stood Bracebold, roaring in rage—and all around his feet were dead or dying bowmen. The damned beasts *were* going for the archers.

"To me!" Olondyn shouted, from another direction. "My men, to me!"

A moment later, he added in lower tones, "Narbrel! Yon torch!"

Narbrel dropped his own bow and hastened to pluck up the torch and apply its flames to the arrow Olondyn held ready. The shaft streaked aloft, its brief light showing the warriors more than a dozen lorn in the sky, flapping or diving.

Arrows sang up at them from six or seven places.

"To me, and I'll send up another!" Olondyn cried. "To me!"

Askurr launched himself into a gasping run toward the archer, knowing that any lorn who hadn't sense enough to flee would be streaking down at Olondyn in the next few breaths.

There were a lot of senseless lorn here this night, it seemed, but by leaping high he managed to catch one of them with the tip of his sword, and send it off-balance and flapping sideways—

to where Bracebold, also lumbering toward Olondyn, clubbed it to the ground. It didn't even have time to shriek before the warcaptain from Telchassur crashed down on it with both knees, to pin and butcher it.

Lorn were racing out of the darkness from all directions now, but the archers were ready for them. Shaft after humming shaft found its mark, and lorn fell to their deaths or squealed and flapped away, trailing blood.

Yet there seemed no end to them; Olondyn and his bowmen had disappeared under a heaving chaos of wings and swords and raking claws.

By the time all the other warriors who'd marched from Wytherwyrm closed in around the knot of lorn to finish them off, thrusting and hewing until they'd cut their way in far enough to rescue the archers, Olondyn stood very nearly alone, only two wounded bowmen still on their feet beside him.

However, that was the lorn done, or almost done; no more of them came hurtling out of the night, and Olondyn's last fire-arrow showed only a handful of lorn left, all of them flapping raggedly back toward the ruins of Malragard, one feathered with arrows and another trailing a dangling, useless arm and much blood.

One of them fell to earth before it could finish crossing the valley, and another two crashed down just shy of the tumbled stones of the wizard's tower, and started feebly crawling deeper into the ruins.

"After them," Askurr ordered curtly. "Never leave lorn alive to come at you again. Ever. Come!"

And he led the way into the night, down from the ridge where they'd fought, and through thornbushes into the water-meadows beyond.

Hastening to catch up, Zorzaerel was frowning and calling, "But the ruins—"

"We can come right back, once we slaughter these last few," Askurr growled. "We need not camp down there. Yet we must do all we can to make sure these don't get away and go and tell more lorn—or something worse—how many of us there are, and what weapons we have, and where we can be found. When slaying or harvesting, finish the task—or it will finish you."

They hastened across the valley.

More than halfway up the far slope, close enough to the outermost scattered stones that Olondyn had one of his dwindling supply of arrows in hand, Bracebold flung up a hand and hissed for a halt.

Ahead of them, they could hear lorn squalling briefly, some thumps and crashes and the ringing of metal on stone—and then a low but unmistakably human grunt of effort, and a satisfied curse.

"Who's there?" Bracebold bellowed, making Zorzaerel sigh with exasperation.

"Me," a familiar voice replied. "I was *wondering* when you'd get down off that ridge—where Malraun's lorn have always liked to roost of nights—and come tramping up to finish them off. Worry not; we took care of that for you."

"Roreld?"

"Who else? I'm too old for disguises and taking on false names and suchlike foolery, so it's Roreld you've found, right enough. Come on up; we've a fire cloaked for the night that we can uncover, though I hope you brought something to sear over it. I lost my taste for roast lorn years ago."

Askurr and Bracebold grew smiles and started trudging up the hill, ignoring Zorzaerel's frantic hiss, "*No!* 'Tis a trap! Don't—"

A moment later, light flared up among the rocks as old Roreld and Tarlund turned back smoldering turf with their swords to uncover a good fire. Sitting beyond the fire, swords ready across laps but not raised in menace, were three men, also of Malraun's former bodyguard: Eskeln, Gorongor, and Glorn.

"This is all of you?" Askurr asked. "What befell the Lady Taeauna?"

Gorongor spat into the coals. "Gone. Magic. At least she took the last Doom—and two other mages we've not seen before, who came striding out of nowhere; they're no 'prentices of Malraun, I swear—with her. Not dead, none of them, so far as we know. Just gone. Through one of those mage-gates, into... somewhere else."

Bracebold grunted, as Olondyn and the few handfuls of warriors they still led—Falcon spew, had the lorn killed that many?—came forward warily to the fire. "Did they go some place you recognized?"

Heads were shaken, on the far side of the fire.

"Could be in Falconfar, could be... farther," Glorn offered. "Boar, anyone? Never mind Roreld's jesting about roast lorn. We found the wizard's smokehouse."

Askurr accepted Glorn's proffered skewer with a grin. "Now *that* is the first welcome thing I've heard said since we left Wytherwyrm."

Many hands reached out for the other skewers Tarlund and Gorongor had set to reheat over the quickening flames, and hungry, weary warriors set about their meal.

It was Zorzaerel who first finished the meat on his skewer, planted the rod in the coals with a satisfied air, and asked, "I don't suppose you found the wizard's ale-cellar, did you?"

"My good marquel!" the king greeted him with a smile, waving him through the doors of the antechamber, and straight to a small sidetable that had been polished as smooth and bright as a mirror.

Upon it, Marquel Gordraun Windstrike saw a tall decanter of the finest luthpurl from far Larsay—unless he mistook that rich emerald hue—shining back the lamplight from between two large and ornate metal goblets. The table was flanked by two identical ornate highbacked chairs.

"Choose a seat," the royal voice added, into his ear, "and unfold your worries—for I can see by your face that some ride you hard. Worries that are fairly bursting to be heard, too."

The young marquel felt himself flush a deep, rich crimson. He hesitated before the two chairs until King Brorsavar firmly took him by the elbow and steered him to one before seating himself in the other.

Watching royal hands pour luthpurl for them both, Windstrike felt emboldened enough to blurt, "S-sire, the Great Court... I'm—I'm worried about your safety. 'Tis your bodyguard. We've not found a hedge-wizard who can do more than light fires by pointing—very close by and only with dry kindling, no less—or conjure glows, and I'd not trust more than a score of our archers to hit a raised drawbridge across your average moat. It's very likely that anyone seeking—forgive me, Sire!—seeking your death will attend Galathgard with more and better archers and *far* stronger magic at their command."

Faltering before a steady, kindly royal regard, the marquel struggled to add, "I—I cannot *begin* to promise even a solemn attempt to guard the safety of your person. Yet I dare not advocate the postponement of this Great Court."

King Brorsavar handed him a full goblet and smiled. "You may freely advocate anything you like, good Windstrike. Your dedication and loyalty have earned you far more freedom than that. Yet I fear I cannot cancel or delay the Court, no—or those who would imperil the realm will grow too restless to stay their hands longer."

The young marquel let out his breath in a loud, unhappy sigh. "I *know* that, Sire, yet no matter how much I think on this—dream of it, and come awake out of dark dreams, time and again—I see only this: that if you attend the Great Court, you may very well perish."

Brorsavar smiled thinly. "My good Windstrike, I don't expect to survive to see the next winter."

Gordraun Windstrike stared at his king. "But... but why did you take the crown, then?"

The old man wearing the crown shrugged. "Someone had to, to keep Galath from collapsing straight away into a land of snarling noble wolves savaging each other—for far too many of us are willing to ruin the realm, in striving to rule it—and give those who merely lusted after the throne time to fall away before the might of those strong and determined enough to seize it. I've given Galath that time."

Brorsavar reached for the heavy goblet, raised it, and studied its intricate chasings, turning it slowly in his hands. A hunting scene, of a stag with a crown caught in its antlers, pursued by many hunters.

Then he smiled.

Windstrike gaped again as he beheld the matching adornment on his own goblet, and realized what he was staring at. He looked back from it to Brorsavar in time to see the royal smile, before the king added, "And I must confess I was finding my dotage increasingly boring. This way, I've had the fun of younglings like you fawning over me, most of the realm hating me, and *everyone* paying attention to me. And isn't that what most of us want, after all—being as we're noble and can afford to want more than just something to fill our bellies—hmmm? Everyone to pay attention to us?"

The young marquel opened and closed his mouth several times, struggling to find an answer, not knowing what to say.

"Drink up," King Brorsavar told him, "and let's go out and hunt us up some lasses, shall we? You need something to take your mind off those nightmares. You may rest assured that I don't suffer from them. I'm looking forward to the Great Court, both as a challenge—and as my last, best source of entertainment."

Windstrike found his voice at last. "Entertainment? Hunt us up some *lasses?*"

"Indeed. You seem scandalized. Well, then, make yourself useful; each one we see, be sure and ask them if they're an archer. Or a powerful mage. Or even mad enough to want to be king, if we put a false beard on them. After all, who knows where the next saviors of Galath may be hiding?"

"WELL, WE *SHOULD* go back there, to retrieve all the arrows we can," Olondyn said, looking over at the night-shrouded ridge where they'd battled the lorn, "but I've no stomach for it now. Leave that for daylight—but *before* we go wading into this wizard's lair, ruined or no, hey?"

"Agreed," Roreld and Askurr said together, each with the firmness of command. The two warcaptains glared at each other, then shrugged, and smiled.

"So let's decide on the watches," Roreld added, looking to Askurr for confirmation.

Receiving a nod of assent, the old bearded warcaptain stood and started to point. "One of us and two or three of you for each, by my counting. We chose this spot because a man here, and another *there*, can block both ways anything without wings can come at it. If you have a third and fourth on watch, and they stand yonder, they can keep eyes on the first two—in a triangle, see?—and make sure if either gets taken down quietly, we all get shouted awake."

Bracebold and Askurr were already nodding, but it was Zorzaerel who dusted off his hands and said, "Fair enough. Where're the jakes? And where does yon archway—right in the heart of our watched-over camp—lead?"

Roreld smiled. "That *is* the jakes. It leads into a little room, all of stone—still has a roof, too. Bare and empty, no doors out. That's where we've been lightening our loads."

"So if it rains, you've fouled the only place with a roof?"

"If it rains, we get wet. Unless we wake and go down that way, to where yon stub of wall is leaning out like a tooth, see? Two chambers there, side by side, still have their ceilings. We can—"

"*Hold!*" One of the bowmen snapped, snatching his dagger from his belt. "Someone comes!"

He was pointing deeper into the ruins, through the gap where one of the watchmen would stand.

In the general rush to heft weapons in hand and turn to face this new menace, Glorn plucked his cloak off a bundle nigh his elbow, and the beam of a shuttered lantern—one of Malraun's best—shone forth. Glorn snatched up the storm-lantern as he rose, sword ready in his other hand, and held it high.

Its light fell on two figures stumbling toward them, out of the ruins. Humans, unarmed or at least emptyhanded, by the looks of them.

One was an Aumrarr they knew, the wingless sometime-bedmate of the wizard Malraun, Taeauna. The other was a white-faced, staggering man a few among them knew to be the Lord Archwizard of Falconfar.

Faces hardened, and swords glittered as they were raised, their wielders striding forward.

"Taeauna, stand away from yon wizard, and we'll kill him for you," Roreld growled. "He's done more than enough dark work already. Or has he enthralled you? I'd hate to have to kill you both."

HURRYING AFTER HIS king, Marquel Gordraun Windstrike found his voice at last, and opened his mouth—then closed it again with a frown. Crazed or not, kindly old Brorsavar was hardly likely to appreciate any of the responses that came to mind.

So Windstrike held his peace, fielded the night-cloak the king flung at him without a word, swung it around his shoulders, and followed the King of Galath through a small side door of the castle, out into the night, and down the steep cobbles toward the waiting lights of the town below.

Chapter Twenty-Seven

"Take him, lads!" Bracebold snarled. "Before he can cast some fell magic on us!"

The foremost warriors surged forward—and found themselves suddenly facing Taeauna, who'd smoothly sidestepped to stand in front of Rod Everlar. A dagger had somehow appeared in her hand.

"I have no quarrel with any man here," she told them calmly, "but this man is under my protection—and *no*, Roreld, I'm not enthralled by him, or anyone. Any warrior who seeks to harm him, I *will* have a quarrel with."

"Stand out of the way," Olondyn snapped at the warriors, "and we three can put enough arrows through the man to slay him. There's only one of her, and we're standing well apart; she can't shield against all of us."

Taeauna smiled thinly. "Tell him, Glorn."

The man with the lantern sighed, and did as she'd asked. "Olondyn, put down your bow. She's awakened the Master's warding; no arrow will now fly anywhere in Malragard. If you loose a shaft, it'll just hang in the air in front of you. Hurled stones and daggers, too; the lot. It's blade to blade or nothing."

"Can we break this magic?"

Gorongor and Glorn shrugged in unison.

"If the Mas—if Malraun is dead, yet the ward lives still, we know not how," Gorongor told them all.

"And 'tis working all around us, the ward," Glorn added. "I can feel it."

"So now what?" the foremost warrior asked, turning to look

at Bracebold and Askurr. "We came here to plunder, not fight *another* battle. Who's to say she can't use other magics of the tower against us?"

"Then she should die," Olondyn said grimly. "That will prevent *that* particular doom."

"All of you," the man behind Taeauna said quietly, "please hear me."

His words fell into a sudden silence.

Rod cleared his throat, stumbled as he stepped forward, put a hand on the wingless Aumrarr's shoulder for support, and announced, "I couldn't harm you if I wanted to. I'm no warrior—and I'm no wizard, either, and never was. I'm *not* the Dark Lord. I'm a healer."

There was a sudden murmur from all the warriors facing him, as quickly quelled by those who'd raised it.

"Yes," Rod said wearily, "and there are wounded men here. My healing can be yours—but not if you harm this Aumrarr. If you mistreat her, or me, my curse—the Falcon's Curse—will fall upon you, however dead Tay or I are by then, and your deaths will be swift... and horrible."

Askurr stepped forward, his eyes narrow. "So just how do you heal, if you can't work magic?"

"I can't cast spells, or unleash magic, but I can steer it a little," Rod told him.

"That's a lie," Zorzaerel spat. "I've heard you've worked magic many a time!"

Rod shook his head. "I used enchanted items taken from the three Dooms. Just as any of you could."

Askurr nodded. "That, I *will* believe. I wondered at some of the tales I heard... just why you did magic the slow, late, and feeble ways you did. So, Lord Archwizard who is no Lord Archwizard, how can we know you aren't carrying a hidden armory of enchanted items on you, right now?"

"My name," Rod replied, "is Rod Everlar. And I swear by the Falcon that I carry no magic."

He held up his hand to quell the murmur of snorts and derisive mutterings, and added, "And I'm prepared to prove it."

Stepping out from behind Taeauna, he started unbuckling and unlacing.

Askurr and Bracebold both made gestures staying the others' weapons, and in silence the men around the fire watched Rod take off his clothes. At the last, he kicked off his boots and held them up so the lantern-beam could shine down inside them, turned them to show the heels, then put them back on. "No magic," he announced.

Askurr nodded. "I'll grant that." He looked inquiringly at the other faces around the fire.

"I believe the man," Roreld announced suddenly. "He could have blasted us all from behind Taeauna, but did not. So I'm thinking he *cannot*, and is telling us truth."

Rod started to get dressed again.

"Not even a knife," one warrior murmured. "Who walks Falconfar without a knife, unless they've got spells?"

"I *had* a knife," Rod replied, "but I lost it. I can't even remember now just when. And to answer your question: a fool does." He sighed. "And I am that, many times over."

"Spare us the performance," Narbrel grunted. "You'll be sobbing and imploring us, next. Why, I—"

"We hear you were with Narmarkoun," Bracebold interrupted harshly, "and we know all about wizards riding men's heads, and turning them into slaves. So tell us: what happened to the last Doom of Falconfar?"

"Dead," Taeauna said flatly. "I beheaded him myself."

Bracebold blinked. "Can you prove it?"

The Aumrarr gave him a withering look. "I have no reason to lie about it, Blade of Telchassur. I could, after all, just as easily pretend he was alive and was coming here, then use your fear of his coming to compel you. No, he's dead."

"Wizards have risen before," Olondyn offered suspiciously.

Taeauna looked at him. "So they have, but when a Doom or any great wizard is slain, spells they've tied to their lives begin to erupt—castles explode and fires burst from them; you've heard the tales. That happened."

"What of the other two mages? The young strangers?"

Taeauna shrugged. "I know not. We saw them not, the other side of the gate."

"Huh," one of Bracebold's warriors growled. "What if they in truth saw no Narmarkoun, either?"

A voice that seldom spoke startled fellow warriors into listening. "The way I see it," the laconic Tarlund said, "we have a chance at healing for our wounded, we face an Aumrarr—and *I* don't want to fight an Aumrarr, ever—and a man who says he's not a wizard, whom I've never seen work any magic, *and* who we have *all* just seen carries no weapons. If they're telling the truth about Narmarkoun, we should be heralding them as heroes, not talking about slaying them. And we *are* standing here talking, when I could be sleeping. In life, we must all trust someone, some time... and *I* trust these two. Who here does not?"

Olondyn opened his mouth to reply, then shrugged and spread his hands in resignation.

Bracebold and Askurr looked at each other, traded shrugs of their own, and lowered their swords.

"Put up your steel," Askurr ordered quietly. "Lord Ar—uh, Rod Everlar? Will you see to our wounded?"

"There are men back on the ridge who are dying but almost certainly not dead yet," Olondyn said quickly.

"He's *one* healer, bowman. Wear him out, and you kill him, and they still die," Eskeln spoke up, from beside the fire. "The dead are dead, and the dying soon will be. Save his strength for the living."

Olondyn sighed, then waved his hand in surrender. "So do this healing, then. Convince me."

"I'll need a bowl, and a knife."

"What are we, cooks?"

"Every armored man carries a bowl," Taeauna said crisply. "His helm. And I'll lend him my knife, if all of you are too frightened of one honest man to surrender yours."

That earned her some glares, but no blades; it was Tarlund who held out his helm.

Rod smiled his thanks, took it, and went to the men hunched over by the fire, who had kept heads down and silent through all the talking. Then he looked up at Taeauna.

"Malraun's wards—will any part of their magic hamper what I'm trying, d'you think?"

She frowned, then shook her head, then turned to Gorongor, Glorn, Eskeln, and Tarlund, who all shrugged, making it clear they didn't know.

Rod sighed, accepted the knife she was holding out to him, and slashed open his forearm, letting the blood run down and drip off his elbow, into the bowl. Men murmured as he handed the knife back, and Taeauna calmly licked it clean.

Then she knelt down swiftly, putting a firm hand on his wrist to prevent him offering the bowl to anyone, and murmured a few words over it, with bent head. Only Rod was close enough to hear what they were: "Pretend to mutter magic over your blood, *now*."

Trying to keep his face expressionless, Rod obeyed, and was surprised when the warriors seemed to relax at hearing him do so.

There was pointing and some murmuring at the state of his arm—already healing itself, the gash closing and fading—but Rod ignored it, holding out the bowl to the nearest wounded man and telling him, "Drink. Just a little at first."

The pain-creased face lifted to glare at him. "Drink *blood?*"

Rod shrugged. "If you want the pain to go away, and your wound with it."

The man stared at him, then drank.

Then sat back with a long, shuddering sigh... and started to smile. "'Tis *gone!* The pain is gone!"

Olondyn knelt and snatched away the cloak the man had bound around his slashed midriff. The bloodstained leathers showed where the wound had been, clearly enough... but the skin beneath was now whole and unblemished.

"Wings of the Falcon!" Bracebold swore. "Now that's worth a dozen preening wizards!"

Rod took the bowl to the next man.

There was eagerness to drink this time, not suspicion, and the other wounded men were shifting themselves closer, reaching out.

"There's blood enough for all," Rod reassured them wryly. "Just a moment more of pain... just a moment more."

"Huh. That's as good a description of my life as any," Askurr said, from close behind him. "Rod Everlar, forgive us our hard words, please. We are... not trusting men."

Rod gave him a smile. "How could you be, with the Dooms at work in Falconfar?"

"Aye, that's right enough." Askurr watched the bowl move down the line, from shaking hand to shaking hand.

"You'll be needing to sleep, I'm thinking."

Rod nodded. "I will. Or I'll likely fall on my face, right soon."

The warcaptain nodded. "We'll work out watches."

BELARD TESMER MADE sure no one was within sight as he used his key.

Slipping through the door and locking it behind him silently, he parted thick overlapping curtains to reach the warm lamplight of the bedchamber beyond, strode to the sideboard and tossed two glowing rings onto the ornate bowl Talyss had set before the mirror. They were still a-drip with blood.

She looked up from the chapbook she was reading. "And whence comes this latest donation? Do they do anything particularly useful?"

"The one hides the face of the wearer behind the seeming of a dragon's snout, upon command, and the other whisks him—or her—across a large room in the blink of an eye."

"The donor will no longer be blinking at anything, I take it?"

"Indeed. Galath may just run out of klarls, at this rate."

Talyss tossed aside her reading, flung back the bedcovers, and spread her arms to him in welcome.

His own name greeted him, freshly written across her bare belly in blood.

Above it, her smile was warm, and her eyes a-twinkle. "Well, then, we'll just have to make new ones, won't we?"

"SO IF THE Dooms are all dead, what then for you?" Roreld's voice was a shade too casual. "Would you be interested in a good life— your own rooms, and food from my table, and coins for garments and what-want-you—in my hold, if you'll work your healing there?"

"I can offer better," Askurr said quickly. "Two swift knife-thrusts, when I get back home, and we can both have grand titles, and several castles each!"

"Telchassur, now," Bracebold growled, as idly as if the thought had just occurred to him at random, "is a great city, a port whose coffers gleam with floods of fresh coins every year, and folk—"

"Will *never* get to sleep," Taeauna said sharply, holding up her hand like a scolding wife, "if they have to listen to you lot making empty promises all night. Save your words, sirs, until the time is better suited. After all, who knows what you'll find in these ruins? You've chosen your watches; if we're all too tired to stay awake in the morning, one lorn could kill us all at its leisure—and this healer you now value so highly, too!"

Into the abashed mutterings that followed, Rod said firmly, "And my reply to all of your kind offers is this: I'll go wherever my lady Taeauna goes."

He gave Taeauna a smile, and she returned it fondly.

Above them, Roreld rolled his eyes and grunted, "For this night, we'd best be giving you two a room of your own, then."

"Don't be assuming anything, Roreld," Taeauna told the old warcaptain crisply. "I sleep in my armor. *All* my armor."

"I assume nothing, Lady Aumrarr," he said quickly, throwing up his hands, his voice ringing with sincerity.

Taeauna favored him with a dark look. "Show us this chamber, then."

Roreld pointed. "Down there, where the wall leans out? There're two rooms, side by side. Glorn, take them there with the lantern, and we'll shift where those on watch stand."

Taeauna nodded. "I think I know those chambers. One will do."

Glorn led them away, and Roreld and the others all watched. They waited a good half-dozen breaths after the healer and the Aumrarr had disappeared, and Glorn was on his way back to them with the shuttered lantern in hand, before the chuckles started.

Only to falter into shocked silence when an answering chuckle—every bit as filthy as theirs—came back to them from the shattered room.

It sounded like Taeauna.

"THAT'S THE LAST of them," Morl said, peering. "Aye, gone. Not much left of the place but a stone-lined pit and a lot of charcoal." He shook his head at the sagging lines of yellow "POLICE LINE/ DO NOT CROSS" tape, now swaying in the quickening breeze. "Weren't they as excited as priests at finding the body, though? Beheaded, yet."

Tethtyn nodded. "They'll be back in the morning. We'd best be gone." He pointed. "I was going to try a spell or two, but look! They're *not* all gone."

Morl stepped cautiously around the tree he'd been hiding behind, bent to peer past one of the trees in the yard, nodded, then came back through the boughs to rejoin Tethtyn, pointing behind him. "That black wagon, with all the lights quenched?"

"Aye," the underscribe from Hawksyl replied. "I watched two of the uniformed men—the ones with the caps—get into it. It's the same one they came in. I think they're watching, in case someone tries to go into the ruins. See that box they set up, and the posts? Those are tripwires, just like the some of the lords use along their fences, to fire bows at intruders with no archers to man them. No bows here, but yon wires'll trigger some sort of warning, if we go through the gate and walk up the yard, I'll wager."

Morl nodded slowly. "A book in the library had drawings of those trip-bows; I only got a glimpse, though, just once, when old Urvraunt had it out. It was one of the tomes he kept locked up."

He smirked. "I wouldn't mind casting a few *appropriate* magics in the direction of Urvraunt's backside, when next we meet."

Tethtyn felt something cold and malicious in the darkness at the back of his mind. A deep glee flooded through him like a chill flood. Lorontar evidently approved.

He found himself nodding and saying, "We leave that wagon be and take ourselves away from here, though, or it'll be like a lord's army sent after us. I'd rather not spend the rest of our time in this otherwhere fleeing like a hunted stag."

"Uh, w-who's there?"

It was a third voice, coming from just the other side of the trees. Around the rear, where the little track ran along behind all the backyards on Bridlewood Lane.

Morl and Tethtyn stiffened, and crouched down, out of sight.

It was unfortunate for Maxwell Sutherland that he'd happened to blunder back home at this precise time, bewildered and exhausted but so governed by curiosity that upon hearing voices in the trees just behind Rod Everlar's gate—and registering the smell of burning—he had to go and investigate.

Morl and Tethtyn exchanged glances, and smiled unpleasantly.

They stepped out of the trees together to face the lone, disheveled man standing before them, raised their hands, and began to cast the same deadly spell.

Max blinked furiously, but the two men—smiling wolfishly and gesturing much like Muriel had, after the one and only belly dancing class she'd attended—did not disappear.

So he settled for letting his jaw drop, and staring at them in utter disbelief.

Yet despite the misfortune that had led him into this imprudent meeting, Maxwell Sutherland's fortunes were taking an abrupt turn. Earth is not Falconfar, and some magics—not all, but some—do not work quite the same way in the vicinity of Bridlewood Lane as they do in the Falcon Kingdoms. Or, in fact, at all.

So the bolts of magic that should have slain Max merely set his sweat-soaked shirt on fire—so swiftly that it was down to collar and cuffs before he felt the heat, or any pain. A brief fall of ash down his bared front marked the loss of much of his thick pelt of chest hair.

"Cultists!" he stammered, finding his voice at last, and raising a shaking arm to point at the strangers. "*That's* what you are! Sus-susssatanic cultists!"

He meant to scream Muriel's name and run to her, plunging past her into the house and safety as she flung open the door with shotgun in hand to deal with this latest horror of modern life. Then he would dial the emergency number and be a hero. He would... he would...

Maxwell Sutherland settled for bravely rolling his eyes up in his head and fainting. He collapsed into a noisy, untidy heap in the trodden weeds.

Morl and Tethtyn traded glances again, shrugged, and turned away.

Their spells had worked, after all... after a fashion. Things were different here.

Yet perhaps not *too* different.

Chapter Twenty-Eight

ROD GROANED. "THIS isn't going to be a comfortable night," he muttered, starting to take off his clothes again.

Taeauna's hand fell across his busily working ones. "Why are you disrobing, Lord Rod?"

"I—uh—well, to give you something to lie on. There's nothing here but stone, and—"

"While you lie there bare and shivering?"

Rod shrugged. "Well, it's only right—uh, the chivalrous thing to do, you know, and..."

Taeauna put her arms around him, and murmured into his ear. "You are one of the kindest men I know. And one of the most prize idiots, too. Which of the two of us is more valuable to Falconfar? A healer and Shaper, the Lord Archwizard foretold... or one Aumrarr who has no wings?"

"Well, uh... ah, but—"

Taeauna put her fingers across his mouth. "But nothing. Now keep silent and spare me your protests. We won't be sleeping here. Just stand very still until I return."

She walked back to the doorway that Glorn had led them in through. Crouching low, she peered out into the night, crawling forward as slowly and patiently as a cat.

And was gone, only to rejoin him after a minute or two, as stealthily as she had departed. "Good," she murmured in his ear. "There're no watchers looking in at us. Glorn—and Gorongor and the rest who served Malraun—are good friends."

"How so?" Rod whispered. "And where will we be going?"

"To Rauthtower."

"*Rauthtower?* But that's a ruin, in Galath, in the forest far from anywhere! It'll take us days—"

"It'll take us a few steps. And it's not far from Galathgard. Going through Rauthtower was Malraun's favorite way into the kingdom."

"Galathgard? *Another* ruin!"

"No longer. At least, not all of it. King Brorsavar will be holding his first—very likely his only—Great Court there. They've been fixing it up for months."

"'They'?"

"The nobles who support him—and some who want him dead and have been busily preparing traps in the place, before all the *rest* of the nobles arrive to see them at that treason. Now hush; enough chatter. Take my hand."

"Where—?"

"There's a gate in yon corner. One that Glorn and the others who served Malraun know very well, though it's far older than Malraun. It links Malragard and Rauthtower."

"A gate linking here with... no, this isn't anything from *my* writing," Rod muttered.

"There *are* other Shapers and wizards of Falconfar, Lord. I know not whose hand crafted this gate, but it was long, long ago. Which means others, perhaps many others—noble families of Galath among them, even—may have heard of it. Perhaps they know precisely where its ends lie, perhaps not, but that it exists, yes. So if I knew a way to swiftly do so that I could work, I'd destroy this gate the moment we were through it. 'Tis a back door into the heart of Galath any foe of the realm can use, if they know how. Yet we may need it to depart again, in haste—after someone kills Brorsavar and all the fun starts."

"Fun," Rod muttered, shaking his head, and took Taeauna's hand. "I *like* Brorsavar."

"So do I," she said grimly. Then she turned back to the open doorway, and stared hard out into the night.

After what seemed to Rod a long time, she nodded as if satisfied, turned back to him, and murmured, "Mharraubrath elue maristru!"

And the darkness around them... changed.

They were standing now, not in the dark corner of a bare stone room, but in a roofless, moonlit hall that had once been very grand. In the soft blue-white light Rod could see that it was long and narrow and high-arched, with balconies above them on both sides and ranks of soaring pillars stretching away down a cracked, stained, and branch-littered floor.

"Behold Rauthtower," Rod murmured, half-mockingly and half in admiration. "So, given its name, where's the tower?"

"Destroyed, long ago. A dragon was involved."

Taeauna's hand was smooth and warm and comforting around his, and Rod made no move to pull away. "Whither now?"

"This way," she replied, keeping her voice as low as his. "'Ware, Rodrel; forest beasts sometimes roam these halls."

She led him briskly between two pillars and through an arch beyond, out of the long hall and up a narrow flight of stone steps. Rod felt a tingling in the air as they stepped through another doorless archway at the head of the stair. Magic, of course.

Archways in various walls led out of the room in different directions, but Taeauna ignored them all. An alcove across the room started to glow the moment she approached, and Rod saw that it was crowded with neatly arrayed clothing.

Well, well. A wardrobe, in a hold that had been a ruin for centuries.

Taeauna took her hand away from Rod's and started calmly stripping off her clothes. "Get rid of those rags you have on," she commanded. "There are suitable leathers here."

Rod obeyed without hesitation, turning his back out of polite regard for her modesty—and, he supposed, his. That prompted a sigh of exasperation and a firm hand on his elbow, turning him back to face her.

"Lord Idiot," Taeauna told him, "you can't find the right clothes if you don't use your eyes!"

She plucked the nearest garment from a hook and held it out for his inspection. "Or you'll find yourself trying to put on something like *this*."

It was a one-piece feminine garment, of glossy blue-black leather intended to cover a wearer from shoulders to mid-thigh—with the notable exception of the crotch and the tips of the breasts, where large holes gaped that were crossed by arcs of fine chain. *Barbed* fine chain. Thongs were sewn into the small of the back, dangling now but obviously intended to be laced up tight around the midriff. Rod felt himself blushing.

"Malraun had it made to fit me," Taeauna told him expressionlessly, "and other things like it." She thrust it back where it had come from.

"But for us, now, by 'suitable' I meant *battle*-leathers. Look well; there's harness here to fit Gorongor and Tarlund—and Glorn and Eskeln, too, and they're both about your size. Now stop being modest, get down to your skin, and I'll help you get dressed. I'm tired, even if you aren't—and 'tis a long walk from here to the armory, because Malraun felt it prudent to hide it. Yes, we'll be sleeping in our clothes, because that's what *I* feel is prudent."

Not for the first time, Rod did as he was told.

"BEHOLD GALATHGARD," JUSKRA said wearily.

Garfist peered down at distant moonlit towers. "We *walk* from here? Wouldn't it be quicker just to fall off?"

"Iskarra, kick him," Dauntra murmured.

"Listen, fat and heavy and incredibly *foolish* old man," Juskra snarled. "We flew all this way instead of taking the rest we should have—in part because you can't empty two tankards without getting into a fight. We're all going to go to get a good long sleep now, in yonder cave, and fly the rest of the way after dusk on the morrow. I thought it a better plan than trying to cross Galath in easy flights, as army after army of nobles and their bodyguards— many of whom are archers, just itching for something to put a few shafts into—converge on the same place we're heading for. Make any sense to you? Any at all?"

"Uh, aye. Aye, that it does. My apologies," Garfist growled.

"Well, he's learning," Dauntra commented. "Slowly."

Iskarra nodded. "It's taken me years to get him this far—but I've managed to keep him alive in the meantime, mind."

"If ever you change your mind about the wisdom of doing so, Isk," Juskra said, dagger in hand as she headed for the cave, "remember: we can change all that."

"MALRAGARD GOT THEM, right? Or some hungry monster, loosed from its cage when this place got blasted apart? Or are there secret passages all over this place that we don't know about?"

Askurr sounded angry.

"Fancied her, did you?" Roreld asked quietly.

"Of *course* I fancied her! Didn't all of us? Falcon Above, I'm only human! She's beautiful enough to make your mouth water, she fights as well as any man—"

"Better," Bracebold muttered, glaring into the empty chamber one more time, as if by doing so he could somehow summon the missing man and Aumrarr. They were all staring into it, except the raging Askurr.

"—and has spirit and wits and all of that, and she's the only woman within reach!"

"Harlhoh's right down there, actually," Olondyn said, waving his hand. "Lots of women there. And Taeauna's not a woman, she's an Aumrarr."

"And what man doesn't dream of lying with an Aumrarr, hmm? Well?"

"Dream, yes. Dare to do it? I'm not ready to die *just* yet," the archer replied. "But aye, of course we all look at her, and wonder." He shook his head. "*I* wonder what she sees in that gutless idiot of a Lord Archwizard."

"Kindness?" Glorn said quietly. "Someone she doesn't have to constantly battle to get her own way?"

"Phaugh! You sound like a woman!"

"I always do, when I'm talking sense. Now, let's put all this jawing behind us. They're gone, and that's an end to them. Leaving us free to get on with plundering Malragard—remember?"

"Whose blood is it this time?" Talyss contrived to sound amused and bored, but her brother noticed how sharply she'd turned to look, the moment she saw the dark stains.

Good. He hadn't yet been deemed expendable.

Though he might very quickly become so, if his dear sister discovered that he'd been behind the sudden and fatal accidents that had befallen the last two jacks she'd sampled. She didn't like pawns who thought—or worse, acted—for themselves. Even less, those who dared to eliminate other pawns. That was *her* right, and no one else's. According to the holy Tome of Talyss.

Belard shrugged. "Some careless Galathan. They seem to object to being asked to work hard around here, I've noticed."

"Indeed." His sister's voice turned very dry. "*I* have in turn noticed how well they *can* work, when deprived of extraneous nobles swaggering around giving them unhelpful orders, picking fights, and hiring away any worker they see whose work seems competent for their own secret little side projects."

She smiled. "Galathgard is coming along splendidly. We'll make a strong kingdom of Galath yet—if a somewhat more sparsely populated one."

BARON ARUNDUR TATHGALLANT'S saddle creaked under him again, and he gave a loud, heartfelt groan. "My *legs!* Falcon, I'm sore! What I wouldn't give for a good coach, with decent spells to cut down on all the shaking and pitching and bumping!"

"Longer ride than you're used to, Tathgallant?" Arduke Mordrimmar Larkhelm mocked, from where he sat his tall dappled gray, just ahead. His liveried armsmen were riding before and behind them, bright pennants fluttering the Lion of Larkhelm from their lances. "I suppose you'll be wanting a halt soon, and winsome wenches awaiting us there with wine and dainty morsels and soothing ointments?"

"They have that, on this road?" Tathgallant joked, trying not to sound wistful. "I should get out and about more often."

"You should. Galath is changing around us, my friend, and those who don't see it are going to have a hard time keeping their heads on their necks, I'm thinking."

The baron frowned. "And by that, you mean... ?"

"I mean," Larkhelm replied pleasantly, reclining easily in his saddle, "that I'm heading for Galathgard with a new edge on my favorite sword and my wits honed even sharper, to find the right time for a little regicide. Just a little treason... but *successful* treason, I'm determined."

The baron felt his mouth fall open and his face grow hot. "Sh-should you be telling me such things, good Larkhelm?"

"Why not? I trust our friendship, and therefore your personal loyalty to me. Nor am I the only one riding these roads with such intent. It's not a matter of which dastardly traitor wants to cut down old Brorsavar, my dear baron, it's who'll get to him first. A lot of us are hungry for change."

Tathgallant looked around uneasily, wondering where the arduke's household wizard was. The mage was riding with them somewhere, he knew; without his conjured ward, they'd be unable to see safely in the dark, or have any protection at all against or arrows out of the night, and would never dare to ride in the moonlight. Not that it was much safer by day, with so many nobles who cordially hated each other on the roads. "Aren't..." He spoke slowly, making sure he chose the right words, "Aren't you worried I'll denounce you?"

"No. I've already prepared a suitable fate for you, if for any suicidal reason you should choose to be so stupid." Larkhelm grinned and rode on.

White-faced, Tathgallant put his spurs gently to his own mount, to keep up to the arduke. Larkhelm's rearguard was riding close behind, and he didn't feel like turning around right now.

He knew he'd see the same ruthless grin on their faces.

THE LEATHERS WERE worn and supple and—damn it, yes—*dashing*. Rod found himself strutting, despite Taeauna's amused look.

The boots and all the baldrics and scabbards were the crowning touch. The pouch at his belt might be empty, and the daggers at his belt and boots and the sword riding his hip might be far more dangerous to Rod than to anyone else, but he felt ready to take on the world, with a merry jest on his lips and a swash or six to his buckle.

Taeauna's amused regard only made him blush a trifle. "Bring Falconfar on," he told her, grinning back. "At least I'll die pretty."

He now knew why so many bad actors—and good ones, too, for that matter—liked to play pirate so much, no matter how awful the movie. By *damn*, he cut a fine figure!

"If you polish my breastplate all night, Lord Rodrel, you just might be able to use it as a mirror, come morning," Taeauna said drily.

She plucked down a cloak that was much too large and threw it at him. No sooner had Rod awkwardly caught it, nearly staggering to the floor, than she threw him a second.

"What're these—? Oh. To sleep on?"

"If we live long enough, yes," Taeauna replied, calmly choosing two more weathercloaks for herself, that looked even larger. She headed out of the room, adding over her shoulder, "Yet they must see another use first."

He hurried to catch up, stepping on the end of one of the cloaks and almost falling.

"Quick but *quiet*," Taeauna chided. "And alert me—quietly!— if you see a beast, or any movements in the shadows."

"Yes," Rod whispered, wondering if there was ever going to be a time in Falconfar when he'd know what was going on.

He concluded that the most likely answer to that was: Probably not. Ever.

But was it any different, for any adventurer?

"HOLD! WHO ARE you? Stand where you are—come no nearer!"

The approaching man stopped, half-cloak swirling. "Stay your sword," he said with a sigh. "I'm seeking the jakes, not murder. I presume you're guarding the doors at your back?"

"I am," the burly knight before the doors snapped, "and no one not known to me may come closer. My lord of Silvershields sleeps within, and his safety is my charge."

"Fair enough. I wish him pleasant snores, and you a safe and uneventful shift of guardianship. Yet I fear the latter stands imperiled."

The knight scowled. "What are you, some sort of wizard? Why all the fancy talk?"

"My manner of speech comes naturally to me, O Sentinel of Silvershields. Particularly when I'm irked."

"Irked, are you?" The guardian's sword came up. "So you dispute my duty?"

"No. I merely observe that this passage leads *past* the doors you guard, not *to* them. I also fail to remember ever being told by Klarl Annusk Dunshar, current Seneschal of Galathgard, that the right of Arduke Helgorr Silvershields to safe slumber extended to barring the use of this passage—the way to the jakes—to others. And when it comes to matters of authority, *he's* only an arduke, and *you're* only a knight."

"Oh?" The knight's sneer was not pretty, and his sword flashed as he hefted it threateningly. "And I suppose you're the High King of Galath?"

"No. Not yet. Just now I'm merely Lordrake Haemgraethe Sarlvyre. If you'd been more polite, you might even have lived long enough to see my coronation. As it is, however—"

The slim sword darted at the knight, gleaming low. The knight slashed down at it, but it was gone, darting up and over his blade to thrust deep into his left eye.

It found the right eye, too, before the guardian could sag all the way to the floor.

Then it was wiped clean across the dying man's slack, gaping mouth, and resheathed, because even a lordrake needs both hands to unclasp his codpiece. It was still a long way to the jakes.

With a satisfied sigh, Sarlvyre finished emptying his bladder and glanced at the closed doors beside him, toying with the idea of passing through them to kill Silvershields. He'd never liked the man much... but no, it was early days yet.

Let Brorsavar's head roll first, and then the *real* fun could begin.

Chapter Twenty-Nine

"**H**ERE," TAEAUNA ANNOUNCED suddenly, thrusting her cloaks atop the ones Rod was already holding, and paying no attention as their weight took him to his knees. "Your task, Lord Rod. I'll be needing all of them flapped out horizontally—like a rug or a coverlet you're trying to let fall more or less unfolded, to cover all the floor you can. Move around as much as you can without getting in my way or taking a blade through you, and cover as much floor as you can. Right in front of the door, where we find them."

"*Taking a blade through me?* And finding what?"

The Aumrarr pointed. "Those." She was indicating a number of slender things on the floor, strewn in front of a lone dark door in front of them. That closed portal stood in gloom on the far side of a band of bright, cool moonlight, but it looked massive. The things on the floor were slightly curved, and gleamed.

Swords. He was looking at six or seven—or more—swords, lying on the floor.

"They guard the armory," Taeauna explained calmly. "I doubt the command words I know will still work, so when I approach too closely, they'll rise and dart at me. Unless you want to die, take great care to stay a little farther away from the door than I am, as you throw the cloaks. Be sure not to trip me up or get in my way as you do so, because I'm going to have to move quickly. The moment the cloaks are down, no matter what sort of a tangled mess you make of them, run right over *there*—"

She pointed again.

"—to the pillar standing at yon corner. You'll find a snarling lion face carved in the stone, at about chest level for you. Pull its tongue *down*, firmly. And please don't waste any time doing any of this, or we'll both die." She eyed him. "Got all that?"

By the Falcon, she was as calm as if she were giving directions to find a jar of raisins in her pantry.

"When the swords rise," he replied, finding his mouth suddenly dry, "throw cloaks down in front of door, covering as much of it as I can but keeping out of your way and farther from the door than you. Then run to the pillar as fast as I can and pull the lion's tongue down."

His heart was starting to race.

"I have a very bad feeling about this," he blurted out, the cloaks feeling even heavier now.

"Not nearly as bad as *I'll* feel, if something goes wrong," Taeauna told him, flashing a sudden smile.

God, it lights up her face like the sun. I'll do *anything* to make her smile like that.

Even fight off swords that fly around trying to stab me.

"And just who thought *these* up?" Rod asked, jerking a thumb in the direction of the swords lying so still and innocent on the floor. "Holdoncorp?"

"Malraun," the Aumrarr replied. "Ready with the first cloak yet?"

Rod sighed and bent to arrange the cloaks in three side-by-side rolls, hefting the fourth roll ready in his hands. He was hoping he could flick it open in midair like the red carpets in cartoons, but he already doubted things would go that smoothly. Rod's life was Rod's life, and cartoons were... cartoons.

Taeauna gave him a grin that startled him—did she know what he was thinking? If so, how the *hell* had *she* ever managed to see Saturday morning cartoons?—hefted two of her daggers, and stepped forward.

On the floor, like the brooms in *The Sorcerer's Apprentice*, the swords stirred.

"Aras *hrack*," Taeauna announced crisply. "Taerlo muhaervo haras hrack."

She started forward—and the swords, seven of them, rose from the stone floor like sleepy dogs shaking themselves awake, hanging points down for a moment, then sped to the attack.

"*Now*, Rod," she snapped, charging at them and smashing aside the nearest flying blade with her dagger.

Then she was ducking, darting and dancing in the heart of them, leaping about wildly in acrobatics Rod scarcely saw as he focused on tossing cloaks, swirling them out and letting them go. The damned things hung in the air so *long*, settling ever so slowly...

Steel rang on steel to his left and he heard Taeauna panting with the effort. Rod sidestepped hastily to where he could snatch and throw the second cloak, then the third, not waiting at all for the second to settle. He was way over to the right now, probably pretty close to that snarling lion pillar, and the fourth cloak was going to be useless unless he darted in, trampling down the third one, to cast it closer in...

To the Falcon with staying farther from the door than Tay! Surely he could outrun a few swords...

Rod raced in, let the cloak unroll as he took a step back, then let go, spun around, and ran like hell.

Fear rose chokingly in his throat as he panted along, cursing himself for being a fool, and ran for the pillar for all he was worth.

Picturing glittering swordpoints behind him, Rod flung his left arm wide to catch hold of the pillar as he ran past it, and raised his right hand to slap down the tongue, hopefully as he swung around the pillar, to get its thick stone between him and the swords.

It worked, as smoothly as if he'd practiced it. The tongue grated a bit but came down readily enough—and just as the foremost sword crashed off the pillar right in front of Rod's nose with a shriek that sent stone chips spraying, the swords all... fell.

Just fell, in mid-dart, to bounce and slide to a stop on the floor, the nearest four of them ringing loudly on bare stone. The cloaks muffled the noises of the others.

Not that Taeauna, standing alone behind them all, watching him with her mouth open to scream, looked all that impressed.

"*Idiot!*" she hissed, furiously stabbing towards the armory door with her daggers. "*Get* to that door! *Now!*"

Rod got.

"All Rauthtower heard that," she snarled, opening the door. "Thanks to *you*. Can't you even follow simple comm—instructions?"

"I guess not," Rod gasped apologetically, starting to shiver at what a reckless idiot he'd been. "Sorry."

"You may well be, if we have to fight our way out of here in the morning," the Aumrarr said darkly. "Now stand in this doorway and *don't move*, until I rush in past you. You will keep the door open while I collect the cloaks."

"Collect—?"

"To sleep on, remember?"

Rod watched her toss her daggers past him into the armory— he didn't dare turn to look where they fell—and race around snatching up cloaks.

By the time she burst past him with the untidy bundle of cloaks, reaching out to pluck at his leathers and drag him into the armory on her heels, Rod had his next question ready.

"Fight our way out of here through who?"

The armory door slammed behind them, plunging them into utter darkness.

"Not 'who,' but 'what,'" Taeauna snapped, through its echoes, from somewhere close to his nose. "And let's just hope you never find out, hmm?"

Falcon, but she was angry...

"S-sorry, Tay," Rod mumbled, really meaning it. He'd heard from her voice that she was moving on, away from him, and hesitantly followed her into the chill blackness.

A faint amber glow kindled as they approached, emanating from the tops of smooth marble ledges, running around three sides of the square room. An astonishing array of weapons lay on the shelves, in neat rows.

The fourth wall held a rack of polearms by a long row of suits of plate armor, each on its own stand. Between the suits smaller shelves thrust out from the wall, holding helms, gauntlets and other odd pieces of armor.

This was an armory, all right. Just the swords, right here by his elbow, must be worth a small fortune...

"So, which weapons do we take?" Rod asked, a little doubtfully. He knew that lugging around a lot of heavy stuff was dangerously foolish, and that it was best to find light, balanced weapons that suited one's strength—for him, that would probably mean swords meant for twelve-year-olds, if they made such things—but as to *how* he could decide what was balanced for him—

"Leave that for the morning," Taeauna told him, a little less curtly than a moment ago. "Sleep first. After we find the most useful piece of armor here, that is."

"Oh? What's that? Something enchanted?"

"No, though we'll each be taking one of those, on the morrow. Enspelled codpieces that will hurl back one spell each that's cast at us, then melt away."

Rod shook his head and grinned wryly. "Of *course*. I should have known someone would think of such things. And the armor that's more useful than that?"

"Ah," the Aumrarr replied briskly. "*This* one." She went to one of the jutting shelves and hauled a great helm that looked as if it was fashioned for a giant off it, clasping it to her breast.

Then she turned and shuffled to the bare table in the center of the room—a worktable, Rod supposed. Before he could move to help her, Taeuna braced herself, grunted, and heaved it up onto the table.

Falcon! It was larger—and probably heavier—than an old deep sea diver's helm. Taeauna leaned on it, pointed at Rod, and then over his shoulder at some more helms. "Fetch me that one and *that* one—and those two immediately beneath them, too. *Don't* try to bring them all in one trip."

"Four? How many heads do we have, anyway?"

"Those two are for our muddy wastes," Taeauna told him flatly, "and those two for yellow-wine wastes. To use the polite terms."

"Oh," Rod said, discovering he was starting to blush. Again. "So do they go on the floor somewhere?"

"Pick a corner for each of us. Where we aren't likely to knock something down on our heads when we get up."

"So, uh, we'll be wiping ourselves with our hands?"

Taeauna gave him a disgusted look, then drew four scarves from her bosom, one after another. "From the wardrobe. Hues I never liked. Leave one beside each helm."

Wings of the Falcon, she thought of everything.

When Rod was done arranging things, he came back to Taeauna and the massive helm on the table by her elbow.

"This is it," she told him patiently. "The most useful thing here."

"Really?" Rod asked, peering at it. Taeauna was already tipping it over to expose the underside.

The helm had two dangling strings of overlapping plates attached to it, that hung down to protect the wearer's throat, and neck... and the plates had been latched together, turning the helm into a sealed sphere.

Taeauna was trying to undo the latches and fold back the plates.

"So," Rod asked curiously, watching her struggle. "Do we bathe in it, or is it for carrying the crown and all the royal treasure?"

Taeauna didn't bother to answer, because she had just won her battle and swept the plates open.

A strong, sharp smell assaulted Rod's nose. Cheese.

The Aumrarr lifted a wrapped disk out of the helm and onto the table, and started unwinding it. Even before Rod saw the wedge-shaped segment missing from the disk, through the cloak, he knew what he was staring at. A large wheel of cheese.

Which proved to be green and veined in purple.

It also proved, after two deft slices of Taeauna's dagger had cut off a sliver and separated the evil-looking green rind, to be the best cheese he'd ever tasted.

"Nothing," she told him tartly, "is more useful than a good meal. Eat until I tell you to stop, and then sleep."

Rod felt like groaning with pleasure. He had *never* tasted anything this good. "Is—is it magic, making this so tasty?" he asked, almost begrudging the time it took to speak instead of chewing more cheese. "And is there anything to drink?"

"No," the Aumrarr told him briskly, pulling other packages out of the helm and inspecting them. "And yes. That is, there's no magic, just lurmbrauken cheese from Elskurn, beyond the Sea of Storms. And yes, there's water in yonder earthen jugs—that suit of armor on the end isn't a suit of armor at all, but an armored carryall with earthenware on shelves inside it. It won't taste nice, but it won't kill you. Eating too much of this cheese might, so you *will* stop when I tell you to."

"Or else?"

"Or else the painful duty will fall to me," Taeauna told him, not quite smiling, "of teaching a Lord Archwizard that even he must obey limits."

Rod decided it must be lack of sleep that was making him so reckless. That, or knowing his house was burned, and everything he had—everything he'd saved and collected and surrounded himself with, all the souvenirs of a life he'd on the whole quite enjoyed—was gone. "Teaching how, exactly?"

"Ah. That—for you—will be the painful part."

Rod smiled.

GARFIST WAS RISING from a very pleasant dream. Soft hands were caressing him, running gently over his flanks and the corded muscles of his chest and the great mound of his belly, and then lower...

"Yes," Isk said with a sigh of relief, from close above him. "No wounds at all. It's all someone else's."

"Good," Juskra said, from off to his left. "I thought so."

It was then that Garfist smelled the blood, and woke with a start. "Hurrh? Whahuh?"

"Hush, Old Ox. Lie still; go back to sleep. I'll tell you all about it in the morning."

"No," Garfist growled, "I *know* that tone, Snakehips. Tell me *now*." He felt for the hilt of his sword, but Juskra's steel-strong hand was suddenly holding his wrist immobile.

"It seems some Galathan noble's hired wizard knew about this cave, and crafted a gate to bring the noble and his men through it, to camp here and march to Galathgard come morning."

"What noble? Which wizard?"

Gar felt her shrug, through her firm grip. He tugged, testingly, but it hadn't loosened in the slightest.

"I know not and care not. The wizard is dead, and most of the armsmen who came through with him. His death collapsed the gate, and the noble—shouting some *very* unkind words at us, I thought—and the rest of his guards and toadies were left where they'd started from, back the other side of it. Unless he can find another mage right speedily, and I suspect they're hard to come by right now, he'll have to start riding horses to death come morning, to have any chance of getting here before the Great Court begins. At any rate, they came tramping across us, and stabbed at us when they felt us under their boots, and we had to kill them all. Which is when someone's blood got all over you."

"And *you* slept through it all," Iskarra added, and Garfist couldn't tell if her voice was accusing or envious or both. Probably both.

"Huh," he rumbled slowly. "Could we go back to the part where one of ye was running yer hands all over me? Ye didn't quite finish, as I recall..."

Chapter Thirty

THE GUARD HAD already gone white with fear, but was standing his ground in front of the closed—and undoubtedly locked—doors.

"I am *very* sorry, Lady Maera," he said again, sounding as if he really was, "but the Lord and Lady Tesmer are *not* to be disturbed." He was, yes, starting to tremble.

The tall, slender woman facing him took another step forward. "On whose orders?" she asked flatly.

"Theirs, of course, Lady. I would turn away a Tesmer on no lower authority."

Maera Tesmer regarded the sentinel coldly. "My mother and father are not in the habit of chanting like novice minstrels, Haelgon. There is no 'theirs' in this; either Lord Tesmer or Lady Tesmer gave you those orders. Which of them was it? And what *precisely* was said to you?"

"I..." The guard flushed as red as the draperies flanking the doors. "It would be indiscreet of me to say. Lady."

Maera Tesmer's eyes flashed and she took another step forward.

"Haelgon, you have no idea just how indiscreet *I'm* going to be in a moment, if you fail to answer my question. I *am* a Tesmer, whom you're sworn to obey—and find myself positively *afire* with spells that I'm just itching to use, that might do almost anything if I lose my temper, from turn you into a frog to blast you to drifting ashes."

Her sharp, lashing voice dropped to an intimate, conspiratorial purr. "I might even just force my way into your mind and learn what I want to know that way, leaving you forever a drooling idiot lacking all control over your bowels... the sort of man-beast that would so disgust my mother that she'd see you chained naked, just out of earshot of Imtowers, to be a chew-toy for our war-dogs—and, of course, a lesson to all of our subjects about the folly of disobeying a Tesmer. Oh, there are a *lot* of things I might do. Unless you answer me, right now."

"Uh—I—uh—L-lady Tesmer told me to let no one—no one at all—pass these doors and disturb them, upon pain of death. Then she turned to Lord Tesmer and said... something I tried not to hear."

"But obviously did. *What was it?*"

The doorguard blushed an even darker red, shook visibly, and mumbled unhappily, "'Get yourself disrobed right quick, Irrance, so you can take your time baring me properly.'"

Maera nodded. "I thought as much. So the doors behind you are locked from without right now, and barred and bolted within?"

"Y-yes, Lady."

"Tell me: if Imtowers caught fire, what would you do then? Stand like a statue at these doors, silently guarding them, because you knew you were not to disturb my parents? Or use your key, and thrust your sword in through the gap to lift the bar, and pound on the doors and bellow to rouse them or their maids to shoot the bolts and so survive?"

"I—uh—Lady, *please* don't bait me so! I but—"

Maera Tesmer smiled wickedly. "Faithful Haelgon, I'd not dream of doing so. You have been most loyal to my parents, and most helpful to me. I'll not even demand those door-keys from you. Oh, no."

Eyes still gleeful, she murmured something, made a swift and intricate gesture, and—

The doors behind the sentinel exploded outwards in eerie silence, the blast that destroyed them contained in an invisible sphere.

Haelgon was slammed against the inner curve of that magical prison, bowed gorily outwards along its arc and flattened in an instant—as well as impaled by many wooden shards and splinters.

Then the sphere melted away, spilling the limp, bloody body of the guard out into the passage, leaving no trace of the doors at all.

"Fool," Maera told the boneless remains coldly. "The rules in Imtowers, behind my parents' backs, haven't changed in years. Obey me and live; defy me and die. It's quite simple."

She stepped over the mess and through the hole where the great doors had been, into a draperied outer chamber where two uniformed maids lay broken, sprawled amid spreading blood and the splintered remains of their chairs, their limbs lying at strange angles and jagged, broken ends of the chair-legs thrust through their bodies.

Through the blood-spattered silks on the chamber's far side could be heard Lord Tesmer asking feebly, "What, by the glorking Falcon, *was that?*"

Only to be answered by the sharper tones of his spouse. "Rance, *I care not.* Just you put your tongue back to what it was doing."

Maera sighed, struck aside the draperies, and strode across the opulent and deserted receiving room beyond to one of the half-dozen archways around its richly paneled walls.

She passed her hand in front of her, murmured something, and heard a faint singing in the air that told Maera her parents' swirldagger shield had faded before her assault.

The eldest child of Lord Irrance and Lady Telclara Tesmer smiled tightly. So she was still stronger in her wizardry than the best mage her parents could hire. That was gratifying.

She conjured a hand-shield—just in case; in younger days, her mother had been known to be quick indeed with thrown daggers, and to keep them well-poisoned—and walked through the last set of draperies, into her parents' bedchamber.

Lord Tesmer was spreadeagled face up, naked and bound, between the four posts of a new and grander gilded bed than they'd had the last time Maera had been in here—furtively and alone, testing her spells against the wardings that were laid thickly upon the chamber. Lady Tesmer was also naked, and as beautiful as ever. Her hair unbound, she was straddling Lord Tesmer's face on widespread knees, languidly lashing him over her shoulder with a whip that looked like a horse's tail.

Her mother turned blazing eyes on Maera and stiffened in anger, but wasn't given the time to draw breath and launch into a tirade.

"Satisfy her, Father!" Maera snapped. "She'll not be in a listening mood until she's felt the full fire of her pleasure. As for yours, some other time will have to suffice, or a handy maid, later. I've something important to show you both; *yes,* important enough to interrupt you this way."

Keep them off-balance, unable to start shouting at her in concert.
"So, Lord Irrance Tesmer, ply that tongue! *Ply*, I say!"

"*Maera Harilda Mehannraer!*" her mother hissed. "How *dare* you?"

Maera gave the Lady Telclara Tesmer a cool look. "Very easily, Mother. After all, I learned daring—to say nothing of rudeness—from you. Yet kiss the Falcon and take calm, both of you, and spare me all the snarling and storming. When you see what I've discovered, you'll understand why it just wouldn't wait. This concerns the very future of House Tesmer."

Her mother looked angry enough to dispute that, and opened her mouth to say so—but then stiffened, panted as her eyes went very wide, sobbed as a spasm of pleasure shook her entire body... and collapsed backwards atop her helpless spouse.

Maera strode over to tower over her parents, ignoring her father's stunned stare. Taking hold of her mother's breast, she squeezed the nipple sharply, evoking another spasm of thrashing pleasure, then squeezed it again. Harder.

Lady Tesmer's eyes flew open this time, glaring at her daughter.

Maera gave her a nod, as though greeting her on the road, and snapped, "Free him."

"*Maera!*" her mother responded sharply, "I'm not your servant, and your sheer—"

"*Free him!*"

Maera turned away from the bed in a swirl of sleeves and skirts, and snatched up and hurled aside a padded stool and a broad armchair. When she had enough space cleared among the overlapping fur rugs, she began a long and intricate casting.

"Insolent daughter—" Lady Tesmer began, then fell silent abruptly as she recognized what was forming in the air of her bedchamber.

It was an upright, palely glowing oval, not a gate but the largest and most powerful sort of farscrying "eye." Something far beyond any hedge-wizard.

Keeping her back to them and trusting to her hand-shield to protect it against anything they might hurl, Maera allowed herself a tight smile.

The mere nature of this spell boasted to her parents just how mighty their eldest daughter—their *heir*, and if any Tesmer thought that only sons mattered, she'd soon eliminate them—had become in matters of magecraft. Which was why she should swiftly demonstrate her loyalty to her parents, and keep herself clean of any apparent involvement in the deaths of her brothers. It would be tiresome to have Lord and Lady Tesmer hate and fear their most capable offspring more than they appreciated her talents.

Time to begin this mending.

"I have no wish to embarrass either of you farther," she said, trying to sound both apologetic and loving, "which is why I'm keeping my back turned. If this wasn't of such immediate importance, I'd not have *dreamed* of disturbing your privacy. Mother, Father... I love you both, and am loyal to you. I think first of service to you, and secondly of the strength and reputation of House Tesmer. I hope you know that."

She could hear whispers of energetically tugged silk behind her, yet it seemed a long time before her mother replied coolly, "We thought we did know that. Yet in recent days, so much of what we thought we knew to be true has proven otherwise. Trust, once lost, is harder to regain than you might think."

Had there been an ever-so-slight emphasis on that "you"?

"Turn around, Maera," her father said, as calmly as if he'd been offering her wine. "You have something to show us?"

He *was* offering her wine.

It would be poisoned, of course, but Maera had prepared for that. The spells that would protect her were surging bright and strong within her, so she smiled and took the proffered goblet with a smile as genuine as she could feign.

And drank deeply, matching their alert smiles with one of her own that told them, as clearly as if she'd shouted it, *I know what you did to this otherwise superb wine.*

Her mother's smile changed slightly. *Of course you do, daughter,* it seemed to say. *You* are *a Tesmer.*

Lord and Lady Tesmer were both wearing robes now, though neither of them had bothered to do them up. Interestingly, her father's manhood still stood proud; perhaps poison wasn't the only thing in their wine.

Maera's scrying oval had achieved its full size, and now floated upright like a tall door, stretching from about the height of her knees to just above her head, and about half as wide as it was high. It glowed milkily at one end of the space she'd cleared, showing only swirling clouds to the bedchamber.

"I do indeed, Father. I did not reveal this to you both earlier only because I did not think it was possible, without knowing—or guessing correctly, and I readily admit I tried to guess—where the persons one seeks have gone. Until a stray notion occurred to me that proved to be correct."

"Your demonstration that you can match your mother's mastery of cryptic speech is sufficient, Maera," Lord Tesmer said dryly. "I take it you mean to say that you've been curious as to the whereabouts of our runaways, Belard and Talyss? And acting upon some stray notion proved successful?"

"*Yes*, Father," Maera told him warmly.

His eyes twinkled. "So what was this notion?"

Maera took all the time she needed to reply, choosing her words carefully, and looking to her mother as she did so. "From time to time, although no one is supposed to know, both of you have dealings with a certain wizard. Whose skin is blue. I suspect that both of you in turn know very well that this same wizard, from time to time, has appeared to various of your children—almost certainly including Belard and Talyss, and definitely including me—for his own reasons. I have always thought he was judging us, both individually and as part of House Tesmer, and therefore have obeyed him utterly."

Lady Tesmer stiffened.

"I've not found it necessary to obey him in that way, Mother; he has never asked that of me. Nor has he instructed me in working magic, beyond telling me that something he had seen me doing—without my knowing he was scrying—was right or wrong, futile or dangerous, or worth pursuing. With one exception."

They were both watching her very alertly now, leaning forward, and Maera saw menace in their eyes. If she said the wrong thing, the next few moments would undoubtedly be... interesting.

"The blue mage taught me just one small magic, and encouraged me to practice it often, telling me it would someday be quite useful. The magic is a small spell that does nothing at all, except elude most tracing spells that seek out magic, until a particular sort of spell reaches out to it. A tracer spell, cast by the same person who cast the first spell."

Her parents had relaxed. A trifle.

"So you cast this small spell on many portable items in Imtowers," Lady Tesmer said. A statement rather than a question.

Maera nodded.

"And either Belard or Talyss is unwittingly wearing or carrying some thing that you prepared in this manner right now, so you can—and have—traced them."

Maera nodded.

"Very clever, Maera. Leave telling us what the item might be, and about our Master's involvement with you, for another time. We, too, have work to do and other matters planned for our day than the pleasure you interrupted. So you've found Talyss and Belard, and are ready to show us where they are and what they're up to—and this, you believe, is vital to the future of the family. Well enough. Show us, and let us know and judge.

"Oh, and Maera? Well done."

Maera blinked, and felt herself blush. That was a little distressing, considering she thought she'd mastered control of her face and voice long ago, but then, praise from her mother *was* astonishing in itself.

"One moment," Lord Tesmer said crisply, astonishing her again. *Isn't he supposed to be the weak one?*

"I want this spell of yours banished in an instant, without showing us anything, if you know of any spell that can be used— by a Doom of Falconfar, say, not just by you or a lesser mage—to trace or identify us through it. Or even be aware of our scrutiny as we watch. Will they be able to see and hear us?"

Maera shook her head. "No, Father, they won't, and no, I know of no such spell. If I did, I'd never have dared try to find them in the first place. One thing neither Talyss nor Belard lack is malice."

"Show us, then, Maera," Lady Tesmer said gently, almost fondly. "I have missed our *dear* little Lyss. And Bel, too."

Maera almost winced at the acid in her mother's voice, but managed to keep her face expressionless as she nodded, turned, and waved her hand.

The roiling mists fell away like a dropped tapestry, leaving the three of them looking into another chamber as if through a window.

It was a high-roofed, formal room, and Talyss Tesmer was kneeling in it.

One of the watchers in Imtowers growled in rage.

Surprisingly, it was Lady Telclara Tesmer.

Chapter Thirty-One

IT WAS A high-roofed, formal room. Pillars lined its walls in elegant clusters, soaring up to an ornately carved, vaulted ceiling.

In front of a broad bed flanked by man-high branched candlesticks, Talyss Tesmer was kneeling on a thick, bright, new rauthen-fur rug, right in front of a man.

He was a Galathan noble, by his looks, clad in a puff-sleeved jerkin and sleek hose, his crisp new garments the very height of fashion. His cheeks were rouged and his hair oiled; he was doused in scent. He was sneering down at Talyss in triumph as her slender fingers worked the laces of his ornate codpiece, and using the riding-whip in his hand to flick the translucent silken sleep-robe from her shoulders, so that it fell around her, attached only to her forearms.

"Power," she was purring. "I admire power so *much*, Lord Telgurt."

"I begin to see what Dunshar's been seeing in you," the noble replied, smirking as his adornment was loosed and swung down and aside, and the woman kneeling before him breathed warmly on what was now exposed.

"I hope so, lord," she murmured, and thrust her head forward to apply her tongue.

"If I feel your teeth," the noble snapped, sudden steel in his voice, "rest assured you'll feel my whip. Bear that in mind."

Her reply was a wordless, murmured affirmative, and Lord Telgurt started to relax and give himself over to pleasure.

"One thing more," he muttered, his voice less curt and threatening. "Deceive or seek to harm me in any way, wench, and you'll be sharing pleasure with me no longer. Instead, you'll be giving pleasure to my knights and armsmen—all two thousand of them who rode here with me. Understand?"

"I do," Talyss breathed. "Oh, I do."

In Imtowers, Maera glanced at her father to see how he was taking this, and saw the same eagerness as on Telgurt's face. Her mother's hand was stealing over to the open front of Lord Tesmer's robe.

But of course.

THE KING OF Galath studied the list that had just been handed to him. It was not a short one.

"Larth," he murmured, arching his brows in surprise. "But he's my age! He *knows* what harm is done when Galath fights over this throne. Oh, well, I suppose they're paying him well enough... who *is* paying him, by the way?"

"We're not sure, Majesty, but we're leaning to it being either House Duthcrown or House Yarrove. I say the families to you, Sire, because we can find—as yet—no hint that the heads of those houses are directly involved.

"Beyond the fact that those loyal lords can hardly help but notice that infamous wizards are sitting down with them at their feasting-tables, drinking their wine of evenings, and so on," King Brorsavar said dryly. "Well, they've coin enough, to be sure. And here's Memmurth, of course, and Darlamtur, too. Hmm. It certainly seems as if every mage in Falconfar who knows where Galath is has found his way here. I feel almost honored. Now if some mighty mage would just step in through yonder door with a spell to shield me against all of *their* magics, I could relax and enjoy a decent spell-battle, until the inevitable dagger finds me."

"Sire!"

"Oh? Am I not supposed to know what's afoot in Galath? Isn't that what kings do, when they're not busy tyrannizing their people?"

His steward coughed. "I believe siring royal heirs also comes into it somewhere, Your Majesty."

"So it does, so it does. You obviously know the tasks, good Ravalan; why don't *you* put on this crown and ride to Galathgard? The realm needs someone young, vigorous, and—"

"Expendable," Windstrike murmured from behind the king, before he could stop himself.

There was a moment of shocked silence in the chamber, as Ravalan recoiled in horror from the royal suggestion, and everyone else gaped at Marquel Windstrike.

Except Brorsavar, who pounded his fist on the table and roared with laughter, long bellows of mirth that no one dared join in.

"Now *that*," the King of Galath gasped, when he found breath enough to speak again, "was almost worth dying for. By the Falcon, I'm going to miss this, when I'm gone!"

IN THE SCRYING oval, they heard Lord Telgurt groan in pleasure, as loudly as if he was in a bedchamber.

"Maera, dear," Lady Tesmer murmured then, "you *are* going to tell us where Talyss is, aren't you? And are we seeing something captured by your spell, earlier, or something befalling right now?"

"The room is somewhere in the castle of Galathgard, in the heart of Galath," Maera replied. "As you can see, it's not as ruinous as the tales have always told us. And what we're seeing is happening right now, as we watch."

Her mother smiled and nodded, gaze never leaving the image.

"Shall I—?" Talyss gasped to the arduke then, taking her mouth off him for a moment, "or would you prefer—?"

She waved at the bed behind them both.

"Take it. Take it, then fetch me wine," Telgurt said roughly. "I've some powder; it works swiftly, and then we can do the other."

He glanced swiftly back at the bed, nodded his head as if it met his standards—and then stiffened as her hot, wet mouth closed on him again, and a slender finger thrust gently up his backside.

Arduke Brasgel Telgurt was not a man used to curbing his reactions, and he threw back his head and shouted his satisfaction. Talyss murmured loudly, too, repeating the same muffled sound of satisfaction several times ere the noble backed away from her and sat down heavily on the bed, panting.

"F-Falcon, *yes*, that was—magnificent! Hurry with that wine, lass! No, cast aside your silks—I want to see you run for it naked!"

"Takes after her mother, she does," Lord Tesmer murmured, in the bedchamber in Imtowers.

Maera turned swiftly to see how murderous her mother's face was, but Lady Tesmer was smiling.

ROD EVERLAR CAME awake sweating, out of a nightmare of Lorontar the archwizard smiling at him and bending to kiss him. As those bearded lips bent to his, they became gap-toothed bone, and the wizard's face a grinning skull, as his laughter thundered all around him...

"Go to sleep, Lord Rod," Taeauna said soothingly, from beside him. She was pressed right against him, shoulder to shoulder, leather on leather. Sometime after he'd drifted off, she must have shifted over to join him, amalgamating their cloaks and their warmth.

Rod lay staring up at the dark ceiling, gasping for breath and trying to slow his racing heart. "I had a... had a nightmare," he panted.

"I know," the Aumrarr beside him said soothingly. "Lorontar giving you the skullface, yes?"

"How—how did you know?"

"He always does, to someone trying to sleep here. Some sort of taunting he worked on Malraun, long ago. 'My magic prevails over yours,' I guess. 'You may control this armory, Malraun, but you'll never take refuge in it.' That sort of thing."

Christ. These wizards. Reaching out beyond death, across half a world to sneer into each other's faces. Warning what they could do, even from beyond the grave.

AT THE DOOR of the many-pillared bedchamber in Galathgard, Talyss turned, her mouth open wide to show the arduke what was on her tongue.

She swallowed with obvious relish, and with an almost fond smile said, "My lord Telgurt, I mind scampering through this castle bareskinned not at all; I will be proud to tell anyone I meet that I do your bidding, and have just enjoyed your prowess—but have you no concern that some rivals may use this against you? Deeming your prudence too shallow for high office, when... when high office beckons, as so soon it shall?"

The arduke barked with laughter. "Hah, wench! You worry for me? How sweet! High office is given to those who seize it! And as for my reputation once I have it, or my misuse of it thereafter; my dear little playpretty, misusing it is what high office is *for*." He sat up and sketched a mocking bow in her direction.

"So I *thank* you for your kind concern, bed-lass, but require you now not to worry, but rather to race like the wind to the sour-faced cellarer I bribed not long ago, and request of him what he agreed to provide me—just a decanter right now, mind; I don't want him following you with two hairy lads and a keg! Why, I— IiiieeeeeEEE!"

A slender sword thrust up through the bed from beneath, piercing Arduke Brasgel Telgurt almost up to his lungs.

Belard Tesmer rolled out from under the bed grinning as Talyss raced across the room to wrap herself around the arduke's face, embracing him tightly and muffling his screams as he died.

Then she thrust Telgurt's corpse back onto the bed and tore away the lace that adorned his chest, to wipe herself clean of his blood.

"Overperfumed pig," she said dismissively. "His seed tasted like butter."

"Did it now?" Belard replied. "He died readily enough—and look! It seems he didn't need his powder, after all! Should I leave you two alone together?"

Talyss looked back at the corpse. "Don't tempt me, brother." Her gaze lingered. "Hmm. Perhaps you should, at that."

THE LONG, RAGGED scream brought Garfist awake in a rush, sitting up with his sword in his hand.

"Isk? *Isk!*" he shouted into the darkness.

"Easy, Old Ox mine," his longtime partner replied, from the mouth of the cave. "Everything's fine. Go back to sleep." The two Aumrarr stood at her shoulders, drawn swords in their hands.

"Who screamed?" he growled. "Someone screamed—I know they did!"

"Dark Helms," Juskra replied disgustedly, landing on her knees beside him. "It was Dark Helms, this time. I'd take us to another cave, but there *isn't* another cave."

"Besides," Dauntra put in, "Being right here to kill everyone arriving through the gate is quite... efficient."

Garfist yawned. "An' ye Aumrarr are known for yer efficiency, aye." His next utterance was a snore.

Juskra smiled down at him, then at her fellow Aumrarr. "Efficient. I quite like that."

"CHARMING," LADY TESMER commented, gazing at the bedchamber in Galathgard through the scrying-window. "Maera, will it harm your magic if we send a spell of our own through it, to destroy—or at least maim—your wayward siblings? I'd—"

"No, Mother!" Maera said sternly. "If I try that, I'll be certain of two things: destroying this farscrying, *and* allowing anyone who has any magic at all in Galathgard—and wizards in the hire of nobles have arrived in the castle by the dozens, perhaps scores, by now—to trace us, even after the scrying has ended. *Not* wise.

"And I doubt that I'd succeed in doing anything to Talyss and Belard beyond letting them know we're watching them."

"Ah. Very well. I ache to destroy them, but perhaps a better time will arise."

"Oh, it will." Maera smiled sweetly, and added, "Lyss and Bel want one thing above all else: power. They're in Galathgard right now so as to be properly situated to control whoever rises to rule in Galath."

"Does not Brorsavar rule?"

"Until the first dagger finds him, a few days from now. I think even *he* knows that. Were I him, I'd be butchering nobles right and left, and using wizards to cow the rest into cringing obedience... but he's an old man; I think he's looking for a way to die swiftly and soon, that he can feel truly noble about. Either that, or he's insane or being made so by some wizard no one saw conquer his wits."

"Complicated intrigues you spell-dabblers embrace, to be sure," Lord Tesmer murmured. "So we let Talyss and Bel sink their claws into the new king of Galath... and then?"

"Once the struggle for the throne has sorted itself out—the first claimant after Brorsavar falls may be far removed from the ultimately successful one, ere everyone sickens of the slaughter and depart Galathgard—we strike, taking down my traitor brother and sister. Thereby gaining control of Galath *and* taking our rightful revenge, at one stroke."

"'Our'?" Lady Tesmer's voice was deceptively mild.

"Mother, they stole magic and coins from me, too." Maera held up her hand. "One amendment to my words, though. I should have said not 'my traitor brother and sister,' but rather '*these* traitors.' I think you'll find your other sons have been even more disloyal, if you look closely. I've noticed a few things, recently, but was more intent on working on my magic than in by thrusting my nose where it wasn't wanted."

"I'd be surprised if any of my children were *not* engaged in intrigues in their own interest," Lord Tesmer observed, "but have my thanks, daughter. We shall... look more closely."

Maera nodded. "I'm surprised the hedge-wizard you hired a while back hasn't reported anything of this to you. I'd be concerned about his loyalties, if I were you."

"Well, actually, *no*, dear," her mother said gently. "He's been reporting often and diligently, and we think highly of his performance."

"Oh?"

"Yes, dear. He's been watching you."

Maera snorted, shook her head, and said, "I see."

"Precisely." And on that note, Lady Tesmer rose demurely, nodded farewell, and strode to her robing room.

Maera looked at the scrying-window. Belard and Talyss had rolled the arduke's corpse off the bed and were putting it to good use, bloodstains and all. "I take it Mother feels she's seen enough?"

"It seems that way," said Lord Tesmer, then seemed on the verge of saying something more.

She looked at him, and he smiled thinly and added, "You can also take two things more, Maera."

Something in his tone made Maera stiffen and look at him sharply. His gaze, on hers, was as mild as ever, even approving. She waited, crooking an eyebrow when he remained silent.

That earned her a dry smile.

"End your scrying," he directed.

She did so, and he continued, "The first, patient daughter mine, is that your mother and I agree with your views on dealing with Belard and Talyss. We should plan this together, scrying often in the next few days and talking together often."

Maera bowed her head in acknowledgement and agreement. "And the second?"

Lord Tesmer rose to stand facing her, open robe swirling and hands clenched into fists. "If this is the first step in a bid to seize

Imtowers and become head of the house, dearest Maera," he said quietly and coldly, "be *very* cautious. You are my favorite. I would hate to have to destroy you."

He opened his right hand to her then, palm up, and an emerald glow appeared out of nowhere to fill it.

The radiance was coming from a symbol now visible on his hand. A magical rune.

Maera stared at it, horror clear on her face for her father to see, but could not stop. It was unmistakable.

She had come upon this symbol thrice down the years, in the pages of the most secret and powerful of grimoires she'd managed to get glimpses of—but she had never expected to see it aglow with power, on anyone's hand, in Falconfar.

It was the rune of the long-dead archwizard Lorontar.

Yes, it's mine, said a cold voice inside her, then. The gloating voice Maera had heard in her head for as long as she could remember, not often but whenever her life depended on knowing something. Something it had always provided.

Which meant that her inner voice, the thing that Maera Harilda Mehannraer Tesmer had always taken to mean she was truly special, was not the Falcon or a guardian ancestor but the legendary first Lord Archwizard of Falconfar.

Lorontar, who was not dead, but lived on. Inside her.

Maera would have cried then, if she'd dared. Would have fainted, or turned and fled, shrieking, if a cold claw hadn't suddenly tightened its grip on her mind, controlling her utterly. Making her stand right where she was, still and silent.

Greetings, little pawn. Yes, be as grateful as you know how. I kept you alive all these years for this.

Her father's eyes glowed a piercing, emerald green, a terrible rictus of a smile on his face.

Maera screamed, long and silently, inside her own head, but heard only echoing, gloating laughter.

Chapter Thirty-Two

"HO, ASKURR! WHAT d'you think?"

Bracebold was holding up some kind of triple-pronged sword, whose blades appeared removable, although whatever else could be fitted in their place was missing from the rubble.

Askurr shrugged. "If it were me, I'd put that down *very* gently and carefully, and run far away from it. If it's not a coin or a gem, I don't want it. Being as this was a wizard's abode, anything else could mean some horrible doom for me, that I might not even notice coming until too late. But that's just me. You suit yourself. One man's refuse is another man's plunder."

Bracebold scowled. "I was looking for some words to hearten me, not bid me walk away emptyhanded."

"Then talk to Glorn, or Zorzaerel. They're always eager for treasure and adventure and doing the daring thing, so they'll probably tell you to keep it, carry it off, and find out later what it does. Just remember you'll be learning its purpose the hard way, and don't come crying around my door when you do—if you have anything left to cry with."

Bracebold growled, flung down the three-armed thing, and strode away across the rubble.

He was a good nine strides away when it exploded.

MORL FROWNED DOWN at the man sprawled on the gravel in front of them. "So why did he die, when the other one just fainted?"

Tethtyn shrugged, and spread his hands. "And I became an expert on this 'Earth' place when, exactly?"

Morl sighed. "I wanted one we could question."

"So heave this one into this metal bin that smells so bad, set fire to it, and let's be gone from here and trying to find another man to question," Tethtyn suggested patiently. "I think I heard him call it a 'dumpster.'"

Morl gave his fellow wizard a dubious look. "Nothing says 'A wizard did this' as loudly as a body that's been burned to ashes."

"True, in Falconfar. Yet if they have no wizards here, they'll hardly think the same way about a mysterious killing, will they?"

"Now, now; all we know is that *this* man hadn't heard of wizards, except in something called 'Diznaekartouns.' Didn't the other one call us kulkists, or something? Sussussaetannik kulkists?"

"*Cultists*," Tethtyn corrected, frowning. "Yes, he did. You think that's the local word for wizards?"

Morl shrugged, spread his hands, and grinned. "And I became an expert on this 'Earth' place when, exactly?"

"BEHOLD," DAUNTRA SAID gently as they regarded the sprawling encampments. "The stormclouds gather at Galathgard."

Garfist shrugged. "I care not, if all of them bring sausages."

Iskarra gave him a sour look. "Sausages you'd not be having, nor the eggs, either, if I hadn't persuaded yon cook to part with them."

"Persuaded, hey? How soon is he likely to wake up? That crack ye gave him was a good hard one—an' the skillet was sizzling when ye did it, too!"

Her look a silent question, Iskarra turned to Juskra.

Who shrugged. "Who knows? I'm no expert on the skulls of strange men. 'Twas me swooping he saw, though; they'll not be looking for Isk."

"Leaving me free to tackle the *next* camp kitchen," Iskarra concluded triumphantly. "There seems to be no end to them."

"There certainly seems to be no end to the nobles, to be sure," Dauntra said darkly. "Gar, are you about finished? I'd like to get gone from here, up onto the castle roof yonder, before too many more of them wake up and happen to notice Aumrarr flapping around. We're none too popular—and I've noticed no shortage of archers serving these nobles, either."

Garfist thrust all six sausages into his mouth, chewed triumphantly for a moment, then managed to say around them, "Ready. Ye fly, Jusk, an' I'll chew—or is it cuddly little Dauntra's turn to fly me about?" He leered.

Dauntra rolled her eyes, then gasped in mock breathlessness, "I've a notorious weakness for men with sausages; however did you know?"

"YOU WORKED FOR him," Zorzaerel said almost accusingly. "You should know where his jewels are!"

Glorn sighed. "Tell me, bold swordcaptain: how many wizards have you worked for? Have you ever met even one who trusts *anyone*? Still less, anyone who wears a sword and a dagger, and knows how to use them? He was a glorking *Doom* of Falconfar, not a lackwit!"

Zorzaerel sighed, nodded, and waved his hands in exasperation. They were standing in an inner room of Malragard, ankle-deep in the shifting rubble of its fallen ceiling.

"I just thought it would all be different," he grumbled. "Easier to find, harder to get in. Where are the guardian beasts, the trap—"

"Youngling," a voice rasped from behind him, "clamp your jaws!"

Bracebold was wild-haired and blackened from head to toe, the rear of his leathers and armor a scorched ruin. He now limped, or stood still, his customary restlessness gone. His every word was tight with pain.

"Aye," Gorongor called, from the far side of the room. "Tempt not the Falcon!"

"As it happens, I agree," Roreld said, from a distant doorway, "but as the *last* thing I want is for us to end up daggers drawn over any takings, hearken: Tarlund and I have found some gems. A *lot* of gems. Some of them glowing—and one of them winking like a signal-lantern."

"Get well away from that one," Glorn snapped, "and take the rest of the gems with you. Three or four chambers away, at least."

"My thinking too," Roreld agreed, half-grinning at the sudden eagerness with which all the hireswords were now converging on him, "but you may as well see, first."

They all came, and crowded around, and saw. The winking gem was an angry rose-red and the size of a small man's fist, and in common accord they clawed in the rubble around the other stones—all different, none of them anything like as large; loot from many places, to be sure—until they were sure the room held no more. Then they bore the gems away, using what was left of Eskeln's overleathers as a sack for them. One-and-thirty, in all.

More than one man looked back at the winking gem, sitting alone now, the rubble cleared away from it for several strides all around. Its inner light pulsed, silently and tirelessly, seeming to watch them.

No one wanted to stay within sight of it.

"Back the way we came," Roreld said firmly. "I'm not blundering in deeper when we're all thinking of gems instead of watching for perils. Besides, we know not if anything guards these stones, and will come after us; I'd prefer to fight on ground I know."

"Well said," Gorongor agreed, amid approving murmurs from the rest. They hastened back out to where they'd camped on the edge of the ruins, sat down in a half-ring facing shattered Malragard, and unfolded the improvised sack to look at the gems again.

They sighed with satisfaction. They were gazing at enough wealth, properly sold, for them all to retire in idle comfort. So long as they lived to depart the ruins, and got a fair share. The sidelong looks began.

Roreld saw them and moved to quell that trouble right away, by clapping a gentle arm around Bracebold's shoulders and growling, "This, swordbrothers, is just a start. Yet consider—before we decide whether or not to risk our necks going on busily plundering Malragard—how many wizards may already suspect Malraun has fallen, and be on their way here *right now* to seek a Doom's magic."

That turned the narrowed gazes at each other into peerings over shoulders and up into the sky, and the oldest of the warcaptains smiled; deed done.

"Well," Tarlund said, stepping into the ploy, "if the Dooms are truly all gone—*if*, I say—then there's Empherel of Skoum, Lyrandurl—he of the golden, scented beard and arm-bangles like a dancing-lass—Roskryn who enspells swords to fight for him, and... ach, 'twon't come to me; that one in Tauren, he who took down Skelt Tower with his spells..."

"Halavar Dreel," Olondyn supplied rather grimly. "I fought against him once. We were a very small part of an army he destroyed in, well, moments." He shook his head. "Aye, I've fought him—for a few volleys, before we all gained sense enough to run. If I see his face, I'll not be standing my ground to dispute with him, know you!"

"Dreel of Tauren, aye," Bracebold muttered. "I've heard... things."

"He took to killing hedge-wizards, didn't he?" Askurr put in, peering closely at the gems and then sitting back hastily, his hands spread wide to show everyone they were empty.

"So he did, for a time, but he'd have to spend several lifetimes slaying, morn through even, to reap *that* crop," Eskeln commented. "There are hundreds—thousands—of jacks and lasses in Falconfar who can cast a few spells, and pretend to be able to work more. Enough of them that every noble in Galath who isn't terrified of magic can hire one or two, and be certain of finding others if he fires those he's paying."

"And all a hedge-wizard would have to do is whisper a hint of strong magic for the taking, to get permission—and swift horses and a strong bodyguard—from glorking near *every* noble in Galath," Zorzaerel said disgustedly.

"No," Gorongor disagreed. "Not now. Any other time, I'd agree, but not right now. Not when a Great Court's been called, and every noble of Galath needs to be seen there, to stand loudly loyal at the side of whoever wears the crown when it's done. Nobles don't trust underlings to go hunt down powerful magic behind their backs, when they need them—wizards and bodyguards both—as their shields instead. A mage who comes to plunder Malragard now is a mage whose only master is himself—or who has slipped away to see to this, probably on some other pretext."

"I'd not want to be anywhere near Galathgard right now," Bracebold muttered.

Zorzaerel nodded. "Aye! What if some noble decides to fling more coin than any of us will ever see in our lives, and hires one of the *real* wizards, from across the sea? This Taervellar of the Talons, now, or the wizard-king, Ommaunt Barlaskeir?"

Glorn nodded, but raised one wagging finger. "Tales have a way of growing in the telling. I wonder, now, just how powerful those two truly are."

Eskeln shrugged. "Takes cunning and strong spells to stay king for long," he said, eyeing the gems. "Otherwise, those who fear you always move from thinking they'd be safer if they put a blade through you to doing it."

"Takes real power to sink four ships sailing hard up your behind," Tarlund added, "So I'd say this Taervellar is full coin for their fear of him."

"I," Roreld said grimly, "fear someone else rather more: Lord Archwizard Lorontar. Whom I have a strong suspicion is not as dead as we all hope him to be."

TETHTYN ELDURANT SMILED the sort of bright, ruthless smile he'd seen the Lord of Hawksyl use, when politely giving men a choice between obeying him or dying. "*Tell* us, man! Or—"

He raised his free hand like a claw, fingers jabbing at the man's face as though casting a spell, and tightened his other hand around the man's throat.

Morl Ulaskro gave the man a matching smile, over Tethtyn's shoulder.

Their captive gargled helplessly. Still maintaining his grin, Tethtyn loosened his grip, so the man could speak.

"Tell you *what?* You're a pair of fucking *lunatics*, you know that? Wh—"

"If this 'loonatiks' means wizards, yes we are," Tethtyn agreed. "Which means you know quite well what we can do to you. Which in turn means, I trust, that you will give us an answer— the *right* answer, your best answer, holding nothing back—to our questions. Now, I'll ask again: where is this 'Diznaekartouns,' the fortress that holds Saetannik cultists?"

The man stared at him, then at Morl. "This is a joke, right? Hidden camera, you'll be showing it on the Internet, all of that?"

He looked desperately from Morl to Tethtyn, and then back again. Then he twisted and squirmed in a sudden frenzy, and slammed his leg up into Tethtyn's crotch, in the hardest kick the underscribe's inexpensive codpiece had ever endured, and tore his way free.

Tethtyn flung out one hand to grab the man's shoulder—and found himself clutching a torn scrap of collar as the man sprinted away across the parking lot.

Morl sighed, raised his hand, and firmly declaimed the words Lorontar's cold voice had whispered in his head.

The air around the running man erupted in a sudden burst of flame, as severe as it was sudden. Legs ran crazily beneath a writhing, darkening fireball, then collapsed into a rolling mass that settled to the pavement amid greasy smoke.

Tethtyn and Morl exchanged glances, and then sighs.

"Do they all *want* to die?" Tethtyn waved his hands in exasperation. "Is answering questions that hard for them?"

Morl shrugged, frowned and dropped into a crouch, peering past Tethtyn. The other mage spun around to see the new peril.

It was one of the warriors in the dark uniforms with the caps, popping up from behind a parked car with a gun aimed at them, held in both hands.

"*Freeze!* Police! Get down! Face down on the ground, hands above your head and spread apart!"

The yelling continued. "I *saw* that! You killed him! Dealer gone bad on you, huh? Goddamn druggies, think you can—"

"Put the wand away," Tethtyn ordered crisply.

"The... gonne!" Morl snapped. "Drop it! *Now!*"

The cop thought he'd been shouting as loudly as he knew how, but disbelieving rage lent him new reserves of volume and authority.

"*You* don't give orders here!" he bellowed, waving the gun. "*I* do! Now get down! Down on the ground, with your hands away from your sides, or I'll shoot!"

Neither Morl nor Tethtyn even bothered to point their fingers. Two spellbolts streaked to the same target.

The explosion was louder, brighter, and shorter this time.

Tethtyn just sneered and turned away, but Morl strolled to where he could look down on the smoking corpse, and told it gently, "*Wizards* give the orders, fool. That's how it *works*."

"MY LORD?" His most loyal bodyguard—Hondreth, the only one he trusted enough to have here in the room with him—was offering him a large goblet.

Lordrake Anthan Halamaskar waved away the proffered wine impatiently, shifted in his large and comfortable chair, and went on gazing into the fire blazing lazily in the great hearth. "No, no more. I'll need a clear head for this. One does not treat with mighty wizards casually. Or rather: not twice."

"I'm sorry, Master," Hondreth murmured. "It was just that you seemed, ah, a trifle unsettled—"

"I *am* a trifle unsettled. He should be here by now, if he's coming at all... and if he's not coming, has he decided to tell someone else of my offer?"

"Never think that, Lord of Maurpath. I do not tell tales."

That voice was as cold and sharp as it was unexpected, and made both lordrake and bodyguard flinch, the latter aghast that someone had managed to somehow enter the room without his knowing. He should have at least *sensed—*

"You can take your hand off your blade," the same voice informed him calmly, "or you can die. Choose wisely."

The bodyguard flung his hand away from his sword as if its hilt had caught fire, looking around the room wildly for the intruder. The fire was casting wild shadows in the lofty lodge chamber, which was crowded with man-high mirrors and life-sized statues, but he'd not *seen—*

Quite suddenly, a lean, sharp-featured man with the gleaming black eyes of a hawk, peering out from beneath bristling brows, was standing calmly before them, hands hooked through the belt of his black leathers.

"Halavar Dreel, I presume?" Lordrake Halamaskar asked dryly, suddenly wishing he had that goblet in his hand after all. To toy with. Or clench.

It wasn't that he was a complete stranger to treason. Far from it, if truth be known, but wizards were... wizards.

Chapter Thirty-Three

WITH THE CASTING almost done and the last few words coming with careful precision, Belard Tesmer allowed himself a wry smile.

The trick hadn't been worming how to cast a mind-swaying magic out of the wizard. A simple bag of gems had taken care of that.

Nor had it been killing Sarchar "Lord of Spells" to get the gems back, afterwards. His dagger was sharp, and throat-slitting was almost routine for him by now.

No, the trick was catching his sister asleep. Well and truly asleep, deep enough in slumber that he could stand over her, murmur things, and even touch her without having her wake before his casting was done. There were times, these last few days, when Belard had begun to think Talyss Tesmer never slept. He'd tried tiring her out by pouncing on her for slap-and-tickle again and again, but beyond making her yawn a little amid her delighted gasps and squeals, that only achieved wearing *himself* out.

Yet he'd managed it at last, largely by finding a loft in one of the ruined wings of Galathgard and getting a good long sleep while Talyss was scampering around the castle spying on who was arriving, what dangerous knights, mages, and skulkers they'd brought with them, and who most hated whom.

It had hardly been news to discover that very few Galathan nobles loved their fellow highborn enough even to be civil to more than a handful of closest allies, but Belard and Talyss needed to know which hatreds ran deepest, and who would be more pragmatic than vengeful, when it came to regicide and the scramble for the crown that was sure to follow.

They had agreed it was time to draw back into the shadows and just watch and wait, as more and more of the mighty of Galath arrived for the Great Court. It was time to let Dunshar take the blame for their actions. Feuding Falconaar of any realm had a habit of standing together long enough to hurl down strangers, before turning back to savaging each other.

He had to touch her to complete the casting, and did so now, trusting in his lowered breeches and where he was touching her to fool her, should she awaken.

Talyss stirred, moved languidly among the tangled linens, then smiled faintly and fell still again.

Quelling a sigh of relief, Belard caught up his breeches and turned away in silence, to get himself out of the room before Talyss should awake.

Sarchar hadn't played him false. Belard had read over this spell often enough after killing the dusky-skinned Tammarlan to be sure of that.

So when he needed his sister's obedience, in time to come, all he need do is speak the secret phrase—and Talyss would be compelled to obey him utterly.

Well and good. Another step forward.

There'd need to be some careful steps ahead, to be sure. Deciding when and how to tell Talyss about the unfortunate accident that had befallen Sarchar, for one.

She'd been gleefully looking forward to devising new and interesting uses they could put the self-styled Lord of Spells to, in the unfolding years to come.

Slipping like a shadow down one of the dark servants' passages that ran through the darkness of Galathgard's back chambers, Belard decided it was a pity, in a way, that Sarchar was going to miss them.

"HALAVAR DREEL, I presume?" the noble sitting in the great chair before the fire asked, trying to sound dry and confident and fearlessly amused.

"Of course," the lean man in black leathers replied, his voice sharp. "Just as you are one of all too few lordrakes in Galath, and this is your most trusted bodyguard, Palavar Hondreth—

trust that is well-placed, by the way. And while we're indulging in pleasantries, know this, too: I don't think much of your taste in hunting lodges, Lord of Maurpath."

He waved at the mirrors and crudely sculpted statues arranged around the room, then overhead to include the dusty menagerie of animal heads hanging from the rafters.

"I inherited it," Lordrake Halamaskar replied shortly. "The lodge, not the taste. After all, *I* deal with wizards."

"I have not failed to notice that doing so has become fashionable among the highborn of Galath. Yet you at least demonstrate the discernment to look to *me*—and, if things have not changed, meet my terms?"

"Things have not changed," Halamaskar replied curtly. "Your payment awaits beneath yonder tabletop. Thirty-six stormstones, none of them smaller than my eyeball. One stone for each year of your life, Lord Wizard?"

"Thus far," came the dry rejoinder, accompanied by a casually imperious gesture, directing that the tabletop be lifted.

"Thus far," the lordrake agreed, waving Hondreth forward to see to the table.

Slowly and carefully the impassive bodyguard swung the smooth, polished top of the table upwards. It moved on concealed hinges, rising to reveal a shallow recess half-full of fading maps—upon which had been arranged, each on its own scrap of finest linen, thirty-six gleaming stormstones.

One could have a large keep built for what it cost to buy just one stormstone. Stormstones drank lightning, and magics that hurled lightning, and held a winking, smoky-silver radiance that shamed the finest jewelry. Only a handful of men in Galath—none of them not highborn—could have afforded, even sacrificing most else, to buy more than three or four stormstones outright. Dreel did not ask the lordrake how he'd come by so many; he had long ago learned to quell the curiosity of his youth.

"They're real," Halamaskar said confidently.

"I know," Dreel replied flatly.

"So as I understand your scheme," he added, "I am, in exchange for these stones, to impersonate King Brorsavar as we ride into Galathgard together. At that time, and thereafter so long as we remain in the castle, you will surround us both with your bodyguard. Who will strive to protect me every whit as diligently as they defend you."

"Yes," the lordrake agreed eagerly. "And while wearing the likeness of the king, you'll follow my directions as to which nobles to summon to your side for private parley, one by one."

"When I'll slay them with my spells—privately—and so eliminate those of your fellow Galathan nobles you most want dead. Which may well include those most likely to stand between you and the throne of Galath."

"Quite likely," Halamaskar replied calmly, nodding. He frowned slightly, and added, "Yet I see another query in your eyes, Lord Wizard. As we're speaking plainly..."

Dreel inclined his head politely. "Just this: what place will I have in your Galath?"

The lordrake frowned. "Place?"

"Reception, then. Rest assured I have no intention of dwelling in your kingdom, holding any rank in Galath, or challenging your authority, Lord of Maurpath. Yet I should like to know if I'll be denounced as a foe of King Halamaskar, a man to be hunted—or a resident of a land Galath is likely to invade as its new king casts about for some tasks for its more warlike nobility."

"I have no intentions of denouncing or attacking you, Lord Wizard. Nor eliminating you to conceal our agreement, in future. For one thing, Galath will care not, and for another: if half my fellow highborn react as I think they will when I proclaim myself king, I may soon have need of you again. I am not so foolish as to mar or cast aside a weapon I may soon sorely need."

"Good. Your wisdom outstrips your reputation, Lord Halamaskar."

The man in the chair stiffened. "I am glad to hear it," he said shortly. "We have agreement, then?"

"We have agreement. If you'll prick your finger."

The lordrake frowned. "Just what magic... ?"

The bodyguard stirred, but fell still and silent again at a glare from his master.

"A simple blood-binding," the wizard replied curtly, plucking a needle-like spike from his belt buckle and sinking it like a dart into his own forefinger. He held up the bleeding digit.

And waited.

Slowly, his eyes never leaving Dreel, Halamaskar drew his belt-knife and did as he was asked.

Dreel nodded, murmured something—and a streak of blue flame briefly flickered between the two fingers, causing the lordrake to curse and snatch his hand down to clutch it, and the bodyguard to glare at the mage and start to move again.

Both wizard and lordrake raised hands to stay him.

"We are now bound," Dreel said flatly. "If my blood spills, so does yours. If mine boils, yours suffers the same fate. If you fall enspelled, so do I. You might say we can now truly trust each other—which will probably prove a novel experience for you, as it would any lordrake of Galath."

Halamaskar stared at the wizard, frowning. "Your words scorn both my kind and this great realm—"

"They do nothing of the sort. I but speak plain truth about Galath. And in the continued spirit of doing so: when you venture outside, you'll discover certain of your men now lack swords—and hands. They presumed to raise their blades to me."

The wizard turned away, then looked back over his shoulder and added, "I'd kill them, were they mine, but I've noticed many nobles of this land seem to enjoy keeping fools as servants. Presumably to make themselves feel more competent. So I spared yours. This time."

Dreel inclined his head in farewell, and strode towards the door—but faded to nothingness long before he reached it.

"Just buckle it on over your leathers," Taeauna directed calmly, adjusting the buckles of her codpiece. Rod looked down at his own, shrugged, and started to cinch it tight around his waist. Turn back one spell and melt away, huh? He could live with looking a little more like an idiot, for that.

"If you've finished sitting on your helms, that is," she added calmly. "It might be a fair while before we have leisure again to squat anywhere—or dare to leave behind anything a tracking-beast can smell."

"Tracking-beast?"

"Many of the nobles of Galath enjoy hunting men. And women. Some of them have bred or had wizards twist beasts to help them in their hunting. And we're walking straight into where the nobles are all gathering."

Resplendent in her codpiece, the wingless Aumrarr strode across the armory to take Rod firmly by the elbows and gaze into his eyes. She looked calm, but fiercely determined.

"Lord Rodrel, please heed me, and stop wandering about like a man with no wits. Our lives will depend on doing the right things, quickly and quietly. I'd rather not die because you feel the need to play the idiot."

Rod grinned wryly. "Hey, we all play to our talents."

"*Indeed.*" Taeauna drew her sword, plucked an oddly shaped token of metal from a row of them hanging from hooks beside the door, and looked back over her shoulder.

"Ready?" she asked. "New sword and daggers and all?"

Rod nodded. She gave him a withering look.

"What? Oh." He drew his own sword. She nodded briskly and waved him up to stand beside her.

"Stand there," she ordered, "so you're *not* right in front of the open door. Keep your sword up in front of you, but don't move until I call you. I'm going out first."

"You're making this sound like we're the last survivors of a platoon, deep in enemy territory," Rod muttered.

Taeauna gave him a level look. "We are."

She kept on staring at him until Rod looked down. "*Ready,* Lord Archwizard?"

"Ready," he murmured, hastily stepping away to the spot she'd indicated and holding up his sword in front of his nose, as if he was an officer on parade.

Taeauna took a dagger from her belt, bent, and laid it silently on the floor to the right of the door. Then she straightened up, put her sword between her teeth, clamped the token-thing between two fingers, and used both hands to slowly and quietly lift the heavy metal latch of the door. All around the door, a framework of other latches lifted, connected to Taeauna's by metal bars.

When the door was unlatched, the Aumrarr hauled the door open, leaning a half-step to the side as she did so—and kicking the dagger out into the huge pillared hall beyond.

Swords whirled up from the floor in a sudden storm, as the dark, shaggy shapes waiting outside the door roared and charged—and Taeauna drove her shoulder against the door and closed it again, bare moments before something crashed heavily against it.

There were two more blows, lower down the door each time.

When she opened the door again, the floor outside was awash with blood. The swords hovered and circled like wasps, trailing a bloody mist. The air reeked of fresh butchery.

Taeauna swung the door wider and looked out, then nodded as if satisfied, and tossed the token out into the lake of blood. It landed with a *clink*—and the swords all fell to the floor in a collective clatter.

Her sword in hand, Taeauna ducked low and darted through the door. A moment later, she looked back in and said to Rod, "Take one of those tokens—just hold it in your fist—and come."

Rod obeyed. The gore was slippery underfoot, and sticky at the same time, and the smell was stomach-turning, but Taeauna was ignoring it, so he did, too. The armory door clanged shut behind them of its own accord, making him jump.

Taeauna took the token out of his hand before he could drop it, thrust it down one of her boots, and waved at him to follow her.

Swords drawn, they walked down the hall. Rod looked back. Yes, they were leaving bloody bootprints.

"I know," Taeauna murmured, before he could say anything. "We'll stop at one of the pumps before we go to the gate."

She led him through another side-door and down a dark stair, going first and indicating that he should keep a firm grip on the cold stone stair-rail with his free hand, and look back behind them often. "Keep close," she whispered in his ear, "but don't run into me, if I stop suddenly."

As they turned on a landing, a level down from the armory, Rod looked back over his shoulder into a vast hall, and saw dark shapes gliding through the air, like long-tailed, headless bats larger than horses.

As they left the stair, he hissed, "Tay, there were flying things back there—"

"I know. They'll head for the slaughter in front of the armory, though. We'll soon be long gone."

Then she ducked through another archway and into a room that smelled of mildew, a room where water ran down a wall and across the floor.

"Stand in that," the Aumrarr murmured in Rod's ear. "We won't have to work a pump after all. Looks like one of them's leaking."

Rod nodded, and stood in the water. "Less noise than pumping, right?"

She nodded, putting a finger to her lips, set her sword point-down on the stone and bent to rinse the soles of her boots. Repressing a shudder, Rod did the same, straightening when Taeauna did and silently obeying her wave to fall in behind her, as they went on.

Back out of the pump-room, into deeper gloom, and down a hall to a place where Taeauna stopped him, and carefully led him down three steps. She then sheathed her sword, took hold of his belt with one hand, and led him slowly forward into the darkness. Rod felt her hand slap something more than he heard it. As they passed, he reached out and felt what she'd struck: the cold, smooth curve of a pillar.

Taeauna found another pillar, and then another. When she reached the fourth one, she drew Rod right against her, hip to hip, and said into his ear, "Put your free arm around me, and hold your sword out behind you. We're about to end up in a closet in Galathgard, and I'll need you to be *very* quiet, no matter what we find there."

When he'd done as she'd directed, Taeauna did something to the pillar right in front of them and stepped forward. Rod found himself stumbling along with her as his arm around her waist carried him forward.

It seemed as if they were falling, then, through a silent but star-shot emptiness. And then, quite suddenly, they were stumbling against and falling onto something heaped underfoot. Rod didn't need the lines of light coming through a pair of narrow closed—but ill-fitting—doors to tell him what they'd both just landed on. He could feel, and he could smell.

The closet was full of dead men. Very recently dead men.

Outside the doors, they heard shouts of alarm.

"*There* they are!" someone cried.

Oh, shit.

Rod swallowed—and promptly dropped his sword with a clang.

Chapter Thirty-Four

KLARL ANNUSK DUNSHAR spun around. He *had* heard something, after all.

Men in full plate armor were streaming through a far archway into the High Feasting Hall—or what would be the feasting hall, once the chairs got done and the tables set up. Right now, all he had were a score of crude log benches, and he couldn't think of a single Lord of Galath who'd want to sit on *them*.

Men in plate, with visors down, waving swords and handaxes, and not a badge or blazon in sight. Motley armor, too, of all ages and conditions. Hireswords.

"Rondarl! Bresker!" he bellowed, whipping out his own sword. "Stand guard in yon arch, and hold those men back! Cathgur, sound the war horn! I'll be wanting every man who's not up a ladder or hefting stones here, right swiftly, with whatever weapon they can find! Galathgard is *under attack!*"

The war horn promptly howled, a blatting call that echoed around the high vaulted ceilings in a horrible cacophony.

The advancing intruders slowed at the sight of men arrayed against them, some of them turning to wave spearmen up through their ranks.

And every Falcon-glorking one of them visor-down, menacingly anonymous; fourscore of them, at least, with more still streaming in...

Dunshar cursed bitterly. There were enough of them to butcher all of the men at his command, and quickly—perhaps too fast for him to flee, if Rondarl and Bresker went down right at the first clash. Glork it all! He'd expected no end of trouble from nobles, right enough, but—

307

Hold! Someone was shoving his way through those ranks, face uncovered and a rich cloak streaming from his armored shoulders. A noble, right enough, though it was no one whose face Dunshar knew.

Faces... all he could see, whenever he took this thoughts away from what was right at hand, was the Lady Talyss smiling languidly at him, hair flowing freely over her bared... bared...

He swallowed hard and shook his head as he hastened forward, hefting his sword. A few strides took him to where he could peer over Rondarl's shoulder and get a better look at the man, who saw him, pointed, and shouted, "And who by the spewing Falcon are *you*?"

"Klarl Annusk Dunshar, of Galath. Seneschal of Galathgard, and commander here until King Brorsavar himself sets foot in this castle," he snapped back, matching the man stare for stare. "So in the King's name I ask in turn: who are you, to come striding in here arrayed for battle?"

"Uruld Ruthcoats, Marquel of Galath," came the reply.

Then Ruthcoats flung up his arm and called, "Down blades, men."

There came a collective sigh of relief as swords were grounded and visors swung up. Through it, the marquel called to Dunshar, "So, where's food to be had, in this place? And where are the jakes?"

Dunshar pointed. "Jakes down yon hall. Go right to the end; if things get too bad in the days ahead, we'll abandon that wing, a room at a time, until the smell dies down and the flies stop swarming. As for the food... we're still working on that. If your men can help feed hearthfires and pump water, we've some roast boar and deer that can be scorched enough to eat, and sarnsnips aplenty to go with them."

"Sarnsnips? Boiled *sarnsnips?*" The marquel's snarl was less than happy. Dunshar shrugged. "Or you can have boar with drippings and naught else. The ale's still on its way."

"The ale's still—? Man, *what have you been doing?*"

"Rebuilding Galathgard before it falls on our heads," Dunshar snapped back. "Oh, and removing trap after trap from under the throne, every glorking *day*. Some of our fellow nobles are far more determined than subtle."

Ruthcoats shrugged. "That's a highborn Galathan for you, right there."

He turned away, to follow the general rush to the jakes. "Sarnsnips," he muttered again, shaking his head.

Cathgur came rushing into the feasting hall behind Dunshar, then, at the head of a pitifully small handful of scared-looking men with daggers and cudgels in their hands. "Lord Seneschal?"

"Get all the deer onto spits, and fires going beneath them," Dunshar growled. "Yes, I know they've just been hung."

From another direction, distant war horns sounded—deeper horns than any Dunshar had, or knew.

He groaned, covered his face for a moment, then snapped, "Get *going*, Cathgur! Rondarl, Bresker, come with me! Someone else is making their grand entrance, and if it happens to be someone Marquel Ruthcoats regards as a sworn enemy, I don't want to get caught between them. Everyone else: barricade yourselves in the kitchens!"

Men scrambled to obey—all except young Vethlar, who inevitably danced along beside the hurrying seneschal, asking excitedly, "Anything else, Lord?"

"Glork glork glork glork *glork*," Dunshar snarled at him, not slowing. "Go! *Get to the kitchens!*"

The youngling went pale and fled, presumably to glork someone in the kitchens. Right now, the Seneschal of Galathgard didn't much care. As long as it didn't involved pitched battles in his lap...

"That'll start on the morrow, Lord," Rondarl said grimly.

Dunshar winced. He'd said that aloud, had he? Oh, Falcon *spew*...

The clang of Rod's sword was deafening in the closet, but an even louder racket was arising in the room outside, a chaos of ringing steel and screams.

Taeauna was already on her feet, wading over dead men as if they were a discarded heap of boots, her own sword out and ready. She put her head to one of the cracks to see into the room beyond, peered for a moment, then turned her head and hissed, "Stay *here*, Lord Rod!"

Before he could even start to reply, she'd charged out of the closet, bursting its doors wide and sprinting hard.

The room beyond was large and largely bare, furnished in wood shavings, a few sawhorses and sections of tree-trunk seeing use as rude tables, and a litter of felled saplings leaning against one wall. In the middle of this clutter, men in armor were, yes, hacking at each other with swords, the two at the heart of the fray going at each other with snarling ferocity.

They *really* hated each other, by the looks of it—and one of them, the one farthest from Rod but facing the closet, was a man Rod knew: Baron Darl Tindror.

"I just slew your herald and your banner-knight, Tindror," his scraggle-bearded foe snarled, as they circled face to face, raining blows on each other's blades, and started to pant and stagger. "And now... huff... now I'm going to butcher *you!*"

"You're going to—huhh!—*try*, Murlstag," Tindror replied, wheeling, the clang of their blades never slowing, "but you've not managed it in—uhhh!—all these years, so—"

A man screamed shrilly nearby, startling both barons into turning.

The scream had come as Taeauna reached a Murlstag warrior, run right up his back from behind and toppled him, forcing his face into the sword-swing of the armsman of Tindror he was fighting. He fell messily forward, but she was well past by then, and chopping open the shoulder of the next man.

Rod couldn't tell one warrior from another, men of Murlstag from their foes of Tindror, but Taeauna evidently could, and without the slightest hesitation.

When she'd plunged out of the closet, Tindror had been charging at five men with only two armsmen at his side, but Taeauna had just evened the sides, and wasn't done; she was carving up men of Murlstag as fast as she could move. One of them was fleeing, and Baron Murlstag was glancing away from Tindror, his yellow eyes flashing in alarm. He started retreating, grabbing at his belt as he did so, parrying now rather than attacking.

His hand came up with a small war horn, and he blew a weak, wavering blast on it as he stumbled breathlessly back from Tindror.

It was the last thing he did, as his longtime foe stepped forward and struck him so hard that both swords broke, shards flying away, and kept on coming, crashing into him and slamming him to the floor.

"Die, Mrantos Murlstag!" Tindror roared, pinning his enemy with this knees. "For all the bloodshed you brought to my lands, *my* people, my barony—*die!*"

Then Darl Tindror drove the broken end of his sword into his foe's face, once—twice—thrice.

Blinded and gurgling blood from a sliced mouth, Murlstag struggled feebly, pawing ineffectually at Tindror's sword as the Baron drew its edge cleanly across his throat.

Murlstag coughed and choked, Tindror raining punches on his ruined face—and died, never knowing that his feeble horn-call had brought the rest of his men into the room at a run.

Too late to save him, but not to avenge him.

One of Tindror's armsmen had already fallen; the other cried out in despair as he saw twenty fresh foes charging across the room.

Taeauna screamed defiant laughter, and raced alone to meet them.

"No!" Rod shouted, bolting out of the closet waving his sword. "No, Tay! *No!*"

With a great rolling crash, the wingless Aumrarr sprang high—and swept aside the raised blades of Murlstag's men with her own sword, to plunge into their faces kicking and punching.

"No!" Rod shouted again, knowing he was too late. "*No, Taeauna! You'll be killed!*"

He was always too late.

"Blackraven! Blackraven!" the small knot of warriors surrounding one rippling banner chanted.

"Snowlance! Snowlance!" others shouted, from another archway.

"Make way for Teltusk! Arduke Teltusk is among you!" still others called, from down a passage.

Gleaming armor and fluttering banners were crowding the lofty halls, men milling and shouting and shoving. From one high balcony, two sweating maids stopped at a rail to peer down at it all, wince, and curse softly.

"All the castle's like this," one said. "Like tussling lads, they are!"

"So many nobles," the other said gloomily. "And all their bodyguards, cooks, and manservants, too. And every last man-jack of them of them'll be wanting clean sheets!"

"Huh. Wait 'til the coin-dancers and the lords' hired playpretties get here," the other replied darkly. "Clean sheets aren't in it!"

They uttered despairing sighs, and rushed on again.

Perched unnoticed on a crossbeam above them, Iskarra turned to the two Aumrarr lounging in the angles where two of the rafters met crossbeams. "Haven't seen many archers, yet."

"Oh, they'll be there," Juskra said bitterly. "More than enough of them. And *nothing* hurts more than an arrow through a wing, believe me."

"Heh-heh," Garfist growled happily, from somewhere in the rafters behind them. "Did ye hear? Playpretties."

His companions rolled their eyes in unison.

OFF TO ROD'S left, Baron Tindror was running to Taeauna's aid, too, and shouting at his surviving armsman, "To me! Protect the Aumrarr! To me, Naurlond!"

Rod pounded across the room, well aware of how clumsy he was, how hopeless this was, how stupid and dangerous—

Taeauna was raging through the Murlstag warriors, wreaking grand slaughter, moving so fast that men couldn't keep track of her in the press of men and swords. "Murlstag! Murlstag!" someone was bellowing.

"*Die!*" Taeauna hissed.

"Falconfar!" Rod shouted. "For *Falconfar!*"

Idiot. A warrior who might never have known he was coming in all the fray and its din, turned and saw him—and swung his sword viciously as Rod came pelting up to him.

Rod tried to duck under it, lost his footing, and slid helplessly in under the boots of about a dozen warriors.

Most of whom stumbled—Falcon, their knees and heels were hard!—kicked out wildly, shrieked curses, and fell. All of them on top of Rod, by the feel of it, in a great tangle of bodies that cleared a space behind Taeauna for a moment. The Aumrarr used it to turn and drop out of reach of a dozen Murlstag swords.

One blade sliced through her streaming hair and glanced harmlessly off one shoulder of her leathers—and she was gone.

Rod rolled for his life, just trying to hold onto his sword as he kept moving.

He came to his feet in a stumbling run, on the far side of the Murlstag warriors from Baron Tindror, his lone armsman, and Taeauna. Three Murlstag men advanced on him.

Rod ran to an open door. There was one thing he did know how to do, and that was run. Time to play to his strengths again.

As he ran past the door, he caught hold of its edge and swung it, hard, to close it in his wake. Almost immediately there was a dull crash right behind him, and a curse.

Rod grinned. Just like the movies! He pelted out through the doorway into a passage outside—and found himself about two strides away from a coach.

A Falcon-glorking *coach*, that some noble was riding in, right down one of the halls of the castle! With an escort of matching knights or armsmen on the far side, spears glittering—

He sat down hard, still at a full run, bounced bruisingly off his behind, scraped his nose on the coach's dried-mud-spattered underside, and... was out the other side, a little dazed, just ahead of the large, heavy rear wheel.

His pursuers weren't so lucky.

After the second one had slammed into the side of the coach, rocking it violently, the guards inside were up and slashing through the windows. Rod was able to weave between three of the startled spearmen marching along on the far side of the coach, go round behind the conveyance—it was emblazoned with two crossed war horns, which was a badge Rod didn't remember at all—and emerge again.

He was in time to see two of the Murlstag men down and looking dead, a third cursing and clashing swords with a guard who'd just leaped down from the coach, side door still swinging in his wake, and the fourth Murlstag warrior fleeing back the way he'd come.

Rod ran after him, slashing the man fighting the coach-guard across the side of the head as he passed. The warrior reeled with a groan, and the guard pounced on him. Not looking back, Rod kept on after the fourth man, back into the room he'd just fled from.

Only to come to a skidding halt as the last warrior stopped right in front of him, very suddenly, and started whimpering.

A moment later, Rod saw why. The tip of Taeauna's sword, dark with blood, was protruding from the man's leather-clad back. The man was shuddering from head to toe, his sword tumbling from spasming fingers.

As it clattered to the flagstones, Rod passed the man, his own sword up, and saw his clumsy swordplay wouldn't been needed.

Tindror and his armsman and Taeauna were all still standing, and everyone else in the room was sprawled on the floor, silent and bleeding copiously.

Taeauna tugged her sword free of the warrior and let him fall, and rounded on Rod, eyes blazing.

"*You!*" she snarled. "I told you to stay in yon closet!"

Rod stared at her a little sheepishly, spread his hands—almost dropping his sword in the process, which made the watching baron snort—and said, "Sorry, Tay. I... I guess Lord Archwizards just aren't very good at taking orders."

The wingless Aumrarr stared at him, face tight with rage... shook her head in resignation, and then broke into wry laughter.

Rod grinned back at her the moment he dared to, and Taeauna's laughter grew.

By the Falcon, but she was beautiful.

THE RINGING CLANGOR of swords was rising loudly from a room off to the left, and right below them, four bowmen had just come running out on a balcony.

"There! *That* man!" the oldest one snapped, pointing into the jostling press of men below, and bows were bent and loosed in haste.

A man cried out as an arrow sprouted in his shoulder. Twisting around, he waved at the air in agony and went down—atop another man who'd fallen silently, with five shafts in him.

The bowmen ducked out of sight.

"Don't know who the wounded one was, but ye got the wizard," the elder bowman said with satisfaction. "Now, let's be away from here, before anyone comes looking!"

"Kulduth! *Kulduth*, you motherless defiler of virgin goats! Know that I, Thalander, am your doom!"

The shout was unnaturally, magically loud, and came rolling down the hall from afar.

Right behind it came a burst of rolling, spitting lightning. Men screamed and writhed in their armor, blue-white fire crawling all over them—but it was a haughty-looking man in purple robes who winced as the lightning closed around a cone of air around him. The cone held briefly as lightning lashed it and the air around it roiled, then collapsed. Kulduth didn't even have time to scream.

Thalander screamed, though, as warriors stabbed into him from all sides. He tottered, spewing blood, and fell limply to the ground.

"Well, 'tis indeed nice to know that virgin goats will henceforth be safe in Falconfar," Garfist Gulkoun rumbled from his perch in the rafters, sounding almost contented.

"Hush," Iskarra murmured in his ear. "We're *hiding*, remember?"

"Stormserpent!" someone roared, from the press of men below them. "*Stormserpent, I'm coming for you!*"

"I tremble!" a man in gilded armor called back, almost merrily. "And I, you fat boar of an excuse for a velduke, am coming for *you!* Forward, men! Forward and carve up yon windbag of a Felldrake for me!"

"Oooh, 'tis as good as a minstrel show," Garfist chuckled. "Wizards and nobles dying right and left—when will it all end?"

Chapter Thirty-Five

"THAT'S THE THIRD pitched battle," Iskarra pointed out. "If this keeps up for another day or so, Galath is going to run out of nobility!"

"*Trouble*," Juskra snapped, throwing out one long arm to point as something dark and batlike swooped through the cobweb-shrouded crossbeams and angled rafters of the great hall of Galathgard.

"Lorn!" Garfist and Dauntra spat, in unison.

"'Ware! Dark Helms!" Iskarra added, pointing down at the balcony, and the warriors in black armor with closed black visors on their helms.

The Helms that were already looking up at the four occupants of the rafters.

"Get right in to a joint of the rafter," Juskra warned, "and use its upright as a shield. Dauntra and I can fly if we fall, but you two—"

"*Thank* ye for reminding me!" Gar growled sarcastically. "I was just working my way around to asking ye how many services I'd have to do for the Aumrarr before I was granted wings of mine own, when ye—"

"*Gar!*" Iskarra snapped, slapping at him. "*Watch out!*"

The first lorn slashed at them with a sword as it skimmed past, banking away sharply when Juskra leaned out to thrust at it— and as expected, there was a second lorn swooping down at them right behind the first.

The Dark Helms on the balcony started jabbing at Juskra with some overlong pikes, but she was out of reach.

317

The second lorn darted one way, then the other, Juskra shifting back and forth to keep her sword up and in front of her.

Even before it closed with her, Dauntra had realized what was odd about it, and was clambering along the rafter to join her fellow Aumrarr.

"I *know*," Juskra had just enough time to hiss at her, before the lorn made one last, darting swoop, changed direction again, and—came to a sudden halt, still straining to reach her.

Its talons melted into a human hand as the two Aumrarr watched grimly, holding their swords out as far from themselves as they could with the heavy weight of the dying lorn spitted on them.

If those fingers touched them, the spell borne on the fingertips would do its deadly work. They braced their swordarms as the lorn that was not a lorn slowly turned back into a slim, long-limbed man. He spewed blood at them as he slid messily off their swords, to tumble down through the air onto the helmed heads of the knights and armsmen packed into the hall below.

"Shapechanged wizard," Garfist growled, peering down. "Wonder which noble sent him?"

"*Precisely*," Juskra snarled, turning to give Dark Helms a sneer. "We'd best relocate to a quieter rafter. In the next hall, say. Before every balcony we can get down onto is crowded with Dark Helms!"

"I *hate* Dark Helms," Iskarra said, nodding.

"Come, Gulkoun!" Juskra called, waving a beckoning arm. "Watching nobles butcher nobles is fun, but also foolishness—more than enough foolishness for us. Here comes that first lorn again!"

The flying beast didn't even come close to them this time, with four blades arrayed against it. The moment it was past, they clambered along the rafters, heading down the hall from the balcony of Dark Helms.

"The trick," Juskra explained, as they swung onto an empy balcony, Dauntra striding to the door to look for approaching Dark Helms, "is to keep hidden until the king arrives, and all attention shifts to him."

As if her words had been a cue, the hall rang with a sudden great fanfare, a splendid blaring that made all four of them wince as it echoed deafeningly off around the rafters.

Banners glowing with spell-light were advancing into the hall through the tallest archway, carried by a wedge of men in bright armor. The foremost was the deep blue and silver of the Crown of Galath, and behind it was the red-and-purple of House Brorsavar, flanked by a crimson banner marked with six silver crescents.

"Halamaskar," Juskra murmured. "And there's the lordrake himself, riding right beside Brorsavar. Pah. I don't think much of the company the new King of Galath keeps. I thought he was wise enough to know better."

At that moment, the crown on the head of the aging man riding beside Lordrake Halamaskar began to glow brightly, and he stood up in his stirrups, spread his arms, and said grandly, in a voice made loud and impressive by magic, "Loyal Galathans, I am your king! I—"

Whatever else King Brorsavar might have been going to say was lost forever in a sudden tumult of bright spell-bolts, bursts of magical flame and drifting smokes of various hues, and a hissing onslaught of arrows from all corners of the hall, all converging on him.

So savage was the onslaught that the Lordrake Halamaskar's shielding, where he stood beside the king, flared into a bright pillar of flame, and a dozen or more fully armored knights riding just behind the king were blasted to blackened and twisted remnants atop bucking, headless horses.

The tumult swiftly faded and collapsed into black, oily smoke that sought the floor, leaving everyone staring at Brorsavar.

Or rather, a dead wizard in dark leathers, shattered neck leaving his head lolling brokenly on one shoulder. There was no sign of a crown on the scorched head, and above it, the glows on all the banners winked out.

"*Dreel!*" an arduke spat disgustedly, looking around at the wizards and archers who'd lashed out at the disguised wizard— all following separate noble orders to slay the King of Galath on sight. "Halavar Dreel! *We've been tricked!*"

As they all stared, starting to murmur angrily—far above them, Juskra snorted in disgust, shaking her head at all the murderers who were irked because they'd been duped, not ashamed in the slightest of trying regicide—Dreel's corpse melted into an eerie green-gray smoke and drifted away, emitting distant shrieks and wails as it dispersed.

Then it was gone—and so was the pillar of flame that had raged beside it. The lordrake sat on his saddle with his wards quite gone, burned away in the storm of spells.

All eyes turned to regard him.

"Don't look at me!" Lordrake Halamaskar shouted desperately, seeing the disgust and fury on many faces. He waved one hand wildly at the dead horse and empty saddle beside him.

"Yon foul mage enspelled my wits!" he cried. "I'm innocent of this! I—Hondreth, hold them off!"

He hauled hard on his reins, turning his rearing horse to flee, and the bodyguard beside him obediently turned his own horse into the space where the lordrake had been. Hondreth's face was as sad as it was despairing—in the brief moments it could be seen.

They were men in armor, no longer shielded by any magics, so they and their horses were barely recognizable shapes when the chaos faded. Blackened husks, feathered with arrows, that collapsed silently on the spot.

"So," Garfist whispered hoarsely, as they ducked down behind the balcony rail, "shall we wager on the necks of nobles? As in, who'll still have theirs, by end of day?"

Dauntra gave him a withering look. "That," she observed disdainfully, "is *very* bad form."

Beside her, Juskra's scarred face split into a sudden grin. Giving Garfist a wink, she asked, "How much?"

THE MUSIC WAS deafening, the lights a lurid red that lit only the tiny stage, and Tethtyn Eldurant and Morl Ulaskro were glad when a buxom woman in a shimmering dress, with a tiny flashlight in her ample cleavage and a very wide red smile, asked them breathlessly if they were interested in "a private booth" for "something a little extra."

They nodded, not even needing to glance at each other to confer.

"It's a hundred?" the woman asked, a little warily. There was something *odd* about these two.

Not creepy odd, though, so she gave no signal to the bouncers in dark suits who were nursing watered-down drinks at the bar.

Boldly seizing the hand of the taller, quieter one—Tethtyn—she led the way, turning away from the noise and writhing bodies of the stage, and slowed to brush against him with her hip once or twice.

"Cherry is my name," she told them huskily. "*Very* Cherry."

They merely nodded politely.

"Are you guys... police?" she challenged them, a little uncertainly, as she led them through a door.

"No," the shorter one said firmly. "Nothing like that."

Alarmed that this might mean they were the opposite of police, she murmured, "Are you here to see... the Man?"

"No," the one whose hand she was holding said with a smile. "We like lasses."

Lasses? Very Cherry managed to quell her slight frown, and led them into the booth.

With the door closed behind them, the pounding din fell off abruptly. The booth was very dimly lit, hiding the none-too-clean state of the thick carpet on its walls and floor. Around the walls marched continuous dark vinyl seating, with a small, round freestanding table at one corner. The seats flared out into a bed of sorts just to the right of the door, with a few rather flat cushions. Towels hung discreetly from wall-hooks beside the bed.

The two men ignored Cherry and the bed with equal single-mindedness, going straight to the table. They sat down on either side of it and faced each other. For all the attention they were giving her, she might not have been there at all.

"Shall I...?" she asked them uncertainly.

"Please," one of the men said politely, then leaned an elbow on the table, put his chin in his hand, and said to the other man, "So most of our spells just don't work—or do odd, feeble things, not what we intend."

"Enough do that we can seize things more or less at will, force some to obey us, and slay if we must," was the reply, "but yes, we cannot trust magic here. We still have much learning ahead of us."

Nutbars. She'd *thought* so.

On her knees beside one of the men, trying to gently unzip his fly and wondering what sort of guy bought such an expensive suit and didn't bother to take the sale tags off it, Cherry tried not to listen. Sometimes the Man paid her very well to hear very well, but this wasn't one of those times, and...

They went on talking about magic and killing and who held real power in this Earth place, just as nutty as those guys on the sidewalk who shouted that aliens had landed and we must repent now or be doomed, or whatever. However, what she freed from within the zipper and the underwear—soft black silk womens' panties, but a lot of guys were kinky like that—showed her unmistakably that nutty or not, they were just as human as the next guy, and the sort of men who liked women, too.

As it happened, Cherry liked her work and was good at it, and she applied skilled fingers and a soft mouth to the task at hand.

Above her, they were talking about what they should do next, like businessmen. Geez, listening to the guy she was pleasuring, you'd never know from his voice that she was there at all!

Irked and well aware that she had another client, Cherry roamed oh-so-gently with her fingers, licked her way clear of what had been in her mouth, and turned to the other zipper.

Where her other hand, discovered that the shorter guy was carrying no less than *six* wallets.

She hesitated, just for a moment. What...?

Above the table, Morl felt the warm mouth on him go slack for a moment as its owner stiffened.

She's decided there's something wrong with us. Really wrong.

He tapped Tethtyn's hand with his own, then pointed downwards with his thumb. Tethtyn shrugged.

Morl nodded, flexed his hands, and cast a spell as quietly as he could, muttering the incantation and performing the gestures with exaggerated precision.

Under the table, Very Cherry stiffened again—as the world went away. Forever.

Morl felt her mouth and hand begin their work again, this time repetitively, exactly duplicating their last actions, over and over. Good; her mind was burnt out, and she'd be telling no one what she'd seen and guessed.

The endless repetition started to hurt, so Morl calmly pushed her away. That left her fingers discomfiting Tethtyn, so he thrust at her shoulder, backing her out from under the table.

Where she went on making love endlessly to empty air, staring at nothing with eyes the color of smoke.

The two men went on conferring as if nothing at all had occurred.

"Yet with all that," Tethtyn was saying, "I *like* this Earth. A huge, wide kingdom with, as far as I can tell, no wizards in it."

"Precious few swords, too," Morl sniffed. "No shortage of pompous fools, though."

"Which is *precisely* why we can flourish here. All we have to learn how to do is blend in enough to pass unnoticed. Then we can work whatever mischief we desire!"

Both excited now as they warmed to plans of mischief, neither of them had realized that Lorontar had stirred in their minds, firmly bidding them stay in the strange kingdom of Earth.

"DARL," TAEAUNA SAID fondly, embracing the blood-spattered, sweating Baron Tindror and kissing him, "'tis good to see you again!"

"I feel the same, Lady," he replied. "Still finding trouble at every stride, I see!"

Taeauna chuckled. "It seems to follow the Lord Archwizard here, and I'm... still responsible for him."

Tindror gave Rod a respectful nod. "My lord, I wish you continued health."

"Yeah," Rod said, a little shakily. "Me too."

"Walking with us is likely to get you killed," Taeauna said warningly to the baron, who grinned ruefully.

"Lady Taeauna, just having a title and being here in Galathgard is likely to get me killed! But aye, now that Murlstag's dead—taking some good men of mine with him, glork him—I think it best if I more or less hide, out yonder in the ruins, until the Great Court is well underway. I take it you have other plans?"

Taeauna smiled, clapped him on the back, and stepped away from him. "We do indeed. Fare you well, good Lord Baron. Galath needs more like you."

Tindror bowed his head again. "Lady, you flatter me, but 'tis good to hear."

They saluted each other with their swords, and Taeauna turned and firmly led Rod away. Out a door in another direction from the passage where the coach had passed, up a short flight of stairs, along a dark, mildewy passage, around a corner, and through another door.

"Anyone following?" she asked Rod.

"I—I don't think so," he replied.

"I don't, either," she agreed encouragingly, towing him confidently across a dark room.

"T-Tay," Rod asked her hesitantly, as he trotted on into the darkness, barely able to keep up with the Aumrarr, "where are we going?"

"We're heading for a secret passage that should enable us to get close behind the throne. There we can watch and listen in hiding, to what bids fair to be—*ah!* Here."

Taeauna had found what she was groping for, in the dark. She pushed on a block of stone, hard, and Rod heard the faintest grating sounds, and felt a slight breeze spring up around his ankles.

"Keep hold of me," Taeauna murmured in Rod's ear, then stepped to the left. Rod kept hold of her hand, and found his left shoulder brushing a stone wall. She was leading him along it, down a passage they could feel more than see.

A long way, straight and level, before it angled to the right. Rod stumbled once or twice, and Taeauna squeezed his hand sharply each time in what he took to be a signal to be more careful and quiet. Rod tried. They came to a sudden stop, Taeauna hissing a curse.

"Stand still," she told him, and Rod felt and heard her moving around just in front of him.

"Walled up," she muttered. "Recently."

"A dead end?" Rod asked.

"Dead for some, certainly," a cold, unfamiliar voice said from behind him.

Light flared, as lanterns were unhooded. Four—no, five—of them, held by knights in splendid matching armor. Six in all, with drawn swords and smiling unpleasantly. Two richly dressed men were with them, unarmored but for codpieces and breastplates; nobles, without a doubt. Rod peered at the blazons on their chests.

The smiling one was Arduke Mordrimmar Larkhelm, and by the badges they wore, the knights belonged to him. The younger man, who looked decidedly unhappy to be there, was Baron Arundur Tathgallant.

They were advancing slowly and carefully, taking care to keep their swords to the fore and the lanterns raised. As they closed to perhaps four strides away, the arduke took the baron by the elbow and steered him firmly to the forefront.

"I'm very much afraid, Lady Aumrarr," Larkhelm said to Taeauna, "that witnesses are something we just can't afford. Wherefore your life is forfeit. Tathgallant, kill her."

"No," Tathgallant replied simply.

Larkhelm unhesitatingly ran him through from behind, leaning hard on his slim sword. The baron gasped, staring wild-eyed at Rod and Taeauna, and toppled over.

The arduke stood smirking, blood running off his sword. He shrugged, sighed theatrically, and told his knights, "I guess I'll just have to murder her myself."

"You're welcome to try," Taeauna replied, her cold smile matching his own. She glided forward to meet him, sword in hand.

Chapter Thirty-Six

THE CLASH AND clang of arms in the hall was deafening. Everyone was fighting everyone, armored men crushed together shoulder-to-shoulder in the hall, almost too packed to fall when they were slain.

Four pairs of eyes gazed down from the balcony. The bone-thin woman now snuggled against Garfist Gulkoun's shoulder murmured warningly, "We could be burned alive up here if some fool sets fire to the castle—and someone always does, when thrones are toppled."

"Then come," Juskra said to them. "With me. Now. Back this way."

They obeyed, scuttling off the balcony bent low and following the Aumrarr in haste back through lightless and crumbling passages, out into bird-fouled rooms where the rafters stood open to the sky.

"Where exactly are we heading?" Garfist growled.

"Just one room farther," the battle-scarred Aumrarr told him. "Through this arch, then turn to the right, everyone, to put yon wall at our backs. That should be far enough."

"For what?"

"For talking freely without being overheard—and without some bloodthirsty knight or noble happening along with a lot of friends," Juskra replied.

Gar nodded. "Right. Talk."

"I think we need to agree on what we should do here," Juskra said firmly. "Given yon bloodbath, and no king in sight yet."

"I don't think he's coming," Garfist growled. "*I* think he's decided to lure all the nobles here to Galathgard to cut each other's throats, so he only has to deal with survivors, after it's all done."

"No," Dauntra disagreed, "that's what *you'd* do. I've met Brorsavar. He'll be here, all right, even though he knows he's coming to his death. And yes, with all those swords and bowmen and wizards, someone *will* get him."

Juskra nodded. "I read things unfolding that way, too. Wherefore I hope we can resolve some things, here and now, about what we're going to try to do."

Iskarra shrugged. "Fine. As Gar said, talk."

"Well, I think we should help hasten the deaths of the most ambitious and ruthless nobles—the ones we *don't* want to ever see on any throne, anywhere in Falconfar—before anyone departs Galathgard. More than that, if Brorsavar does fall, I propose that we should *try* to head off a messy civil war by making perhaps the best of the younger nobles into the new King of Galath."

"Who?" Garfist asked bluntly.

"Velduke Darendarr Deldragon."

"I agree," Iskarra said quickly. "Him I *would* like to see on Galath's throne."

Garfist nodded. "So, now, tell me one thing: why did ye Aumrarr not just put him on that throne, long ago, an' avoid all this?"

Juskra hesitated, but Dauntra said to her, "Speak, Sister. The time for secrets is past."

The scarred Aumrarr sighed and nodded. "We—we Aumrarr—came to suspect, some time ago, that he'd fallen under the sway of a Doom. Which meant, once encrowned, he'd be as much a tyrant, or waste, as Devaer was. We need only trick him into a swift and simple test, to make sure no one else has taken him over now that the Dooms are all dead."

"Right, I agree—an' we all agree, hey?" Garfist asked briskly. "So let's get ourselves back to that balcony, an' see who's died while we've been away. I don't get to see high-nosed lords slaughtered by the dozens every day, ye know!"

They all hastened back the way they'd come. Under their boots, as they trotted, Galathgard shook more than once, the stones rattling under deeper thunders. The wizards were settling down to work.

LARKHELM'S SNEER HELD, but as Taeauna strode forward, he backed away just as swiftly, his knights parting to let him pass through, and closing in front of him, holding out their lanterns like shields.

Taeauna never slowed.

Swords thrust at her, but she flung herself to the left and chopped backhand at the head of the leftmost knight.

He cursed and swung himself all the way around, barely parrying—and her foot hooked his heel and brought him crashing to the floor, Taeauna ducking past him and thrusting her sword up into the next knight's neck and jaw as she went.

He tried to scream but managed only a gurgle, and staggered, tripping over the fallen knight—who was frantically trying to crawl away—and crashing down atop him.

By then, Taeauna had fenced for a moment with the third knight before driving the point of her blade through his throat. Larkhelm was backing away, calling one of the knights—Torth—to fall back with him.

Rod trotted after Taeauna, slicing his sword through the throat of the first knight, who was struggling to get out from under the weight of his dying fellow. Three down, one retreating, two knights left—who ducked to either side and hacked at Taeauna fiercely.

She cried out in pain as a sword bit into her side, slicing through her leathers, and staggered sideways—but the knights were too eager to follow her and strike her down to really notice Rod, and he flung himself atop the nearest one, bringing him crashing to the floor. Which left the other one turning, startled—so Taeauna could hack at his neck, and send him reeling away, choking on blood and dropping his sword.

Viciously Rod swarmed up the struggling knight, knowing the man was stronger and heavier than he was, and if he got Rod off him and turned over, Falconfar's newest Lord Archwizard would be doomed. He chopped awkwardly at the man's face with his sword, again and again, as if he was dicing onions, and was still at it when Taeauna's sword slid in past his, right into the man's snarling mouth.

An instant later she was gone, swept away by the charging Torth, whose vicious swing took her under her breasts and sliced upwards, flinging her back and away amid a great spray of blood.

Rod heard her sword clatter across the floor as he struggled to his feet, slipping and sliding on blood-drenched armor underfoot, and flung himself on Torth, hard.

He came down on the knight's legs and drove him headlong to the floor, down atop the first two men he and Taeauna had felled. Torth stopped struggling, very suddenly, and collapsed.

Rod clawed his way up, bloody sword in hand and breathing hard, and whirled around.

Arduke Mordrimmar Larkhelm, who'd been creeping up on him with a sword raised to strike, halted warily.

"Taeauna?" Rod called, waving his sword to keep the noble at bay. "Tay?"

There came no reply. Larkhelm sneered.

"Calling for your Aumrarr nursemaid, not-wizard? What a pitiful little figurehead *you* are! Plaything of the wingbitches, strutting simpleton..."

He feinted with his sword, and Rod desperately sought to parry; the arduke's sword slid past his clumsy blade and almost kissed his throat. Rod frantically leaned away.

"You are no man of Galath," the noble purred, advancing a menacing step and forcing Rod to retreat. "In fact, you are no *man*."

"Ah," Rod replied, rage rising in him, "but at least I'm human. Unlike most of the nobles of Galath."

Larkhelm laughed, feinting again. This time Rod sidestepped and tried a cut of his own. It was turned aside with casual ease. "Ooooh," the arduke grinned at him, "you taunt like my sisters used to—before I ruined and then killed them. Which I believe I'll do to you, not-wizarrr—"

Rod lost his temper and smashed at Larkhelm's blade as if he was wielding an axe. The startled arduke fell back hastily, clawing at his sword with his other hand to keep from dropping it—and Rod tried what he'd seen Taeauna do. He ran past the noble, lashing out backhand from behind.

Larkhelm parried, turning to do so. Rod kept running, circling. The noble was defending now, taunts gone, face tight with determination... and fear. Rod smashed at him again, then danced away before the arduke's counter-thrust could reach him. And in again.

This time, Larkhelm's retreat took him back into Torth's feet, and he stumbled.

Rod rushed in, raining clumsy blows on the noble's swords and arms and face, rage mastering him at last.

"I did not create you for *this!*" he spat. "You're a Falcon-spitting evil *bastard*, harming Galath with every swindle and sneer! Die! *Die*, you—you creep!"

Larkhelm gurgled through the blood streaming down his face, pleading.

Rod swung his sword two-handed, biting through Larkhelm's throat.

The noble toppled over backwards, staring disbelievingly at the ceiling.

Leaving Rod panting for a moment, the last one standing in the gloomy chaos of blood and bodies.

He didn't feel like a hero. He didn't even feel like the victor. Not when his Tay had fallen...

Rod spun and raced to her.

She was sprawled on her back, her chest a lacerated ruin—but rising and falling. Feebly.

Her eyes were closed, her mouth slack, more blood everywhere. Rod crashed down on his knees beside her and sliced open his palm, wincing at the pain. His hand filled with wet stickiness, eerie sky blue glow coming off it like smoke, and he tipped it into her mouth.

She coughed, shuddered, mewled with pain, and coughed again.

Rod looked down at his palm. It was almost whole again already. Impatiently he cut himself again, deeper this time, the pain sickening... and gave her more.

Taeauna's eyes opened.

"*Tay?*" he cried, bending close to her. "*Tay?*"

She seemed to be staring at him from a distance, her eyes dull as if a mist hung between the two of them.

"M-more, if you please, Lord," she whispered.

Rod cut his arm this time, carving deeply, gritting his teeth to keep from retching. Blue fire streamed down him and into her greedy mouth, and she seemed to be raising herself by pulling on him, gaining strength as she sucked and swallowed.

"Lord Rod, you have saved me," she told him, sighing with relief. "Again."

Rod nodded at her, managing a smile through a sudden, pounding headache. He felt weak and empty—and when he turned, almost toppled over.

Strong hands caught and held him. Taeauna rose and hauled him to his feet, as strong and supple as ever.

Rod smiled at her again, took a step toward his fallen sword— and stumbled, almost falling.

A hand like iron held him and dragged him upright again.

"Come, my Lord Archwizard. We must find another way than this."

"Way to where?"

"We need to find a good place to watch from."

"Watch what?"

"You'll see!"

Rod had to be content with that; she'd turned away, kicking Larkhelm's sprawled body as she passed it.

Shaking his head ruefully, he puffed along in Taeauna's wake, admiring—and not for the first time—her shapely behind as she raced away from him.

"BY THE FALCON!" Garfist Gulkoun growled. "What d'ye think we've missed?"

As they came out onto the balcony, bodies were spattering and thudding into the rafters—knights and armsmen and nobles, flung high into the air by spells.

Dozens of lorn were flapping and cartwheeling among them, wings smashed by the collisions, and here and there among the hurtling bodies were Dark Helms. The floor of the hall, below, was an almost continuous maelstrom of explosions and the flashes of spells going off.

Gar, Isk, Dauntra, and Juskra exchanged looks. From the sounds coming from the balconies below theirs and the passages behind them, it seemed that all Galathgard had become a battleground.

Several people came out on the balcony right beneath theirs. Juskra flung out an arm to warn her companions back, and they sank down and fell silent to listen.

"But—but why *me*? I'm only a klarl, hardly someone of wealth and power enough to—"

"Dunshar, we *know* that," someone replied firmly. Male, like the klarl; the next speaker was female, her voice melodious and cool.

"Annusk, I value your candor. Your judgment is every bit as sound. If we had the leisure, we would indeed try for a higher-ranking and better-known lord of Galath. I thank you for your concern; you *do* care for your realm above all else."

"Lady Tesmer, I—I always have, I swear..."

"In all this tumult," the other man interrupted, "we dare not reach for anyone higher. Take heart, for you just might turn out to be the best king Galath has ever known."

Juskra tapped the others, pointed back the way they'd come, and started crawling, holding her sword with great care to prevent the slightest sound.

Not that she need have worried much. A miscast magic roared up to the rafters in a tower of glowing smoke, and burst half the hall away, sending splinters and shards and roiling dust crashing past the balconies in ear-splitting cacophony.

When they could hear again, several rooms away, Juskra murmured into the ringing heads bent close to hers, "I know those voices. Belard and Talyss Tesmer are here, and coaching their own puppet noble—Klarl Annusk Dunshar—as to how to behave, as they try to put him on the throne."

"Tesmers? From Ironthorn?" Gar rumbled. "Falcon, *all* the troublemakers are gathering!"

"Which is why," Dauntra told him sweetly, "*you're* here."

STRIDING INTO HER chambers in Ironthorn, Maera Tesmer stopped suddenly as something dark and cold uncoiled in her mind. She stiffened, drawing in her breath with a gasp. Lorontar.

It's time.

Trembling, she hastened back to bar her door, then put her back to it, faced the silent rooms, and cast a shielding to end all scrying on her.

It took effect, rolling silently out from her like a wave. Nigh the door to her bedchamber, there came the sudden flare of a spell collapsing, and a faint, momentary whisper, just a snatch of a heartfelt curse.

Smiling, she turned to a lectern and threw back its cloth cover, revealing an old, heavy tome. It held a spell that would enable her to trace her parents' hedge-wizard, if she moved *very* quickly, and—

No. Gather your magics faster than that. You are now going to disappear from Ironthorn. Swiftly.

Maera stiffened again. "To where?" she whispered.

You'll see.

Maera waited, but the cold voice in her mind said no more.

The silence deepened, and she crossed her chambers and started snatching grimoires and wands and bulging pouches out of hiding places.

Warmth was rising in her, spreading through her limbs. Power. Dark power.

The true Lord Archwizard of Falconfar was awakening.

THEY WERE BOTH panting by the time they reached the top of the stairs. Taeauna reached out, clasped Rod's hand in hers, and towed him to the left, into some ruined rooms Dunshar's workers had not yet touched. Mildew, old animal dung, and a litter of small bones and torn birdnests lay strewn everywhere.

"Good," the wingless Aumrarr said, surveying the wreckage. "Unfinished. We should be able to move swiftly, then."

"Where are we going?" Rod gasped.

"Onward," she snapped back, then added a grin. "As always."

IT WAS A small army, and on foot, but it was moving fast. Warriors in motley armor, with only a handful of knights. Some of those who wore leather war-harness and bore swords were hedge-wizards who had spells ready, but were determined not to look like wizards—or as the king had dryly termed mages, "targets."

Marquel Gordraun Windstrike led the dozen-strong bodyguard of old loyal knights who strode in a ring around two men. One was the King of Galath, and the other was a man in long dark robes, with a face like a hatchet and eyes like angry fires. Half Falconfar could have identified him by the claw badge on the breast of his robes: Orothor Taervellar of the Talons, wizard for hire.

They slew all who defied them, as they advanced through Galathgard, but there were few enough; skirmishes were raging through various far-flung wings of the castle, but the great rooms at its heart were now heaped fields of the dead.

"This next one," King Brorsavar announced calmly, "is what we're looking for. The throne room."

The doors stood open, and a haze of smoke hung heavy in the air. Armor-clad bodies lay everywhere, with here and there a pain-wracked armsman or knight moving feebly amid the gore.

Briskly the king's warriors spread out, ranging through the room. No one still alive looked to be a wizard or a noble of consequence, so they lit torches and set them in wall-brackets, heaved the press of bodies in and around the throne aside—lordrakes, ardukes, and veldukes all lay thickly there—and lifted one man off the throne itself whose backside, by the looks of things, had triggered one last trap, and driven four swordblades right up through him. He—if it had been a he—came away in slabs of meat that trailed bones and intestines, and Marquel Windstrike was nearly sick several times.

Some of the knights set about hammering at the upthrust swords, but Taervellar of the Talons shook his head, waved them away, and cast a spell that turned the metal to a mist that drifted slowly away.

"'Tis safe now of all metal," he announced, cast another spell, and after a moment nodded and added, "And lurking magic, too."

Windstrike looked to the king, received a nod, and turned to point at certain armsmen, who lifted war horns from their belts and blew a long, roaring succession of blasts.

Then they stood waiting.

It did not take long. Running boots could be heard approaching, and occasional clangs of swords glancing off stone, to the accompaniment of curses.

Then noble after noble, wild-eyed and blood-spattered, came panting into the great chamber, bloody swords in hand.

Windstrike waited a little longer, glanced at the king and received another nod, and signaled to the hornsmen again.

The fanfare, this time, was loud and splendid. Amid its rolling echoes, more men came crowding into the room.

The marquel stepped forward. "King Melander Brorsavar hath arrived!" he announced grandly.

Behind him, the smiling man sat down on the blackened, bloodstained throne of Galath and said in a voice both gentle and—thanks to his hired wizard's magic—heard from end to end of the hall, "This, my Great Court, has now begun."

The blood-spattered nobles stared at him open-mouthed for a long and wavering moment.

Then bellowed as one man and charged to the attack.

Chapter Thirty-Seven

TAERVELLAR OF THE Talons stood under an unlit torch, his back to the wall, wearing an unlovely smile. Magical flames had sprung into being out of nowhere into his hands, and he was almost casual in blasting down every noble or knight, or armsman who got too close to the throne.

Pillars of fire sprouted from the stones, men shrieking as they died, until there were no more.

"We will have order," King Brorsavar said calmly. Those who shouted defiance of those words were Taervellar's next targets.

Greasy smoke drifted away down the throne room in the uneasy silence.

For now, at least, order had been achieved.

"The *rightful* King of Galath welcomes his *loyal* nobles to this, his first Great Court," Marquel Windstrike announced.

King Brorsavar stood up, smiled down at the crowd in the room—which was growing again, as late arrivals came hesitantly in—and told them, "I don't expect to survive this gathering, my lords of Galath. Yet we have much to celebrate, whatever befalls. Our realm has been cleansed of many lorn and Dark Helms, and—"

"Now!" a noble shouted, and magics were unleashed from all over the chamber. Not spells, but the stored powers of ring, wand and helm.

The magics were sent not at the king, but at Taervellar, who struggled to keep his feet in the jaws of a growing conflagration that raged savagely around him, howling and tightening.

Suddenly, in the roaring heart of the rending magic, he fell. With nothing to strike at, the magics that had killed him whirled outwards, lashing the knights and armsmen guarding the throne.

A door beside the throne opened, stone grating loudly, and an unwilling servant was thrust out. Marquel Windstrike's sword was in the man's heart in an instant—leaving him defenseless against Belard Tesmer, who thrust his blade over the dying servant's shoulder and into Windstrike's mouth before he could even shout a warning.

"*Now*," Talyss Tesmer said, voice triumphant—and Belard hurled both dying servant and marquel aside, to race past the throne and hack at the nearest knights.

In his wake came Klarl Annusk Dunshar, charging the throne with daggers ready in both hands. King Brorsavar had just time to draw his own knife before Dunshar's blades sank deep into him.

Brorsavar reeled, and Belard Tesmer took time from slaughtering knights to lash out backhanded at the king, breaking the royal neck and driving the dying man forward into Dunshar's unwilling embrace.

"For... for Galath," the old king struggled to say, through welling blood. And died.

Nobles all over the room were sprinting for the throne, hacking at everyone in their way.

Brorsavar's guards went down quickly, and wild slaughter raged across the throne room once more, the nobles protecting themselves and settling grudges in the melee.

Garfist Gulkoun came out on a low balcony with Isk and the two Aumrarr, and shouted, "'Tis Galath, all right. Conducting their lords' business very much as usual."

TAEAUNA WAS STRONGER than ever. Rod struggled vainly in her grasp, raging for all he was worth but unable to get free of her or move anywhere.

"I've *got* to get out there!" he shouted at her, trying to break free of her and get out on the balcony. "They're all killing each other! In another ten-twenty minutes, there won't *be* any lords of Galath!"

"And if you run out there," Taeauna snarled at him, shoving him away from the balcony, "in a lot less time than that there'll be no more Rod Everlar!"

"Tay, I've got to do *something!* I just can't—"

Taeauna shook him.

"Listen to me!" she hissed. "You can do something that will help Galath—help *Falconfar*—greatly. You can get back into one of these rooms here and sit down and stare at the wall, while I stand guard over you, and gather your will and Shape again! That's what you do, Rod Everlar! That's how you made Falconfar great, and that's how you can save it now!"

"But—but Shape what?"

"Just quell all magic in yon throne room, so no wizard can cast anything!" Taeauna hissed at him. "Just that! *Do it!*"

Rod nodded. "Right," he said. "I will. Lead me."

"THERE!" JUSKRA SNAPPED, pointing past Garfist's shoulder. "There's Deldragon! Over there, across from the throne—see? Get to him! We must protect him!"

"*Us?* Protect *him?*" Gar shouted, staring at her. "*Look* at him! Just how do y'see someone like that needing *our* protection?"

Velduke Deldragon was hacking his way across the hall like a man possessed, ignoring challenges and shrugging off thrown weapons. He was making for the throne.

The throne and the steps around it had become slick with fresh blood; even the Tesmers winced at the affray and ducked back through their secret door, vanishing. The moment Klarl Dunshar saw their departure, he turned and sprinted the other way, abandoning crown and throne in his desperate need to get away.

Deldragon abruptly changed direction in the fray, and started hewing himself a path down the hall rather than toward the throne. It became clear to the four watchers on the balcony that the velduke wasn't after the crown *or* the throne.

He was after Dunshar, the slayer of his king.

"MAGIC," TAEAUNA MURMURED, "looks like a steady fire, shot through with lightning. A blue-white glow, when raw; other hues when spells make it so. Keep to the blue-white. You want it to be extinguished, to go dark. Shape it thus, Lord Archwizard. Shape it so, Rod."

Eyes closed, lying on a cold stone floor, Rod saw glorious blue-white in his mind—and did his best to kill it.

Melting it away from Galathgard was easy, but thrusting its destruction outwards was harder. *Much* harder. He couldn't do it, he... Wait. Malraun had done this, once, when linked to Rod's mind, and—yes. *Yes!* It was like shattering ice, so it could be shoved back and aside.

And *this*, now, this casting that Rambaerakh had done a time or two; if he could Shape the same results...

He *could*. Well, then, all men's ties to magic could be burned away. Like this. Things of magic would survive, until broken or worn out, but no spell would work, ever again, once his work was done.

Not that it would be easy. It hurt—God, it hurt!—but he was doing it. Someday he might want to bring it back, but not if there would be other Dooms.

No more Lorontars.

Only Rod Everlar, the greatest Doom of all. Because he'd taken all magic away.

The *pain*. Perhaps burning his own life to do it...

Well, he wasn't going to stop. Not now, not after all this, after so many dead.

Oh, but it hurt.

"KINGSLAYER!" DELDRAGON ROARED, hacking aside a screaming knight, and thrusting his dagger at an armsman, who fled before him—and suddenly there was no one between the velduke and the fleeing klarl.

"No!" Dunshar cried, finding his way blocked by men fighting among themselves. "No! I—I didn't mean to do it! They made me do it, the Lady Tesmer and her—"

"I saw *you* go for the king," Deldragon said coldly, a sweep of his sword striking Dunshar's dagger away and taking most of a finger with it, "and I saw *your* daggers take his life. *You* slew him, Annusk Dunshar!"

"And for that crime..." Garfist Gulkoun murmured eagerly, leaning well out over the balcony rail to watch.

Dunshar turned and tried to flee again, babbling incoherently, then shrieking as Deldragon's sword caught him in one shoulder, spinning him around, and slapped his cheek hard when he tried to turn again.

They were nose to nose again, and Deldragon's face was terrible.

Dunshar's was white and drenched with sweat and trembling. "Don't kill me! Don't—I'll do anything! Anything! I'll—I'll—"

"A song I've heard too many a time before," Deldragon said coldly, swinging his sword twice.

Dunshar toppled silently, head almost severed. A strange lull occurred in the battle, and Velduke Deldragon found himself standing over the man he'd slain, stared at by men all around.

"Dunshar killed Brorsavar," a lordrake cried, "and he just slew Dunshar. So he's the king—get him! Get him, and the crown is ours!"

"'Ours?'" Dauntra asked. "Just how big is this crown, anyway?"

One or two men just beneath the balcony chuckled at that—but everyone else was surging forward, shouting, swords rising against the man who stood alone.

Deldragon shook his head in disgust, and ran to meet the nobles. Best take down the worst of them, if today I must die...

"Enough of this," Dauntra said suddenly, swinging herself over the balcony rail. "Are you with me?"

"Aye!" Garfist roared, shaking his fist—and toppling over the rail to crash down atop a baron, flattening the man to the ground and causing two more men to stagger, as Deldragon's blade cut down a corrupt lordrake.

Juskra plucked up Iskarra with one hand and dropped her lightly to the ground behind Deldragon—where the bone-thin woman found herself staring into the eyes of a dozen onrushing armsmen.

Nine: Juskra swooped, cutting throats as she came, and landed hard on the rearmost man, stabbing him.

All four were down amid the blood and the dead now, hacking and hewing, guarding Deldragon's back and flanks.

"Aumrarr!" someone shouted. "The wingbitches are among us!"

"Pah! A handful! Hew them down! *Hew them all down!*"

Slapping at their knights and armsmen with the flats of their swords, the few surviving nobles urged their men forward. None of them had ever been so close to the throne before; just a few more deaths might land them on it! Just a few—

"For Deldragon! For Galath!" someone roared from beyond the closing ring, slashing a noble's neck and sending him reeling. "King Deldragon, for Galath!"

It was Baron Tindror, one weary, bloodied armsman grinning at his side, and even before the lords could turn to face him, two of them lay dying underfoot, and the ring was broken.

"Wizards? Where the *glork* are our wizards?" one of them cursed. He cast about and saw a man in robes, far off across the chamber, staring down at his empty hands in disbelief—before Deldragon's sword silenced his question forever.

There were only a few nobles left fighting, now, a knot of desperate men. The little magics they'd trusted to see them out of a tight spot were failing them, now; doom was upon them. Leaving them just one satisfaction—

An Aumrarr in their midst, this one without scars, whose beauty had distracted many an armsman just long enough for him to take a wound...

Could not possibly fend off all their blades. Even as she sent a knight reeling back, six swords slid into her.

"*Die*, wingbitch!"

"Sister!" Dauntra screamed and sobbed, eyes bright.

"*No!*" Juskra howled, bounding into the air and clapping her wings to buffet men backwards in all directions. "No!"

Her sword felled two nobles as if they'd been dry firewood, and she flung it down to cradle Dauntra.

"Sister..." Dauntra gasped.

And died.

"No!" Juskra howled. "*No!*"

Arms around Dauntra, she sprang into the air—and she was gone, up and out of the throne room.

MAERA KNEW WHERE she was heading now.

The flat, thrusting stone in the forest.

There it was, just a glade ahead. The Tesmer knights following her no longer mattered; her parents' anger no longer mattered, either. Lorontar was strong within her, and he would—he would—

The power within her suddenly roiled and faded, sending her staggering. The grim knights behind her stopped and drew their swords, approaching warily.

Bent over and helpless, Maera stared at them. "No!" she spat. "Not now! This can't—*no!*"

Lady Tesmer turned to her husband, horror in her face. "Do you—Irrance, do you feel it?"

"I do," Lord Tesmer said grimly. And sighed. "I guess it's back to swords, then. And I'm getting no younger."

Lord Luthlarl raised one eyebrow. He'd never liked wizards much, and this one was no exception. The man's fee was staggeringly high, and now he was standing in Dlarmarr's best garden with both hands raised theatrically—and nothing at all was happening.

"Is there," he asked silkily, "a problem?"

"The spell," the wizard mumbled, looking sick. "It just... won't work."

Lord Luthtarl smiled. The gesture he made to his bodyguard was almost leisurely.

Perhaps wizards made good fertilizer.

"You failed my lord!" the knight said angrily. "And now he's dead. You'll not see one coin of your fee!"

The wizard smiled. "Oh, no? While all of you go on butchering each other here in this Falcon-forsaken castle, I'll just whisk myself back to your arduke's bedchamber and take that coffer of gems he's so proud of. Along with, perhaps, that lush-bosomed wife of his, too!"

The knight snarled, sword grating out of its scabbard.

The wizard sneered, raised one hand, and murmured something.

Then, with a look of astonishment, tried it again.

He was still trying, a third time, when the knight drove his blade hard through his chest.

All around him, bloodied armsmen roared approval.

There weren't more than a score of men still standing in the throne room, from one end to the other. Wizards were scuttling off in all directions like frightened rats, but everyone else looked more dazed than anything else, leaning on their swords wearily.

Baron Tindror was looking for something. When he found it, he trudged across the bodies and strewn weapons, stopped behind Deldragon, and held it up.

It was the crown of Galath.

Gently, almost reverently, he settled it on Deldragon's head.

"All hail King Deldragon of Galath!" he bellowed, and struck the nearest shield, almost toppling the tired armsman holding it. It rang like a gong. "All hail King Deldragon!"

"All hail!" other men took up the cry, Garfist among them. Iskarra clung to him, still crying too hard to say anything. Juskra and Dauntra were gone, and she cared not who kinged it anywhere.

"YOU DID IT," Taeauna said happily, and her arms were warm around him.

Rod nodded vaguely. He was so tired...

She was kissing him, wasn't she?

"I—I DON'T WANT the throne," Deldragon said slowly. "I am much the junior to many good men—"

"Darendarr," said one of the oldest surviving nobles, "shut your jaws and sit on that throne. I'm glorked if I'm going through *this* again."

"Aye," said another. "I pledge my allegiance to you, King Deldragon. Rule long and well."

"Yes!" quavered another, who was older still. "And we know Tindror's loyalties, and I hear no one disputing, so..."

"Well, all right," Deldragon said reluctantly, "but—"

A ragged cheer drowned out whatever else he'd intended to say, and then another.

After the third he smiled, shook his head, and went to the throne, limping a little.

"Right, then," he said, turning before it to look down on them all. "Hear then my first decree: I want only one wizard to set foot in my land without my express invitation: Rod Everlar, who I name High Wizard of Galath."

There were some mutterings, but Deldragon asked, "Any of you care to wear this crown?"

The mutterings ended abruptly. "Right," he said with a weary smile. "More radical yet: I want an Aumrarr to be my Lady Herald. Many of you know her already: Taeauna."

"OH, *SHIT*," TAEAUNA said suddenly. "No."

She let go of Rod, only to take firm hold of his hand.

"What's happening?" he asked, a little bewildered. "Where're we going?"

"You'll see," she replied briskly, and towed him off into the gloom. Again.

"WE CAN'T FIND them anywhere, Your Majesty," the knight said wearily. "And I mean *anywhere*. They're gone."

Deldragon looked furious. "Have the trails around the castle scoured," he snapped, "and quickly! They can't have got all that far—"

He blinked. There was a fat, shaggy man he'd seen before standing in front of him, with a rail-thin woman at his side.

"Uh, Lord King?" Garfist rumbled.

"Not *now*," Deldragon began, but the fat man held up one shovel-like hand.

"Understand ye're short a High Wizard, an' a Lady Herald?"

Deldragon stared at him.

"Well," Gar rumbled, "*we're* here. Not an Aumrarr nor any sort of wizard, to tell truth—but we're here, an' the ones ye seek are... not. And I daresay we've wiles enough to outstrip what they have, four or five times over."

"*That's* true," Isk commented, folding her arms across her breast.

Deldragon stared down at them both—and burst into sudden laughter, gripping the arms of the throne.

"It... it just might work, at that."

"WHERE IS SHE now, Jusk?"

The voice behind her was soft and gentle, and Juskra knew the speaker. She went on staring up at the moon from the battlements above the Ironthar forests, but replied finally, "I buried her yonder, on the hill. With Glaelra and Maethe and too many others."

"That was rightly done," Taeauna murmured, and put her arms around Juskra.

The Aumrarr sat like a statue for a moment, and then dissolved into wracking sobs.

It might take days before she was done crying over Dauntra, but Taeauna was patient.

"I KNOW WE have no appointment," the taller of the two men told Holdoncorp's receptionist, "but we have something vital to the future of your corporation. We really do need to speak to the project manager."

She looked up at him over her glasses, as severely as she knew how. "And your name might be?"

"Tethtyn," was the smiling reply. "And this is Morl."

The other man smiled, and waggled two fingers, ever so slightly.

The woman across the gleaming desk pushed a button almost eagerly.

"Bert? Bert, can you come out here straight away? There are two men here to see Sam; it's very important."

Bert wore shirt-sleeves and looked distracted, but he led them to Sam happily enough.

The last he saw of the two strangers was of them striding into Sam's office. One of them was saying, "We've come to you with a proposal I think you'll find *very* interesting. It's about Falconfar..."

The project manager closed the door then, leaving Bert one last glimpse of the two visitors. They wore identical mirthless smiles.

TAEAUNA DREW DAGGERS from around her person—so many places, as she went on, that Rod stopped unrolling blankets to watch in open-mouthed fascination.

When a dozen gleaming knives lay around her, she gave him a wink. She raised her hands, wiggled her fingertips in the air in a deft pattern, and murmured something.

In silent and stately unison, the daggers all rose into the air, to hang in a ring floating above her. As Rod watched, they drifted out unhurriedly to surround him and the blankets and everything else, just within the walls of the tent.

"Ready to attack any intruders?" Rod murmured. Taeauna nodded.

"I thought you had no magic left."

"Nor did I," she purred triumphantly, crawling forward to where she could start to unlace his tunic, "but while you were rolling around drooling after working the dream-gate to take us from your Earth home to Malragard, *I* was plundering one of Malraun's private caches of magic. Falconfar needs no more wizards... and with spells gone, there'll be none. But I have a small armory of enchanted items, and know how to use them so most men won't know I'm not casting spells. It's been centuries since Falconfar has had a sorceress of power—and when the last Queen-Sorceress reigned, this world knew peace and prosperity. I'd like to bring that happiness to Falconfar again."

"Starting with just one Falconfar man?" Rod teased, as she tugged away his tunic and pushed him down onto his back, straddling him on her knees as she started to unlace her leathers.

Taeauna froze, her fingers halting amid the thongs as she stared hard at him.

She bent low, her intent, serious face close to his.

"Do you consider yourself a man of Falconfar, then, my lord?" she whispered.

"Oh, yes," Rod Everlar growled, reaching out to tug her bodice apart and out of the way. "Yes, I do."

Here ends Book 3 of the Falconfar Saga, the tale of the awakening of Rod Everlar, how he came to know that fantastic worlds can be all too real, and how much in the end he loved having learned that.

DRAMATIS PERSONAE
[named characters only]

"See" references occur where only partial character names appear in the novel text (such as when a surname is omitted). Not all folk in Falconfar have family names; Aumrarr, for example, never have surnames.

These entries contain some "spoilers" for FALCONFAR, and for maximum enjoyment of this book, should be referred to only after two-thirds or more of the text has been read.

A note on the nobility of Galath: from lowest to highest, their ranks are knight, baron, klarl, marquel, arduke, velduke, lordrake, prince, king. A knight is a "sir," but barons and up are addressed as "lord" (it is acceptable to call the reigning monarch "Lord of All Galath," but "the Lords of Galath" are the collective nobility of the kingdom). Outside Galath, the "Lord" of a place is usually its ruler.

Albrun, Xandur: warrior of Darswords, who fled the independent hold when it fell to the army of Malraun the Matchless.

Arlaghaun: "the Doom of Galath," a deceased wizard who was widely considered the most powerful of the three Dooms (Falconfar's wizards of peerless power), and for some years the real ruler of Galath. Arlaghaun inhabited Ult Tower, the black stone keep of the long-dead wizard Ult, in Galath, and with his spells commanded armies of lorn and Dark Helms, as well as every utterance of King Devaer of Galath. Some judged his power so great they called him "the Doom of Falconfar." He was slain at the end of DARK LORD.

Askurr, Endramace: tall and proud commander in Malraun's army. A capable, well-respected, kindly veteran warrior.

Aumrarr, the: a race of wingéd warrior-women who fight for "good." They seem human except for their large, snow-white wings, and fly about taking messages from one hold to another, battling wolves and monsters, and working against oppressive rulers. They are dedicated to making the lives of common folk (farmers, woodcutters, and crafters, not the wealthy or rulers) better, and laws and law-enforcement just. Their home, in the hills north of Arvale, is the fortress of Highcrag, where most of them were slaughtered, early in DARK LORD.

Baerold, Darvus: big, bristle-browed, and deep-voiced warrior of Darswords, who fled the independent hold as it fell to Malraun's army. A wary, suspicious man.

Barlaskeir, Ommaunt: the wizard-king of the distant Falconaar realm of Aundraunt. Very powerful in his magic but only rarely seen outside Aundraunt; his rare journeys occur when he desires gold and gems, and agrees to hire out his magical services to someone wealthy enough to pay his very high fees.

Blackraven, House: noble family of Galath, whose head is a marquel.

Bloodhunt, Aumun: Velduke (noble) of Galath, an angry, conservative old man who lost a leg at the siege of Bowrock in DARK LORD.

Bloodhunt, Haerelle: Velduchess (noble) of Galath, the deceased wife of Velduke Aumun Bloodhunt. An accomplished wizardess who died of winter-fever, and is entombed in a pavilion in the Bloodhunt gardens, abutting the Velduke's mansion.

Bracebold, Olgur: "Blade of Telchassar," a veteran mercenary warcaptain from the rich port of Telchassur who has taken service in the army of the wizard Malraun. Loud, belligerent, and sometimes jovial, a man of simple pleasures.

Bralgarth, Melvo: aging, limping commander in Amaxas Horgul's Army of Liberation, who was installed as Lord of the independent

Rauklor hold of Hawksyl by Horgul after the army conquered it. A cold-eyed, cynical, brutal and ruthless man.

Bresker, Ilmos: a large, capable warrior of the household of Klarl Annusk Dunshar.

Brorsavar, Melander: Former Velduke of Galath, a stern, just, "steady" and therefore popular Galathan noble, well-respected by most of his fellow nobles. Large and impressive-looking, having shoulders as broad as two slender men standing side by side, he was crowned King of Galath by several fellow nobles at the end of DARK LORD. Some Galathan nobility were slow to accept his authority; although civil strife is still raging in his kingdom, he is slowly gaining wider acceptance.

Buckhold, Tamgrym: a tall, terse, stealthy commander in Malraun's army, a veteran warrior whose face is disfigured by dozens of crisscrossing sword-scars.

Carroll, Rusty: the grayhaired, honest, follow-the-rules Head of Security at the headquarters of Holdoncorp, on Earth. Note: a fictional character.

Cathgur, Darmeth: a warrior of the household of Klarl Annusk Dunshar.

Dark Helms, the: warriors, aptly described as "ruthless slayers in black armor." Living men and (increasingly, as their losses mount over time) undead warriors, these enspelled-to-loyalty soldiers are the creations of Holdoncorp.

(Daera: see *Quevreth, Daera*)

(Darlamtur: see *Paelendrake, Darlamtur*)

Dauntra: an Aumrarr; once the youngest, most beautiful, and most saucy of "the Four Aumrarr" who flew together, seeking to avenge the slaughter at Highcrag, now one of two survivors of that quartet (the other is Juskra).

Deldragon, Darendarr: Velduke of Galath (noble), who dwells in the fortified town of Bowrock on the southern edge of Galath, which surrounds his soaring castle, Bowrock Keep. A handsome, dashing battle hero, of a family considered "great" in Galath, who defied King Devaer and the wizard Arlaghaun, and was besieged because of it. Near the end of DARK LORD he was brought back from the verge of death by the wizard Narmarkoun, who (unbeknownst to Deldragon and everyone else in Falconfar) cast magics into Deldragon's mind, to make him Narmarkoun's slave henceforth.

(Derek: see *Welver, Derek*)

(Devaer: see *Rothryn, Devaer*)

Dooms, the: wizards so much more powerful than most mages that they are feared all across Falconfar as nigh-unstoppable forces. For decades there were three Dooms: Arlaghaun (widely considered the most powerful); Malraun; and Narmarkoun. During the events recounted in DARK LORD, Rod Everlar came to be considered the fourth Doom, and Arlaghaun perished.

Dreel, Halavar: sadistic, ruthless wizard of Tauren, famous for destroying Skelt Tower with his spells. Short, lean, and sharp-featured, he has gleaming black eyes like those of a hawk, and is always gloved and dressed in black leather.

Dunshar, Annusk: Klarl of Galath, an arrogant, cruel, ambitious, bullying noble, widely disliked by his peers. A burly warrior who spied on Galathans for the wizard Arlaghaun in DARK LORD, and who has been named Seneschal of Galathgard, and put in charge of the rebuilding of that royal castle to prepare it for King Brorsavar's Great Court.

Duthcrown, House: a small but well-established noble family of Galath (its head holds the rank of marquel). The Duthcrowns have recently (and quietly) built themselves great wealth through shrewd land purchases.

Dzundivvur, Aumundas: a commander in Malraun's army; an old, hollow-eyed veteran merchant and mercenary warrior of Stormar who's ailing from a variety of sicknesses. His miserly nature is almost legendary, and he fears wizards and has purchased various magical protections against their spells over the years, that he wears strapped to himself in a profusion of crisscrossing baldrics and weapons-belts.

Eldalar, Baerlun: Lord of Hollowtree, a independent mountain-vale hold north of Arvale and northeast of Galath. A stiff, gruff old warrior who likes and trusts Aumrarr but strongly dislikes and mistrusts the neighboring realm of Galath—and all wizards, everywhere.

Eldurant, Tethtyn: youngest underscribe to Bralgarth, the Lord of Hawksyl appointed by its conqueror Horgul. A young, lazy, stammeringly uncertain man.

Empherel, Jalren: wizard of Skoum, an ambitious and arrogant man who frequently prowls Falconfar looking for magic—and wizards wounded or weak enough he can slay them and seize their magic.

Enfeld, Hank: honest and a trifle slow-witted, but the largest and strongest of the custodians (janitors) at the headquarters of Holdoncorp, on Earth. Note: a fictional character.

Esdagh, Lanneth: the more charismatic and talkative of the two "Brothers Esdagh," commanders in Malraun's army. A quick-witted, swift-tongued, persuasive and capable warrior; a burly man who customarily fights with an axe.

Esdagh, Mulzurr: the more silent of the two "Brothers Esdagh," commanders in Malraun's army. A veteran warrior with customarily fights with an axe, and Lanneth's elder brother by some years. A patient, determined hunter who "never forgets nor forgives."

Eskeln, Candram: longtime bodyguard of the wizard Malraun, a talkative warrior of swift wits and loyalty.

Everlar, Rod: hack writer of novels, who believed himself the creator of Falconfar. During DARK LORD, he discovered he was one of its creators; in Falconfar, he is a "Shaper" (one whose writings can change reality), though non-wizards tend to think he is one of the Dooms (powerful wizards). He was referred to as "the Dark Lord" (the most evil and most powerful of all wizards, a bogeyman of legend) by the other Dooms, to blame him for their misdeeds. Considered to be the Lord Archwizard of Falconfar by the Aumrarr (the first Lord Archwizard since Lorontar). The Aumrarr Taeauna brought Rod (whom she often calls "Rodrel," the closest Falconaar name to "Rod") into Falconfar and was his guide until the wizard Malraun captured her at the end of DARK LORD; as ARCH WIZARD begins, he sets out to regain her.

Falard, Onzril: senior hoist-jack in a Galathan stonemason's crew.

Falcon, the: THE deity of Falconfar, the embodiment of all things, and fount of inspiration, wisdom, daring, and splendid achievement. All-seeing and enigmatic. Also known as "the Great Falcon," to distinguish it from lesser, mortal birds that share its shape, and as "the Lone and Flying Falcon."

Felldrake, Ollund: Velduke of Galath, a fat, coarse, boar-like noble ruled by his gluttony, greed, and lust.

Forestmother, the: recently-risen deity of Falconfar, gaining swift and wide popularity, and standing for wild ways and the unspoiled forests, against excessive woodcutting, land clearances, and despoiling overhunting and farming.

Glaelra: battle-slain Aumrarr of Galath.

Glorn, Branlabult: longtime bodyguard of the wizard Malraun, an ugly but good-natured veteran. Kindly and worldly-wise.

Gorongor, Indragar: longtime bodyguard of the wizard Malraun, a handsome, dashing warrior. Keen of hearing and attractive to women.

Gorult, Jelgo: farmer of Darswords, who fled that independent hold when it fell to the army of the wizard Malraun.

(Great Falcon, the: see *Falcon, the*)

Gulkoun, Garfist: Often referred to as "Old Ox" or "Old Blundering Ox" by his partner Iskarra Taeravund, this coarse, burly and aging onetime pirate, former forger, and then panderer later became a hiresword (mercenary warrior), and these days wanders Falconfar with Iskarra, making a living as a thief and swindler. "Garfist" is actually a childhood nickname he took as his everyday name, vastly preferring it to "Norbryn," the name his parents gave him.

(Haelgon: see *Xindral, Haelgon*)

Halamaskar, Anthan: Lordrake of Galath, a cultured but unprincipled noble who seldom leaves his castle of Maurpath (and its surrounding forest, where he likes to hunt).

Hallowhond, Mespur: Velduke of Galath, a burly, wealthy noble who owns many rich farms and fine lumber forests.

Hammerhand, Amteira: daughter of Burrim Hammerhand, she fiercely insists on riding on hunts and taking war-training like any man. She has shoulders as broad as many men, long brown hair, startlingly dark eyebrows, and snapping blue-black eyes.

Hammerhand, Burrim: Lord of Ironthorn, a large, prosperous, militarily-strong hold in the forests north of Tauren and northeast of Sardray, that for years has had three rival lords, ruling from three separate keeps. Gruff and shrewd, Hammerhand is the strongest of the three, a large, hardy, capable warrior and battle-leader. He rules the northernmost part of Ironthorn, a small demesne that includes the market town of Irontarl and the north bank of the Thorn River, from his crag-top castle of Hammerhold. His badge is an iron gauntlet (a left-handed gage, upright and open-fingered, on a scarlet field).

(Hank: see *Enfeld, Hank*)

Holdoncorp: a large computer gaming company that licenses the electronic media games rights to the world of Falconfar from Rod Everlar, and develops a series of computer games that increasingly diverge from Everlar's own vision of his world. (Holdoncorp is NOT based on any real-world corporation or group of people. The Falconfar tales are fantasies, not satires of, or swipes at, anything or anyone real.)

Hondreth, Palavar: the only bodyguard of Lordrake Anthan Halamaskar that the Lordrake trusts (and a loyal warrior who is fully worthy of that trust).

Horgul, Amaxas: warlord, leader of an "Army of Liberation" marching north from the Sea of Storms to conquer Raurklor hold after Raurklor hold. Said to hate and fear all who wield magic, and to execute all hedge-wizards and altar-priests he finds. Described as "more boar than man, a brawling, rutting lout governed by his lusts and rages," but a great warrior who dominates battlefields and warriors, inspiring and commanding swift and unquestioning obedience.

Imdael, Narbrel: a mercenary archer in service to Olondyn of the Bow. Young, agile, and loyal.

Insenjones, Bert: a game programmer at Holdoncorp. Note: a fictional character.

(Iskarra: see *Taeravund, Iskarra*)

Jaklar, Cauldreth: the Lord Herbal of Hammerhold, in Ironthorn. Priest of the Forestmother, a cruel, nasty, and ambitious young man, vigorous and judgmental by nature.

Jenkins, The: nearby neighbors of Rod Everlar on Bridlewood Lane (on Earth). Note: fictional characters.

Juskra: Aümrarr; the most battle-scarred, hot-tempered, and aggressive of the "Four Aumrarr" who fly together, seeking to avenge the slaughter at Highcrag.

(Lord Herbal, the: see *Jaklar, Cauldreth*)

Korauth, Orlryn: the loudest and most aggressive of Malraun's army commanders (in the Army of Liberation formerly led by Horgul). His fearless, fiery-tempered manner makes him the most feared and disliked by others in that army. A burly, glowering warrior of skill and charisma, easily recognized by his flame-red hair, scowling brows and full beard. Lord of the minor hold of Balember, and a blusterer who has little use for women as warriors.

Kulduth, Hazandros: ambitious hedge-wizard of Stormar.

(Lady Icycurses Wingwench: see *Juskra*)

Laeveren, Waend: warrior of Darswords, who fled the independent hold as it fell to Malraun's army.

Larkhelm, Mordrimmar: Arduke of Galath, a carefree, glib, unprincipled noble whose family banner displays a roaring lion.

Lionhelm, Halath: Arduke of Galath, a handsome and principled noble.

lorn, the: race of winged, flying, horned predatory creatures that dwell in rocky heights such as castle towers and the Falconspires mountain range. Often described as mouthless by humans because their skull-like faces have no visible jaws, they typically swarm prey, raking with their talons and even tearing limbs, bodies, or heads off or apart. They have bat-like, featherless wings, barbed tails, and slate-gray skin. Arlaghaun, Malraun, and many lesser wizards discovered or developed spells for compelling lorn into servitude.

Lorontar: the still-feared-in-legend first Lord Archwizard of Falconfar, once the fell and tyrannical ruler of all Falconfar, and the first spell-tamer of the lorn. Long believed dead but secretly surviving in spectral unlife, seeking a living body to mind-guide, "ride," and ultimately possess. So greatly is his memory feared that no one, not even a powerful wizard, has dared to try to dwell in his great black tower, Yintaerghast, since his disappearance and presumed death.

Luthtarl, Maraumedurr: Lord of Dlarmarr, an independent port on the Hywond Shore.

Lyrandurl, Raelen: wizard of Sardray, a hedonistic dandy who sports a golden-hued, scented beard and many golden arm-bangles of the sort favored by dancing-lasses. Deceptively jovial and apparently careless, he has destroyed many who have thought him an easy target. Often feigns drunken helplessness, to lure others into attacking him—whereupon he blasts them to flaming ash.

Lyrose, House: one of the three rival ruling families of Ironthorn (the others are Hammerhand and Tesmer). Much was seen of the Lyroses in ARCHWIZARD.

Lythrus, Handro: chief scribe to Bralgarth, Lord of Hawksyl. An old drunkard of failing eyesight and cynical disposition.

Maethe: battle-slain Aumrarr of Galath.

Malraun: "the Matchless," wizard, one of the Dooms of Falconfar. A short, sleek, darkly handsome man who dwells in Malragard, a tower in Harlhoh, a hold (settlement) in the green depths of Raurklor, the Great Forest. Malraun is served by lorn and spell-subverted traders, and after the death of his chief rival Arlaghaun, increasing numbers of Dark Helms he's magically bound to himself. At the end of DARK LORD he captured the Aumrarr Taeauna, and with Arlaghaun dead, set in motion bold plans to conquer all Falconfar north of the Sea of Storms.

Markel, Imbrelker: an unprincipled merchant of Stormar. Agile and handsome, but a cold-blooded swindler and murderer of many rival traders.

(Memmurth: see *Velaskoon, Memmurth*)

Merek, Dranth: young, good-natured painter and warrior of Darswords, who fled that independent hold when it fell to the army of the wizard Malraun.

Millers, The: former (deceased) nearby neighbors of Rod Everlar on Bridlewood Lane (on Earth). Note: fictional characters.

Moon Masked, The: a secret society of wizards opposed to the Archwizard Lorontar. Their name derives from their shared ability to magically cloak their faces with pearly radiance like moonlight to avoid being identified. They have no leader, are located all over Falconfar and several "otherwheres," too, and have only one common purpose: opposition to Lorontar. Long silent and hidden, or perhaps vanished entirely.

Mrelbrand, Larguskus: tavernmaster of The Stag's Head roadside tavern in western Galath.

(Narbrel: see *Imdael, Narbrel*)

Narmarkoun: wizard, one of the Dooms of Falconfar; a tall, blue-skinned, scaly man who dwells alone in a hidden subterranean wilderland stronghold, Darthoun, a long-abandoned city of the dwarves—alone, that is, except for dead, skull-headed wenches animated by his spells. He breeds greatfangs (huge dragon-like scaly flying jawed lizards he uses as steeds) in the hollowed-out mountain of Closecandle, and maintains several other strongholds (notably his first tower, Helnkrist), where "false Narmarkouns" (doubles of himself) dwell, that he has fashioned from his undead servitors so that Malraun and other foes will attack them, and not him. Most mysterious of the Dooms, and always popularly regarded as the least of them in magical might, Narmarkoun is an accomplished, patient magical spy.

(Norbryn: see *Gulkoun, Garfist*)

Norgan, Vaerant: warrior of Darswords, who fled the independent hold when it fell to the army of the wizard Malraun. Sour of face and nature, he hates Baerold of Darswords.

Norgarl, Uldur: the old, hairy, and ugly senior commander in Malraun's army, who brought the largest number of warriors into that force. A coarse "old boar" who considers the Aumrarr far less than human, and that women should be subservient to men, he inspires intense loyalty from his men (from the coastal hills of Parlath).

Olondyn, Relse: "Olondyn of the Bow," a proud, sneering, hot-tempered Raurklor mercenary, an archer and forester who leads other archers and foresters; he joined Malraun's army and became one of its commanders.

Ondrelt, Susan: "Very Cherry," a dancer and prostitute of Earth.

Quevreth, Daera: dead but magically-animated pleasure-slave of the wizard Narmarkoun. Gray-skinned and sleekly curvaceous, she is one of many such "skull-wenches" who serve the wizard in his castle of Darthoun. In life, she was the daughter of a farmer in lands Narmarkoun ruled, before he seized her from her home by force. By means of his spells, he can inhabit her body or those of any of his other "playpretties," at will—but will do so only in emergencies.

Paelendrake, Darlamtur: wizard-for-hire who dwells in a fortified rock that juts out of the harbor of the southern port of Hrathlar. A polite, kindly-seeming but coldly ruthless man.

Raenor, Yenbresk: (Sir), a knight of southeasternmost Galath, a cruel veteran warrior, unscrupulous and ruthless.

Rambaerakh: "Slayer of Dragons," an undead wizard now little more than a floating, talking skull. Once the founder and ruler of Rauryk, the Realm of Tall Trees (that has now become the wild forest of Raurklor). Creator of the first Dark Helms and builder of the tower that became Malragard, home of the wizard Malraun the Matchless.

Ravalan, Selder: steward to King Brorsavar. A young, vigorous, and loyal man, customarily urbane. He is tall, thin and unremarkable of appearance.

(Roar: see *Taroarin, Delkur*)

(Rodrel: see *Everlar, Rod*)

Rondarl, Tarace: a capable, veteran warrior of the household of Klarl Annusk Dunshar.

Roreld, Duthdaer: old, growling, bearded mercenary warcaptain, who joins Malraun's army.

Roskryn, Velnar: a fork-bearded, dapper, polite wizard who enspells swords to fight for him, always has several escape schemes and contingency magics lurking up his sleeve, and stealthily seeks magic he can take for his own. Often finds dying or dead wizards from afar and appears at the site of their deaths soon after they fall, ready to take all he can.

Rothryn, Devaer: deceased King of Galath, a young, handsome, and haughty wastrel youngest prince who became the puppet of the wizard Arlaghaun (after the Doom of Galath slew all of Devaer's kin, to put him on the throne of Galath). Utterly controlled by Arlaghaun, he became widely known as "the Mad King" because of his apparently nonsensical decrees, pitting noble against noble. He was slain during DARK LORD; Velduke Melander Brorsavar succeeded him on the throne of Galath.

Ruthcoats, Uruld: Marquel of Galath, a middle-aged, conservative noble of patrician tastes and ever-increasing cynicism.

Sarchar: "Lord of Spells," a dusky-skinned, always-smiling wizard of middling skills but peerless greed and ambition who recently relocated from the southern land of Tammarlar to Galath.

Sarlvyre, Haemgraethe: Lordrake of Galath. An ambitious and bold noble known for his deadly skill with a sword.

Sargult, Tammur: nasal-voiced, sarcastic horse-tamer and warrior of Darswords, who fled that independent hold as it fell to Malraun's army.

Silvershields, Helgorr: Arduke of Galath, a noble of haughty pride and sneering sophistication, a stickler for the privileges of rank and station.

Smiths, The: nearby neighbors of Rod Everlar on Bridlewood Lane (on Earth). Note: fictional characters.

Sollars, Pete: a pleasant, stolid, and a trifle slow-witted security "eyes" (monitor watcher) at the Corporate Headquarters of Holdoncorp, on Earth. Note: a fictional character.

Snowlance, House: old but minor noble family of Galath, whose head is a klarl.

Sortrel, Ingresk: warrior of Taneth, a mercenary warrior in the army of the wizard Malraun the Matchless.

Stormserpent, Laskrar: Arduke of Galath, a tall, muscular, darkly handsome warrior noble who spends much of his leisure time hunting.

Sutherland, Maxwell: a short, balding, thickly-bespectacled, goatee-sporting real-estate broker. Rod's next-door neighbor on Bridlewood Lane (on Earth). A nerd, known to one and all as "Max" (and more than a little crazy), who owns a Chihuahua named Honeybell. Note: a fictional character.

Sutherland, Muriel: the snobbish, domineering, loud-voiced wife of Maxwell Sutherland. Note: a fictional character.

Taeauna ("TAY-awna"): Aumrarr, who in desperation "called on" Rod Everlar and managed to bring him to Falconfar to use his powers as a Shaper to deliver her world from the depredations of the Dark Helms and the Dooms (wizards) who control them. A determined, worldly, experienced Aumrarr who harbors secrets yet to be revealed, she was captured by the wizard Arlaghaun, and then, at the end of DARK LORD, by the wizard Malraun.

Taeravund, Iskarra: best known as "Viper" from her thieving days in the southern port of Hrathlar (her longtime partner-in-crime, Garfist Gulkoun, prefers to call her "Vipersides" or "Snakehips"), this profane, homely woman has been a swindler all her life, and has used many false names (including "Rosera"). Possessed of driving determination and very swift wits, she is as "skinny as a lance" (in the words of Garfist Gulkoun), but usually wears a false magical "crawlskin" (the magically-preserved, semi-alive skin of a long-dead sorceress), that she stole from a wizard in far eastern Sarmandar, and can by will can mold over herself to make herself look fat, lush, or spectacularly bosomed (and cover leather bladders in which she can hide stolen items). She now makes her living as a thief and swindler, wandering Falconfar with Gulkoun.

(Tamgrym: see *Buckhold, Tamgrym*)

Tarlund, Muskrum: longtime bodyguard of the wizard Malraun, a loyal, laconic warrior.

Taroarin, Delkur: cooper (cask maker) and warrior of the independent hold of Darswords, who fled as it fell to Malraun's army.

Taervellar, Orothor: "Taervellar of the Talons," an almost-legendary wizard of Falconfar, known to be very powerful and to (rarely) hire out his services for staggeringly high sums. His nickname comes from the huge flying talons—and a menagerie of smaller monsters—he can conjure out of thin air to fight for him, when the need arises. Hatchet-faced, he has blazing eyes, and his badge is a beast-claw.

Taether: long-dead wizard of Falconfar, the creator of wands known as Taether's Talons, that can conjure up claws of force out of empty air, to rake and rend the wand-wielder's foes.

Tathgallant, Arundur: Baron of Galath. A noble of middling wits and wealth, who is a friend of Arduke Mordrimmar Larkhelm.

Telgurt, Brasgel: Arduke of Galath, a cruel and forceful noble who mistreats all women and most servants. He douses himself in scents, and thinks himself both clever, and irresistible to all womankind.

Teltusk, Tethgar: Arduke of Galath, a young, well-intentioned noble.

Tesmer, Belard: eldest of the sons of Lord Irrance Tesmer and Lady Telclara Tesmer, but won't inherit the lordship unless his three elder daughters predecease him. Darkly handsome, sardonic and "sophisticated" (dabbling in all the latest fashions, and cultivating a mastery of the arts, finance, and "knowing all that it's important to know"), Belard is deadly with both his sword and a cutting insult, and has discreetly sampled many of the women of Ironthorn, of high station and low.

Tesmer, Delmark: fourth son of Lord Irrance Tesmer and Lady Telclara Tesmer. Nondescript of appearance and quiet in his movements and speech, he's quick-witted, sharp-tongued, deceitful, lazy, resentful of his kin's successes, sadistic, and a "sneak" (spy) and tattletale.

Tesmer, Feldrar: sixth and youngest son of Lord Irrance Tesmer and Lady Telclara Tesmer. A handsome wastrel, prankster, liar, and dashing wencher and swindler.

Tesmer, Irrance: Lord of Ironthorn, one of three rival lords of that isolated Raurklar hold. Tesmer is the husband of Telclara and the father of (in order of precedence, eldest to youngest): Maera, Nareyera, Talyss, Belard, Ghorsyn, Kalathgar, Delmark, Ellark, and Feldrar (however, see Tesmer, Telclara). He rules the southeastern Ironthar valley of Imrush, from his keep of Imtowers. (The valley takes its name from the River Imrush, that flows down its heart to join the Thorn River where the Tesmer lands end and those of Lyrose begin.) Formerly owner of all the gem-mines in Ironthorn, and a buyer of many slaves. His badge is a purple diamond on a gray field.

Tesmer, Kalathgar: third son of Lord Irrance Tesmer and Lady Telclara Tesmer. Of middling size and nondescript appearance, he is often forgotten and overlooked, and resents it. Taciturn and farsighted, capable with his hands and in matters of war and trade-tactics. Scornful of his kin and restless to depart Ironthorn for a better life elsewhere—almost anywhere elsewhere.

Tesmer, Maera Harilda Mehannraer: eldest daughter and heiress of Lord Irrance Tesmer and Lady Telclara Tesmer. Of haughty manner and coldly-cutting speech, she has raven-black hair, sharp but beautiful features, and brains almost as sharp as her mother. She never lets anyone forget for a moment that she is first in standing among the risen generation of Tesmers.

Tesmer, Nareyera ("Nar-RARE-ah"): second daughter of Lord Irrance Tesmer and Lady Telclara Tesmer. Even more darkly beautiful than her sister Maera, she has long, glossy raven-black hair, flashing eyes (black pupils flecked with gold that seem to flash when she's excited or angry), and is sharp-tongued. She devotes her every waking moment to scheming to gain wealth, power, holds over people, and greater influence in the Tesmer lands and beyond. She thinks herself the smartest of all the Tesmers, who will (she believes) one day rise to attain far more power than even lordship over all Ironthorn.

Tesmer, Talyss: third and youngest daughter of Lord Irrance Tesmer and Lady Telclara Tesmer. Tall, quiet, long-haired, and graceful, her movements always seeming languid, she resents being overlooked, pushed aside, and thought "feminine" and so brainless and subservient. She is vicious to others whenever she dares to be.

Tesmer, Telclara: Lady of Ironthorn, one of two living women to use that title (the other being Maerelle Lyrose). Many Ironthar rightly say Lady Tesmer rules her husband, and has the keenest wits in all Ironthorn. Two of her children weren't sired by her husband; although this has long been rumored around the Tesmer lands, she doesn't admit it, or identify which two, until near the end of ARCH WIZARD.

Thalander: an arrogant, ambitious hedge-wizard of Hywond.

Tindror, Darl: Baron of Galath (noble), a gruff, decent, law-abiding man who governs the small farming barony of Tarmoral on the eastern edge of Galath, on the Falconspires mountain range border with the neighboring land of Arvale. Tindror's castle is Wrathgard, and his longtime foe is a neighboring Galathan baron, Mrantos Murlstag.

Torth, Nuth: loyal and brutal knight of the household of Arduke Mordrimmar Larkhelm of Galath.

Tresker, Feldren: old and bitter warrior of Darswords, who fled that independent hold when it fell to the army of Malraun the Matchless.

Ulaskro, Morl: tomekeeper of the private library of Lord Luthtarl of Dlarmarr, an independent port on the Hywond Shore. A young, book-loving dreamer.

Ult: deceased wizard of Galath, who built Ult Tower, a black stone keep in the heart of the realm that he magically linked to himself, stone by stone, so the tower was like his skin; he could feel what was done to it and see out of it. Before the events recounted in DARK LORD, the wizard Arlaghaun took over Ult's body and conquered his mind, inhabiting both, and so gained control of Ult Tower.

Urvraunt, Imglur: locklar of the private library of Lord Luthtarl of Dlarmarr. Old, near-blind, increasingly deaf, and waspish of voice and temper. The superior of Morl Ulaskro.

Velaskoon, Memmurth: a young, energetic, ambitious, and very busy wizard-for-hire, who dwells (in disguise) in dozens of Stormar ports and other cities, moving about often and delighting in maintaining scores of identities. He has a voracious appetite for wealth, reportedly seeing it as a means of crafting new and titanic magics, and is always hiring himself out to many patrons in need of battle-spells or magical protection.

(Very Cherry: see *Ondrelt, Susan*)

Vethlar, Narangel: a young and callow warrior of the household of Klarl Annusk Dunshar.

Welver, Derek: a sarcastic but sensible veteran policeman of Earth, desk sergeant at the local precinct in which the Holdoncorp Corporate Headquarters is located. Note: a fictional character.

Windstrike, Gordraun: Marquel (noble) of Galath, young, earnest, and loyal to King Brorsavar.

Xamdaver, Sam: a project manager of Holdoncorp's gaming division. Note: a fictional character.

Xindral, Haelgon: senior guardsman of House Tesmer, trusted with guarding the doors of the private apartments of Lord Irrance Tesmer and Lady Telclara Tesmer, in the fortress of Imtowers.

Yarrove, House: wealthy, swiftly-rising junior noble family of Galath.

Yorl, Larth: elderly wizard-for-hire, from the island realm of Jorannuth.

Zorzaerel, Kalahark: youngest and boldest of the commanders in Malraun's army, a sharp-tongued, decisive warrior.

ABOUT THE AUTHOR

Ed Greenwood is best known for his role in creating the
Forgotten Realms setting, part of the world-famous Dungeons
and Dragons franchise. His writings have sold millions of copies
worldwide, in more than a dozen languages. Greenwood resides
in the Canadian province of Ontario.

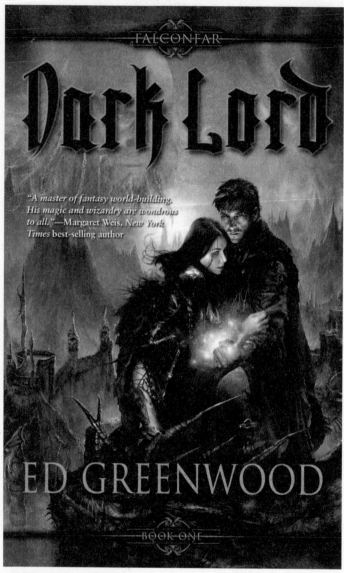

UK ISBN: 978 1 906735 63 0 • US ISBN: 978 1 844167 64 7 • £7.99/$7.99

Having been drawn into a fantasy world of his own creation, Rod Everlar continues his quest to defeat the corruption he has discovered within. With the ambitious Arlaghaun now dead, he sets off in pursuit of the dark wizard Malraun, only to find that he has raised an army of monsters and mercenaries in order to conquer the world...

 WWW.SOLARISBOOKS.COM

Follow us on Twitter! www.twitter.com/solarisbooks

BRIAN LUMLEY

HAGGOPIAN
AND OTHER STORIES
A Cthulhu Mythos Collection

UK ISBN: 978 1 844167 62 3 • US ISBN: 978 1 844166 79 4 • £7.99/$7.99

Prior to his best-selling Necroscope series, Brian Lumley built his reputation by writing stories set against H. P. Lovecraft's cosmic Cthulhu Mythos backdrop. These dark and frightening tales appeared worldwide in some of the most prestigious genre magazines, and this volume contains some of the very best of Brian Lumley's works. Collected together, it confirms his place as a master of horror fiction.

 WWW.SOLARISBOOKS.COM

Follow us on Twitter! www.twitter.com/solarisbooks

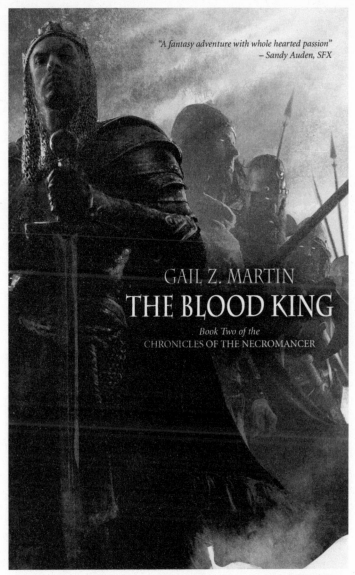

"Black Magic Woman is the best manuscript I've ever been asked to read. Keep an eye on Justin Gustainis. You'll be seeing more of him soon."

Jim Butcher

BLACK MAGIC WOMAN
A MORRIS AND CHASTAIN INVESTIGATION
JUSTIN GUSTAINIS

www.solarisbooks.com   ISBN: 978-1-84416-541-4

Supernatural investigator Quincey Morris and his partner, white witch Libby Chastain, are called in to help free a desperate family from a deadly curse that appears to date back to the Salem Witch Trials. To release the family from danger they must find the root of the curse, a black witch with a terrible grudge that holds the family in her power.

SOLARIS DARK FANTASY

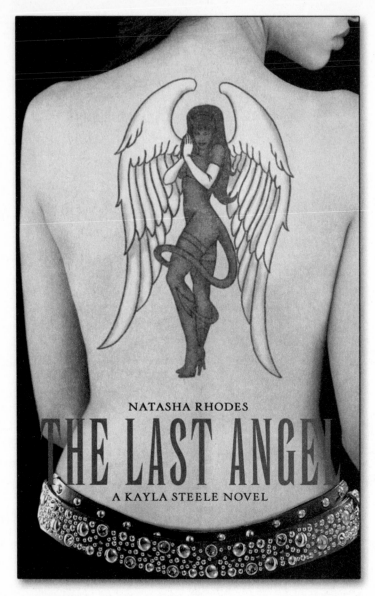

NATASHA RHODES

THE LAST ANGEL

A KAYLA STEELE NOVEL

www.solarisbooks.com   UK ISBN: 978-1-84416-646-6   US ISBN: 978-1-84416-577-3

An angel is found murdered on the streets of Sunset Boulevard. To the media gossip mongers, it's the biggest story ever. To the Hunters, an underground monster-fighting hit-squad, it's just another case of "whodunnit". To Kayla Steele, their newest member, it means a last chance to bring her murdered fiancé back from the dead, and to others with a far darker purpose it is the means to destroy the human race.

☾ **SOLARIS** DARK FANTASY

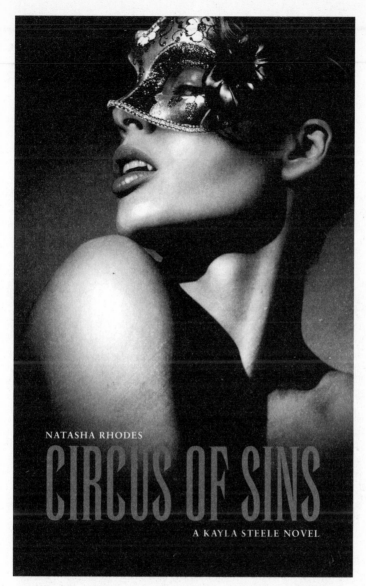

NATASHA RHODES

CIRCUS OF SINS

A KAYLA STEELE NOVEL